D0365268

THE
MIDNIGHT
GATE

THE MIDNIGHT GATE

HELEN STRINGER

FEIWEL AND FRIENDS
NEW YORK

A FEIWEL AND FRIENDS BOOK
An Imprint of Macmillan

Library of Congress Cataloging-in-Publication Data

Stringer, Helen.
The midnight gate / Helen Stringer. — 1st ed.
p. cm.
Twelve-year-old Belladonna Johnson, who lives with the ghosts of her parents,
once again teams up with her classmate Steve, whose mother has suddenly disappeared,
when they are given a dangerous assignment by a ghostly monk involving the return
of the Dark Times.
ISBN: 978-0-312-38764-8
[1. Supernatural—Fiction.   2. Ghosts—Fiction.   3. Orphans—Fiction.
4. Schools—Fiction.   5. England—Fiction.]   I. Title.
PZ7.S9182Mi 2011
[Fic]—dc22
2010036476

Book design by April Ward

Feiwel and Friends logo designed by Filomena Tuosto

First Edition: 2011

1 3 5 7 9 10 8 6 4 2

mackids.com

For my parents, who always believed

The Visitor

"MR. EVANS!"

No answer.

"Mr. Evans!"

Belladonna sneaked a look over her shoulder to the back of the classroom where Steve and his friends usually clustered. He was far away, gazing out of the window and down at the football field below. The cloud-cloaked sun was low in the sky, throwing the trees at the end of the field into stark relief and making the frost on the grass sparkle.

"Am I talking to myself?" Madame Huggins suddenly had that dangerous sarcasm in her voice, the tone that generally went before a detention, or worse—a trip to Miss Parker's office. Not that Steve was a stranger to either penalty.

Silence settled on the classroom like a heavy blanket, but still Steve was oblivious.

Jimmy Wright shoved a bony elbow into his ribs and Steve jumped back to life, first shooting an angry stare at Jimmy, then gradually becoming aware of the silence in the classroom. He slowly turned his head to look at Madame Huggins. She had drawn herself to her full height, a difficult feat for someone so resoundingly round.

"Good morning," she said, her voice dripping with sarcasm.

Titters from the rest of the class.

"Did you have a good rest?"

Steve just stared at her, sullen indifference writ large on his face.

"Now, give me an example of a genitive charge."

Steve stared and then cocked his head to one side and shifted in his seat.

"In Latin?" he said finally.

"No, in Greek. Of course in Latin! This is a Latin class, you stupid boy!"

Madame Huggins's face had turned entirely red, except for the very tip of her nose, which was as white as snow. Belladonna began to suspect that she might explode, but instead she took a deep breath.

"Look," she said, her voice strangely calm, "you don't know how lucky you are. Most schools dropped Latin from the curriculum years ago. But it's a great foundation, it really is."

Belladonna bit her lip: Dr. Ashe had said the same thing the first time they'd seen him on the Other Side and that hadn't ended well at all, what with the Hound, poisonous Night Ravens, and the imprisonment of all the ghosts. She glanced back at Steve again to see if he registered the same memory, but he was busy staring at Madame Huggins, his face a mask of obstinance.

"Alright," said Madame Huggins finally, "let's see if you have even managed to grasp the basics. A genitive charge—in English."

"He nearly died of boredom."

Madame Huggins opened her mouth to pour scorn and then stopped. A barely suppressed giggle ran around the classroom.

"Um . . . yes," she said, clearly amazed. "Yes, that's right. But if you know that, then why didn't—"

But she was destined never to know what made Steve Evans so impossible in class when he was clearly one of the brightest students in it. The bell rang for the end of the lesson and the end of the day. Steve scooped up his backpack and was out of the door in a flash and on his way down to football practice with the rest of his cronies.

Belladonna packed up her Latin grammar, her exercise book, and her pencils. She glanced at Madame Huggins as she stuffed them into her pink backpack. The old lady had slumped into her chair behind the desk, exhausted by the sheer effort involved in trying to get a bunch of twelve-year-olds to take any interest in Latin. Belladonna smiled as she passed by, but Madame Huggins didn't notice; she just stared toward the back wall of the class.

Belladonna walked through the empty corridors of Dullworth's, her steps echoing on the old wooden floors and the crisp tile of the entrance hall. It was amazing how quickly several hundred students could vacate a building when they were really motivated. Of course, not everyone had gone—there were always the after-hours classes. Tonight it was orchestra practice, and the sound of chairs being dragged across the parquet floor of the assembly room was soon followed by the whining, huffing cacophony of twenty erstwhile musicians attempting to tune up. Belladonna winced as she hurriedly retrieved her coat from the cloakroom, stepped out into the late afternoon gloom, and headed home.

She hadn't gone very far before it was completely dark. She kicked at a stone lying in her path and pondered the misery that was February. It may be the shortest month of the year, but it always felt like the longest. By February she always felt as if winter would never end, days would always be short, and the sun would never shine again. It didn't get light until close to nine in the morning and by three it started to fade, all without the actual sun putting in a single appearance, just the endless lowering, lead-gray sky.

At which point in her reverie, the skies opened and a freezing rain began to descend.

"Oh, great," muttered Belladonna, pulling her hood up, "that's just great."

By the time she got home, her fingers and nose were almost blue with the cold, her feet were soaked, and her black hair was hanging in dripping strings down the sides of her face.

"I'm home," she said, hanging her coat up on its hook in the hall.

"Oh, my heavens!" said her mother, materializing near the sitting-room door. "You're soaked to the skin! Get those wet shoes off and get in front of the fire. Dinner will be in five minutes."

Belladonna pulled her shoes off and left them at the

bottom of the stairs before wandering into the sitting room, where her father was sitting, or more accurately hovering, an inch or so above his easy chair, watching the television. He took one look at her and let go with a single guffaw.

"Ha!" he said. "You look like a drowned rat!"

Belladonna glared at him and sat on the floor in front of the gas fire. The news was on, of course, but it wasn't very interesting. She looked up at her father, who was watching attentively, and wondered why he was so fascinated. It wasn't as if any of it affected him—he'd been dead for nearly two years.

After dinner, she went up to her room to do her home-work, but her heart wasn't in it. She just couldn't bring herself to care about the establishment of the monasteries. Her thoughts kept going back, instead, to Dr. Ashe and his efforts to open a doorway to the Dark Spaces. Sometimes, at night, when everything was at its most silent, she would still wake up, her heart racing with the awful sensation of the thrumming, pounding power that had changed the Dream Door to a door of nightmares. She remembered the smooth, cold surface of the second Nomial, the honey-colored Silex Aequoreus, as she had raised it above her head. And most of all, she remembered the way the Words had made her feel as she defeated the dark emissary of the Empress of the Dark Spaces and reclaimed the Dream Door for the ghosts and for the living. It had seemed like such a great victory, but the uneasy feeling she'd had since then just wouldn't seem to go away.

She shook her head and tried to make herself

concentrate. She carefully traced the outlines of a typical medieval monastery and started labeling the various buildings. Then she stopped and glanced out of the window. The rain was beating against the glass like impatient fingers and she could just make out the trees on the road, bending and lashing about in the wind.

She watched it for a while and the reason for her mood slowly dawned on her.

It was because everything was back the way it was. She walked to and from school alone and was still the "weird girl," the one no one really wanted to talk to. Sophie Warren and her friends still lay in wait and poured scorn on her every chance they got. She was still only an average student and she wasn't showing any signs of "blossoming," as her mother had promised. And to cap it all off, Steve, the only person who knew her as anything other than the girl whose parents had died, had apparently stopped speaking to her.

Which, of course, was the way things had been before they'd found the door to the Other Side.

She chewed on the end of her pen and looked at the diagram of the abbey. Things must have been so simple then. You just became a monk or a nun and spent the rest of your life reading books and copying them out. And praying. There was a lot of praying, and an unreasonable amount of it seemed to take place in the early hours of the morning. That wouldn't be so great. But still . . . they didn't have to worry about exams, and some of them got to work on the farm. Although perhaps that wouldn't be so great either, seeing as there wasn't any farm machinery.

Belladonna sighed. She still didn't know what the Spellbinder really was, even though she was it. There had been others before her, she knew that much. Had they been left in the dark as well? Or had they known exactly what to do and when? It seemed that all she had done was react to something that had happened, and that really didn't strike her as the best way to go about things. It was like her dad with their old car—every time something went wrong, he would get it fixed, but he never did any maintenance (unlike Peter Davis's Dad, who spent so much time under *their* family car that Belladonna suspected Peter didn't even know what his own father looked like). The result was that the Johnson family car slowly fell apart. More slowly than if he'd done nothing at all, of course, but it fell apart all the same.

It all gave her the feeling that something was missing, that there really ought to be someone who could explain what she should do. Or perhaps it really would just come to her—maybe she'd sort of ripen, like an apple in a brown paper bag. Though, if that was the plan, it was a very haphazard one. She sighed again. Everything seemed so complicated and yet dull at the same time. She filled in the names of the kitchen, the dormitory, and the chapter house. But perhaps it was always like that, no matter what time you were born in. The past always seemed simple, the present was always slightly disappointing, and the future was always just a little bit scary.

The next day it was still raining, so she pulled on her boots, at her mother's insistence, shoved her shoes into her grubby pink backpack, and trudged off to school for another dismal day. She hung up her coat and was just taking off her boots when Lucy Fisher suddenly appeared at her elbow. Lucy was probably the only girl in school who was even more shy than Belladonna. She was tiny for her age, and pale as a charnel sprite, with a tangled mop of blond hair surrounding an ethereal face.

"Hey," she said, "did you hear?"

"What?"

"Mr. Watson's taking us on a field trip to some old monastery next Tuesday. It's an all-day thing, so you know what that means!"

Belladonna looked at her blankly. Lucy glanced around to make sure no one was listening, then leaned in.

"No Latin," she whispered, grinning lopsidedly. "Isn't that great?"

Before Belladonna could answer, Lucy was gone, off to spread the good news in her endless, futile efforts to be accepted. Belladonna sighed and hoped against hope that she didn't give the same impression.

Sure enough, when History rolled around, Mr. Watson handed out permission letters to be signed by parents and informed everyone that they had to be at the school by seven in the morning the following Tuesday and to bring sandwiches for lunch because they would be gone all day.

Belladonna shoved the note into her bag.

As soon as school was over, she walked to her grandmother's house on Yarrow Street. Approvals, permissions, and sick notes all had to be signed, and seeing as her parents were currently residing (so far as anyone else was concerned) in a shared grave in the churchyard, their signatures didn't carry much weight. Everything of that sort had to be handled by Grandma Johnson, who took her responsibilities very seriously.

Belladonna rang the front doorbell and saw the familiar twitch of the curtains in the séance room, shortly followed by the sound of the latch and the sight of Grandma Johnson flinging the door wide.

"Well, Belladonna!" she said, beaming. "What a surprise! Come in, dear, come in. Get your wet things off and go into the back room. I've got a client. Won't be a mo."

Belladonna nodded, relieved that it was just an ordinary séance. Ever since she'd discovered that her grandmother was a senior member of the Eidolon Council, she was never quite sure how many people she'd find in the house. The Council were supposed to work with their opposite number in the Land of the Dead, the Conclave of Shadows, on things that affected both worlds, but Belladonna was still not entirely convinced that they really achieved anything much at all.

She took off her coat, hung it on the end of the banister, and squeezed past all the assorted junk in the hallway to the back sitting room. Grandma Johnson smoothed Belladonna's dark hair with her hand as she passed, then winked and returned to her séance room, resuming a session that involved rather more than the usual amounts of hooting, table thumping, and moans, while Belladonna tried to find something to watch on the television.

Grandma Johnson was the only person Belladonna knew who still had an indoor aerial. Her parents had been dead for two years, but at least they had satellite. She pushed the wires of the rabbit-ear antennae from side to side, up and across, until she managed a configuration that brought in a grainy picture that she thought might be a cooking show. Or something about cars. No . . . interior design.

She sat in a hard wingback chair and squinted at the screen as the rain stopped outside and silence settled over the house. Except for the moaning next door, of course. Belladonna smiled—whoever the client was, they were getting the full four-star treatment, though she knew that the witch bottles hidden under the front and back steps meant that there wasn't a ghost anywhere in the building.

After about fifteen minutes, she heard the front door click shut, and her grandmother bustled into the sitting room.

"Right!" she said, rubbing her hands together. "What about some cake?"

"Yes, please," said Belladonna. "I'm starved!"

She followed her grandmother into the ridiculously small kitchen at the back of the house, and watched as she took a box out of the fridge and unpacked a small sponge sandwich cake. Grandma Johnson never cooked. If you couldn't get it pre-made at the local supermarket, then she wouldn't have it. Belladonna had a feeling that her Dad had never had a home-cooked meal until he married her Mum.

Grandma Johnson cut two huge slices, made them each a cup of tea, and herded Belladonna back into the warm sitting room.

"Now," she said, once they had each had a few bites of cake, "what brings you here? Does something need signing?"

"Yes," said Belladonna a little sheepishly, aware that she hadn't been seeing her grandmother as often as she should. "There's a trip to Fenchurch Abbey next Tuesday."

"Ah," said her grandmother. "Establishment of the monasteries, eh? Or is it dissolution? I can't remember where you're up to."

"Establishment," said Belladonna, pulling the permission slip out of her bag.

Her grandmother took it and then spent about ten minutes looking around for her glasses, which turned out to be inside a particularly ugly pottery vase in the shape of a yellow-eyed cat.

"Let's see . . . hmm . . . sandwiches, eh?"

"It's an all-day trip," explained Belladonna.

"I can see that," said her grandmother, peering at her over the top of her glasses. "Well, it all sounds alright. Though I can't imagine why they have to have these trips in the middle of winter. You're going to absolutely freeze up there. Make sure you wear two extra pairs of socks."

Belladonna shuddered at the thought of anyone seeing her bundled up like a four-year-old. She'd be suggesting mittens on a string next.

"And mittens," said her grandmother, right on cue. "They're so much warmer than gloves."

Belladonna smiled and took another bite of cake.

"Now," said her grandmother, leaning forward, "how are things going at school?"

"It's boring," said Belladonna.

"Boring? How can it be boring?"

"It just is," said Belladonna.

"Nonsense," said her grandmother, handing her the signed permission slip. "These are the best years of your life. You'll see. It'll get better."

Belladonna finished her cake and wondered if her grandmother had ever been to school and if it had been different then. Maybe things really were interesting in the olden days. Maybe everyone had been nice and played hockey and had midnight feasts and ripping adventures, but Belladonna doubted it. Something told her that once people left school, a sort of selective memory kicked in and all the bad stuff, all the teasing and humiliation, all the tedious classes and endless mounds of homework, were forgotten in favor of half-recalled sunny summer after-noons filled with laughter, tennis, and surprise picnics.

"I'd better get going," she said.

"Goodness, is that the time?" said her grandmother, leaping to her feet and nearly knocking over a nearby occasional table crowded with china figurines. "I've got a new client coming at five! Off you go. Say hello to your Mum and Dad."

She hustled Belladonna out of the sitting room, helped her into her coat, and practically shoved her out the front door. Belladonna sighed and zipped up her coat. The rain might have stopped, but the wind was still icy cold and cut to the bone. She hoisted her backpack onto her shoulder and walked down the front steps just as the new client arrived.

It was a woman. Belladonna could tell that from the shoes, but almost nothing else was visible behind the capacious black coat with its high collar and the wide plaid scarf that encircled her neck and the lower part of her face. The woman swept past Belladonna, and for a moment, as the fabric of the coat brushed against her hand, she shuddered, her feeling of February gloom somehow magnified. She glanced back and saw the woman reach up and ring the doorbell with a long leather-gloved hand. Grandma Johnson opened the door and ushered her in, all smiles and happy conversation, but Belladonna noticed that as she did so, something fell from beneath the woman's coat and landed on the top step.

She waited until the door had clicked shut and the orange "séance light" had come on in the front room, then she quickly scrambled up the steps to see what the mysterious new client had lost.

It was still there, gleaming slightly in the sickly glow from the old streetlamps. Belladonna hesitated for a moment, then reached down and picked it up, a knot forming in her stomach.

It was a large black feather.

2

The Black Feather

THE WEEKEND SEEMED to go on forever. Belladonna kept the feather in her backpack at first, but on Saturday evening she decided to show it to her parents. Their response was not quite what she expected. Her mother just thought it was dirty and that she might catch something from it, while her father thought it was probably from a crow. When Belladonna pointed out that it was far too big to have come from a crow, he just shrugged and suggested that it might be from a raven.

"A raven?" she said, images of dive-bombing Night Ravens leaping into her mind. She remembered them swooping out of the night sky in the Land of the Dead, minions of Dr. Ashe.

"Yes," said her Dad calmly, "a raven. Like they have at the Tower of London. Those things are huge."

Belladonna stared at him. Was it really possible that he had forgotten about the Night Ravens? But her Dad just turned his attention back to the television.

"Have you seen this?" he said. "They've decided to widen Ellsmore Road."

"What's wrong with that?" asked her mother. "It's needed it for years. I mean, it's all very well having motor-ways and bypasses, but if you can't even get to the things without a half-hour wait in traffic, what on earth is the point?"

"Yes, but now?" interrupted her father. "In the middle of winter? The days are so short, it's going to take for-ever. And cars'll be sitting there in rush hour, not moving, with their heaters on and—"

Mrs. Johnson smiled indulgently as the ghost of her husband turned a peculiar shade of red.

"You don't have to do it anymore, dear," she pointed out gently.

"That's not the point," he said. "*Someone* does."

Belladonna sighed and slowly twirled the feather, watching the glossy black surface shimmer from blue-black to ebony in the flickering light of the television.

"Really, Belladonna," said her mother, looking con-cerned, "throw it away. It's probably got vermin."

Belladonna nodded and walked into the kitchen. She flipped open the top of the trash bin and was about to drop it inside when something stopped her. She had no idea what it was, but she just knew that this was important and it shouldn't be consigned to a collection of potato peelings, crushed frozen-food containers, and yesterday's tea leaves. She glanced back toward the living room. She could hear her parents talking softly, followed by the theme tune for

Staunchly Springs. They wouldn't be out for at least forty-five minutes once the saga of betrayal, death, and scandal set in a street of reasonably priced homes picked up where Thursday's episode had left off—with Mrs. Carpenter bundling what she thought was her husband's dead body into the deep freeze, except that (as her mother had pointed out) he almost certainly wasn't actually dead.

Belladonna crept down the hall and slipped the feather back into her backpack. She waited for a moment by the door in the chilly hall, listening to the sounds of home, and couldn't help but wonder why she felt the way she did. When she was in the Land of the Dead, all she could think about was getting home and returning to a normal life, but now that she was back and everything had returned to the way it was before she had found the door marked seventy-three, she couldn't shake a sense of apprehension and the feeling that something, somewhere wasn't right.

The next morning she raced through breakfast and told her parents that she was going to the park for a walk.

"Wear your boots," said her mother in that matter-of-fact tone that only people who don't actually have to go outside on freezing cold days use.

Belladonna pulled on her wellies and picked up her backpack.

"Scarf!" yelled her mother from the kitchen.

Belladonna sighed and looped the scarf around her neck. She hated the scarf. It was a kind of a dull greenish plaid and was far too long, but once she was outside, she was glad she had it. The morning air cut like a knife through all her careful preparations and she hadn't gone two meters before her toes felt numb and her fingers tingled. She pulled the scarf up over her freezing nose and headed off down Lychgate Lane toward the town center.

It was another typical February day, freezing and grim with a low gray sky that constantly threatened rain and would almost certainly deliver it before the day was out. Belladonna shoved her hands in her pockets and wished she'd remembered her gloves.

The Christmas lights were still up in the High Street, but now that the holidays were over, they seemed more sad than cheerful, with grubby-looking snowflakes and reindeer that were missing more than a few lights and had clearly suffered in last week's storms. They swayed slightly in the icy wind, still grinning above the street, but the shoppers were all oblivious. Life had moved on, Christmas was over, and the endless gloom of February was making everyone feel that spring would never come and the sun would never shine again.

Belladonna shivered on the wet pavement and darted into Gimball's to warm up. Gimball's was a rather old-fashioned department store, with a giant circular staircase where most shops had escalators. It still had long counters where gloves were sold even in the summer, and the ladies' toilets had a sitting room with couches and elegant occasional tables. Belladonna drifted among the glass-topped counters until the feeling returned to her fingers, then made her way back outside and up the street.

Evans Electronics was at the far end. Her mother always referred to it as the "shabby end" with a sort of sneer in her voice that Belladonna suspected had more to do with her failed efforts to save the old theatre than anything else. Though, as she walked up the street on this cold February day, Belladonna did have to admit that the further she went, the more dismal things got. The fresh, bright windows of the shops near Gimball's gave way to grubby panes of glass shielding displays that hadn't changed since the summer. Sad travel agents showed peeling posters of faded Spanish beaches and washed-out cruise ships on barely blue oceans; shoe shops crowded their windows with rank upon rank of high-heeled shoes, near enough to the fashionable styles to make people pause and look, but not enough to make anyone actually go inside; while small boutiques promoting perpetual sales crowded against grubby newsagents and the sort of small would-be department stores that always seemed to be announcing that "Everything must go!"

A cold misty rain began to fall as Belladonna approached the electronics shop in the old theatre. She heard it before she saw it, of course: the raucous clatter and clang of DVD players, stereos, and televisions spewing out of the shop and across the pavement like a barbarian army. The window was circled with flashing colored Christmas lights, and little arcs of white had been painted in the corners in a vain imitation of snow.

She stepped inside and blinked for a moment in the bright fluorescent glare. Mr. Evans was helping a customer and smiled thinly at her as she walked toward him. He had always been skinny, but since his wife had left him, he seemed to have almost faded away. His face was gaunt, with shadows under the eyes, and his body seemed to strain against some unseen weight.

Mrs. Evans had taken off soon after she and Steve had returned from the Other Side, leaving only the briefest of notes on the kitchen table. When she'd first heard about it, Belladonna had wanted to tell Steve that his mother had seemed to know more than she really ought to when she'd tried to stop them going through to the Other Side, but somehow the moment never seemed right.

Steve's Dad was devastated and initially spent his days standing at the front of his shop staring into space. After a few weeks of that, he pulled himself together and decided that Steve would have to take up the slack in the family business, which meant that apart from school and football practice, Steve had to spend every spare moment helping in the shop.

"He's in the back, love," he said as she approached. "He's supposed to be bringing up some of them new MP-whatsits, but he's been gone long enough to make the things by hand."

Belladonna smiled and made her way past the crowded ranks of screaming machinery to a small door at the back of what had once been the town's only theatre. She pushed it open and stepped into the cool semidarkness. Around her, where the seats had been, ranks of boxed electronics were stacked like the hedges in a maze. Other than the boxes, the theatre was frozen in time—even the gilded cupids on the front of the dress balcony looked like they were waiting for the evening performance. Belladonna glanced up at the stage. The old scenery was piled at the back where she and Steve had left it, and the doorway "flat" that had been their first entry into the Land of the Dead lay on the stage where it had fallen when Belladonna had struggled with Steve's mother. She could still make out the marks on the dusty stage floor where they had fought, though since October, new dust had settled over them like a drift of fresh snow. Soon any sign of their skirmish would be gone.

Belladonna turned away from the stage, pushed her hair behind her ears, and walked slowly past the rows of boxes, peering down each narrow canyon, looking for Steve.

All was silent.

She strained to hear anything that would indicate someone was in here looking for something, which was, after all, what he was supposed to be doing.

Nothing. She took another step forward and something cracked under her foot. It was only an old piece of plastic packing, but in the empty theatre, it sounded like a gunshot. Steve's head shot up like a meerkat on the savannah.

"I'm just getting them!" he said. "Oh, it's you."

He disappeared once more behind the bastion of boxes. Belladonna sighed and made her way between the narrow rows to where Steve sat surrounded by the garish colors and detailed specs of DVD boxes and televisions, reading a comic and eating a packet of chips. He barely glanced up.

"What do you want?" he said grimly.

"What are you doing back here?" said Belladonna, ignoring his surly tone. "It's freezing."

"Taking a break," he muttered.

"Your Dad said you were supposed to be bringing some stuff up to the shop."

Steve looked up darkly and Belladonna decided against pursuing the subject. This wasn't going at all as she'd imagined, and it seemed like the best option was to forget about what Steve's Dad wanted or had said or anything to do with the shop. She let her hair drop down from behind her ears, curtaining off her face until all that was visible were her dark eyes.

"I found something," she said finally. "Mum and Dad said it wasn't anything, but . . ."

Her voice trailed off. She suddenly felt really stupid standing there among all the boxes, talking about feathers.

"Never mind," she muttered. "Sorry."

She turned on her heel and started making her way back down the narrow canyon of boxes.

"Wait!" said Steve.

Belladonna ignored him. She wished she'd never come. She should have thrown the feather away like her mother said. She squeezed past some particularly large projection TV boxes and was just about to step out into what had been the theatre aisle when her way was suddenly blocked.

"I'm . . . I'm sorry, okay?" said Steve, shoving his hands into his pockets. "It's just . . ."

They stared at each other for a moment, then Belladonna swung her backpack to the ground.

"I found something," she said, and proceeded to tell him about her grandmother's new client and the mysterious feather.

Steve seemed about to make some smart remark about people who went to séances in general and her grandmother's clients in particular, but his expression changed when she got to the part about the feather. Belladonna thought he blanched slightly and she definitely saw a muscle in his jaw tighten.

For her, much of last October's adventure had been about discovering why Dr. Ashe had captured all the ghosts, trying to prevent the long-dead necromancer from opening a door to the Dark Spaces for the Empress to return, and realizing that she, Belladonna Johnson, really was the Spellbinder. But she knew that for Steve the most vivid memory was of the Night Raven's poison scorching through his veins, and she suspected that he still woke up in the night with his heart pounding at the memory of hovering near death with the evil Dr. Ashe administering just enough antidote to keep him alive, but never enough to make him well.

"No," she said hastily, "I don't think it's a Night Raven. It's too big."

She flipped open the top of her backpack and rummaged around. Where was it? Why was nothing ever easy? She threw her notebook, six packets of Parma Violets, and two cans of Tizer onto the floor, pushed aside the remains of last Wednesday's sandwiches (some kind of nasty avocado spread), and finally retrieved the long, blue-black feather.

Steve looked at it, then took it from her and turned it over slowly.

"D'you think it could be a—"

"A Kere?" It was the one thing that would be worse than Night Ravens, for the Kere had said she was the bringer of Death itself.

"Yeah." He handed it back. "But it couldn't be. We killed her or sent her back to wherever she'd come from."

Belladonna nodded dubiously and bit her lip.

"What?" said Steve, starting to get annoyed.

"Don't you remember what she said? She said she was one of the Keres, bringers of death. *One of.* What if there are more?"

"More?"

He made her feel that it was somehow her fault. She began shoving her belongings back into her backpack.

"Did she have wings?" asked Steve as Belladonna slid the feather into a side pocket and zipped it closed. "The woman, I mean. The visitor. Could you tell?"

"She was wearing a big black coat," said Belladonna. "But . . . no, not that I saw."

"Well, she can't have been a Kere, then, could she? I mean, you'd hardly miss wings that size, would you?"

Belladonna looked at him. She was almost certain that a creature like a Kere would have no difficulty concealing her wings from mortal eyes, and she was just as certain that Steve knew that. But there was a sort of eagerness in his eyes, a desire for things to return to the way they had been before they found the Door. Could he really feel that way? Only a few months ago he'd joined her quest to find her parents on the Other Side with almost fearless glee. But perhaps that was the problem—she had found her parents, but he had returned to discover that his mother had gone. Just gone. In that ordinary human way that happened every day and that no amount of questing or adventure could fix.

"No, you're right," she said, smiling. "I was just being silly, I suppose. She probably didn't even drop it."

"You said it was nearly dark."

Belladonna nodded and swung her bag over her shoulder. Steve walked with her to the front of the shop.

"See you on Monday, then," he said.

"Yeah, see you," said Belladonna and headed for home.

A slow drizzle had started and the icy wind clawed at her face and ears. As she trudged up the street, she could hear Steve's Dad asking him where the MP-whatsits were and what on earth he'd been doing in the storeroom all that time and didn't he know that there was a sale on and he couldn't see to every customer himself and . . .

The sound of his voice gradually faded into the general babble of voices and sounds, and Belladonna walked quickly home, hoping that Steve was right but knowing that he wasn't.

The Chair

THE WEEKEND'S DRIZZLE had developed into a full-fledged downpour by Monday morning. Belladonna gazed grimly out of the kitchen window as she ate her cereal. Her father was leaning against the doorjamb, watching the steady rivulets of rainwater cascading down the kitchen window.

"Sorry I can't take you into school, Belladonna," he sighed. "You're going to get soaked through."

Belladonna smiled encouragingly. She knew her parents hated the fact that they couldn't take more part in her life, but given that they were dead, she thought they did a pretty good job.

"It's okay," she said. "I'll just take an umbrella."

The umbrella was purple with two broken spokes and a small tear on one side. It did nothing to belie Belladonna's image as a fashion disaster, but it did keep some of the rain off as she trudged through the gloomy streets to school.

By the time she got there, she was freezing, her hair hanging down like rats' tails and her shoes soaked through. She hung her coat and scarf on a hook in the cloakroom and made her way to the classroom. Sophie Warren and her friends were already there, of course, warming the backs of their legs on the radiator. Sophie's Dad drove her to school every day, so she always looked flawless, though she was the kind of girl who never seemed to get ruffled at all. Netball, lacrosse, tennis, Sophie came through it all with the sleek aplomb of a supermodel. On days when outdoor sports combined with pouring rain and slicing wind, and every other girl in class ended up looking like they'd been dragged through a hedge backward, there was still hardly a hair out of place on Sophie's blond head. Though Belladonna suspected that, given the opportunity, the Wild Hunt would easily take her down in a chase to the death. She smiled a little at the thought of Sophie running for her life, pursued by a howling mythological horde, horses and riders thundering out of the sky, their huge dogs baying beside them, but she was soon brought back to earth by the sound of barely suppressed giggles.

She glanced up. By the way they were all looking at her, Belladonna guessed that Sophie had just said something terribly funny about her sodden appearance.

She dumped her bag by the side of her desk and sat down with a thump.

The day pretty much went downhill from there, and by the time lunch rolled around, Belladonna was feeling gloomy and frustrated, and the cheese and onion pie on offer in the school cafeteria didn't help at all.

She put her coat on and wandered outside, avoiding the main areas of the grounds and walking instead along the side of one of the Victorian houses that made up the school buildings. It was a little dark and considerably colder than the rest of the playground, but there was a small bench nestled beneath some leggy, overgrown bushes, where she knew no one would bother her.

At least that was what she thought.

"Belladonna!" The familiar voice sounded more than usually excited.

Belladonna sighed and looked up. Elsie was leaning out of a window near the back door. The window was closed, but that was neither here nor there for Elsie, given that she'd been dead for nearly a hundred years.

"What?" said Belladonna, a note of irritation creeping into her voice.

"It's Sophie," said Elsie, "that odious Warren girl."

"I'm not interested in her," sniffed Belladonna. "I'm trying to read."

"Oh, right. Fine, then. You can find out the hard way."

"Find out what?"

"Oh . . . nothing."

Elsie was clearly miffed. Belladonna stood up and walked over to the building. She couldn't risk anyone seeing her shouting in the direction of an empty window, and Elsie couldn't leave the school buildings that she had chosen to haunt.

"Find out what?" repeated Belladonna testily.

Elsie looked away, toying with one of her luxuriant brown curls. Belladonna sighed loudly and turned to walk away.

"She and her friends are planning a trick," said Elsie hastily.

"What else is new?" muttered Belladonna, turning back.

"You're not going to just *let* them?" Elsie looked at Belladonna in amazement.

"They're always doing it," explained Belladonna. "I'm used to it."

"But . . ."

"It's just easier," she explained. "They get their jollies and then redirect their energies onto some other target. It's okay."

"No, it isn't!" Elsie sounded genuinely shocked. "You can't let people walk all over you just because they can! That's not the attitude that won the Empire!"

"Britain doesn't have an empire anymore."

"Aha! Well . . . exactly!"

Elsie folded her arms triumphantly.

"No," said Belladonna. "We didn't lose the empire because we didn't . . . Look, fighting doesn't prove anything."

"Yes, it does," said Elsie with the kind of certainty that made Belladonna a little jealous. "Fighting proves who is strongest. And cleverest. But anyway, I wasn't suggesting fighting. I was thinking more of 'own's back.'"

Belladonna looked at her. There was something undeniably tempting about getting back at Sophie Warren, even if it did mean that her life would be made thoroughly miserable afterward.

"What is she planning?" she asked finally.

"She and those friends of hers have been working a chair apart. Loosening the joints. They've had it hidden in the caretaker's closet. They've been working on it since last week, but I just saw them take it to the classroom. They took your chair away and put the wobbly one in its place."

Belladonna sighed. Now that Elsie had told her, she knew she'd have to do something. She reached forward and opened the door into the dark stairwell. Elsie was waiting, practically glowing with anticipation.

"What are you going to do?" she asked, following Belladonna up the stairs, the enormous black taffeta bow bobbing in her hair.

Belladonna didn't answer, she just peeked into the room to make sure no one was there before creeping in and walking up to her chair. She laid a hand on it and rocked it lightly—everything wobbled and one of the stretchers fell off.

"Right," she said, grim determination in her voice.

She dragged Sophie's chair away and carefully slid the broken chair into its place, leaving plenty of room between the chair and the desk so that Sophie wouldn't have to move it to sit down.

"A little more to the right," said Elsie. "You should try to make it look just the way she left it."

"Why do I think you've done this before?"

"It's a classic," beamed Elsie. "The collapsing chair. The classics always work."

"I'm going to get into so much trouble for this."

"No, you won't. No one except Sophie will know it was you, and she can't tell on you without revealing that she tried to do it to you first."

"I meant Sophie," said Belladonna, going to the door and admiring her handiwork from afar. "Sophie will make it her life's work to make my life miserable. Yes, I think that'll work."

"I thought she already did that."

"Well, yes, but . . ."

At that moment the bell for the end of lunch blared through the school and across the grounds, and children began to meander indoors, fingers and noses nearly numb from the cold.

Sophie and her friends walked in and took up their usual positions in the window with their backs against the radiators. Belladonna knew that they were looking at her, but she tried to adopt an air of nonchalance and wandered to the opposite window. She stared out across the wintry park as if she were really curious about something. As if a herd of wildebeest had suddenly decided to migrate through the middle of the playground while unbeknownst to them a cheetah lurked behind the broken fountain.

For a few moments it seemed that the whole world and everything in it had stopped. As if time itself had paused. But, inevitably, Mr. Watson eventually strode in, books, folders, and handouts under his arm.

"Right, everybody," he said, dumping his papers onto

his desk, "I'm going to be collecting your permission slips for the abbey in just a moment, but first Miss Parker would like a word."

At the name of the redoubtable headmistress of Dullworth's, everyone scuttled to their desks and stood at attention.

Oh, no! thought Belladonna. *No! Not in front of Miss Parker!*

Miss Parker walked into the room. As usual she was wearing a crisp navy blue suit, with a skirt that reached exactly three centimeters below her knees. Her shoes were black and sensible, and around her neck was a string of pearls that was neither too small to be worth the bother nor so large as to be ostentatious. Her expertly cropped hair curled into two spikes at her jawline, perfectly framing her pale face with its gimlet eyes and pursed red mouth.

She stopped in front of Mr. Watson's desk and nodded to him before turning back to the students.

"I just want a word or two about the responsibilities of Dullworth students when they are out on school trips," she said. "You may sit down."

There was much scraping of chairs on the floor as everyone sat down. Miss Parker had taken to delivering these brief words of warning ever since the Year 11s had visited Fordham Farm on the same day as a group from Beeston Secondary and ended up tossing several of them into the pigstys. Belladonna sank into her chair and tried not to look across at Sophie, as if her not looking might prevent the inevitable.

It didn't.

There was a yelp and a crash and the roar of laughter as everyone in the room luxuriated in the most undignified fall of Sophie Warren. Everyone except Belladonna . . . and Miss Parker. Even Mr. Watson could barely conceal his delight, and as Belladonna turned slowly to look at Sophie, she had to admit, even in the midst of her foreboding about what would happen next, that seeing her nemesis sitting on the floor, surrounded by the constituent parts of her chair, her legs stretched out and her perfectly coiffed hair hanging over her stunned face, was almost worth the amount of trouble she was about to be in.

She turned around and glanced at Steve, confident that he would be impressed with her achievement.

But he wasn't. He wasn't even looking at Sophie. He was looking at Belladonna, and his face was shocked and serious and perhaps a little angry.

Belladonna turned away. Why was he looking like that? Could it be that he really liked Sophie? He certainly spent plenty of time with her, but Belladonna had always assumed that it was because his friend Gareth was her brother.

"Quiet!" Miss Parker's voice cut through the giggles and guffaws like a hot knife through butter. "Get up, Miss Warren. There appears to be a spare chair over there."

Sophie scrambled to her feet and retrieved what had been Belladonna's chair from the front of the room.

"Right." Miss Parker raked the class with a humorless glare. "This is exactly the sort of behavior I do *not* expect from Dullworth students. Tomorrow you will be out in public for an entire day. I am confident that your behavior will be exemplary. Am I correct in feeling so confident?"

There was a pause, then a mumbled "Yes, Miss" rolled around the room like the distant lowing of cattle.

"Right. Carry on, Mr. Watson."

She raked the class with a final steely stare, then turned and walked out, closing the door behind her with a click. Mr. Watson sighed, then turned to the blackboard and began writing a list of the different orders of monks. Benedictine, Cistercian, Dominican . . .

Belladonna opened her textbook and glanced around. Everyone was copying down the list in their workbooks. Everyone except Sophie Warren. Sophie was chewing on the feather-maned pink velvet pony that adorned the end of her pencil and staring at Belladonna with unalloyed hatred in her eyes.

"Right," said Mr. Watson, turning around. "Who can tell me the differences between the various orders of monks?"

Several hands shot into the air, but Belladonna didn't hear what was said. She turned slowly to see what Steve was doing, but he was gazing out of the window as usual. She turned back and began to doodle on her exercise book. The minutes ticked slowly by. She turned to look at Steve again. This time, he was looking at her. His face was grim and as she caught his eye, he shook his head slightly and looked away. She looked at the clock above the door. The lesson wasn't even half over. Why had she done it? She'd been managing alright before. Why did she listen to Elsie?

The minutes ticked by. *You know,* thought Belladonna, *I'm probably making this worse than it really is.* After all, Sophie played practical jokes on loads of people. She probably didn't think anything of someone doing it back. And it must have happened before, though she had to admit that she couldn't think of a time when it had. Still, Sophie was just an ordinary girl, and Belladonna was the Spellbinder and really ought to stop being so gloomy about everything.

Belladonna had almost talked herself into feeling alright about the whole thing when there was a loud *CRACK* to her left.

Sophie Warren had just bitten the head off her pony.

4

The Last Paladin

"WHAT ON EARTH were you thinking?"

"I don't know. It seemed like a good idea. Like it would serve her right. Elsie said—"

"Oh, right!" Steve rolled his eyes. "I should've known!"

They were huddled in the library, near the shelves of classics and the hidden entrance to the Sibyl. Belladonna had hurried in there as soon as History ended, on the basis that the library was the last place she would expect Sophie to go. Steve had soon joined her, throwing his backpack on the floor and earning a hissed "sh!" from Mrs. Collins, the librarian, as she popped in to sharpen a pencil. Mrs. Collins never spent any time in the actual library, which she found claustrophobic, instead preferring to linger in the much larger study hall next door.

Belladonna and Steve pretended to be looking for books until she'd gone.

"Anyway," said Belladonna, starting to get angry, "why is it such a big deal? She does it to other people all the time."

"Didn't you notice that no one ever retaliates?" asked Steve.

Belladonna shook her head.

"We were in the same junior school," he whispered. "One day, Gareth played some joke, I can't remember what. We all thought it was really funny. Anyway, a couple of days later, Gareth didn't come to school. He'd broken his leg."

"Broken his leg?"

"Yeah, they both took riding lessons and she loosened the . . . the thing that holds the saddle on . . ."

"The girth."

"Yeah, the girth. And he fell off and broke his leg. And that was her own brother! And they're twins—twins are supposed to be really, you know, close."

Belladonna sighed, then looked up and tucked her hair behind her ears in what she hoped was a convincingly defiant gesture.

"Well," she said, "it's done now. I'll just stay out of her way, that's all."

She smiled swiftly and strode out of the library and off to double Geography.

It was all so stupid. Sophie Warren was just a girl. She wasn't a Kere or an evil alchemist. She didn't have magic powers. Still, by the time the school day ground to a close, Belladonna was ready for a warm fire and her tea, and she barely felt the rain as she splashed through the streets, straining to hold on to the purple umbrella as the greedy wind tried to snatch it from her grasp.

She paused by the church and watched the rain

pounding on the old gravestones, as the wind whipped through the yew trees, scattering the floral tributes. For a moment she thought she saw someone on the opposite side near the church, but when she looked again, no one was there. She shrugged and turned for home—it was probably just a charnel sprite taking a break from conducting the dead to the Other Side.

The weather was no better the next morning, though the wind seemed to have died down a bit, and Belladonna didn't feel quite so much like an arctic explorer as she made her way to school. She paused at the gate to the church-yard again and strained to see if any charnel sprites were about, but they apparently had more sense than to linger in the long grass on a dismal day.

She reached into a side pocket of her backpack and pulled out a packet of Parma Violets. She'd had a perfectly decent breakfast, of course, but there was something about rainy days (or any days, for that matter) that just cried out for sweets on the way to school.

Almost everyone was on the bus by the time she rounded the corner, and Mr. Watson was gazing anxiously up the street, attendance sheet in hand. He waved her on, exasperatedly tapping his watch.

"Late again, Johnson," he said as she scrambled onto the bus.

Belladonna looked around. The only seat left was next to Peter Davis, who was sitting on the aisle, deeply en-grossed in the handheld game that he'd got for Christmas. He swiveled around to let her have the window seat but didn't look up. So far as Belladonna had been able to make out, he never looked up. The most any teacher had been able to get out of him was the occasional grunt, though he always did well on tests. Belladonna glanced at him as his fingers sped over the small machine and wondered if he was like this at home and if he'd ever spoken a complete sentence.

Mr. Watson did a final quick head count, tapped the driver on the shoulder, and the bus lurched off. The decibel level immediately skyrocketed and Belladonna hunkered down, trying to cut herself off from the cacophony by concentrating on the view from the window.

It wasn't much of a view. First there were city streets as they made their way through the gray town, then the highway on-ramp, and after that, nothing but road and cars and steadily pouring rain streaking across the windows.

"Hey, Belladonna," hissed a voice at her ear.

She turned around. The face of Sophie sidekick Louise Pargiter was pressed into the space between the two headrests.

"What?"

"Why did your mother name you after a *weed*?"

Belladonna rolled her eyes and turned back to the window, but Louise wasn't going to be put off so easily.

"I suppose you thought that chair thing was funny yesterday?"

Belladonna didn't respond.

"Huh. Well, enjoy your last day of freedom."

"Shhhh!" Sophie yanked Louise back into her seat. "You'll spoil it!"

Belladonna sighed. Great. Now she'd be spending the whole rest of the day waiting for Sophie's revenge. She wished she'd just do whatever it was and get it over with.

"Idiots."

Belladonna glanced to her left in surprise. Peter looked up from his game.

"They're idiots," he said, smiling. "You probably already know that."

Belladonna nodded and smiled back, but he had already returned to the delights of his game. His concentration gave him a certain sense of calm, which Belladonna couldn't help but begin to share. Even among the whizzing uproar of the rest of the class on the bus, their two seats seemed somehow apart and silent. She settled down and gazed out of the window at the wet roads and the cars and the occasional distant house, its windows bright against the gloomy morning.

After about an hour, the noise level declined and people started reading or sleeping. In another half hour, the rain had begun to subside and the coach left the highway and began to wend its way down narrow country lanes, past green fields, tumbledown farm buildings, and verdant clumps of trees whose low-hanging branches scraped across the roof like eager fingers. Gradually the number of buildings declined and the trees closed in ever more tightly. The road was only one lane wide now and Bella-donna wondered what on earth would happen if they met something coming the other way.

Finally, as the road began to descend into a narrow valley, Mr. Watson stood up.

"Alright!" he said. "Pay attention!"

The ones who had been sleeping looked up bleary-eyed as Mr. Watson pulled a sheaf of handouts from his bag.

"Pass these around," he commanded, shoving the stack into the hands of Alison Jones, who beamed at him. Alison always sat near the front on Mr. Watson's trips—she'd had a crush on him since her very first day, and her faithfulness showed no signs of abating. It made her the target of a great deal of Sophie Warren's spite, but she didn't care. For his part, like almost everything else to do with his students, Mr. Watson was blissfully unaware.

"Right," said Mr. Watson, once everyone had a copy. "On page one, as you can see, there's a brief history of Fenchurch. Not too much detail—you should all know this already. Page two is a ground plan of the abbey. I expect you all to name the different parts before we leave today. Finally, there are three essay questions. Pick one. One. And you needn't look at me like that, Evans, this isn't a pleasure trip. One essay each, due next Tuesday. Got that?"

There was a general grumbling assent as the bus pulled into the gravel car park and ground to a halt under an aged oak tree. The doors crashed open and everyone piled out for the usual quick head count.

Belladonna looked around. There wasn't a sign of an abbey, just the car park and a rather grim-looking visitor center. And it was cold. Really, really cold. She zipped up her jacket and pulled on her gloves as Mr. Watson led them all into the visitor center.

After a quick word with the woman behind the cash

register, he led them past a few salvaged pieces of stone carving and out the opposite side of the building.

The whole class stopped and gasped. Reading about the scale of the old monasteries was one thing, but to actually see the massive ruins of one was something else altogether.

"Right," said Mr. Watson. "Has everyone got a watch? If you don't, find someone who has. I want everyone back at the picnic area over there by noon for lunch. Noon, got that? Half an hour. Right, off you go."

It was like a reenactment of a Viking raid: The whole class whooped and ran across the wet grass toward the towering buildings. Belladonna ran too, the grass whipping against her legs and the cold wind stinging her face. Then she slowed and finally stopped as the impossibly slender red sandstone arches of the nave soared skyward around her and almost blotted out the feeble February daylight. It was stunning. Each stone fit so perfectly with its neighbor and each piece of carving was so flawlessly executed, it was hard to believe it had all been done by hand over eight hundred years ago. She wandered through the nave and out onto the grass. She could see a cluster of her classmates near the exposed lower half of a monk's sarcophagus. They were taking turns lying in it and taking one another's picture. Nearby an elderly monk watched, sadly shaking his head. Belladonna caught his ghostly eye and smiled. He stared at her for a moment, clearly taken aback, then vanished.

Belladonna shrugged and turned back to the abbey.

She wrote *Nave* on the plan and set out in search of the refectory.

By lunchtime she'd found the refectory, the lay brothers' dormitory, the infirmary, and the kitchen. The monks had diverted a piece of the small river that ran through the valley so that it flowed through the kitchen. A kitchen with running water in the Middle Ages—it wasn't what she'd imagined.

She was just adding a sketch of the river to the plan when she heard a bell start to toll. She glanced at her watch. It was noon. Time for lunch.

It wasn't until she was halfway back to the picnic ground and walking through the nave that it occurred to her: There was no bell. There couldn't be—the monastery had been in ruins for over four hundred fifty years.

But there was. Deep and sonorous, the single spectral bell rang out from the empty air above the nave where once there had been a magnificent tower. Then she heard them. A hundred voices chanting plainsong. And there was a smell, a faint whiff of incense. She turned around and saw rank upon rank of shadowy monks in their white robes walking into the church and down what must once have been the aisle to their places for midday mass. Their voices echoed through the vast space as if the church were whole, which to them it was.

Belladonna watched them, almost hypnotized by the deep sound of their voices and the slow mesmerizing song. And then it was over. A bunch of kids charged through the ruins on their way to lunch, and the monks, the incense, and the song vanished. Belladonna sighed and made her way to the picnic area.

Everyone else was already there, and Mr. Watson gave her a stare and glanced at his watch as she made her way to an empty seat, brushed the accumulated dead leaves and gunk off it, sat down, and opened her sandwiches. Her mother had made them. They were brie with slivers of blanched almonds and probably seemed like a good idea to her mother, but after being in Belladonna's backpack for four hours, the almonds had gone sort of soggy and the cheese had nearly all run out of the sandwich and adhered to the plastic bag. Belladonna ate as much as she could stand while everyone listened to Mr. Watson talk about the founding of the monastery and how the Cistercian monks had broken away from the Benedictines—all of which they had already covered at length since the beginning of term.

After what seemed like an eternity of rambling, Mr. Watson finally announced that lunch was over and they had one more hour to finish marking their plans and decide on their essay topic.

Belladonna drifted through the abbey buildings again, slowly filling up her abbey plan with the building names: night stairs, bakehouse, brewhouse, cloisters, garden, garderobes (toilets, which also had running water), and the abbot's house. Eventually the only room missing was the chapter house. The chapter house was where the monks would meet to discuss the business of the monastery and it was usually on the east side of the cloisters, which would put it just about as far away from where she now was as it was possible to get. Belladonna looked around from the slight rise where the abbot's house had sat. Her feet were absolutely freezing, even with the boots and two pairs of socks, and she was wondering if she could get to the chapter house without walking on the wet grass. A collection of low stone foundations zigzagged their way through the grounds and seemed like her best option. She climbed onto the nearest one and set off.

It was nearly the end of the trip. The light was beginning to fade and she could see her classmates making their way back across the monks' cemetery to the visitor center. She walked quickly through the refectory again, and crossed the cloister toward the chapter house. It was very quiet. She glanced at her watch—she was late. Everyone else would be back now, maybe even climbing on the bus.

There was a low arched tunnel leading from the cloister into the chapter house. Belladonna hurried through it . . . and stopped.

She could hear voices, but something told her it wasn't ghosts. She stepped into the shadow of the tunnel and peered into the chapter house. The voices were low, but she recognized one. It was Steve.

She walked into the chapter house and peered through the gathering gloom. It had obviously once been a spectacular room. Unlike the nave, it wasn't daunting in size or scope, just a good-sized octagonal hall, its double arched windows still nearly complete, each with a huge delicately carved rosette between each arch. The center of the room was dotted with the bases of the carved pillars that had once supported the roof, now sadly reduced, like great trees in the aftermath of a forest fire. She looked around for Steve. He was standing near a small niche, like a bay window, deep in conversation with someone she couldn't quite make out.

She crossed the room, oblivious to the freezing ground. Steve saw her coming and stepped back. As he did so, a figure emerged from the shadows, too solid to be a ghost, but somehow not quite alive either. It was a young man in the distinctive white robes of a Cistercian monk, but his careworn face and sturdy build spoke more of a life lived outside the cloistered confines of a country abbey.

"Is this her?" he said, his voice soft and sad.

"Yes," said Steve. "That's Belladonna."

Belladonna looked him, waiting for more, but before he could speak again, the young monk stepped forward and bowed. Not the awkward bow of compulsory country dancing classes, but the graceful, easy bow of one for whom it is the most natural movement in the world.

"I am Edmund de Braes," he said, "the last Paladin."

"Um . . . hello," said Belladonna, glancing quickly at Steve, who seemed both pleased and worried. "I'm Belladonna."

Edmund de Braes smiled slightly and nodded.

"You are the Spellbinder," he said.

"So people keep telling me," said Belladonna, trying to keep the annoyance out of her voice.

"Your Paladin and I have been discussing you," continued the young monk. "I was just telling him that—"

"Yes, well," interrupted Steve, "he was, um . . . he was saying that he's been waiting for us. For . . . um . . . ."

Edmund glanced at Steve, clearly surprised, but quickly regained his calm demeanor.

"For over six hundred years," he said.

"Six hundred years," said Belladonna. "But you're not . . . That is, you don't seem to be . . ."

"No, I am not dead," explained Edmund. "But neither am I alive. She came to me and bade me stand sentinel against a change in the tide. I have been waiting here for your coming. Now you are here and the Dark Times are upon us again."

"A change in the tide?" asked Steve.

"Hang on," said Belladonna. "First, who is this She, what are the Dark Times, and what are we supposed to do about it? And why is everything always so cryptic?"

"You do not know?" said Edmund, clearly taken aback.

Belladonna and Steve both shook their heads.

"But who has the care of your teaching? Have you not been trained in the ways of battle?"

"No," said Steve, grinning. "We've been trained in the ways of Math, English Lit, and double French on Wednesdays. Most schools these days kind of frown on the ways of battle."

"Not that it ever stopped you," said Belladonna.

"What is this?" said Edmund. "You jest in the face of all that is dread?"

"Look." Belladonna took a deep breath. "If you'll just explain, clearly, what is going on, why you have been waiting, and what we have to do, preferably before Mr. Watson comes and drags us back to the bus, then maybe we'll take it all a bit more seriously."

Edmund looked from one to the other and nodded. "So be it."

Belladonna hardly dared breathe. Was he really going to make everything clear?

"In the last of the Dark Times, I was Paladin to Margaret de Morville of the Priory of Gwybod in the Welsh Marches. I was tasked, like all the Paladins who preceded me, to protect the Spellbinder from those who would do her harm. But all was not as it seemed, and I was too slow in perceiving the danger. By the time I awoke to the peril, the whole world was helpless before the pestilence and death that destroyed all in its path. Yet all was not lost, for it came to pass that in due course the forces of light beat back she who fashioned herself Empress, and she, along with all her minions, was imprisoned in the Dark Spaces. But She Who Knows All perceived that they would return and that they would seek and this time find the Instrument of Life. So I was charged with waiting until the next Dark Times in order to warn the Spellbinder and Paladin who would then appear and give them this that they might prevent her return, find the instrument, and conceal it anew."

Belladonna and Steve stared at him.

"Clear as mud," said Steve finally.

Belladonna had to agree. As explanations went, Edmund's was right up there with Miss Venable's "clarification" of quadratic equations. She took a deep breath.

"Look—" she began.

"Evans? Johnson?" Mr. Watson's voice rang through the abbey.

Edmund reached into one of his capacious sleeves and produced a rolled parchment.

"There's no time," he whispered. "Take this! And tell no one!"

He handed it to Steve, and as he did so, a look of relief replaced the worry on his face.

"It is done," he said.

"No . . . wait!" Steve looked at the parchment and then back at Edmund, but it was too late. He was already transparent; in another moment he would vanish altogether, gone on his long-delayed journey to the Other Side.

"Evans! Johnson! What the devil are you doing here? Couldn't you hear us calling?"

Mr. Watson had that mix of fury and gratitude that Belladonna had noticed grown-ups frequently had on locating wandering children. She turned toward Mr. Watson and smiled sheepishly.

"Sorry," she said. "We were just—"

"Listen!" hissed Edmund, suddenly grabbing Steve's right wrist with a surprisingly strong grip. "Always carry the Rod of Gram. That was my error. Always! Do you hear?"

And he was gone. Steve stood frozen for a moment, then hastily shoved the parchment inside his jacket as Mr. Watson strode through the sodden grass in the chapter house.

"You were just what?" he demanded.

"We couldn't hear you," said Belladonna. "It's really quiet in here."

Mr. Watson stopped and cocked his head slightly

sideways, listening. There was no sound but the distant cry of a lonely seabird and the faint rustle of wind.

"So it is," he said, surprised. "How odd."

He listened for another moment, then glanced at his watch and clicked his tongue.

"We should be halfway back by now," he snapped. "Your parents will be beside themselves if we're late!"

Belladonna could see his regret as soon as the words were out of his mouth.

"Sorry, Johnson. Ah . . . let's be having you. Come on."

He herded them ahead of him across the chapter house, through the low archway, and out into the main part of the abbey grounds. Once they were outside, they could hear the shouts of the other kids looking for them, as well as the chiming of a distant church bell and the sputtering cough of the idling bus.

"Found them!" he shouted. "Everyone onto the bus!"

The trip back seemed shorter than the one in the morning, though it was nearly dark by the time the bus pulled up outside school. Belladonna was lost in thought, her forehead against the misty window and her mind racing. The last Paladin! And the last Spellbinder! They had names! And something was happening. Or was going to happen. For all that she'd longed to return to her normal life while she was in the Land of the Dead, she now longed for something new. Something important. Something where more was expected of her than just turning her homework in on time. Perhaps that was what she wanted, after all, not an escape from ordinariness but a way to be more alive. Even if it meant spending a lot more time with the Dead.

"Johnson!"

She jumped to life and sat up, startled, her head leaving a circular mark in the steam on the window where she'd been leaning. The bus was empty.

"We're here! Come on, off you go."

She scrambled out of her seat and headed toward the front of the bus, where Mr. Watson was waiting.

"Didn't you have a bag?" he asked, rolling his eyes and looking at his watch.

Yes. She turned back and retrieved the battered pink backpack, then scurried past him and out onto the pavement. The shrill February wind whipped around her face and froze her fingers almost as soon as she stepped out. Most of the other kids had gone, whisked home by waiting parents in family cars. Steve was still there, of course, huddled near the tree on the opposite side of the road with his friends. These days he always seemed to wait until the last possible moment to go home.

Belladonna smiled at him as he glanced toward her, but he pretended he hadn't noticed and returned to his conversation.

Boys! thought Belladonna cheerfully as she turned up the road and headed toward Lychgate Lane and home.

5

Care

"HOW WAS THE monastery?" asked her father as soon as she was out of her wet things, into warm clothes, and huddled by the fire, waiting for the feeling to return to her nose and fingers.

"Cold," said Belladonna.

"I'll bet it was. Did you see any ghosts?"

She shrugged. "A couple of monks."

He nodded and returned to watching the television. Belladonna stared at the fire, wondering why she hadn't told him about Edmund de Braes. It wasn't as if he didn't know about the Spellbinder stuff, after all.

"Actually . . ." she began.

"Dinner's ready!" said her mother cheerfully, sticking her head through the wall from the kitchen.

Belladonna scrambled to her feet and hurried in. She was starving and almost wishing she'd eaten the awful brie and almond sandwiches.

"Nothing fancy," said her mother as Belladonna pulled

her chair up to the table. "Just a little vat of beef bourguignon to warm you up from the inside out."

Mrs. Johnson was working her way through all the great cookbooks of the world in alphabetical order. She said it gave her something to do and that being dead could get a little dreary if you didn't keep yourself occupied. She had always been a good cook, but now every evening was a gastronomic adventure. Belladonna loved almost everything (except liver and tripe and the seedy parts of tomatoes) but couldn't help longing for some good old fish and chips once in a while.

Still, this beef thingy showed every sign of being a keeper. It sat dark and gloopy in her plate, slightly red and soaking into the potatoes, and the smell was fantastic. She picked up her knife and fork and dived in. Yes, this one was definitely a winner—the chunks of beef positively melted in her mouth, and the carrots, mushrooms, and onions melded with the garlic to create something sweet, sharp, and fragrant all at the same time.

Mrs. Johnson smiled as she watched her daughter eat. Belladonna grinned back.

"This is amazing!" she said, wiping a trickle of glutinous ooze from the corner of her mouth.

"Even the carrots?" asked her mother.

Belladonna nodded enthusiastically and continued wolfing down what was, basically, a stew, but so much better than any stew she'd ever had before. She had almost finished before she noticed that her father was being unusually quiet.

"What is it?" she asked.

"Something happened today, didn't it? What were you going to tell me?"

"Nothing," said Belladonna.

She had intended to tell him, but right now she just wanted to hold on to this—to dinner in the kitchen and everything normal and comfortable. She suddenly felt as though she were in a fairground on the roller coaster, and the car was just about to reach the top of the first climb. For some reason she knew that it was all about to start again and that the moment she actually began to talk about it, everything would rush out of control. And even though she was excited and eager to find out about Edmund de Braes's parchment, right now, here, in the warm kitchen with her parents on a cold, windy evening, she wanted nothing more than a little bit of quiet and to pretend that they were just an ordinary family sitting together and having dinner.

Her father nodded and was about to say something else when her mother shut him up with a stern stare.

"Would you like some more?"

"Yes, please."

Belladonna had seconds, then thirds, and then a piece of apple tart with ice cream. Through it all, her father smiled and made casual conversation, but she could tell that he was worried and was just waiting. Finally, as she finished the last bit of ice cream, he smiled, glanced at his wife for the almost imperceptible "go ahead" nod, and turned to Belladonna.

"Who did you see at the monastery? It wasn't just the ghosts of monks, was it?"

"No. Wait . . . how do you know?"

"You're our daughter, Belladonna," said her mother softly. "We always know when something is bothering you."

Belladonna looked from one to the other, not sure if she should say anything. After all, it wasn't as if their response to the black feather had been even remotely helpful.

"We've been talking," said her mother suddenly, "your father and I. And . . . well, there's no denying that you are the Spellbinder . . . and there really isn't any point in trying to protect you from all that."

"All what?" asked Belladonna.

"The things that you need to know. Deirdre always says that knowledge is power. . . ."

"I think she picked that up at one of those business seminars she's always going to," said Mr. Johnson, grinning.

"That doesn't mean that it isn't right."

"Sorry."

"Anyway, it's all too dangerous for you to take on alone. You need help and advice and —"

"And it's pretty foolish of us to pretend that things like that feather are just from crows or ravens or whatever," interrupted her father. "That's not what you need now, is it?"

Belladonna shook her head slowly.

"It's all very dangerous, and ignoring it isn't going to make it less so. Did you throw the feather away?"

"No. I was going to but . . ."

"That's alright. Why don't you fetch it here."

Belladonna smiled and went into the sitting room to get her backpack. She retrieved the feather, but as she stood up, she thought she saw a movement. Was it in the garden? Or was it the road? It was hard to see outside, the thin winter daylight had all but faded and the bright lights of the sitting room made it almost impossible to make anything out.

There was a car near the gate. That's probably all it was, thought Belladonna. But she drew the curtains anyway and made her way back to the kitchen.

"Yes," said her father, taking the feather and turning it over, "it's a pretty good size, isn't it?"

"Too big for a crow," said her mother.

"Or a raven, really."

"Steve and I were thinking that maybe . . . well, do you think it could be a Kere?"

"I've no idea," said her father. "I've never seen one. We were . . . indisposed, if you recall, when . . ."

"They're these women, well, not women, obviously, but they look like them. They have pale skin and their hair is dark blue and they have wings . . . huge black wings. The one at the House of Mists said that the Keres were bringers of Death and that no one commanded them except the Empress of the Dark Spaces. Then today," said Belladonna, rushing forward with her story, suddenly eager that they should know everything, "today, when we were at the monastery, we met Edmund de Braes."

Her parents both looked blank.

"He said he was the last Paladin."

Mr. and Mrs. Johnson glanced at each other, clearly worried. Belladonna smiled in what she hoped was a reassuring I'm-not-bothered-by-this-at-all way and told them all about the last Paladin and how he said he'd been waiting for over six hundred years and how, now that she and Steve had come to the monastery and he had given them the parchment, his job was over.

"And where is the parchment?" asked her father.

"Steve has it."

"So you don't know what it's for?"

"No." Belladonna shook her head. "Edmund said we had to find something and then hide it again. He called it the Instrument of Life. Do you think it could be some kind of a map?"

Her parents glanced at her and then at each other. Mrs. Johnson seemed to blink back tears, then suddenly left the table and began sweeping dishes into the dishwasher with irritable waves of her elegant hands.

"This is too ridiculous!" she said finally, wafting the pans into the sink with a clang. "She's twelve, for heaven's sake! How can she be the Spellbinder? What can she possibly do? It's too dangerous! You have to talk to her."

"To me?" said Belladonna, suddenly confused.

"No," said her mother, turning to her father, desperation in her eyes, "to HER. You have to go to the House of Ashes. You have to explain. . . ."

"I'm not sure I can," said her father quietly. "I don't think we're allowed to."

"Who?" asked Belladonna. "Who is 'her'? And what's the House of Ashes?"

The question brought a sudden halt to what was shaping up to be a full-blown argument between her parents, and Belladonna's mind raced. Who could they mean? Mrs. Jay? She had certainly seemed to know all about the Land of the Dead, the Nomials, and the Empress of the Dark Spaces when she'd called them into her office last October. But if they meant Mrs. Jay, then why wouldn't they be allowed to talk to her?

"Tell her," said Mrs. Johnson, an unfamiliar tone of stern command in her voice.

Mr. Johnson nodded and turned to Belladonna, but before he could speak, there was a sharp rap on the front door, followed by an extended ring of the doorbell.

They fell silent for a moment and just stared at each other.

"Who could that be?" muttered her father. "What time is it?"

"It's probably just your mother," snapped Mrs. Johnson, "forgotten her key again. Go and let her in, Belladonna."

Belladonna nodded and left the kitchen. Once she was in the hall, she could see the tops of two heads through the stained-glass fanlight on the door. It couldn't be her grandmother. She'd never bring someone else and, anyway, she wasn't tall enough to be seen in the fanlight.

She ran back as quietly as she could.

"It's not Grandma," she whispered. "It's two people. Two tall people."

The words were hardly out of her mouth before there was another sharp rap on the door.

"You'd better see what they want. It's probably just salespeople."

Belladonna nodded at her father, who tried to smile encouragingly, but the anxious look on her mother's face told her that she needed to be very careful. She wasn't supposed to be living here. So far as anyone else was concerned, Belladonna lived with her grandmother on Yarrow Street. This house was supposed to be empty.

She walked slowly to the door, then glanced back. Her parents were huddled in the kitchen doorway watching. She reached up and opened the door about four inches. The first face she saw was that of a woman, tall and slightly overweight, wearing a gray skirt and a brown anorak.

"Are you Belladonna Johnson?" asked the woman.

"Yes," said Belladonna suspiciously.

"Can we come in?"

"No," said Belladonna, a knot developing in the pit of her stomach. "I'm not supposed to talk to strangers."

"Quite right," said the woman, rummaging in her bag and producing a small identification card. "Here you go."

Belladonna looked at the card. It had a photograph of the woman that looked like it had been taken quite a few years before, along with her name, Donna Lazenby. But that wasn't what made Belladonna's blood run cold.

It was the words written in bold black print at the top of the card: CHILD PROTECTION SERVICES.

"We've had a report that you're living here alone," said the woman, smiling.

"I'm not," said Belladonna. "I live with my grandmother."

"Is she here?" asked the woman, straining to see past Belladonna.

"Not . . . not at the moment."

"Well, we'd like to come in and wait for her."

"No! I mean, can't she call you?"

"We can't leave you here alone," said the woman in tones that she clearly hoped were soothing. "Let us in, there's a good girl."

Belladonna hesitated, but before she could answer, the other figure stepped forward into the light. It was a policeman. He looked stern and was clearly not interested in wasting any more time on this than he absolutely had to.

"Open the door."

"Don't . . . um . . . don't you need a warrant or something?"

"Not if we think a child might be in danger," said the woman.

Belladonna glanced back at her parents.

"It's alright," said her father. "Let them in, then phone your grandmother. She'll sort it out. And remember—you can't see us."

He smiled encouragingly. Belladonna tried to smile back and was just about to open the door when it was shoved sharply from the other side. She stumbled back and hit her head on the stair banister.

"Ow!"

"Constable Dodd!" said the woman, shocked. "That really wasn't necessary. This is a child, not a bank robber!"

She helped Belladonna to her feet.

"That's a lovely smell," she said. "Has your grand-mother been cooking?"

"No . . . um . . . I have." Belladonna winced inside. That didn't sound even vaguely like the truth. Why was she so rubbish at lying?

"Really? How clever! Now, I'm Mrs. Lazenby and this is Constable Dodd. My office received a call telling us that you were living alone."

"But I'm not. My grandmother—"

"Yes, I am aware that your grandmother is your guardian," said Mrs. Lazenby. "But this isn't her address, is it? According to our records, she lives on Yarrow Street. This was your parents' house, wasn't it?"

"Yes, but . . ."

"But what, dear?"

"But . . . that's her work address."

"Her work address? But I thought—"

"It *was* her house," blurted Belladonna, thinking as fast as she could. "But after the . . . after the accident, she thought it would be nicer for me here, so . . . we live here, but she still has her business at the old house."

"Well done, Belladonna!" whispered her mother.

"And what is her business?" asked Mrs. Lazenby.

"She's a . . . that is . . . she holds séances and . . . things."

"Really? And she can make a living at that, can she?"

Belladonna nodded.

"Do you think you could phone her, then, and get her over here?"

Belladonna tried to look confident as she crossed the hall and picked up the phone, but the knot in her stomach was getting bigger. She glanced back at her parents.

"Don't worry," said her mother. "Your grandmother will sort everything out."

Belladonna started to dial.

Mrs. Lazenby smiled and turned to Constable Dodd.

"Have a look upstairs," she said. "See if it looks like anyone else is living here."

Dodd nodded and pounded up the stairs. Belladonna listened as her grandmother's phone rang . . . and rang . . . and rang. Then there was the familiar click as her answering machine came on: "Hello, you have reached the home of Jessamine Johnson. I can't come to the phone right now, so please leave a message and I'll return your call as soon as I can."

"Hello, Grandma, it's Belladonna. I'm sorry to bother you when you're probably . . . busy . . . but there's a lady here from Child Protection Services and she wants to talk to you. I told her that you do live here with me and just work there at your old house but I don't think she believes me. So . . . please call."

She hung up and turned back to Mrs. Lazenby.

"She was busy."

"Very good," said Mrs. Lazenby, smirking a little. "And a quick message to make sure you get your stories straight."

The policeman pounded down the stairs. "Looks like only one room being used."

"Right. Let's go and see Grandma, shall we?"

Belladonna tried to keep the tears from her eyes as she reached for her coat.

"Don't cry, baby," said her mother, looking like she was about to start crying herself.

"It'll be alright," urged her father. "Your grandmother will give them an earful and you'll be back home before you know where you are."

Belladonna tried to feel confident, but something felt wrong. She walked down the path and out of the gate, and as she got into the back seat of the police car next to Mrs. Lazenby, she couldn't keep the panic out of her mind. What if they took her away? What if they wouldn't let her come home? It was the only place she could see her parents. It was the only place they could be together.

She stared out of the window as the car sped through town, willing herself not to cry but unable to keep the tears away. When they stopped at the traffic light at the end of Yarrow Street, she wiped her eyes and looked up. There, on the street corner, sitting on his bike with his friends, was Steve. His jaw dropped when he saw her, and he started to move toward the car, but no sooner were his feet on the pedals than the light had turned and they were gone.

"Do you have a key?" asked Mrs. Lazenby as they pulled up in front of Grandma Johnson's house.

"Yes," murmured Belladonna, "but I usually ring the doorbell."

Constable Dodd double-parked the car and they

trooped up to the front door. Mrs. Lazenby rang the bell. No answer. She rang again.

"Sometimes it's hard for her to hear if she has a client," explained Belladonna.

Mrs. Lazenby rang again. No answer. She was about to try again when Constable Dodd reached between the two of them and grabbed the door knocker. He pulled it back, obviously intending to deliver a really loud crack, but the door just swung open. Belladonna gasped. Something was terribly wrong—her grandmother *always* locked the front door.

They stood on the step for a while, then Constable Dodd strode forward and led the way into the house.

"Hello?" he bellowed. "Anyone home?"

"Mrs. Johnson?" called Mrs. Lazenby in somewhat more friendly tones. "Mrs. Johnson? Hello?"

She pushed open the door to the séance room and glanced inside before making her way to the sitting room. The fire was on, but no one was there.

"Mrs. Lazenby," called Constable Dodd, "come look at this."

Belladonna trailed after Mrs. Lazenby into the kitchen. There was a bacon sandwich on a plate on the counter next to the teapot. Constable Dodd felt the pot.

"It's warm," he said. "It's weird. It's like she was just here."

"Yes, well, she isn't here now, is she? Check upstairs, would you?"

Dodd nodded and strode out of the room.

"Do you have anyone else?" asked Mrs. Lazenby. "Any other relatives we could call?"

Belladonna shook her head. The only other relative she knew of was Aunt Deirdre, but she hadn't been seen since she'd gone off after the Wild Hunt in October.

"Two bedrooms," said Constable Dodd, striding back into the kitchen. "Looks like only one is lived in, though."

Mrs. Lazenby looked at Belladonna sympathetically.

"She wasn't living with you, was she? You were staying in your parents' house alone."

"No, I wasn't!" Belladonna knew that no matter what happened, she had to stick to her story. Perhaps Grandma Johnson had gone to a friend's or nipped out to the shops, maybe someone had broken in while she was out or maybe something worse. But no matter what the reason, Belladonna had to believe that she would come back, and when she did, they had to have a plausible story.

"It's alright," said Mrs. Lazenby gently. "Losing your parents is a terrible thing."

"But —"

"Wanting to stay in the house that you shared with them is perfectly normal, it really is. But you can't do that. You can't stay there all alone. You do understand?"

"But my grandmother —"

"She isn't here. And when she comes back, we'll have to have some serious discussions with her."

"Can I go home now?" asked Belladonna, knowing perfectly well what the answer would be but still clinging to one last desperate hope. "Perhaps she's there. She could have got my message and tried to call back but we'd already left."

Mrs. Lazenby shook her head and said exactly what Belladonna had known she was going to say:

"No. I'm sorry, Belladonna, but I'm afraid we're going to have to take you into care."

6

Shady Gardens

ELLADONNA HAD BEEN sitting outside the office
for what felt like hours. As soon as they'd arrived at the
gray concrete building, Mrs. Lazenby had signed in at
the door, thanked Constable Dodd for his help, and led
the way back through a maze of narrow corridors and cubicles to a small office with a window that looked over the
car park. She hadn't taken Belladonna into the office,
though. She'd just smiled and directed her to a seat on a
row of plastic chairs that had probably once been colorful
but were now rather grimy and depressing.

Mrs. Lazenby had gone into her office, removed her
coat, sat at her desk, and picked up the phone.

Since then, there had been a great deal of to-ing and
fro-ing, all of which Belladonna had been able to see
through the large glass window in one wall. One woman
had come with a fat folder, which Belladonna assumed was
her file. Mrs. Lazenby had looked at this, then made several phone calls, none of which appeared to have been answered. Then another woman had arrived, smiled briefly

at Belladonna, then gone in and talked with Mrs. Lazenby for what seemed like ages. While that was going on, a very young man had come and asked her if she'd like a cup of tea or some juice. She declined.

The woman left, then returned with a stack of folders. She and Mrs. Lazenby talked for a while, then started making phone calls. These calls seemed to be answered, but judging by the expression on both women's faces, they weren't getting the results they were hoping for.

Belladonna squirmed on the chair. The seat was really hard. Why couldn't they provide cushions? She glanced up at a clock on the wall. If her grandmother had gone out, she'd be back by now and have heard her message. But if that was the case, Belladonna knew the old lady would already be here, storming the halls and hauling her granddaughter back home again.

"What happened?"

She jumped. For some reason, she hadn't expected to see a ghost here. Though, of course, there was no reason why she shouldn't. She turned slowly and looked at the boy. He was younger than her and wore a dark green sweater that had holes at the elbows. He was wearing the gray shorts children used to wear back when her grandmother was young, and his knees were a mottled red and blue from the cold. Gray socks wrinkled around his ankles, and his brown shoes were scuffed and worn. His face was round and a little mournful.

"My Mum and Dad are gone," said Belladonna. "They can't find my Grandma."

Neither of these was exactly true, but Belladonna

couldn't think of what to say. How could this have happened? How could she be here?

"Hmm," said the boy thoughtfully, "that's what happened to me. Sort of."

Belladonna didn't find this at all comforting.

"What d'you mean?" she asked quietly, after glancing around to make sure that no one could see her talking to the air.

The boy sniffled and wiped his nose with the sleeve of his sweater. The youngish man came scurrying along the hall with another fat folder and took it into the office. He smiled at Belladonna when he left.

"My Nan died," began the boy.

"I'm sorry," said Belladonna.

"That's alright," said the boy, smiling slightly. "She'd been very poorly. I was poorly too. I had a sister and they were trying to find her."

"Did they?" asked Belladonna, knowing the answer but wanting to be friendly.

"No." The boy shook his head. "I had to go to the hospital. They said I had p-new . . . p-new : . ."

"Pneumonia?"

"Yes. There's a p in it somewhere, though."

"You don't pronounce the p."

"Oh. Well, anyway, I died of it."

Belladonna smiled in what she hoped was a sympathetic manner and glanced up into the office. Mrs. Lazenby was on the phone again.

"But why did you come back here?" she asked finally.

"Couldn't you have picked somewhere nicer? Did anyone explain that you could only haunt one place?"

"Course they did," shrugged the boy. "I just thought she might come. My sister."

"But she didn't."

"Not yet."

Belladonna stared at him, her sense of gloom growing.

"I'm not getting you down, am I?" asked the boy, attempting a smile. "It's okay here, really. They have a color television in the break room. I'd never seen a television at all before I died and now I watch color television all the time."

"That sounds nice."

"Belladonna, would you come in here for a moment?"

Mrs. Lazenby was standing in the open doorway.

"Off you go, then," said the boy. "I hope they find your Grandma."

Belladonna nodded to him in what she hoped was a discreet manner and joined Mrs. Lazenby.

"Were you talking to someone, dear?"

"No," said Belladonna. "Just . . . you know . . . telling myself a story."

Mrs. Lazenby nodded but looked unconvinced and a little worried. *Great,* thought Belladonna, *now she thinks I'm a loony.*

"Have a seat."

Belladonna sat in the only other chair in the tiny office.

"This is Miss Kitson," said Mrs. Lazenby. "She's a colleague of mine."

"Have you found my grandmother?" asked Belladonna.

"No, dear. Though according to our records, you also have an aunt, living in London. Why didn't you tell us about her?"

Belladonna looked from one to the other and shrugged. It was late, she was tired, and she just couldn't think of stories or excuses anymore. All she wanted to do was go home and get into her own bed and have this all be over.

"Well, as it happens, we haven't been able to reach her either," said Mrs. Lazenby in a tone that implied that if Belladonna had mentioned it earlier, they would certainly have been able to do so.

"So . . . ," began Belladonna with a sinking heart, "what does that mean? Are you going to send me to an orphanage?"

"No, dear," said Miss Kitson, smiling. "We try not to do that these days. The family unit is important, so we try to place our . . . clients with families."

"Families?"

"Temporarily," said Mrs. Lazenby quickly. "Foster homes, they're called."

"But, I don't want to. . . . My Grandma will be back; she must've just gone somewhere. Have you looked?"

"Of course we've looked," said Mrs. Lazenby. "And if she's still missing by this time tomorrow, we'll let the police know that she's a missing person, but until then, we have to deal with you. That is, we need to find you some nice people to stay with."

Belladonna just stared at them. She knew that if she tried to speak, she'd burst into tears.

"Most of our foster parents are up to their ears, unfortunately," said Miss Kitson cheerfully. "But by sheer chance, the Proctors are completely available."

Belladonna didn't say anything. The two women looked at each other.

"The Proctors are really wonderful people," said Mrs. Lazenby, patting the fat file in front of her. "You're a very lucky girl."

"They've been on our books for years," added Miss Kitson. "And they live quite close by, so there'll be no problems with school."

"So," said Mrs. Lazenby, standing up, "let's get you over there and into a warm bed. I'm sure things will look much better in the morning."

Miss Kitson jumped to her feet as well, as if their display of energy would make Belladonna feel better, which of course it couldn't.

She picked up her backpack and stood up slowly. Mrs. Lazenby steered her out of the office, pulling a face at Miss Kitson on the way that she thought Belladonna couldn't see but which communicated her feeling that this particular "client" was being just a bit too sulky and ungrateful for her liking.

"Best of luck!" called Miss Kitson brightly as they disappeared into the maze of cubicles and corridors. "Not that you'll need it!"

Belladonna followed Mrs. Lazenby back toward the entrance. It was dark outside now and even the air inside felt cold. She glanced to her left as they neared the front door and found herself looking into the break room. There were old couches, chairs, and tables scattered about and a television suspended from one wall. It was playing cartoons and there was the ghost of the sad boy lying on the couch, not looking sad at all. He waved as Belladonna passed.

And then they were outside in the dark, and the chill February wind whipped around their faces.

"Ooh!" said Mrs. Lazenby, shivering. "It's starting to feel like it might snow. This way: My car's just over here. You don't look very warm. Are you warm?"

"I'm fine," muttered Belladonna as Mrs. Lazenby unlocked an old hatchback and cleared papers, sweets wrappers, and empty coffee cups from the front seat.

Belladonna slid into the passenger seat and closed the door. Mrs. Lazenby adjusted the rearview mirror and smiled encouragingly.

"Here we go!"

Belladonna felt a little guilty. Mrs. Lazenby was trying really hard to be cheerful and it seemed a bit rude not to at least respond with a smile, but somehow she couldn't muster even that. How could this have happened? This morning, everything had seemed fine. And there was the trip to the monastery. Had that been today? It felt like weeks ago.

The car lurched forward.

"Oops!" said Mrs. Lazenby. "Reverse would probably be a good idea."

The monastery . . . There was something . . . Belladonna

racked her brains. No, it wasn't at the monastery, it was on the bus, on the trip there. It was something Louise Pargiter had said: "Enjoy your last day of freedom."

Could that be it? Could all this be Sophie Warren's revenge? Belladonna felt the anger beginning to boil in her veins. She took a deep breath . . . no, it was silly. Sophie didn't know she was living at her parents' house, and even if she did, how would she know that her grandmother didn't live there too? And anyway, who'd listen to a schoolgirl?

Unless Sophie had told her mother. Maybe Mrs. Warren . . .

"Here we are!"

Belladonna looked up.

"What is that?" she blurted as the shadow of a huge building loomed before the tiny car.

"It's Shady Gardens," said Mrs. Lazenby. "Isn't it spectacular? I'd thought they were going to demolish it, but apparently it's being saved. They say it's an architectural treasure, though when I was growing up, we always called it the Bullring."

It was much more like a bullring than any shady gardens Belladonna had ever seen. It wasn't that it was tall — no more than four stories high so far as she could make out in the dark. But it was circular, spreading out on either side like a huge gladiatorial arena. Mrs. Lazenby drove through a wide arch on one side and into the center of the building. There were a few yellow lights scattered about near the entrances to stairwells, but all they really did was add to the general feeling of gloom.

Mrs. Lazenby parked the car, and Belladonna got out. There were a few scrubby bushes straining for life in the concrete, and near the middle was bit of beaten earth with a swing set on it. There was only one swing, though, swaying slightly in the breeze, the sound of its chains echoing around the courtyard. Belladonna pulled her jacket close, picked up her backpack, and followed Mrs. Lazenby to one of the stairwells.

"They're up here," she said. "The lifts don't work, apparently. There's some big architectural firm from London coming to do the actual refurbishment. Mr. Proctor is just keeping an eye on the place. Don't suppose any of us will be able to afford to live here when they're done. Who would've thought, eh? I was sure it was going to be knocked down. Ah, here we are!"

She stopped in front of a bright green door. The doorknob was brightly polished and Belladonna could see a row of ornamental china dogs ranged across the windowsill. There were dark red curtains that had been drawn closed, but a few streaks of light broke across the walkway, and the sound of a television could be heard.

"Now, don't worry," whispered Mrs. Lazenby. "Like I said, the Proctors have been on our books for years and have lots of experience. They're really nice people; you'll really like them."

"Yes," said Belladonna, as some sort of response seemed to be expected.

"They've been on our books for years," repeated Mrs. Lazenby.

Belladonna glanced at her sharply. There was something odd about the way she said it, but Mrs. Lazenby just smiled and rang the doorbell.

The door was opened immediately, as if Mrs. Proctor had been standing just on the other side, waiting. But if Belladonna was doubtful at first, all of her concerns were soon swept away in the warmth of the greeting as she and Mrs. Lazenby were hurried into the sitting room, urged to sit down in front of the old gas fire, and given cups of tea and cream cakes.

Mr. Proctor was sitting in a sturdy wingback chair near the fire. He was thin and gangly and didn't seem entirely comfortable as he folded up his newspaper and tried to appear welcoming, but his wife more than made up for his awkwardness. Unlike her husband in almost every way, Mrs. Proctor was small and round, with glowing rosy cheeks and dark hair just starting to turn to gray, which was pulled back into an untidy bun that seemed to be held in place by two pencils.

"Well, now, you must be Belladonna!" she said, beaming. "I know this must be terribly hard for you, but don't worry, I'm sure you won't be here long. Better here than in some horrible cold office, eh?"

Belladonna tried to smile. She wanted to be polite but she wasn't sure how convincing she was being.

"Right," said Mr. Proctor. "D'you have any bags?"

"Oh, er, no," said Mrs. Lazenby, a little sheepishly. "It was all rather sudden, I'm afraid. We'll pick some things up for her in the morning. Why don't you give me your key, dear?"

Belladonna's heart leapt at the thought that a stranger

would be rooting through her home, but she handed over the key without a word. It was as if a piece of her thought that Mrs. Lazenby might discover her parents, though she knew that was impossible.

"Well, let me show you up to your room anyway," said Mr. Proctor, smiling. His eyes were a piercing pale gray that seemed all the paler in his tanned face. He smiled easily and winked at Belladonna as he led the way upstairs.

"Here you are," he announced, pushing a door open. "The bathroom's right there, and me and Flo are across the hall there."

Belladonna stepped into the room. It was bright and airy and clean as a new pin. It seemed to have been decorated with a mind to suiting anyone who might come, and Belladonna found herself wondering how many other children, frightened, worried, or relieved, had found a welcome here.

She turned and smiled at Mr. Proctor. "Thank you."

"No problem at all. You settle in now, Belladonna. . . . That's a very long name, isn't it? Is there something they call you for short?"

"No, I'm just Belladonna."

"Hmph. Well, you settle in. Flo'll come up and see to you in a bit. There are some girls' night things in that second drawer."

Belladonna kept smiling until the door clicked shut, then she dropped her backpack next to the bed and sat down. Somehow the niceness of Mrs. Lazenby and the

Proctors made it worse. It would have been so much easier if they'd been horrible. Then she could have run away and . . . and . . .

And what? She couldn't stay at home all the time. And what had happened to Grandma Johnson? Aunt Deirdre's disappearance had been one thing; she hadn't really known her, and everyone had always said she was odd, so it didn't seem so strange. But Grandma Johnson wasn't strange. She was reliable and responsible. She wouldn't just vanish. Not without saying something. Phoning. Or leaving a note. And the teapot was still warm!

"Is everything alright, dear?" Mrs. Proctor peeked around the edge of the door. She wasn't smiling now, she just seemed concerned. "Mrs. Lazenby's gone, but she'll be back tomorrow to check that everything's alright. Did Stan tell you about the girls' night things?"

"Um . . . yes, thank you."

"I think you've probably been through a lot today, haven't you?"

Belladonna nodded.

"Well, you just get to bed. I'll bring you some hot chocolate. I spoke to Mrs. Lazenby and we both think it would be best if you stayed off school tomorrow and got your bearings a bit."

"Thank you."

"Right. Well, hop into bed and I'll be back with the cocoa."

The door clicked shut. She waited for a few moments, then checked the drawer with the "night things."

She picked out some pajamas, changed into them, and scrambled into bed just as Mrs. Proctor returned with the hot chocolate.

"There you go, love," she said.

Belladonna took the mug and sipped some of the chocolate. It was velvety and soft and slid easily down her throat. For the first time since the doorbell had rung at home, she actually felt safe. She smiled at Mrs. Proctor.

"Thank you."

"Alright. Well, you settle down. It'll be morning before you know it."

7

Shadows

BELLADONNA WOKE slowly the next morning. For a moment she thought she was back in her own bed at home, listening to the clatter of dishes in the kitchen as her mother created some new breakfast surprise. But the clatter wasn't her mother, it was Mrs. Proctor, and the room wasn't her own, just a generic kids' room always ready for whatever waifs and strays came its way.

She got out of bed, feeling a little guilty and ungrateful. She had to remember that she was a guest and that it was really nice of the Proctors to take her in. She made her way to the bathroom and was surprised to see herself looking so tired. There were unfamiliar circles under her eyes and she seemed pale. *Well,* she thought, *probably only to be expected.* She cleaned her teeth and went downstairs.

Mrs. Proctor was waiting in the small kitchen, a packet of bacon in one hand.

"Good morning, sleepyhead!" she said cheerfully. "You've had a good sleep; it's past ten o'clock. What would you like: bacon and eggs or cereal?"

"Um . . . cereal, thanks," said Belladonna, sitting down at the table.

How could it be after ten? She always got up early. . . . But perhaps it was just the body's way of coping with things. Just sort of shutting down and letting you recharge. Except she didn't really feel recharged; she felt just as tired as when she'd gone to bed.

She ate her breakfast in silence as Mrs. Proctor talked about her morning and how Mr. Proctor had gone to visit the company that was going to be restoring the building, and how Belladonna must make herself at home, and had she noticed that there was a bit of a playground.

Belladonna listened and nodded at the appropriate moments and smiled when it seemed expected. By the time breakfast was over, she knew that the Proctors had lived here for over thirty years and had seen the old place fall into decline. She'd heard all about how they'd campaigned to save it (with more success than her mother had experienced with the theatre) and how they had been given the job of living on site while the architects did the preparatory work, and that they'd been promised one of the new apartments when it was all done.

"There now!" said Mrs. Proctor, finally. "Just listen to me go on! I'm sure you don't care a jot for old buildings. Why don't you go outside and play while I get on with the dishes?"

"I can help," suggested Belladonna, noticing that there wasn't a dishwasher. "I could dry."

"Oh, no, no, no," gushed Mrs. Proctor, smiling. "You need some fresh air. Out you pop and have some fun."

Belladonna wondered what kind of fun Mrs. Proctor thought she could have the day after she'd been taken from the only home she'd ever known, but she dutifully put on her coat and went outside.

The day was cold but bright, with a sickly sun shining low in the sky. Belladonna closed the front door and leaned over the low concrete wall. It was even more like a Roman arena from here. She almost expected gladiators to march out and salute before fighting each other to a grim death. The idea cheered her up a little and she decided to go in search of some ghosts. After all, the building was nearly sixty years old, loads of people must have died here and some of them *must* have decided to haunt the place, so there had to be a few ghosts wandering about. And given the lonely state of the building, they'd probably quite like to have a chat.

She started by walking all around the same level of the building. Most of the old apartments had been boarded up, but a few were open, the wind whistling through from front door to rear window. They seemed sort of sad—hollow and expectant, with hardly any sign that they'd ever been lived in, except for the occasional broken mug or three-legged chair.

But no ghosts. Once, she thought she saw something out of the corner of her eye, but when she turned around, there was nothing there. She made her way down the narrow concrete stairs to the central arena and wandered over to the swing set. She sat down on the single swing and began to turn around slowly, winding the chains supporting the swing into a spiral tangle. Seen from this angle, the whole place seemed even bigger and more impersonal. You could barely see all the front doors, just the top foot of colored paint, then nothing but dull bricks and more concrete.

She took her foot off the ground and spun slowly as the chains unwound. The rotting concrete and brick smoothed itself out as she spun faster and faster. Perhaps that's what it looked like when it was new: sleek and modern, the very latest thing in urban living.

And that was when she saw them, loads of them. Shadows standing in doorways or in the arches that led to the road and on to town. Tall, lanky shapes that were definitely people but without any definition—there were no faces, clothes, or shoes. Just shapes.

She put her foot down suddenly and stopped spinning, but as soon as she did so, the shadows vanished and the building was as empty as it had always been. But it wasn't. They were still there, just out of sight on the edge of her vision. What were they?

Belladonna walked slowly toward one of the doorways where she was sure she'd seen a shadow but nothing was there. She closed her eyes and felt around. Was it colder on one side? She opened her eyes. Probably not. She went back to the swing, wound it up, and spun again. Yes. There they were. She put her foot down again and stopped. Gone. Picked her foot up, spun . . . and there they were.

They couldn't be ghosts, she thought. If they were ghosts, she would be able to see them properly and talk to them just as she always did. And there was something about them . . . something uniform. They didn't seem like individuals; there weren't tall ones and short ones, thin ones and fat ones; they didn't seem like the shadows of actual people. She got off the swing and walked toward the huge archway where she and Mrs. Lazenby had driven in the night before. There had been at least three shadows lurking there, but, just as with the doorway, by the time she got there, they were gone.

What were they? And why were there no ghosts?

She squinted her eyes to see if she could see them more easily that way, but before she could decide if it was helping or not, a car horn suddenly blared behind her. She leapt to the side of the road and spun around. It was Mrs. Lazenby.

"Hello, Belladonna!" she yelled cheerfully, rolling down her window. "How are you feeling today? I brought you some things."

She rolled through the archway and parked the car in the same place as the night before. Belladonna followed her back to the Proctors's and soon they were both in the warm sitting room drinking cups of tea and eating homemade scones still warm from the oven. Mrs. Lazenby nodded toward a small suitcase she'd left in the hall.

"I stopped by your . . . by the house," she said, smiling, "and picked up a few things for you."

Belladonna stared at her.

"Say thank you, dear," said Mrs. Proctor.

"Thank you," said Belladonna, glancing at the bag. Mrs. Lazenby had been inside her house and rooted around in her bedroom. Her Mum and Dad had probably been watching. Belladonna was consumed with a mixture of sorrow and anger.

"Are you still looking for my Gran?" she asked, trying to keep the sullenness out of her voice.

"Of course, dear!" said Mrs. Lazenby, patting her hand. "And your aunt. As soon as we locate them, you'll be on your way home. Well, not right away, of course—they're both going to have some explaining to do."

She winked at Mrs. Proctor as though the fact that they thought Belladonna's grandmother had behaved irresponsibly was somehow not grasped by Belladonna herself.

"Have you reported her missing to the police? You said you—"

"It hasn't been twenty-four hours. She could have just gone off to see friends or something. She could still come back."

"She wouldn't do that," said Belladonna, unable to stop her anger from seething into every word. "She's never done anything like that. And she has clients, she wouldn't just go. Something's happened, I know it has!"

"Well," said Mrs. Lazenby, her voice getting a little tense, "I hardly think that being a psychic is like being a doctor. I imagine her 'clients,' as you call them, can manage quite well without their weekly dose of crystal gazing."

She flashed Mrs. Proctor the aren't-children-silly smile again, and the older lady tittered obligingly.

"Well," she said, "I must be off. Lots to do. Don't worry, Belladonna. I'll come by every day to make sure everything is alright and let you know what's happening."

"Oh, that's alright," said Mrs. Proctor, following Mrs.

Lazenby to the front door. "We're getting on like a house on fire, aren't we, Belladonna?"

Belladonna just stared at them both, unable to muster even a meaningless smile.

"Yes, of course," said Mrs. Lazenby. "But I do have to see her every day. You understand."

"I think a daily phone call will do," said Mrs. Proctor, smiling and placing a friendly hand on Mrs. Lazenby's arm. "After all, you've known us for years."

Mrs. Lazenby didn't say anything until she'd opened the door and stepped outside, then she turned back.

"Actually," she said, "I think a daily phone call will do. It's not like you've never done this before, and I've known you for years. I'll talk to you tomorrow. Good-bye, Belladonna!"

The door clicked shut and Mrs. Proctor stepped back into the sitting room.

"Well, that was nice, wasn't it?" she said, sitting down and pouring herself another cup of tea. "It's always nice to have visitors, I think. You must learn to control your temper, though, Belladonna. Little girls really ought to be polite to their elders and not grill them as though they are criminals."

"I'm not a little girl," muttered Belladonna.

The teapot stopped in midair and Mrs. Proctor dropped her smile.

"Yes, you are," she said, an edge of steel suddenly in her voice. "Now, why don't you take your suitcase upstairs and unpack?"

Belladonna stared at her for a moment, then stood up and picked up the suitcase.

"And while you're doing that, why don't you have a think about the proper respect due to your elders? There's a good girl."

She smiled cheerily as Belladonna started up the stairs. The bag wasn't heavy but she took her time getting to the room. She had a feeling that something important had happened and she'd somehow missed it. It wasn't Mrs. Proctor's remarks about "little girls." That was just irritating. It was something else.

Something Mrs. Lazenby had said.

She unpacked her clothes, then tried doing some of her Math homework and made a start on the monastery essay, but had difficulty concentrating. By the time she heard Mr. Proctor arrive home, she had given up entirely and was looking at some of the books in the room. How many children had been exactly where she now was, taken from everything familiar and plonked down with strangers? She imagined that for some children it was an escape, the best thing that had ever happened. But for others, like her, it was their worst nightmare come true.

That night at dinner, Mr. and Mrs. Proctor chatted with each other happily, but Belladonna couldn't pretend anymore. She wanted to be alone. To think.

"I'm sorry," she said, pushing away a plate from which she had eaten two small mouthfuls, "I'm really tired. I think I'll go to bed early, if that's alright."

"Of course it is, dear," said Mrs. Proctor. "I'll bring you some hot chocolate."

"That's alright. I'm not really —"

"Nonsense! All children must have a hot drink at bedtime."

Belladonna climbed the stairs to her room again. She sat on the bed, racking her brains. What had Mrs. Lazenby said that was so important? What had she missed?

"Here's your cocoa, dear."

The Parchment

THE NEXT MORNING, Belladonna woke up with one thought—school. She'd never thought she'd actually be happy to go, but the idea of being in a place she understood, with people she knew, suddenly seemed like the best thing in the world. She scrambled out of bed and into the bathroom. Her reflection in the mirror still looked tired, but perhaps not quite so bad as the day before. She'd had plenty of sleep, after all, even though it was far from restful slumber. A succession of dreams had left her feeling exhausted and wrung out with a slight headache, but who cared about that? Now it was morning and she could get out of this house and away from all the people trying to do what was "best" for her.

She wolfed down some toast and a cup of tea.

"What do you do for lunch?" asked Mrs. Proctor. "Do you need me to make something?"

"No, thanks, there's a cafeteria," smiled Belladonna, throwing on her coat and picking up her pink backpack.

"Do you know the way from here?"

"Yes. I'll be fine."

"See you at teatime, then!"

"Bye!"

And she was out. She didn't actually have any idea where school was in relation to Shady Gardens, but she ran all the same. The wind caught at her black hair as she went, whipping and tangling it. She was sure she looked even more of a mess than usual, but it was so wonderful to be running. There was the church! And the corner of her own road! Now she knew where she was.

She ran through the front door, hung up her coat, and dashed toward the classroom, waving to a surprised Elsie as she passed. She just made it to her desk as the bell sounded for the first class, so it wasn't until forty minutes had passed that she noticed that everyone was staring, and by the time break rolled around, her initial elation at being away from the Proctors had evaporated and she was back to feeling like the odd girl out.

And her head was pounding.

She went to the school nurse and got a couple of aspirins, then made her way around the back of the school to her favorite bench and sat down with a thump.

"Where have you been?" asked Elsie, poking her head out of the art room wall.

"She got arrested."

Belladonna looked up. Steve was leaning against the wall, looking grim.

"I told you Sophie would get you back for the chair."

"So it *was* her?"

Steve nodded.

"How do you know?"

"Her brother Gareth told me this morning."

Elsie looked from one to the other with rising frustration.

"What? What happened? What did she do?"

"She followed Belladonna home and saw her go into her old house instead of going to her grandmother's. She watched for a while to make sure she was really living there, which wasn't hard because apparently the Johnsons don't have enough sense to draw the curtains, and then she went home and told her mother."

"Why should we draw the curtains? It wasn't dark yet."

"Because you're twelve and you're living alone in a house with two ghosts."

"Yes, but why should anyone want to spy? And why are you so narky?"

"I'm not narky."

"Yes, you are. You've been in an absolutely filthy mood ever since the beginning of term."

Belladonna felt glad that she'd finally said something about it, but Steve looked at her as if he was trying to decide whether to say something or just give up and stalk back to the football field.

"I'm fed up," he said finally.

"About what?" asked Elsie.

"Nothing. Everything. My Mum for leaving me and my Dad. My Dad for making me work in the shop all the time. You . . ."

"Me?" said Belladonna. "What've I done?"

"All of this!" he said, waving his arm around vaguely.

"It was all so simple before. And now . . . What if it doesn't work out? What if you die? Or I die? It could happen."

"What's wrong with being dead?" asked Elsie, clearly annoyed.

"Nothing . . . I mean . . . well, it's not the being-dead part, is it? It's the actual dying. This isn't some story with happy endings and stuff. It's real and it's getting worse."

"Worse? How do you know? Did Edmund de Braes say something?"

"Yes," began Steve, then changed his mind. "I mean no. I mean I don't need him to tell me. Look, if the Paladin's job really is to protect the Spellbinder, like he said, then don't you think the Spellbinder is supposed to have at least a tiny bit of common sense?"

"What?"

"Well, there's that feather for starters. It's obvious that a Kere is wandering around here somewhere, but do you even have the sense to draw the curtains or take any care at all? Noooo."

"It isn't obvious that there's a Kere here," hissed Belladonna angrily. "And that stupid feather had nothing to do with me being taken into care. That was all Sophie's fault. It wasn't magic, or Night Ravens, or winged women, or evil apothecaries, just a mean-spirited, spoiled little girl. And if you think—"

"Enough!" Elsie's voice echoed around the buildings and even though both Belladonna and Steve knew that no one else could hear her, they both gasped, glanced around, and then smiled a little sheepishly.

"Yowza!" said Steve. "Enough with the shouting. Who knew ghosts could be so loud?"

"So," continued Elsie, ignoring him, "Steve says you met a monk at the monastery and he gave you a parchment."

Belladonna nodded. "He's got it."

"Have you looked at it yet?"

"Yeah," said Steve. "Can't make head or tail of it. It just looks like streaks across the paper."

"Well, why don't we look at it at lunchtime, then. In the library."

Steve looked dubious.

"Oh, for heaven's sake," said Belladonna, rolling her eyes, "it's not like anyone ever goes in there. I think you'll be able to preserve your reputation."

Steve smiled slightly in spite of himself as the bell for the end of break sliced through the winter air.

"Okay." He shrugged.

"And no more shouting," said Elsie.

By the time lunch rolled around, Belladonna was glad to escape to the library. Sophie Warren had spent the bulk of the day so far either smirking knowingly across the room at her or giggling with her friends. Belladonna had never really been in trouble for much of anything at school, but she was sorely tempted to punch Sophie. What could have possessed her to get her mother to phone the authorities? Was one little joke with a chair really too much for her fragile dignity?

She stomped down the hall to the library, her mood getting blacker by the moment.

"Whoa!" said Steve as she walked into the small room that passed for Dullworth's repository of all printed knowledge. "Your mood's improved since this morning, then."

"Oh, shut up."

"Hello!" chirped Elsie, materializing near the Ancient History section. "Oh . . ."

"It's alright," sighed Belladonna, dropping her backpack into a nearby chair. "I've got a headache. Let's have a look at this parchment."

Steve extracted it from his own extremely battered bag and unrolled it across the nearest table. Belladonna placed books on each of the corners to hold it flat, but as soon as she looked at it, her heart sank.

"Oh," she said.

"I told you," muttered Steve.

The parchment was yellowed with age and worn around the edges, but the contents were quite clear . . . and utterly meaningless. Instead of the map that she had expected, Belladonna found herself staring at a series of black streaks of ink that seemed to have been smeared at random across the page. The only item that made any sense was a rough drawing of the moon near the center of one long edge.

"I thought that was probably the top," said Steve.

"Brilliant," said Belladonna, squinting at the ink smears.

"I know what that is," mused Elsie.

Belladonna and Steve looked at her expectantly.

"It's a . . . I can't remember the word. It begins with an *A*. We used to have them all over the house. Argh! Why can't I remember?"

They stood around the table and stared at the parchment, as if hoping that by some freak of nature the whole thing would suddenly resolve itself into something legible or leap up vertically like a pop-up book.

"Nuts," said Steve finally.

"Can't you say some Words over it or something?" asked Elsie.

"I don't think so," said Belladonna. "I don't feel anything."

They stared at it for a few more moments, then Steve rolled it up and shoved it back into his backpack.

"I'm going to have lunch," he announced. "I'm starving."

Belladonna put the books away and wandered out into the corridor. Elsie trailed along behind, lost in thought, and slowly vanished.

The lunch room was almost empty by the time Belladonna got there. Except for the chess club, of course. They were always there banging their little clocks and peering earnestly at the ranks of wooden figures. She helped herself to some fish and chips, and some peas that seemed to have the mass of Jupiter, and then selected a table as far from the chess club's perpetually pinging clocks as she could manage. Steve wasn't there. He refused to eat school lunches and had been given special dispensation to bring in food from home. When his mother had still been around, his lunches had been the envy of all his friends, but now that it was just him and his Dad, it was nearly always just a ham sandwich, an apple, and a thermos of tea, all of which he ate outside while watching the under-15s football practice.

Belladonna thought about the parchment as she pushed the food around her plate. She could understand the map being disguised in some way, but why wouldn't Edmund de Braes have given them the key? Or a clue to the key? Or the vaguest of hints? He'd said it would help them find the "Instrument of Life."

She stopped pushing the remains of the fish and chips about and looked up.

No, he didn't, she thought. *He said it would help us prevent her return, find the Instrument, and hide it again.*

Perhaps that was what the map would lead them to—something that would prevent the return of the Empress of the Dark Spaces. That had to be the first thing, surely? But even if that was the case, why not just tell them? Why make everything so complicated? He knew she was the Spellbinder; why not just tell her?

She took her plate back, scraped the remains of the fish and chips into the bin, and put the plate and cutlery into the tub marked DIRTY PLATES in large block letters. She noticed that a lot of people didn't bother scraping off their plates before they stuck them in the tub and reflected that there were worse things in the world than being the Spellbinder.

After lunch it was double English followed by French, by which time Belladonna was having difficulty staying awake while Madame Huggins read some endless passage out of a "very important" book. She had prefaced this by going on at length about how she couldn't understand why none of them had ever read it. Then Steve had piped up brightly that possibly it was because it was in *French*, which everyone had thought was very funny, though he was rewarded for his pains by being forced to sit at the very front for the rest of the class.

Belladonna had just diverted her attention from doodling in her book to gazing blankly out of the window when suddenly Elsie appeared, standing right on Madame Huggins's desk.

"Whoops!" she said cheerily, jumping down. "I've got it! I know how we can read it!"

Steve stared at her in disbelief, but Belladonna managed to maintain a bit more composure as Elsie ran up to her desk.

"Honestly, it's so simple!"

Belladonna sighed, turned the page of her exercise book, and wrote in large letters at the top: *NOT NOW. GO AWAY.*

Elsie read it, thought about it for a few moments, and glanced around the class. "Oh, righto. Sorry. Wasn't thinking and all that. Reconvene in the library at half three, then?"

And she was gone.

"Can you believe her?" hissed Steve as they made their way down to the library after school. "She doesn't have the sense of a turnip!"

Elsie was waiting in the library when they got there.

"Roll it out!" she commanded.

Steve glared at her for a moment but did as she said, placing the books on the corners just as before. Elsie examined it closely, squinting and crouching down until her eyes were at the same level as the tabletop.

"Right," she said finally, straightening up. "I remembered the word. It's *anamorphic*."

"Ana-whatsis?" asked Steve.

"It's a kind of art. My Dad used to collect examples. Prints, mostly, of course. He thought they were really great."

Belladonna and Steve just stared at her.

"Look," she said, "you make a painting or a drawing and then you have to tilt it at a certain angle or you need a mirrored cylinder or something to view it properly. They used to hide secret messages in them or just use them for . . . well, jokes, I suppose. There's a famous one with a skull . . . um . . . by Holbein, I think. He was the court painter to Henry VIII. Is there a book on him here?"

Belladonna scanned quickly along the half shelf of books dedicated to art.

"I'm not . . . ," she began.

"There it is!" said Elsie triumphantly, pointing to a slender volume with a green cover. "*English Art in the Sixteenth Century*! Gosh, I think that book was here when I was alive."

"Dullworth's does pride itself on being on the cutting edge," grinned Steve.

Belladonna removed the book and placed it on the table.

"Look at the list of illustrations," said Elsie. "See if there's something called . . . um . . . I think it was *The Doctors* . . . or *The Diplomats* . . . or . . ."

"How about *The Ambassadors*?" asked Belladonna.

"Yes!"

Belladonna turned to the page and was surprised to find herself looking at something that seemed perfectly normal to start with: two men in the clothes of the period leaning on a desk covered with papers, scientific instruments, and a large lute, but as her eyes traveled down, she noticed a strange whitish smear that spread diagonally from the center of the picture to its lower left-hand corner.

"What's that?"

"It's the anamorphic part," said Elsie. "Hold the picture up so it's level with your eyes and then kind of look at it sideways."

"It's a skull!" said Belladonna, amazed.

"The picture was supposed to hang on a staircase, so you'd see the skull as you came up the stairs."

"Give me a go," said Steve, taking the book and holding it up. "Huh. Cool. But I thought you said you needed a mirror."

"Not always," admitted Elsie. "But you can sort of see how it works. The ones that needed mirrors were usually drawings or engravings. There'd be a circle or something on the page that told you where to put the cylinder. The moon on our picture is probably where the mirror goes."

"So we need a round mirror with the same diameter?"

Elsie nodded. "I think you mean cylindrical, though."

"Maybe a piece of pipe," suggested Steve, ignoring her. "With foil around it."

"Or maybe—"

Belladonna didn't get any further.

"Seems to be clear," said a voice right outside the library. "I'll just check in here."

Belladonna swept the anchoring books out of the way, and Steve rolled up the parchment and shoved it inside his bag just as Mr. Watson walked into the room.

"Steve Evans! Belladonna Johnson! What are you doing in here?"

Belladonna stared at him, her mind a total blank, but Steve immediately went into trouble mode and picked up the books that had been holding the parchment in place.

"Just getting some books!"

"Really?" said Mr. Watson.

"Yes," said Belladonna. "For a project for . . . Geography."

"Hm. Alright. Don't forget to sign them out. Surprised you know where the library is, Evans."

Belladonna went to the sign-out book and hurriedly listed the titles and signed her name.

"Right," said Mr. Watson. "Off you go, we're locking up."

Belladonna shoved two of the books into her bag and handed the other two to Steve as Mr. Watson steered them out of the library and out of the front door with a hasty "good night."

"Good job he didn't want to know what the project was for," said Belladonna.

Steve looked quizzical, then examined the spines of the two books she had handed to him.

"*A Beginners Guide to Forensic Science* and *Britain's Endangered Species*. Well, maybe we're going to open a detective agency."

Belladonna laughed and for a moment almost forgot that she wasn't going home.

"Where are you staying?" asked Steve.

"Foster parents," said Belladonna, her mood suddenly darkening again. "They're very nice, really. They try. I feel a little guilty . . . but . . . well, it isn't home and . . ."

"Do they live close by?"

Belladonna nodded.

"Good," said Steve. "I have to stay off school tomorrow. My Dad sent a note saying I have to visit some sick relative somewhere, but really it's just to help him get ready for the latest sale. Come over on Saturday and let's see if we can find a way to look at this map."

"Okay," said Belladonna. "Saturday. This is my road."

She stopped at the turn to Nether Street, the long road that led to Shady Gardens, but instead of just saying good-bye and sauntering off home, Steve looked suddenly concerned.

"Down here?" he said, "But there isn't . . . Where did you say you were staying?"

"It's an old apartment building," said Belladonna. "It's a bit grotty, actually, but it's going to be restored, apparently. At least that's what the Proctors said. It's called Shady Gardens."

"Is it round?" asked Steve.

"Like a big arena, yes." Belladonna had noticed the change in Steve's expression. "What is it?"

"You can't be staying there," he said grimly.

"Why not? I mean, it's a bit run-down, but the Proctors keep their house nice and clean and—"

"No," said Steve, "you don't understand. It was demolished three years ago. My Dad took me to see them blow it up. Shady Gardens doesn't exist anymore."

9

Walking

BELLADONNA DRIFTED along Nether Street. Demolished? He had to be mistaken. It must have been another building. Maybe they'd built two. Then the building itself came into view as she rounded a bend in the road and she realized that he *had* to be wrong. Shady Gardens was huge and solid and most definitely there.

She stopped for a moment and stared. Her headache had gone and suddenly she didn't feel like going back just yet. She turned and walked away with every intention of just having a bit of an aimless wander, but before she really knew where she was going she found herself in front of her house. Her real home. She looked around to make sure no one was watching, then opened the gate and slowly walked up to the door.

Out of habit, she reached for her key in the side pocket of her backpack, forgetting for a split second that she'd given it to Mrs. Lazenby. She sighed and pushed open the letter box, peering into the empty hall. It seemed dark and cold and above all empty.

She let the letter box flap shut with a quiet creak and walked over to the living room window, but the curtains were closed. They were closed around the back too and so were the kitchen blinds. Mrs. Lazenby must have done that when she picked up her clothes.

She returned to the front of the house and opened the flap again.

"Hello?"

She was surprised by how small her voice sounded.

"Hello?" she said again, more loudly. But there was no reply. Just silence and the distant tick-tick of the kitchen clock.

Of course, there was no reason why they should be there. They only haunted the house so they could take care of her, and if she wasn't there, they probably just stayed in the Land of the Dead. Still, she'd have thought they might have heard her. But perhaps not. Perhaps she needed to be inside the actual house. She sighed and wished she'd asked them how the whole "haunting" thing worked when she'd had the chance.

She let the flap close and walked away, closing the gate after her. How could this have happened? And after all the trouble they'd had rescuing them in the Land of the Dead! She began trying to think of suitable ways of revenging herself upon Sophie Warren but wasn't having much success. The only things she could think of would probably end up with her getting in even more trouble and Sophie just carrying on as usual. She was starting to wonder what the point was of being the Spellbinder if you couldn't get own's back against irritants in your life, when she realized she was on Yarrow Street. She scurried along to her grandmother's house. That, too, was shut solid, curtains and blinds drawn.

"Belladonna, is that you?"

For a moment her heart leapt, but when she turned around, it was just Mrs. Proctor. She was standing at the gate, holding two heavy shopping bags full of groceries and smiling.

"Oh, hello" was all Belladonna could muster.

"What on earth are you doing here?"

"It's my Gran's house," explained Belladonna. "I just thought I'd . . . you know . . . see if she was back."

"Oh," said Mrs. Proctor, "I see. I'm sorry."

"It's alright." She closed the gate and joined Mrs. Proctor.

"Shall we get home and have some tea?"

Belladonna nodded.

"That's the girl! Why don't you take one of these bags? There you go! We'll be back in no time."

"Have you talked to Mrs. Lazenby today?" asked Belladonna.

"Of course I have!" said Mrs. Proctor in a resolutely cheery voice. "No news, I'm afraid."

"Have they reported my Gran missing? To the police, I mean?"

"I think so."

Belladonna sighed and trudged on beside Mrs. Proctor, who prattled on cheerily about her day and what she did in town and what the latest news was about the restoration of Shady Gardens. Belladonna smiled and tried to pretend to be interested, but all she could think about was finding her grandmother and getting away from the Proctors and Mrs. Lazenby. She knew they all meant well, but they weren't family and they didn't know her.

The one thing that had made seeing ghosts and then being the Spellbinder bearable was the fact that her family knew. So while she had to pretend that she couldn't see the dead at school or out in town, at home she could relax and be herself and talk about it. Without those conversations, that understanding and release, she felt as if she was somehow locked in her own head, peering out at the world and always on guard.

They walked down Yarrow Street, turned the corner up Jeremiah Place, and made their way past the end of Umbra Street. There were ghosts everywhere and it took all of Belladonna's concentration to pretend not to see them. The spirit of old Mrs. Renshaw, who had spent the last twenty years of her life housebound with crippling arthritis, sped by on a ghostly skateboard, her hair flying in the wind.

"Hello, Belladonna!"

Belladonna smiled a greeting but could do no more than that.

Then the Phillips sisters, all four of them, came running toward her. They'd all died in a diphtheria epidemic back in the 1870s and had a beautiful gravestone in the churchyard near her house, complete with a weeping angel and a sad-looking marble puppy.

"Have you seen Mary?" gasped Irene, the eldest.

"She's on one of those boards—the ones with little

wheels," said Rose. "She said we can have a go if we can catch her."

Belladonna glanced back over her shoulder. For a moment the girls seemed puzzled, then Irene got the message.

"Oh, right," she whispered, as if that made any difference. "Sorry. Come on, you lot, she went this way!"

And they were off. Belladonna was almost relieved when they reached Shady Gardens and there were no ghosts for her to pretend not to see. Just the silent Shadow People lurking in doorways and clustered in the arches.

"I think I'll play on the swing. Just until tea is ready." She tried to sound cheerful.

"That's fine," said Mrs. Proctor, smiling. "I'll call you when it's ready. Would you like me to take your bag in for you?"

"No, that's alright." Belladonna smiled brightly and wandered off to the swings. The bag contained everything that was most precious to her now—Dr. Ashe's book, the hunting horn, the bell for calling the Dead, and her rapidly dwindling supply of Parma Violets.

She dumped the bag near the swing, sat down, and slowly wound it around and around. As it spun she could see the shadows clearly, standing in small groups around the building. She did it again . . . and again. There seemed to be more of them. Maybe they were ghosts after all. Then the third time she spun, she saw something else. There seemed to be someone moving around in one of the ground-floor apartments.

She jammed her foot into the hard dirt beneath the

swing and stared. It wasn't possible—the apartment was boarded up. She got up and walked over to it. She pushed on the boards to see if they were loose, but they were all new and firm. It was really weird. She went back to the swing and spun again and while the Shadow People appeared in their ones, twos, and threes, the apartment remained boarded up and blank.

"Tea's ready!"

Mrs. Proctor was leaning over the balcony and waving down at her. Belladonna smiled and waved back, then ran up the stairs for tea. *Tomorrow,* she thought. *I'll have a proper look at that apartment tomorrow.*

But she didn't. The next morning she felt so tired she could hardly get out of bed. Mrs. Proctor said that it was probably just delayed stress and she'd feel better in a day or two. Mr. Proctor gave her a ride to school and picked her up at the end of the day, and even though she still (against her better nature) slightly resented them, Belladonna had to admit that they were being really nice.

The next day was Saturday and she was up early and although her reflection in the bathroom mirror still looked tired, she certainly felt a lot better. She told Mrs. Proctor that she was going out for a walk and headed into town, breathing in the fresh, cold February air and feeling that perhaps everything was going to change and it would all be alright after all.

She stopped by the graveyard at St. Abelard's where the dead leaves and grass crackled under her feet as she walked to her favorite table tomb and sat down. She gazed across the grassy expanse, the graves slightly crystalline with frost, and for a moment it felt as it always had.

"Aren't you cold sitting on that?"

Belladonna looked down. Aya, the charnel sprite, was standing in what remained of the tall grass, her head to one side and the curls of her purplish hair bobbing slightly in the breeze.

"A little," said Belladonna, "but I think it's to be expected in February."

Aya smiled and jumped up beside her.

"I know," she said. "We've been really busy. Lots of people pop off in February."

Belladonna nodded, then suddenly had a thought.

"Has . . ." She hesitated for a moment; there was something dreadful about saying it out loud, but she had to know. "Has anyone from my family been through?"

"Died, you mean?"

Belladonna nodded. Conducting the Dead to the Other Side was just a job for Aya, but Belladonna couldn't share her matter-of-fact attitude. Even though she knew it was alright and that the Land of the Dead was quite a nice place (when it wasn't being turned into slime by evil ex-alchemists), there was still something slightly unsettling about it.

"No, I don't think so," said Aya. "Was it someone in particular?"

"My Gran is missing. I thought . . . you know . . . maybe . . ."

"When did she go missing?"

"I'm not sure. Tuesday, I think."

"No," said Aya, after thinking about it for a bit. "Funnily enough, we haven't had any old ladies this week."

Belladonna felt relieved and a little disappointed. She didn't want her Gran to be dead, but she hated not knowing and couldn't get rid of the knot in her stomach that told her that something really bad had happened.

"Don't worry." Aya was gazing into her face and seemed genuinely concerned. "I'm sure she's alright."

"It's just not like her," whispered Belladonna.

"Look," said Aya, her tiny hand grasping Belladonna's, "I'll ask around. She could have come through when I wasn't there. When I was on break or something."

Belladonna smiled. Most people would have assured Belladonna that her Gran wasn't dead, but in Aya's world it was roughly equivalent to having retired and bought a villa in Spain.

"Thank you."

"No problem," grinned Aya, jumping down. "I'd better get back. I'm supposed to be making the tea."

"Charnel sprites drink tea?"

"Of course! There's nothing like a good cuppa to keep you going. Bye! I'll ask about your grandmother!"

And she was gone. Belladonna waited for a while to see if she'd return, but all was silent except for the faint whine of a distant jet. She got down from the tomb and strolled through the graveyard to the far gate, wondering if charnel sprites had electric kettles or if they boiled the water over an open fire.

She was still pondering the eating habits of charnel sprites and trying to picture them with tiny cups and saucers when she found herself in front of Evans Electronics. The blaring cacophony of competing stereos, TVs, and radios drowned out all quiet thought and banged around inside her aching head like marbles in a jar.

Mr. Evans was with a customer, so she waited until he was finished.

"Looking for Steve?" he said, his voice a perpetual half shout.

"Yes," nodded Belladonna.

"He's in the back. Reading comics," grinned Mr. Evans. "He thinks I don't know, y'know."

Belladonna smiled and made her way past the teetering towers of noise to the small door at the back of the shop and the relative calm of the old theatre. She stood for a moment in the cool darkness, looking over the labyrinth of boxes and cartons.

"Steve?"

"Over here!" His head bobbed up like a meerkat and was gone again.

She picked her way through the maze in what she thought was the right direction but soon found herself at a dead end.

"Where are you?"

"Here!"

The voice seemed further away than when she started.

"Well, stand up so I can see you!"

"I don't want my Dad to see me," said Steve, standing up. "He thinks I'm checking the inventory."

"No, he doesn't," said Belladonna. "He thinks you're back here reading a comic."

She made her way through and finally arrived at a small space among the towering boxes that Steve had cleared for the scroll. It was spread out on the floor, the corners held down by two MP3s, a camera, and a discarded caster from some kind of rolling cabinet.

"Any progress?"

"No," said Steve gloomily. "I made this. . . ." He held up a piece of cardboard tube covered in foil. "But I can't stop the foil from wrinkling, so it's not really working."

"Let me have a go." Belladonna dropped her bag and took the tube. She tested it on the moon drawn on the parchment and it seemed to be the right size. "Have you got any more foil?"

"Yes," said Steve, handing her the box, "but it's getting a little low. I've been trying for ages."

Belladonna carefully removed a piece of foil, laid it on the floor, and slowly rolled it around the tube. She thought she'd been really careful, but when she looked at her handiwork, it was almost as wrinkled as Steve's effort and reflected nothing except the most abstract shapes and colors.

"See?" he said. "It just doesn't work."

"No." Belladonna examined the tube and some of the foil still in the box. "It doesn't even reflect properly when it's not wrinkly, though, does it?"

Steve shook his head and sighed. "Have you got any sweets?"

Belladonna handed him a half-empty packet of Parma Violets and he poured them into his mouth.

"Hey!"

"What?"

"Never mind." She glared at him for a moment, then returned her attention to the parchment. "What we need," she said finally, "is something the right shape that's already shiny, like a piece of chrome off a car or a silver cup or something."

"A cup?"

"Yes, like a—"

But before she elaborated further, Steve leapt to his feet and ran out of the theatre. A few moments later he returned with his school bag.

"Thank goodness I didn't take it home," he gasped.

"Since Thursday?" said Belladonna, incredulous. "What about your homework?"

Steve rolled his eyes and flipped the top of the backpack open. After a few seconds rifling through the contents, he made a small grunt of triumph and produced his thermos flask. Its lid was shiny, tubular, and just about the right diameter.

"Brilliant!" said Belladonna, pushing her hair back from her face and leaning over the parchment as he unscrewed the lid and placed it over the moon.

And then they saw it. A perfect reproduction of a circular, or nearly circular, stone building with a conical roof and tall windows. Walls seemed to extend out from either side and a small skull was lying right next to the large studded door.

"Cool," said Steve.

"It looks familiar," mused Belladonna.

"But . . . hang on." Steve sat up. "I thought it was supposed to be a map."

"Maybe it is. Maybe the thing . . . whatever it is . . . is inside this building."

"So where's the building?" said Steve, a note of irritation creeping into his voice. "Maps are supposed to tell you where things are; drawings just show you what they look like. They only work if you've seen the place before."

Belladonna shrugged. "I don't know, but I feel like we should recognize . . ."

"It looks kind of like a piece of a castle . . . or . . . Yes! It's the —"

"Monastery!" said Belladonna. "It's the chapter house! The chapter house was round!"

They both grinned and stared at the silvery image for a few moments. Then Steve shook his head.

"Typical," he said finally. "We were standing in the chapter house when he gave it to us. Why couldn't he have said, 'It's over there'? We could've got the secret thingy, hidden it somewhere else, and saved everyone from the return of the Dark Times with the minimum of fuss. But noooooo, it has to be on a scroll that you can't read without a silver cup."

"Maybe because there's something else," said Belladonna, sitting up and looking at the whole parchment again. "Maybe the picture isn't the only thing on the parchment."

Steve sat back on his heels and stared at the scroll.

"The margins are very big."

Belladonna nodded—the margins *were* very big. The actual picture of the chapter house occupied only the central portion of the scroll, leaving two wide empty borders on either side. It might have just been the design, but Belladonna felt sure there was something else.

Steve leaned over the parchment until his nose was nearly touching its aged yellow surface. He sat up again.

"I can't see anything."

"What if . . . Did they have invisible ink in the Middle Ages?"

"Yes!" Steve's face lit up. "Yes, I saw this film once; I think they used things like lemon juice. You have to hold the paper over a flame and the heat makes the writing visible."

"So we need a candle or something."

"Yes, although . . ."

"We might set it on fire."

"Which would be bad."

They stared at the parchment, thinking.

"We need something warm," said Belladonna finally. "Something very warm but not so hot that it'll damage it. Do you have central heating here? Maybe if we put it against a radiator . . ."

"Central heating?" said Steve. "You must be joking. There's no way my Dad would pay for that. There's a little electric fire in the shop, but . . . Hang on, I've got it—a car!"

"A car?"

"Yes, a car. They get really hot, well, warm anyway. We

could put the parchment on the hood of a car that some-one's just left. One that's still warm."

"I suppose . . ." said Belladonna, unconvinced.

"Oh, come on, it's worth a try. We could go to that parking lot around the corner."

Belladonna bit her lip and considered.

"Okay."

Steve grinned and put the lid back on his thermos, picked up the various items holding the parchment in place, and rolled it up.

"Let's go out the back."

Belladonna nodded and followed him to the stage and back past the dressing rooms to what had been the stage door of the theatre.

They stepped out into the alley and blinked in the cold daylight. Steve zipped up his jacket and shoved the scroll inside.

"Come on."

They ran up the alley, then out onto Glebe Road and into the throngs of people meandering through town, look-ing for the best Saturday bargains. Steve led the way to the parking lot, dodging through the crowds with the ease of a Dickensian street urchin. By the time Belladonna caught up, he was already waiting impatiently in the entrance of the town's only multistory car park.

"It's pretty full," he said. "Let's go to the roof."

They piled into the tiny lift with half a dozen exhausted shoppers and one screaming baby and waited while it ground slowly upward, stopping on every floor before hauling itself up to the next. By the time it got to the roof, they were the only ones left, though there was a small crowd waiting to descend.

"Ugh!" said Belladonna, stepping out and gasping for air. "Why do they always smell so horrible?"

Steve opened his mouth to speak.

"No! Never mind—I don't want to know."

He grinned and scanned the ranks of cars.

"We need one that's only just got here. And the older the better."

"What about that one? My Gran's got one of those and it's always overheating," said Belladonna, pointing to the top of the entry ramp, where an aged green Morris Minor had just labored its way to the roof.

"Brilliant!"

They watched as the old car crept along the aisles of cars before finally pulling into a parking space in the far corner, then made their way toward it as nonchalantly as they could.

The driver was an elderly man with a pipe, which he removed from his mouth and shoved into his jacket pocket before adjusting his scarf and walking toward the entrance.

"He'll set his pocket on fire doing that," whispered Belladonna.

"No," said Steve. "My Granddad used to do it all the time. It's probably not even lit. Come on."

They scurried over to the car. Belladonna removed a glove and felt the hood.

"Ow!"

"Hot?"

"Yes. I don't think he should be driving it."

Steve smiled and took the parchment out of his jacket.

"Hang on," said Belladonna. "Let me get some paper out. Just in case. If there is any writing, we should write down what it says in case it only appears once."

"Good thinking."

Belladonna rummaged through her bag and produced her Geography exercise book and a ballpoint pen. She opened the book at the back and checked the pen. It worked.

"Okay."

Steve nodded and tried to press the parchment onto the hot hood, but it was too large.

"We'll have to do one side and then the other."

Belladonna nodded and watched as he smoothed the left-hand margin of the scroll over the car and held it in place. For a moment it seemed that nothing was happening.

"I don't think it's going to—"

"Wait! Look!"

Belladonna leaned in and stared as slowly, slowly something began to appear on the margin. At first it seemed like random squiggles, pale brown and curving. Was it another drawing?

"It's words!" said Steve.

"Is it English? Can you read it?"

"It's . . . no . . . it's some other language."

Belladonna leaned in. At first she thought it was going to be Latin, but it was something else, something that she could read but not understand, although some words did seem like English ones. Then the penny dropped—of course she'd seen it before! In all these weeks and weeks of studying about the establishment of the monasteries in England in the Middle Ages, they'd seen dozens of illustrations of old parchments and illuminated manuscripts. Most of them had been in Latin, but a few had been in early versions of English. An English that seemed almost totally foreign now, but it *was* English.

"I think it's Old English," she said, wondering if this whole adventure was going to improve her chances in the History exam at the end of term. "You know, the language they spoke in the Middle Ages."

"Great," muttered Steve. "Now we have to find someone who speaks that."

He stared at the parchment, then suddenly turned to Belladonna.

"Hang on . . . isn't that the language Mr. Watson's been banging on about? The one in . . . what was it called . . . *Beowulf*?"

"Yes!" said Belladonna, unable to conceal her surprise.

"You needn't look so stunned. It had monsters in it . . . and a dragon. Anyway, maybe he'll know what it says."

He picked up the parchment as if to put it away.

"I don't think so," said Belladonna. "He said he'd only read translations of it."

"Rats."

"Wait, I've got an idea. Put it back again."

He put the parchment back and pressed it against the

hood again. Belladonna leaned in closer, held one hand above the parchment and closed her eyes. At first nothing came, but slowly, slowly the Words came to her.

"*Igi ʃi gar.*" She opened her eyes and said it again: "*Igi ʃi gar.*"

"Look!"

Belladonna smiled. The tangle of unintelligible words slowly unwound and twisted on the page, like earthworms on a rainy day, until nothing remained but a pattern of lines. Then, as they watched, the lines curled and twisted again, forming new words—modern English words.

"Yowza," muttered Steve. "What did you say?"

"'Reveal yourself.'"

"That's all?"

Belladonna nodded.

"Read it out."

Steve smoothed the parchment again and began to read.

> "*Thrice times three the cromlechs be*
> *And thrice times three the charm,*
> *Thrice the knight who failed the fight*
> *And thrice be mercy's balm.*
> *But twain is all the angels keep*
> *Though none do they mistrust,*
> *For the last is lost in the land of sleep*
> *In the murksome house of dust.*"

Belladonna scribbled it down, but Steve seemed less than impressed.

"Oh, great. Another stupid riddle. Why can't people just say what they mean and be done?"

"Never mind, never mind!" said Belladonna excitedly. "Do the other side. Quick, before the car cools down."

Steve rolled his eyes and pressed the other margin to the still-hot hood.

"It's not cooling down at all. I'm sure this thing isn't roadworthy. Oh, here it comes."

The brown scratches slowly formed into a new set of words.

> *"Thy beating heart is not the best*
> *For this the darkling perilous quest.*
> *Find one with a heart whose time is through*
> *Yet constant holds with brightness true."*

"Got it?"

"Yes."

He stood back and rolled up the parchment.

"It's weird," said Belladonna, looking at the rhymes. "Edmund de Braes said there was a thing, one thing that needed to be found and rehidden, but this makes it sound like there are nine."

"And one of them, whatever they are, is lost," grumbled Steve. "This is so stupid. Why can't they just—"

"Hey, you!"

They spun around. A tall, skinny man in an ill-fitting uniform was striding across the car park toward them.

"What are you up to?!"

Belladonna glanced up. There were three security cameras focused on the cars.

"Nothing!" yelled Steve, shoving the parchment back in his jacket. "Just frying some eggs! Come on, Belladonna!"

And he was off, dodging between the cars and heading for the stairs. Belladonna hesitated for a second, thinking that it might be easier just to explain, but a quick look at the thunderous face of the parking attendant told her it would be useless, so she took to her heels and raced after Steve.

They banged through the door to the stairwell and racketed down the flights until they burst, laughing, into the street. Another guard leaned out of the payment booth.

"Hey!"

They stared at him for a second, then took off again, running back down the street to the alley and the safety of the old theatre.

Belladonna stopped at the door and glanced at her watch.

"Yikes! I'd better go. I told Mrs. Proctor I'd be back for lunch. Are you around tomorrow? We should probably start working this out."

"No." Steve shook his head. "We're going to my Auntie Viv's for Sunday dinner."

"Your Mum's sister?"

"No, my Dad's. We go every Sunday since . . . well, my Dad can't really cook or anything, so . . ."

Belladonna was sorry she'd mentioned his mother, but a little something had jumped inside her at the thought that Mrs. Evans might have a sister. A sister would mean that she was just an ordinary mum after all and that Belladonna had been wrong when she had suspected that she knew more than she ought to about the door to the Other Side.

"That's okay," she blurted, afraid that his effort to appear cool about everything might fail and subject him to the ignominy of crying in front of a girl. "Monday, then."

She turned to go, but Steve reached out and stopped her.

"Wait," he said as she turned around in surprise. "Um . . . I wanted to give you this."

He unzipped his pocket and pulled out a square envelope.

"It's a DVD. You need to see it."

"Alright."

She took the DVD and put it into her bag.

"Alone," said Steve. "You should watch it alone. Promise?"

Belladonna nodded.

"Okay. See you Monday, then."

He hesitated for a moment as if there was something else he wanted to say, then turned and disappeared into the darkened theatre.

Belladonna felt that she should go after him and find out what it was, but just as she reached for the door, the town hall clock began to strike twelve. Now she really *was* late for lunch.

She hoiked her bag onto her shoulder and took off running.

Gran

IT WAS NEARLY half past twelve when Belladonna finally reached Shady Gardens. She raced across the scrubby grass and worn drive, ran up the stairs, and burst in the front door.

"Sorry I'm late!"

Mrs. Proctor poked her head out of the kitchen. She didn't look very pleased, but managed a smile anyway.

"There you are! We were beginning to worry!"

"Sorry. I was in town and I just . . . I forgot. I'm sorry."

"That's alright. Get your coat off and take a seat. Beans on toast okay?"

"Yes, thanks."

Belladonna hung her coat on one of the hooks in the hall and slid into a chair.

"Mr. Proctor had to go out," said Mrs. Proctor, popping the bread into the toaster. "So we couldn't wait."

Belladonna smiled a little sheepishly as Mrs. Proctor gave the beans a stir and plonked them on top of the toast.

"There you go. Nice and hot for a cold day. D'you

think you could wash your own plate? I have to pop out for a few moments."

Belladonna nodded.

"Right you are, then."

She disappeared into the hall and returned buttoning up her coat and pulling an old woolen hat over her ears.

"Is it very cold?"

"No. Better than yesterday, I think."

"Good. Won't be long. You can watch the telly if you like."

Belladonna smiled and listened for the click of the latch, then ran to the door and waited until she heard Mrs. Proctor's sturdy footsteps marching across the broken tarmac of the drive. She quickly finished her lunch, rinsed off the dish, and retrieved Steve's DVD from her backpack.

She went into the sitting room, turned on the TV, and slipped the disk into the player.

There was a pause and a faint whirr as the disk loaded. The machine was far from new and she was beginning to think that it might not load at all, when the TV screen suddenly sprang to life with the image of a family picnic. A much younger Steve and his mother were sitting on a blanket on a beach somewhere. They waved to the camera happily.

They were just an ordinary family, thought Belladonna. Here, on the beach, Mrs. Evans looked so unthreatening, just another slightly overweight mum out with her family. But why had Steve wanted her to see this? And why did she have to watch it alone?

The picture changed. It was another day and Steve, his

mother, and the beach had gone. Instead of sand, rocks, and the sound of water, Belladonna found herself looking at a building. A window on a building. People were talking, there was shouting. The picture zoomed back and revealed . . . Shady Gardens!

"When are they going to do it?" asked the much younger voice of Steve.

The camera swung down to look at him and he waved at the lens. The camera swung back to look at the building.

"Soon," said his father's voice. "Look, they're clearing everyone out now."

Belladonna could see the tiny figures of the workers running away. It couldn't be the same building. She squinted at the picture, looking for something that would confirm that it was a different circular apartment building. Similar, but not the same. It couldn't be the same.

There was a muffled boom, then another, and another. Clouds of dust and smoke bloomed out of the sides of the building and it slowly collapsed in and down. The site was nothing but concrete rubble and settling dust. There was the sound of a crowd cheering.

Steve's younger voice said, "That was amazing! Did you get it? Show me!"

The screen went black. Belladonna kept staring at it as if the picture was still there. She wanted to shrug and know that Steve was wrong, that it was obviously a different building—the roof was the wrong color, it was taller, it was clearly in a different part of town. But she couldn't, because it wasn't true, and because just before the first explosion, she had seen it—a concrete sign set into the front of the apartments right next to the arched entrance that read: SHADY GARDENS.

There could be no doubt now. She'd seen it with her own eyes. The building where she was now living had been demolished over three years ago. But how could that be? The Proctors were so nice, and Mrs. Lazenby's office had a thick file on them. Mrs. Lazenby herself had said that she'd known them for years.

She took the disk out of the machine and stared at it. Now, more than ever, she needed to speak to her Mum and Dad. She thought about going to the house to see if they were there, but somehow she didn't think she could bear calling through the letter box and hearing nothing in reply. She had just put the disk back in her bag when there was the sound of the key in the front door lock and Mrs. Proctor came back in, carrying a plastic shopping bag containing a single pint of milk.

"Here we are!" she said cheerily. "And look who I found! I didn't have to walk after all."

Mr. Proctor smiled as he followed her inside. Belladonna managed a small smile as they hung up their coats with much stamping of feet and exclamations about how cold it was and how sometimes it seemed like spring would never come.

It was all just what you'd expect and, in spite of what she had just seen, Belladonna found it hard to believe that there was anything strange about the place at all. She needed to be alone and think, but she was soon swept up in the Proctors' Saturday, sitting and watching television while the smell of the evening's dinner meandered out of the kitchen and the late afternoon sun scattered across the sitting room carpet. She sat cross-legged on the floor and finished her homework, then wandered into the kitchen, where Mrs. Proctor was peeling potatoes.

"Do you need any help?"

"No, dear. Everything's under control. Why don't you play outside for a while? Dinner'll be ready in a jiffy."

Belladonna smiled. At last. Now she could think.

She put on her coat and wandered over to the swing. She didn't spin around to see the Shadow People, though. She wanted to pretend that they weren't there and that everything was perfectly normal. Perhaps there had been two Shady Gardens buildings. One had been demolished and the other one—this one—was being restored.

But somehow, even as she repeated it in her head, she knew it was wrong. Two buildings would never have been given the same name, and even though Steve had only been about nine when he'd come with his Dad to see the demolition, surely he would have noticed if there had been another one. She stopped swinging and stared at the silent walls around her, then thought of the parchment and the Words.

What if . . . ?

"Igi si gar." She said it quietly at first, then more loudly: *"Igi si gar."*

Nothing happened. She got off the swing and walked slowly to the center of the circular garden. She stood for a moment, then began to turn slowly, repeating the words over and over. *Igi si gar—Reveal yourself. Igi si gar. Igi si gar.*

When she had turned completely around, she stopped

and waited. And waited. Nothing was happening. Perhaps the building was too big. Perhaps you needed different Words for brick and concrete. She closed her eyes and concentrated again, but the only Words that came into her head were the ones she had said.

And then it started. Imperceptibly at first, as if a haze was settling over the building. Then the structure itself started to shimmer, the concrete and brick quivering like jelly until the massive edifice was nothing but a vague outline of itself.

"Belladonna!"

She spun around. At first she thought it was Mrs. Proctor, but the voice came from ground level . . . and she recognized it. Her eyes searched the shadowy structure, straining to see.

"Over here!"

She turned. It was coming from the flat she'd looked at the other day. The one where she thought she'd seen a movement. She ran toward it, afraid that the building would reconstitute itself before she could reach it.

"Belladonna!"

As she ran, the tears sprang to her eyes. She was here! She was alive!

"Gran!"

Grandma Johnson was standing at the edge of what had been the outer wall of the flat, the only solid thing in a roughly sketched home. She looked alright. A little tired, but not hurt. Belladonna wanted to hug her, to feel her arms around her, but as soon as she reached what had been the wall, she realized that she was dealing with a magic much stronger than her own.

"No!" She wiped the tears away and closed her eyes, desperate for Words that would release her grandmother, but nothing came. She opened her eyes.

"I can't," she said. "Nothing will come. . . ."

"It's alright, Belladonna, it's alright," said Grandma Johnson softly. "I'm fine."

"Are you . . ." Belladonna hesitated, hardly daring to ask. "Are you really there? Here, I mean?"

"Yes, I'm here. Though I must say I really thought I'd seen the last of this monstrosity when they knocked it down."

"But how . . . ?"

"Your guess is as good as mine. But the last thing I remember is that tall woman, Grace Shapwith—"

"Your new client?"

"Yes, she came back for another session. Said she felt the spirit of her mother wanted to reach her. I went to make a cup of tea and . . . then I was here."

Belladonna tried to concentrate and reach across the line of the wall, but it was no good. It was as if the concrete was still there, as hard and gray as ever.

"You're trapped. I can't—"

"You can't do everything."

"I can't do anything!" she shouted, suddenly angry at herself. "I'm supposed to be the Spellbinder and I couldn't even tell that the stupid building wasn't real!"

"It's alright."

"No, it isn't! How can this be alright? What am I supposed to do!?"

"Well," said Grandma Johnson, dropping the soft approach and going back to her usual no-nonsense manner, "you could pull yourself together for a start."

"What?"

"You're no use to man nor beast like this, are you? Wipe your eyes and calm down. Some girls look pretty when they cry, but I'm afraid you're not one of them. And have you combed your hair at all this week?"

Belladonna sniffled and pushed her hair behind her ears. There was something comforting about being told off by her Gran. It made her feel that somehow everything would turn out alright.

"Now," said her grandmother, "the first thing you have to do is get away from here. Those people upstairs are no more human than that stone over there."

"But what are they doing? Why have they gone to all this trouble? Who are they?"

"I don't know. I can't see anything from here. I've been hearing noises at night, though, out in the center of the building there, near the playground. The point is that they've gone to a great deal of trouble to get you and . . ."

She stopped and looked up. The building was becoming solid again.

"There's no time. Belladonna, you have to get away from here. You can't do anything while you're living in their house. Are you listening?"

"Yes," said Belladonna, straining to stand as close to the rapidly solidifying wall as she could.

"You look tired." Grandma Johnson's voice was getting more faint. "You have to get away."

The wall was all but solid concrete now.

"I love you!"

The last word faded away, snatched from Belladonna's ears by the gray stone. She stepped back and took a deep breath. Her Gran was right: There was no point going all wibbly. She had to pull herself together and sort things out.

"Dinner's ready!"

Mrs. Proctor's voice echoed across the empty gardens.

"Belladonna?"

Belladonna stepped back from the wall of the ground-floor flat and waved up to Mrs. Proctor.

"Coming!"

She climbed the steps slowly, unsure of what would greet her. Would the Proctors know what she had done? If they did, what would they do? She hesitated near the top, her right foot frozen in space just above the last step. Maybe she should run. She lowered her foot and began to turn.

"There you are!" Mrs. Proctor was beaming at the top of the stairs, her face glowing from the heat of the kitchen. "Come along now, you don't want it to get cold!"

Belladonna smiled in what she hoped was a normal way, though she had a feeling it might have looked more like a grimace, and walked into the house.

Mr. Proctor strolled out of the sitting room, folding the paper as he came and muttering something unintelligible about the local football team. He smiled at Belladonna and helped her hang her coat on one of the hooks in the hall.

"Don't know why I'm interested in sports at all," he said, smiling and tapping her lightly on the head with the folded newspaper.

Belladonna smiled back and slid onto her chair. The dinner was roast beef with all the trimmings, followed by a jelly trifle. Just the sort of thing that she would usually adore, but today she could do little more than push her food around the plate and sneak glances at the Proctors. They didn't seem to notice her and talked to each other about the architects' plans for the building and when the construction crews were going to arrive.

They were very convincing and Belladonna almost began to doubt what she'd seen. One thing was clear, though—they didn't know she'd discovered that the building didn't really exist. But who were they and why were they doing this? And if they were powerful enough to create and maintain a whole imaginary building, what on earth could she do about it?

"More trifle, dear?"

"Oh, no," Belladonna smiled. "No, thank you. It was really nice. May I leave the table?"

She was anxious to get away, upstairs, outside, anywhere where she didn't have to keep pretending and where she could get her thoughts straight.

"After you help me clear up, there's a good girl."

Belladonna's heart sank, but she did her best to seem willing and cleared the dishes from the table as Mr.

Proctor ambled back into the sitting room. No sooner was the table cleared and the tablecloth folded than Mrs. Procter put a tea towel into her hand.

"You dry," she said.

Belladonna smiled thinly and took up her position to the left of the sink. It seemed to take forever for it to fill with water and then another age to actually wash the dishes. Mrs. Proctor treated each plate as if it was antique Wedgwood, slowly lowering it into the soapy sink and then gently rubbing it, examining it, rubbing it again, and finally setting it into the dish rack. Belladonna then took them out, dried them, and stacked them on the table. Through all of this Mrs. Proctor prattled on about the price of beef these days, memorable meals from her past, the importance of learning to cook, the weather, being tidy, and the general state of the world today. Under normal conditions, Belladonna would have sort of tuned out and lost herself in her own thoughts, but now she hung on every word, looking for a sign that Mrs. Proctor knew she had discovered that everything was a lie. But there was no sign. Everything was just the same as it had been the day before.

"There!" said Mrs. Proctor when everything was finally done. "Now let's go and have a sit, eh? I think there's some kind of talent show on. That'll be fun, won't it?"

Belladonna trailed after Mrs. Proctor and sat on the couch as Mr. Proctor turned the television on and his wife settled down with some knitting. An hour of painful caterwauling followed, interrupted by Mr. and Mrs. Proctor as they exchanged opinions about the relative merits of each of the performers and discussed how modern songs just didn't seem to have any proper structure and who on earth chose the clothes that the contestants were wearing? Then Mrs. Proctor asked Belladonna if she could sew and if she would like to be a costume designer, and Mr. Proctor interrupted, saying that of course she didn't want to be a costume designer, she wanted to be a singer because that's what all young people wanted to be and wasn't he right?

Belladonna smiled and tried to look interested while sneaking looks at the clock on the wall and longing for it to be bedtime. But the clock seemed frozen and the minutes crept by like so many exhausted snails. Then, when it was over, Mr. Proctor insisted that she stay and watch the news because it was very important for children to be aware of the world around them. Belladonna smiled again, but every fiber of her being wanted to jump up and yell and tell them to stop it, she knew they weren't real people, so just stop!

But she didn't, and eventually Mrs. Proctor went into the kitchen to make Belladonna's hot chocolate. Belladonna said good night as politely as she could and climbed the stairs to bed.

Once she was alone she allowed her thoughts to return to her grandmother and the building that wasn't a building. The building where she was living, that she was in right now, this minute, that was nothing but a shadow, a ghost building.

As she got ready for bed a feeling of dread began to creep over her. Could this be something to do with what Edmund de Braes had been talking about? Was this . . . all of it . . . something to do with the parchment and the Dark Times? The Proctors had gone to enormous lengths to get her, even kidnapping her grandmother. But why? What were they planning here, in this ghost of an apartment block? It hadn't even been here in the last Dark Times!

She finished the hot chocolate and lay down, pulling the covers up until only her dark eyes were visible. As scary as everything was, in a way she felt better than she had since Tuesday. At least she knew her grandmother wasn't dead and she knew for certain that the Proctors were up to something—all of which was better than not knowing. On Monday she'd go to see Mrs. Lazenby and ask to be placed with different foster parents.

She just had to take control of her own life.

11

Mrs. Lazenby

SUNDAY CREPT by even more slowly than Saturday, and Belladonna spent the day trying to avoid the Proctors. When she was with them she kept catching herself staring, looking for some clue as to who (or what) they really were. Or were they just innocent bystanders, living in the ghost building yet completely unaware? But how could that be?

She tried returning to the center of the garden and calling for the building to reveal itself again, but nothing happened. It was as if she had inadvertently made it stronger, or perhaps because it had already revealed itself, the Words no longer meant the same thing.

After that she concentrated her energies on the boarded-up apartment where her grandmother was imprisoned, but she couldn't force the boards, and her attempts at communicating by knocking or whispering through the sturdy wood went unanswered.

She returned to the swing set and spent hours trying to decide whether the Proctors were unwitting pawns in someone else's plan or willing harbingers of something dreadful. When the rain got so heavy she couldn't ignore it, she drifted back inside and up to her room, where she pored over the rhymes she'd copied from the parchment.

Thrice times three the cromlechs be
And thrice times three the charm,
Thrice the knight who failed the fight
And thrice be mercy's balm.
But twain is all the angels keep
Though none do they mistrust,
For the last is lost in the land of sleep
In the murksome house of dust.

Nine things . . . there were nine things. But what were they?

Thy beating heart is not the best
For this the darkling perilous quest.
Find one with a heart whose time is through
Yet constant holds with brightness true.

A "heart whose time is through" obviously referred to someone who was dead, so whatever the things were, it looked like they could only be found by a ghost. But "constant holds." What did that mean? And what on earth were "cromlechs"? She got up and wandered over to the bookcase at the far end of the room. There were picture books, comics, a few classics of the kind that people who didn't have children thought they'd like to read, but no dictionary.

At seven o'clock Mrs. Proctor called her down to dinner. Belladonna tried to smile and be polite as she nibbled on fried chicken, mashed potatoes, and broccoli. And that was a clue right there—if the Proctors were really supposed to be such experienced foster parents, would they really have given her broccoli? Only creatures from some other dimension could possibly think that she'd like it.

After dinner, the Proctors insisted that she stay downstairs and watch television with them, so Belladonna found herself watching some murder mystery set in London in the 1920s. It wasn't much good, though—there weren't nearly enough murders. There was only one right at the beginning and then an hour and a half of people talking and driving around in old-fashioned cars. She was relieved when Mrs. Proctor got up to make the hot chocolate. Bedtime at last!

Belladonna said her good nights and went upstairs. She felt optimistic—with any luck, this would be the last night she spent here.

The next morning was overcast and gloomy and, while not actually raining, clearly had every intention of doing so as soon as it got up to speed. Belladonna dragged herself out of bed, feeling as if she hadn't slept at all. She had a pounding headache and the night's dreams were still marching through her head like a slowly retreating army.

There had been stone circles, Shadow People, dark holes, piercing lights, and chanting . . . endless hours of chanting. She couldn't remember what the chanting had been about, though she couldn't shake the feeling that if she could concentrate for a few moments, it would all make sense. Dreams don't work like that, however, and the more she tried to recall the details, the more they slipped away.

When she got to the bathroom, she discovered that the restless night was writ large across her face. A face that, Belladonna had to admit, was never at its finest first thing in the morning, but on this particular morning the contrast between her straight dark hair, dark eyes, and pale skin was accentuated even more by the addition of two dark circles beneath her eyes.

"Great," she muttered, "I look like a refugee from a zombie film."

She dressed quickly and shoved her homework into her backpack. She wanted to take her clothes as well but knew that the empty drawers would set off alarm bells for the Proctors and she thought it was best to keep them in the dark until the whole thing was done. Mrs. Lazenby could pick up the clothes and bring them to the new foster parents, whoever they turned out to be.

The anticipation of leaving for good put a spring into her step and by the time she arrived downstairs for breakfast, she was feeling a lot more cheerful. She even managed to chat with Mr. Proctor about the weather and agreed with Mrs. Proctor that lamb chops for dinner would be nice.

Mrs. Proctor stood at the door and waved as she set off for school. Belladonna waved back and walked down Nether Street until it curved to the right and Shady Gardens was out of sight, then instead of taking the next left, which would have led to Dullworth's, she kept going into town. She wasn't entirely sure where Mrs. Lazenby's office was—she'd been far too upset at the time to notice—but she was fairly sure it was on the far side of town, down a back street. It was a single-story building, she recalled, with a large unkempt parking lot.

Anyway, she thought, *there's bound to be a sign.*

As she hurried up Umbra Avenue, past the launderette that had been Dr. Ashe's apothecary shop, and past the arcade where she and Steve had found the Draconite Amulet, she was struck by how strange it all seemed in the early morning. The High Street was even stranger. She was so used to seeing it bustling with shoppers, traffic, and noise that the silence was really striking. The shops weren't open yet and almost no one was about. It almost looked like the High Street in the Land of the Dead, except that it was a lot grubbier and there was no tree.

She hurried past Gimball's department store and up past Evans Electronics, strangely silent with heavy metal shutters pulled down over the windows. She dodged down a few side streets, but none of them seemed even remotely familiar and she was beginning to wish she'd looked up the address before she'd left. She'd thought about it, of course, but she was worried about attracting attention and being asked difficult questions.

All she wanted was to get out of that house and away from the Proctors.

Then, just as she was about to give up, she turned down the last street before the war memorial and there it was: low-slung and sprawling, the aged pebble-dashing dropping off in chunks and the door and window frames painted dark blue. There was a big sign near the entrance to the car park and a piece of paper attached to one of the double doors at the entrance with *Use Other Door* scrawled on it in black felt-tip.

Belladonna pushed on the other door and was relieved when it swung open. She had been afraid that the office wouldn't open until nine o'clock and she'd be stuck waiting in the car park.

Inside there was a strong smell of coffee that she hadn't noticed the last time, and an air of hushed exhaustion. There was also a small square opening with a sliding window and a sign that said RECEPTION and another that said ALL VISITORS MUST CHECK IN. Belladonna went to the window and peered into the small room beyond. It boasted little in the way of comfort, just an old office chair, a telephone system, and rows of timetables painstakingly drawn by hand and taped to the wall. There was nobody there, but she noticed a small bell just inside the window with yet another sign taped above it: RING FOR ASSISTANCE. Belladonna slid the window open and tapped the bell. It hardly made a noise, so she tried again with more force. This time it made a clang like Big Ben, and Belladonna shrank back, sliding the window closed again.

"Ha!" said a voice behind her. "Everyone does that."

She spun around, half expecting Mrs. Lazenby, but it was just the ghost boy that she'd met before.

"Oh, it's you!" he said, smiling.

"Yes," said Belladonna, not quite knowing what to say.

"My sister hasn't come," said the boy.

"No."

"No. I'm beginning to think that she might never come."

Belladonna opened her mouth to say something encouraging when the glass window behind her slid open with a bang.

"Well, you're up with the lark!" said a friendly voice.

Belladonna turned around to see a round-faced girl wearing an official identity badge and clutching a mug of coffee.

"Yes, well . . ." she began.

"Do you have an appointment?" asked the girl, sitting down and pulling out a large black appointment book.

"No, but I was hoping to see Mrs. Lazenby."

"She's not in yet, pet," said the girl. "But you can wait if you like."

Belladonna nodded.

The girl picked up the phone. "Cheryl, there's a girl here to see Donna. . . . I know she isn't. . . . Yes, she'd like to wait."

She hung up the phone and smiled at Belladonna.

"She's nice, isn't she?" said the boy. "The last one was really mean. I think they moved her to the probation office or something."

Belladonna pretended she couldn't hear him and smiled at the receptionist instead. Then the door to the right of the sliding window buzzed and a woman stepped out, holding the door open. It was Miss Kitson, the woman who had helped Mrs. Lazenby the last time Belladonna was here. She was younger and prettier than Belladonna remembered.

"Hello, Belladonna," she said. "Come on back. Mrs. Lazenby should be here soon."

Belladonna followed her back through the labyrinth of desks and cubicles, past the break room with the television, and on to the row of chairs outside Mrs. Lazenby's office.

"Would you like a cup of tea?"

"No, thank you," said Belladonna, sitting down.

"Juice?"

"No, thanks."

Miss Kitson nodded. "Well, just wait here, she usually arrives about this time."

And with that she was gone and Belladonna was alone with her thoughts.

Not for long, though.

"Why have you come back?" The boy was sitting in the seat next to her, swinging his legs back and forth.

"Because," said Belladonna, who really wasn't in the mood to talk to ghosts. "Isn't there anything on the telly?"

"No," said the boy. "I mean there is, but it's just people sitting and talking."

"You mean the news?"

"I suppose. I don't like the sitting and talking programs, even if they are in color."

"No, me neither." Belladonna smiled at him and he grinned back.

"I like exciting programs, or things where people die. Do you ever watch the one called *Staunchly Springs*?"

"Um . . . yes," said Belladonna.

"There's a lady in that who killed her husband and shoved him in a big box—"

"A deep freeze."

"Yes. Only it turns out that he's not dead and he's got away but she thinks he's still in there. It's really good."

Belladonna smiled. Her mother had predicted that the husband wasn't dead. She wondered how her parents were managing. She knew that they could turn the television on and off—ghosts were good at that sort of thing—but would they even bother? They certainly hadn't been there when she'd gone around the other day.

"What are you thinking about?" asked the boy.

"My Mum and Dad. *Staunchly Springs* is my Mum's favorite show."

The boy stopped swinging his legs and stared at her, puzzled. "Your Mum and Dad? Why are you here if . . . Oh. Are they dead?"

Belladonna nodded and was instantly glad she hadn't spoken her reply because at that moment Mrs. Lazenby marched around the corner. She was carrying a stack of files and a briefcase and was trying to balance a cup of coffee. Even though it was only the beginning of her work day, she already had a frazzled air.

"Belladonna Johnson!" she said, almost dropping the coffee. "What on earth are you doing here?"

Belladonna opened her mouth to speak, but before she could say anything, Mrs. Lazenby dropped some files and her keys.

"Oh, marvelous! Would you get those, dear, and open the door for me, there's a pet."

Belladonna gathered up the files and picked up the massive set of keys.

"It's the one with the yellow plastic thingy . . . yes, that's it."

The door swung open and Mrs. Lazenby staggered in, deposited her belongings, hung her coat up on a hook in the corner, and sat down with a sigh of relief. Belladonna hung back by the door, not quite sure what to do.

"Right," said Mrs. Lazenby, taking a quick slurp of coffee. "Sit down, Belladonna, and tell me why you're here."

Belladonna slid into the chair and . . . hesitated. She hadn't really thought things through past this moment. She couldn't tell Mrs. Lazenby the truth, but how exactly could she make a strong enough case to ensure that she wouldn't have to go back? She knew that what she probably ought to do is make up some dreadful story about the Proctors, but she couldn't quite bring herself to do that, so she found herself rambling on instead about being really unhappy there and it being too far away from school and her friends (she was banking on Mrs. Lazenby not knowing that she didn't actually have any friends except for Steve). By the time she finished, she had genuine tears in her eyes, but as she looked up at Mrs. Lazenby and let one of them trickle slowly down her cheek, she had a sinking feeling that none of it had worked.

"Belladonna," said Mrs. Lazenby, staring at her sternly, "do you have any idea how many hundreds of children we have to take care of every day?"

Belladonna shook her head.

"No, I didn't think so."

Belladonna racked her brain for something to say that might tip things in her favor.

"Listen," said Mrs. Lazenby, "I know it's difficult. I understand, I really do. But there are lots of children in a much worse situation than you and they need my attention too. The Proctors are lovely people; they've been fostering children for years. I really don't think you'd like things any better anywhere else, I really don't."

Belladonna bit her lip and stared at Mrs. Lazenby through the hair that she'd allowed to fall in front of her face.

"Who?" she said finally. "Who else have they fostered?"

"Why—" Mrs. Lazenby seemed about to say something, then stopped, confused. "Well, actually . . . I can't think . . ."

Belladonna's heart leapt: Was Mrs. Lazenby going to realize that the Proctors weren't real?

"Anyway." Mrs. Lazenby shook her head. "Anyway . . . it's all confidential, so that's a question I can't answer. You'll just have to believe me when I tell you that I've known them for years and they are wonderful people."

"But you haven't!" blurted Belladonna. "You've never heard of them before!"

Even as the words left her mouth, she knew it was the worst thing she could have done. Mrs. Lazenby's face hardened into a mask and she stood up, pushing her chair back from the desk.

"I've had quite enough of this," she said. "This office is snowed under with genuine cases of hardship and suffering. I don't have the time to listen to the lies of one little girl who has been pulling the wool over the eyes of all the people who have been trying to care for her for heaven knows how long. The Proctors are wonderful people and you are being unkind and ungrateful."

"But . . ."

"Now I suggest you get to school sharpish. And while you're walking, you can give some thought to your selfish attitude. Close the door on your way out."

Belladonna stood up slowly, hoisted her backpack onto her shoulder, and walked to the door. She glanced back at Mrs. Lazenby, then strode away past the row of chairs and through the maze of cubicles.

"She can close her stupid door herself," she muttered, her eyes stinging.

Why had she thought it would be so easy? She should have known that whatever or whoever was behind all this wouldn't have made it easy for her to get away. She marched past the reception window, banged the wrong door open, and stalked out into the car park. A steady rain had started to fall and it seemed even darker than it had been when she got up. She pulled her hood up and headed for school.

If only she hadn't played that trick on Sophie. If only Sophie wasn't so crabby. What if . . . ? She shook her head. She only had Steve's word for it that Sophie *was* responsible—she could've just said she'd done it because it made her look really powerful in front of everyone else. Steve was definitely right about one thing, though; they really should've closed the curtains in the evening. Even if

Sophie's Mum hadn't called, it would have been easy for anyone to see inside and place an anonymous call revealing that there was a girl living alone on Lychgate Lane.

She strode down the High Street, her mind racing, trying to think of what to do. If only Aunt Deirdre was here. She always seemed to see things so clearly; everything seemed sort of manageable when she was around. If only she hadn't vanished into the night after the Wild Hunt.

And then she was at the front door of Dullworth's. She'd got there much faster than she'd intended, but not fast enough. The distant sound of the buzzer marking the end of the first period could be heard on the street where she stood. She didn't want to go in, but she knew she had to. If she was going to sort this out by herself, she needed to make everyone—particularly the Proctors—think that everything was normal.

She reached up, turned the handle of the door, heaved it open, and suddenly knew exactly what she had to do.

"You want to do *what*?"

"I think it sounds like fun!"

"Yes, well, you're already dead and, anyway, as you can't appear anywhere except in school, you're not going to be in any real danger, are you?"

They were in the attic room above the science labs and Miss Parker's office, and Steve was annoyed because he was having to eat his lunch sitting on a dusty old trunk instead of sitting at the side of the football field (even though it was freezing outside and Belladonna couldn't even begin to imagine why he would want to be there at all). Elsie was sitting cross-legged on one of the roof beams above their heads. Or pretending to—on closer examination she was actually hovering about an inch above it.

"But I can't think of anything else to do! We *have* to call the Hunt!"

Belladonna was trying to keep the desperation out of her voice, but she knew she wasn't doing a very good job.

Steve looked at her and shoved the rest of his sandwich into his mouth.

"I still don't see—"

"It's rude to talk with your mouth full," said Elsie.

Steve glowered at her, swallowed, and tried again.

"I still don't see how it'll work. Doesn't it have to be midnight or something?"

"No," said Belladonna. "It was daytime when we called them in the Land of the Dead, remember?"

"Yes, but that was the Land of the Dead," said Steve. "The rules there are different."

"I can't do it at midnight. The Proctors would notice. And . . ."

Her voice trailed away. This wasn't going at all as she'd planned. For some reason she'd been sure that Steve would think it was a good idea, but now even she wasn't sure. He was right about the Land of the Dead—things were different there. But what else could she do?

"And what?" asked Steve.

"And I have to get away from there!"

Steve nodded and Elsie slowly descended from her perch.

"Of course you do," she said. "I mean . . . ghost buildings! I've been dead for nearly a hundred years and I've never heard of such a thing. And kidnapping grandmothers! That really does take the absolute cake."

"Okay," said Steve, putting the remains of his lunch away and screwing the cap back on his thermos. "Let's give it a go. It's dark by six o'clock, we can go to the graveyard and call the Wild Hunt then."

"But won't there be services?" asked Elsie. "Evensong or something?"

"No, only on Sundays," said Belladonna. "The church is locked the rest of the week."

"Oh. Locked? Really? Well . . . things have changed quite a bit, haven't they?"

"Yes," grinned Steve. "We've got cars and everything."

"We had *cars*. And aeroplanes. Besides, it's not like I can't look out of the windows, you know."

The buzzer sounded for the end of lunch, and Belladonna and Steve headed for the stairs, waving a swift good-bye to Elsie as they went. But she wasn't watching them. She had gone to the dusty window at the far end of the attic and was staring out into a world that had long since ceased to be hers.

"Have you had a chance to look at the stuff from the parchment?" asked Steve as they clattered down the stairs, past the upstairs classrooms and the science labs.

"Yes, I think . . . I mean, the nine things are all hidden in the chapter house, that much is clear."

"But there's no clue about what they are. And why are there nine when Edmund said there was one?"

"I don't know," muttered Belladonna. "I'm so tired. I feel like I can't think."

She became aware that Steve was staring at her intently, so she lowered her head and let her hair fall in front of her face.

"What? Why are you looking at me like that?"

"You don't look well."

Belladonna shrugged. "I'm fine."

Steve shoved his hands into his pockets as they walked on in silence, past the library and the hot drinks machine, through the assembly hall with its faded blue ceiling and golden plaster stars, and along the corridor to the last of the Victorian houses.

"So what are these dreams about?" said Steve finally.

"I can't really remember," said Belladonna. "Last night there was a stone circle, though. I remember that. And chanting."

"Like monks?"

"No . . . it wasn't lots of people."

"D'you think you'd recognize the stone circle? My Mum has loads of books about them. That is . . . had . . . Anyway, they're still at our house."

"I don't know. I can't really remember. . . . There were Shadow People there as well."

"Shadow *what*?"

"Shadow People. That's what I call them anyway."

Steve looked at her as if he couldn't believe this was the first he'd heard of it, and Belladonna did feel a little ashamed for not telling him before.

"I thought they were just ghosts," she said. "But I'm

not so sure now. And there are more of them every day."

"Spill," said Steve grimly.

By the time they reached the Geography classroom, Belladonna had told him everything she knew about the Shadow People. About how they clustered about inside Shady Gardens, how even she could see them only out of the corner of her eye or when she set the swing spinning, and that there were more and more of them all the time.

"And they stay in Shady Gardens?"

Belladonna nodded.

"What's this?" said an all-too-familiar, overly posh voice. "Has Steve Evans got himself a girlfriend?"

Belladonna turned around slowly. There she was: the cause of all her misery. She wanted to be able to do something, to hit her, to say something clever, but as usual she could do nothing except hide behind her curtains of hair and hope that Sophie would move on to other targets.

"Mind you," continued Sophie, "I would've thought you could do a lot better than this sorry excuse for —"

"Back off," hissed Steve, suddenly turning on her. "And take your vacuous little friends with you."

Sophie froze, her mouth hanging open in surprise. For a moment it seemed as if she was going to say something else, but Steve's glare stopped her and she just drew herself up, sniffed, and pushed past them into the classroom.

"Vacuous," muttered Belladonna. "Good one."

"Wait till they look it up," said Steve. "Then they'll be really angry. See you later."

And then he was gone, straight to the back of the class

where Gareth Warren and his other friends were clustered near an open window dropping chalk on passersby. Belladonna waited for a moment, then walked as quickly and quietly as she could to the nearest vacant desk. She glanced at the clock above the door. One o'clock.

It was going to be a long afternoon.

12

Calling the Hunt

THE TABLE TOMB was cold. Belladonna couldn't remember it ever being so cold. Of course she'd never tried to sit on it on a cold winter evening either. She jumped down.

It was six o'clock and as dark as midnight, but there was no sign of Steve yet. She decided to get started without him, then perhaps it wouldn't take too long and she could get back to Shady Gardens at a time when "staying after school to play" might come across as a reasonable excuse. Or maybe she'd have to think of another one.

She walked to a corner of the graveyard, then crossed to the other, dragging a stick behind her in the wet grass to make a visible line. Then she did the same thing for the other corners. She remembered that the last time she'd tried anything like this, she'd ended up summoning Dr. Ashe and things had gone pear-shaped very quickly. Hopefully, tonight would have a better result.

"What are you doing?"

Belladonna looked up. Steve was standing near the yew tree by the lych-gate.

"Casting a circle."

"It looks like an *X*."

"Yes, well, I haven't finished, have I? It's supposed to be in the center of the graveyard, so I have to find that first."

"Okay." Steve dumped his backpack on the tomb. "But aren't circles supposed to protect you from the Dead? The Hunt aren't dead . . . at least I don't think they are."

"Well, we don't really know what they are, do we?" said Belladonna, marking out the circle with the stick. "So I thought . . . you know, better safe than sorry."

"Because this worked out sooooo well with Dr. Ashe."

Belladonna glanced up sharply, but Steve was grinning and clearly just trying to wind her up. She tossed the stick aside and marched back to the tomb. She opened her backpack and rummaged through it, finally producing the green box. She opened it and handed Steve the horn.

"Wow," he said. "Do you carry all this junk around with you all the time? Your bag must weigh a ton."

"Well, I'm not going to leave it at the Proctors, am I?" She led the way to the middle of the circle.

"Okay. Go!"

"Hang on," muttered Steve. "It's freezing. I need to warm it up."

Belladonna sighed and waited while Steve blew on the mouthpiece and held it between his hands. She knew he enjoyed being the only one who could get a sound out of the thing, but he certainly made a song and dance of it.

He glanced nervously at Belladonna.

"Ready?"

Belladonna nodded. He put the hunting horn to his lips, took a deep breath, and let loose with a clarion call that Belladonna thought must have scared the living daylights out of the charnel sprites in their caverns deep beneath her feet.

The sound shot across the grass, wound itself around the shadowy tombstones, and disappeared into the dark blue sky. And then all was silence.

"Should I give it another go?"

"Yes, I suppose."

Steve raised the horn again, but just as he took a breath, Belladonna raised her hand.

"Wait!" she said, peering at the sky above the church tower. "Is that . . . ?"

Steve followed her gaze. "Yes, I think . . . Yikes."

The dark gray-blue of the sky had been flat and featureless except for the occasional star, but as they watched, it began to change, to spin and froth, almost like liquid. Thunderclouds started to form high above the church steeple, small at first, then larger and larger until they rolled across the sky, lightning flashing deep within their core. And then there was more than thunder, more than lightning, there was the flash of hooves, the howl of the hounds, and the crashing jangle of stirrup and bridle as the Wild Hunt roared out of the clouds and down to the churchyard.

As she watched them charge across the sky and then land among the old tombs and gravestones, their horses' flashing hooves pawing at the frosty grass, Belladonna had a sudden feeling that perhaps Steve had been right and this wasn't the best idea she had ever had. *Still,* she thought, as the Leader turned his horse's head toward her and approached the circle, *it's too late to worry about that now.*

"We meet again, Spellbinder," said the Leader, his voice silky with menace and his eyes flashing beneath the rim of his hat.

Belladonna just stared at him. Steve dug an elbow into her ribs.

"Get on with it!" he hissed.

"Um . . . yes . . . I was wondering—" she began, but the Leader was staring at the grass.

"What is this?" he said. "A circle?"

"Yes . . . sorry, but—"

"Hey, boys! She thinks a circle will keep us out!"

The graveyard echoed with the sepulchral laughter of the Hunt. The Leader walked his horse across the circle and right up to Belladonna and Steve, then he leaned down, conspiratorially.

"They only work for the Dead. We're not dead."

"I wasn't sure. So you're alive, then?"

"Alive . . . or somewhere in between." He straightened up, grinning, but the smile seemed joyless. "So why have you summoned us? Be quick—I promised the boys a trip to a campsite in Canada. You should see the way the tent dwellers run. There's nothing like the great outdoors for amplifying fear."

"Is that what you do, then?" asked Steve. "Go around scaring people?"

"No, that is how we entertain ourselves. Would you like to know what we do, boy? There's a horse back there without a rider."

"Um . . . no . . . thanks anyway," said Steve hastily.

"So, Spellbinder," said the Leader, turning back to Belladonna, "why did you sound the horn?"

"I was wondering—" Belladonna hesitated. It seemed like such a stupid question now.

"Yes?"

"I was wondering if you'd seen my Aunt Deirdre?"

For once, it was the Leader who was surprised.

"Your Aunt Deirdre? Do I look like a keeper of aunts, a nursemaid to recalcitrant relatives?"

"No, it's just that the last time I saw her, she was chasing you . . . trying to find you . . . and I just wondered if she—"

"Bad luck for her if she did!" said a gravelly voice among the Hunt.

The rest of them laughed, but the Leader held up a hand and all was suddenly silence.

"This Aunt Deirdre of yours," he said quietly, leaning forward in his saddle again. "Does she have a last name?"

"Nightshade. Deirdre Nightshade."

The Leader didn't move and his face showed no sign that the name meant anything to him, but Belladonna saw a change in his dark eyes, a momentary flash of recognition that was gone almost as soon as it appeared.

"Do you know her?" she asked.

"Once. I did know her once."

"But you haven't seen her? She didn't find you?"

The Leader shook his head and with that slight movement, Belladonna's last hope of escaping the Proctors vanished. There was no one else. Not a single family member who could come to her rescue. She felt the tears begin to sting her eyes.

"Tell me," said the Leader, "why do you seek her now?"

Belladonna glanced at Steve.

"Go on," he said, "tell him."

She nodded, wiped the tears away, and looked back at the Leader sitting high on his black horse, his too-pale face an expressionless mask. Belladonna stared at him for a moment. He hadn't changed, but knowing that he had known Aunt Deirdre had changed her. Suddenly he wasn't quite so daunting. She took a deep breath and the whole story poured out. She told him about Sophie Warren and the chair, about being taken into care and realizing that the building she was living in didn't exist, about the Proctors, the Shadow People, and her dreams of stone circles and chanting. But most importantly she told him about finding her grandmother and the warning that she had to find a way to escape Shady Gardens.

When she finished, the Leader didn't move but continued looking at her as though she were still speaking. Belladonna grew increasingly uncomfortable. Had he heard anything she'd said?

"Tell me about these Shadow People," he said finally.

"They're just shapes, dark shapes but like people. I thought they were ghosts at first, but I can't see them properly. So then I thought they weren't. I've only seen them inside Shady Gardens, but they don't seem to do anything. They just stand around in small groups."

"And does their number remain constant?"

"No, there are more now than there were at the beginning."

The Leader was silent again.

"You know what they are," said Steve, examining the Leader's face.

"Yes. They are Darkness."

"You mean they're bad?"

"No, I mean they are Darkness. The Darkness itself."

Belladonna and Steve looked at each other, mystified. Steve tried again. "Darkness like night? Are they pieces of night?"

"Night isn't a thing, boy," sneered the Leader. "Night is merely a temporary absence of the sun. These creatures are of the Dark Spaces; they *are* the Dark."

"The Dark Spaces?" Belladonna was starting to get a cold feeling in the pit of her stomach. "You mean the place where the Empress is? But I thought that was like a prison. What are they doing here?"

"Who knows? But I'll wager it's something to do with the stones. She always liked the stones. It was the power of the stones that started it all."

"'She'? Who's 'She'? And what stones are you talking about? The standing stones in Belladonna's dream?" The Leader's enigmatic answers were starting to get on Steve's nerves.

"Perhaps. Perhaps not. All I know is that the last time it began with the stones too. She said that the stones were the heart, the whole, the breath of what we were, and that they were the key to what we are and could be. To her, there was no future without the stones, no matter what they might bring—good or bad."

"You're talking about *her*," said Belladonna. "The Empress of the Dark Spaces. That's who it is, isn't it?"

"Hang on," said Steve suspiciously. "You said 'we.' Were you on her side?"

"I'm not on anybody's side, boy. And certainly not on yours."

He wheeled his horse around to rejoin his men, then stopped and turned to Belladonna.

"I'll tell you this, Spellbinder: She may have been condemned to the Dark Spaces, but if enough of the Darkness were here, I daresay she could slide back through. And then heaven help you all."

"But how are the Shadow People getting here?" asked Belladonna. "There are more every day. Is it the Proctors?"

"No." The Leader lowered his voice. "I rather imagine it is you. Take care and keep your wits about you. I shall keep an eye out for your aunt. For Deirdre. Farewell."

He turned his horse's head away again, pointed it to the north, and galloped up into the night sky, followed by his hallooing men, their horses' hooves cracking against the air like thunder, and the hounds running alongside in full, deep-throated cry.

"Such a cool exit," muttered Steve as the roiling thunderclouds gradually dispersed.

Belladonna nodded, walked to the table tomb, and picked up her bag.

"It doesn't help much, though, does it?"

"It gives us an idea of what the Proctors are up to," suggested Steve. "And it sort of underlines that you *really* need to get out of there."

"I know, but I've *tried*. I went to see Mrs. Lazenby this morning, but she wouldn't listen."

"I suppose . . . you can come and stay at mine if you like. I don't think my Dad would mind."

"Thanks." Belladonna managed a smile. "But the authorities would just come and get me, and then your Dad would be in trouble as well."

Steve kicked a nearby stone between two grave markers and sighed.

"That's it for ideas from me at the moment," he said. "Except that I think we should be concentrating on the parchment and the nine thingies. I mean, it's obvious that the Proctors and Shady Gardens and the Empress are connected with the Dark Times that Edmund de Braes was talking about. And there's no way that some overworked social worker is going to be able to do anything about that. Maybe if we find the thingies, we'll know what to do."

They walked out of the graveyard and down the street. Then Belladonna stopped.

"I have to talk to my Mum and Dad."

"What?"

"Could you help me get into the house? Mrs. Lazenby took my key."

"Break into your house? Now?" Steve's voice betrayed that housebreaking was a step too far, even for him.

"Please. I can't go back to the Proctors yet. I need to . . . I just need to talk to them."

"But if we get caught we'll—"

"It's my house."

"Yes, but it's not mine."

Belladonna tried her best big-eyed look, though it had never yet worked on anyone her own age.

"And you needn't look at me like that either."

"Sorry." She let her hair fall back down over her face.

"Oh, alright. Come on."

Steve turned around and strode off down Lychgate Lane toward her house. Belladonna ran to catch up, suddenly elated at the thought of seeing her Mum and Dad.

"Thanks! I'll pay you back sometime, I promise."

"Great," said Steve grimly. "You can come and visit me in jail."

The house looked the same as before, dark and quiet with all the curtains tightly drawn. Belladonna felt a pang of sorrow—it seemed blind and bereft, exuding emptiness.

"We'd better go around the back," she whispered.

"No duh," grunted Steve.

They slipped down the side path, into the back garden, and up to the back door. Steve tried the knob as if hoping someone might have forgotten to lock it. He sighed.

"I was thinking we could break a window," suggested Belladonna. "The latches are at the bottom. Mum always said it was really unsafe."

Steve nodded and they crept to the kitchen window. He took off his jacket and wrapped it around one hand.

"You're going to have to give me a bunk up."

Belladonna made a basket with her hands and Steve stepped in and up to the window. He smashed his hand against it, then fell back down. The window hadn't broken, but there was a long crack across the center.

"What about a stone?"

Belladonna handed him a good-sized rock from the half-completed rock garden. Steve wrapped the jacket around it, and Belladonna gave him another bunk up to the window.

This time it shattered and although the actual break was relatively quiet, the sound of all the glass falling to the ground and into the sink sounded like a waterfall in the evening quiet of Lychgate Lane.

They froze and listened—silence.

Steve reached in, unlatched the window, and hoisted himself inside. Belladonna went to the back door and waited while he slid the bolts back and let her in.

"There's a strange smell in here."

"Ew!" said Belladonna, wrinkling her nose. "Mrs. Lazenby didn't take the trash bins out. And the beef bourguignon is still on the stove! Yuck!"

"Quiet!" hissed Steve.

"Sorry."

She made her way into the hall, peeking into the sitting room and peering up the stairs.

"Mum!" she whispered as loudly as she dared. "Dad! It's Belladonna!"

Silence.

She glanced at Steve, who looked like he wanted nothing more than to be absolutely anywhere else.

"Mum! Dad! Please!"

Silence.

"They're not here," said Steve. "We'd better go before someone finds us."

"Oh, my God! Look at my kitchen!"

"Mum!" Belladonna's face lit up like a lamp as she ran back to the kitchen.

Her mother was standing by the stove, fury writ large on her face.

"What on earth was the woman thinking? We're going to get vermin!"

"Calm down, Elspeth," snapped Mr. Johnson. "There are more important things. Belladonna, how are you?"

"I'm alright. I'm fine."

"No, she's not," said Steve. "She's living in a building that doesn't exist with people who are probably trying to bring the Empress here from the Dark Spaces."

Mr. and Mrs. Johnson looked from Steve to Belladonna.

"Is this true?"

Belladonna nodded.

"Tell us all about it."

For the second time that night, Belladonna told her story, telling them everything that had happened since Mrs. Lazenby had taken her away. As she talked, her mother began cleaning the kitchen. Pots, pans, and dishes flew into the dishwasher, sponges and cloths wiped down all the surfaces, and the contents of the trash bin leapt out in their plastic bag and tied themselves tight.

"I'm so sorry, Belladonna," said Mr. Johnson when she'd finished. "I don't know what to say."

"I think we should go to the abbey and get the nine thing-ies," suggested Steve. "I mean, Edmund said he had been waiting until the next Dark Times to give someone the parchment and he gave it to us—so that *must* mean that the Dark Times are coming *now*. We need to get to the abbey."

"But we don't even know what the thingies are," said Belladonna.

"Yes, but we sort of know where they are, and after we find the first one, we'll . . . well, we'll know more than we know now, won't we?"

"That's not a bad idea," said Mr. Johnson. "Let's see those rhymes."

Belladonna opened her exercise book and put it on the table.

"'*Find one with a heart whose time is through,*'" read her mother. "I think you're right there; that does sound like a ghost."

"Yes, but what does *Yet constant holds with brightness true* mean?"

"I don't know."

"It reminds me a bit of old stories," said her Dad. "You know, the sort where the only person who can do a task is someone with a true heart. In the stories it usually ends up being some boy named Jack who's been a total waste of space up to that point."

"That sounds like me," grinned Steve.

"Nonsense," smiled Mrs. Johnson.

"So a ghost with a true heart," mused Belladonna.

"As to the nine things," said her Dad, "we'll see what we can find out."

"But I don't know if I'll be able to come here again."

"That's alright. It's probably best if you don't. If we find out anything, we'll tell Elsie."

"I don't know," said Mrs. Johnson, slipping into full mother mode. "I don't like the idea of two children going all the way up to that abbey by themselves."

"It's okay," said Steve brightly. "We'll go by train."

"But that's really expensive."

"I'll get tickets, don't worry."

Mr. and Mrs. Johnson seemed somewhat mollified, but Belladonna wasn't so sure.

"You're not going to steal them?"

"Well, firstly, we're supposedly saving the world, so I imagine a couple of half-inched train tickets would probably be okay. But, anyway, I'm not. I've got another idea."

"Yes, but—"

Belladonna never got to finish her sentence. Steve had grabbed her and pulled her down to the floor.

"Hey!"

"Shh! There's someone out there!"

They crouched, hardly daring to breathe. Then they heard footsteps—heavy, booted footsteps.

"You're right! There's a broken window here." The voice was gruff and vaguely familiar, but Belladonna couldn't quite place it.

Mr. Johnson put his head through the wall and had a look outside. When he came back in, his face was grim.

"It's the police. Two of them. Belladonna, you stay here, it's your house. Steve, you'd better hide upstairs."

"But won't they search?"

"Not once they find Belladonna. Now off you go."

Steve looked at Belladonna reluctantly.

"It's okay," she whispered. "I'll be fine."

Steve scurried away and up the stairs. Belladonna watched as the back door opened slowly.

"One other thing," said her Dad. "I think you'd better stop drinking the hot chocolate."

"The chocolate?"

"I'm pretty sure they've been drugging you."

Belladonna was about to say something else, but the policemen were standing in the doorway and she recognized one of them.

"You!" said Constable Dodd.

She stood up slowly.

"See you soon," said her mother, trying not very successfully to keep from crying.

"Chin up," said her Dad. "Remember you're the Spellbinder."

Plans

HER DAD had been right. As soon as Constable Dodd
and his partner found Belladonna, they stopped looking.
Belladonna tried to explain that she was homesick, but neither officer was open to discussion. They led her out to their
car and put her in the back seat, then Dodd called in to the
station to report what they'd found.

Belladonna felt pleased. Perhaps they'd take her to
prison. Maybe she'd never see the Proctors again.

The two officers got into the car.

"We're taking you home," said Dodd.

"No! I mean, don't you have to . . . I don't know . . .
arrest me or something?"

"I'd love to, but word is we take you back to the foster
family."

"But . . . no, please. I don't like them. . . . Couldn't
you . . ."

"Where is it?" asked the second officer, ignoring Belladonna and pulling away from the curb.

"Shady Gardens," said Dodd. "Top of Nether Street, apparently."

"Nether Street? I thought that place was demolished years ago."

"That's where they said she's staying," shrugged Dodd.

A spark of hope ignited in Belladonna's heart. Would they realize that something was wrong? That the building *had* been knocked down?

It wasn't long before the car rolled through the arched entrance, though Constable Dodd's partner was still not happy.

"Honestly," he said, "I could've sworn they leveled this place yonks ago."

"Well, obviously, they didn't."

They pulled up, marched Belladonna up the stairs to the Proctors, and rang the bell. The door was immediately flung open by a thunderous-looking Mr. Proctor, but he quickly rearranged his expression into one of concern when he saw the police. Mrs. Proctor quickly shoved him aside and smiled gratefully at the two men.

"We've been worried sick," she cooed.

"Found her in her old house. Said she was homesick."

"Of course she is, the poor dear."

Mrs. Proctor reached out and pulled Belladonna into the house, hugging her close.

"This . . . I could've sworn this building was demolished." The second policeman looked around, confused.

"Oh . . . um . . . you're thinking of the other one," said Mrs. Proctor. "There used to be two buildings. Thank you so much for bringing Belladonna home."

She reached out and shook the hands of both men and in that instant Belladonna saw all their concerns melt away.

"That's right," said Constable Dodd. "There *did* used to be two buildings. Funny how your memory plays tricks. Well, thank you, ma'am, we'll be off, then."

"Oh! You won't come in for a cup of tea?"

"No. Thank you, but we'd better get back to work."

Mrs. Proctor beamed, the two policemen nodded, smiled, shot stern looks at Belladonna, and then were gone. The front door clicked closed and a few moments later, Belladonna heard their car start up and drive away. Her heart sank.

Mrs. Proctor let her go and spun her around by the shoulders to face them, almost incandescent with fury. What was she thinking? Why hadn't she called? Did she have any idea how worried they had been? And how on earth would they ever be able explain her disappearance to Mrs. Lazenby?

If it had happened the week before, Belladonna realized, she would probably have felt guilty, but now that she knew that the Proctors were . . . well, she didn't know exactly what they were, but they certainly weren't good, and that knowledge allowed her to stand impassive under the onslaught and to simply turn and go to her room when she was ordered to bed.

About an hour later, there was a light tap at the door and Mrs. Proctor poked her head in, the benign smile back on her face and a mug of hot chocolate in her hand.

"Hello, Belladonna," she said softly. "I couldn't let you go to bed without your hot chocolate."

She put the mug on the bedside table and sat on the side of the bed.

"I know it's difficult for you," she said, her eyes large with concern, "but you have to understand it from our point of view. We're responsible for you and we really would be in terrible trouble if anything happened. And we do care about you, you know."

"I know. I'm sorry," Belladonna replied, in what she hoped was the right apologetic tone.

"Good girl. Now sit up and drink your hot chocolate. Tomorrow's another day."

Belladonna sat up and took the mug from the bedside table. Mrs. Proctor was watching her every move, so she pretended to drink, then blew on it, smiling.

"Hot."

Mrs. Proctor watched while she pretended to drink some more, then got up and walked to the door.

"Good night, dear."

"Good night."

Belladonna listened as her footsteps receded down the stairs, then waited until she could hear the television and the low hum of conversation. She crept out of bed and opened the door. They were definitely in the sitting room. She quickly ran to the bathroom and poured the chocolate down the sink, then scurried back to her room and into bed.

It was hours before she heard her door being pushed open. She was lying in bed, curled up and pretending to sleep, but through her eyelashes she could see Mrs. Proctor's slippered feet walking across the floor to the bed.

"Arise, Spellbinder." Her voice sounded different but familiar. It wasn't the voice of Mrs. Proctor, but it was a voice she had heard before. Belladonna kept her eyes closed and racked her brain, but she couldn't think who it was. Perhaps it was just that Mrs. Proctor had been creeping into her room and saying the same thing for nearly a week now.

"Arise, Spellbinder," repeated Mrs. Proctor.

Belladonna pretended to wake up.

"Hello, Mrs. Proctor," she said. "Is something wrong?"

Mrs. Proctor nearly jumped out of her skin and stumbled backward before regaining her composure and managing a thin smile.

"No! Um . . . no. Just checking on you before we go to bed. Did you drink your hot chocolate?"

"Yes, thank you," said Belladonna politely.

"Right. Well, then, off you go back to sleep. It's a school day tomorrow!"

She gave an unconvincing little chuckle and left the room. Belladonna didn't move as the door clicked shut and Mrs. Proctor's feet scurried away down the stairs again. Then she leapt out of bed and peered through the gap in the bedroom curtains into the center of Shady Gardens.

Mr. Proctor was there, setting something out on the ground as Mrs. Proctor ran out of the house. They spoke together, quietly at first, but soon their voices betrayed anger and accusation, although Belladonna couldn't hear exactly what was being said.

She smiled to herself—it might only be a small triumph,

but at least now she felt a little more in control of things. She slid back into bed, intending to stay awake all night but drifted off into her first proper sleep for a week.

Breakfast the following day was tense and silent. The Proctors glared at each other over the toast and cereal, and it was clearly only with much effort that they managed a cheery smile and good-bye to Belladonna as she headed out to school.

It was another gray day, but Belladonna felt as though the sun was gleaming as she strode along the familiar streets. History was first and was interesting as they finally left the confines of monasteries and convents to venture into the much more exciting world of kings, knights, serfs, and feudalism. Then French (boring), Math (confusing— she'd never really got the hang of it since missing all those classes last term), and Biology (clipping bits of paper onto geraniums).

As the lunch bell rang and the assembled hordes charged toward the cafeteria, Steve passed quickly by Belladonna and pointed upward. She nodded and followed him upstairs, past Miss Parker's office to the top floor and the attic.

Elsie was already there.

"Did the Wild Hunt come?" she asked eagerly. "What did they say? Had they seen her?"

Belladonna and Steve filled her in on the events of the previous night as Elsie sat, rapt.

"How did you get out?" she asked, when they had finished.

"As quickly as I could," said Steve. "Before the police car reached the end of the road."

"What about the Proctors?"

"They weren't pleased, but I don't think they suspected anything. Well, until last night."

She told them about pouring the chocolate down the sink and Mrs. Proctor's reaction when she discovered that she was still awake.

"Yowza!" said Steve. "Could you see what they were doing outside?"

Belladonna shook her head. "No, I was too far away."

"We really have to get the nine thingies. They're the only thing we've got to go on."

"Absolutely!" said Elsie. "I mean, really, if you can't trust people to make proper hot chocolate, what is the world coming to?"

"Right," said Steve, delving into his bag. "Train passes! Well, season tickets, really."

He held up two laminated cards triumphantly.

"Where on earth did you get those?" asked Belladonna, genuinely amazed.

"My Dad gets them every year. One for me, one for him, and one for my Mum. For when we visit my Gran in the Lake District. My Mum left hers behind when she left, so you get to be her. I'll be me."

He handed the card to Belladonna, who stared at it in admiration for a moment, then looked more closely.

"Hang on," she said. "This has her date of birth on it."

"That's alright—they never look at them properly. I think we should go tonight."

"What? Tonight? I can't."

"You have to get out of there, Belladonna, and we have to stop the Shadow People getting in."

"I know, but the Proctors are on alert now and we don't even know what we're looking for. And even if we do get them, I'll still have to go back. Plus we don't know who the ghost with the true heart is."

"The what?" Elsie looked from one to the other, confused.

"It's what we think the second rhyme means," explained Belladonna. *"Find one with a heart whose time is through / Yet constant holds with brightness true."*

"Wouldn't that be a monk?" asked Steve.

"A monk?"

"Well, they spent all their days praying, didn't they?"

"Yes, but if you'd been paying any attention at all in History, you'd also know that knights and lords who'd spent their lives rampaging over the countryside, killing and maiming all and sundry, often took holy orders for a few years at the end of their lives to try and rack up some divine goodwill."

"Oh. I missed that part."

"Obviously."

"Well, then how are we supposed to find him/her/it?"

Belladonna shrugged. It seemed like such a ridiculous requirement.

"Umm . . . actually," said Elsie, "I think it might be me."

"What?" said Belladonna and Steve in unison.

"Look."

Elsie opened the purse that was built into her sturdy

Edwardian school uniform belt and took out a small silver locket. She opened it and showed it to them.

On one side was a small sepia photograph of two people who Belladonna assumed were Elsie's parents and on the other an engraving in a formal, spidery script.

"I can't make it out," said Steve. "What does it say?"

"It says *'For Elsie, Our True Heart,'*" said Belladonna.

"I lost the chain," explained Elsie. "They gave it to me on my tenth birthday. I thought it was a bit soppy at the time, but . . ."

"It's brilliant!" said Steve. "Let's go tomorrow. What do you say?"

"How?" said Elsie. "I haunt the school; I can't go anywhere else. I can't even go into the garden."

"Oh. Right."

They sat in gloomy silence for a while.

"There has to be a way," said Belladonna.

"You can only haunt the school?"

"Yes, I said I—"

"What if we take a bit of the school with us?" said Steve.

"What, like a brick?"

"A brick?" said Elsie, her voice rising in indignation. "How am I going to manifest on a brick? I'm a ghost, not a circus performer!"

Steve laughed. "I'd pay money to see that! But it probably shouldn't be anything too heavy. I was thinking more along the lines of the front-door mat."

"D'you think it would work?" asked Belladonna.

"No," said Elsie.

"There's only one way to find out!" said Steve, jumping to his feet. "I'll meet you outside. Round the back, by the bench you go to when you sulk."

"It's not sulking, it's thinking!" said Belladonna, but Steve was already halfway down the stairs.

"Just kidding!" he yelled back.

"This won't work," said Elsie.

"How do you know?" asked Belladonna. "Anyway, why not try?"

Elsie shrugged. "I don't know."

"It's not like you to look on the dark side. You're always Miss Can-do-gung-ho-let's-go."

"Well . . . maybe I don't want to go anywhere."

Belladonna looked at her. For the first time since they'd met, Elsie looked genuinely worried.

"You don't have to," she said finally. "Not if you don't want to."

Elsie looked at her for a moment, then smiled.

"Yes, I do," she said. "This is important. I'm just afraid that if I leave the school, I won't be able to get back. Or that if I try to leave, I'll vanish into . . . I don't know . . . somewhere. But that's the sort of thing soldiers have to cope with every day, isn't it?"

"Well, not the vanishing."

"No. But you know what I mean. The not knowing. And if they got all whiny about it, Britain wouldn't have an empire, would she? And then where would we be?"

"Well, like I said before, we don't actually have a—"

"Right-ho! Down to the garden. Last one there's a rotten egg!"

And with that she vanished. Belladonna sighed. She hated to see Elsie unhappy, but her lows were so brief and her boundless enthusiasm the rest of the time was so . . . bouncy, it was really exhausting just to be around her.

She made her way down the stairs and out to the bench under the bushes. No one else was there, so she sat on the bench and tried to pretend that everything was fine and she would be going home to her parents on Lychgate Lane after school and her Gran would be coming for dinner and then they'd all watch *Staunchly Springs* and she'd go to bed in her own room with the curtains that didn't quite meet and she'd watch the stars through the gap until she fell asleep.

"Hello! What are you thinking about?"

Elsie's face protruded from the wall like a mask, her former gloom now completely gone.

"Nothing," said Belladonna, smiling.

At that moment the door crashed open and Steve appeared with the school's front-door mat rolled up under his arm.

"Sorry it took so long," he said. "I had to wait until no one was around."

He unrolled the mat and lay it on the ground near the bench. It wasn't the usual thick fiber front-door mat but a rectangle of old carpet that usually sat in a sort of trough just inside the front door so that the piece of carpet was level with the floor. Belladonna had always imagined it was left from when the house was just a home. There was something about going to all the trouble of making a trough for a front-door mat that seemed so quintessentially Victorian.

"Right," said Steve, stepping back. "See if you can appear on that."

Elsie nodded and vanished from the wall. There was a long pause and Belladonna and Steve looked at each other in the manner of people who are just about to admit defeat, when all of a sudden Elsie, in all her Edwardian glory, was standing between them in the garden.

"Ta-da!"

"It works!" yelled Belladonna, breaking into a broad grin and then realizing she'd been a bit loud. "Oops, sorry."

"Yes!" said Steve. "Right. I checked the railway timetables this morning at home—"

"Railway timetables!" gushed Elsie. "This is just like Sherlock Holmes!"

"What?"

"He was always checking the railway timetables. Well, the ones he didn't know by heart."

"Riiight," said Steve. "Okay, so there's a train at ten that should get us there at about eleven thirty."

"Can't we go earlier?" asked Belladonna.

"No, the passes are for off-peak. Oh, and we'll have to change at Lancaster."

"Change?" Belladonna's heart sank. She hated changing trains—she was always sure that she wouldn't be able to find the right platform and she'd get left behind.

"Can I sit by the window?" asked Elsie eagerly. "I love trains."

"Erm . . . well, I suppose. If the train isn't crowded."

"So," said Belladonna, "are you taking her home tonight?"

"What?!"

Belladonna grinned. Steve clearly hadn't thought this through.

"Well, someone has to take the mat home and it can't be me."

"I'm . . . um . . . I suppose."

"Oh, this is getting better and better!" Elsie was so excited her curls had started bobbing up and down as she bounced with glee. "We can watch television! I've only ever seen school programming, you know."

"Well, I'm not sure that my Dad—"

"Oh, go on," said Belladonna mischievously. "He won't be able to see her."

Steve glared at her and was about to speak when the bell for the end of lunch sounded.

"Oh, that's you!" said Elsie. "See you later!"

And she was gone. Steve rolled up the carpet and shoved it into his bag.

"It's sticking out," said Belladonna. "Can you fold it?"

He sighed deeply, took it out, rolled it more loosely, and bent it in half. The bag looked ridiculously packed (particularly when you considered that this was Steve Evans and he didn't usually carry much around in the way of books or homework).

"Okay?" he said testily.

"You should've seen your face!" grinned Belladonna. "Are you going to keep it in your bedroom?"

"No, I am not," said Steve. "It's going to be rolled up in my bag by the door ready for morning."

They walked into the building and on to the art room,

where they spent the afternoon trying to draw a vase with some flowers and fruit. Belladonna thought hers wasn't too bad until she got a glimpse of Lucy Fisher's version. Her vase looked shiny and the flowers were perfect and delicate, while Belladonna's looked more like Amazonian trees. On the other hand, Steve's looked like an office building being attacked by huge plant monsters, though she suspected that was probably on purpose. Miss Barnstaple, the Art teacher, tried to stifle a smile when she saw it, but without much success.

At the final bell, everyone handed in their drawings and headed for the exits. Belladonna looked around for Steve, but there was no sign of him. She smiled and wondered if Elsie was going to get to see any proper TV.

14

Trains and Treasure

THE NEXT MORNING, Belladonna felt terrible. The Proctors hadn't offered her any hot chocolate before bed, but they must have slipped whatever it was into something else because the dreams were back, only this time they were worse and she felt as if the Shadow People were pulling her into the standing stones and away to the Darkness and oblivion that the Leader had talked about.

She dragged herself from bed and went down to breakfast, feeling as if she hadn't slept at all. The Proctors, on the other hand, were extremely cheery, joking with each other about the length of time the building was taking but that it would all be done soon and wouldn't that be nice. For the first time, Belladonna realized that they weren't really talking about the building at all.

She finished her breakfast as quickly as she could, then grabbed her bag and headed off for town and the train station. With every step, she half expected Mr. Proctor to pull up in his car and ask her why she was heading in the opposite direction to Dullworth's, so when she saw the old station and the entrance to the waiting room, she dashed inside. She was far too early, of course, but there wasn't anywhere else to go and the station was comfortingly crowded. She stood back for a while and watched the commuters anxiously checking their watches or chatting eagerly on cell phones while they waited for the trains to take them to work.

As soon as there was a seat available, she settled down to watch the waiting room television and wait for Steve.

As it turned out, he was early too.

"Oh, you're here!" he said, as he marched through the door, leaning slightly to one side with the weight of his bag. "Whoa, you look awful! Did you drink the hot chocolate again?"

"No, but I think they put it in something else. I thought you'd sleep in."

"Huh! You must be joking! We watched TV all last night, then this morning my Dad found the mat in my bag and had it spread out on the sitting room floor, so she was right there again, wasn't she? And . . . honestly, Belladonna, I like cartoons as much as anyone, but it's *all* she wanted to watch."

"What did your Dad say about the mat?"

"Nothing much. He didn't know it belonged to the school or anything, he just thought it was odd."

"Which it is."

"I told him it was something to do with an art project."

Belladonna never failed to be impressed by how good Steve was at thinking on his feet. If it had been her in the same situation, she knew she would have ummed and urred and then she'd have got that look on her face, the one that she could always feel whenever she was about to lie. The one that she was sure telegraphed to anyone looking at her that she was not to be believed.

"Did he believe you?"

"Yeah." He dropped his bag on the floor and sat down next to her. "Actually, he's not really bothered that much anymore. Since Mum went, it's like he can't really concentrate."

Belladonna smiled. What she really wanted to do, of course, was tell him her suspicions about his mother, but common sense told her that it wouldn't go down well, so she pretended to watch the waiting room TV instead.

The crowds of commuters slowly thinned as train after train arrived and departed, taking them to offices and businesses all over the region. Then, after what felt like hours, the train for Fenchurch finally arrived, and they clambered on and found some seats in an empty carriage. The train heaved out of the station and picked up speed as it whizzed past office buildings, schools, and row upon countless row of houses. Then it was out in the countryside and past an endless patchwork of wintry fields punctuated by drystone walls and skeletal bushes and trees.

The conductor came by and they flashed their passes. Belladonna was ready to try to explain why she had someone else's train pass, but the conductor barely glanced at them before he continued on into the next carriage. Steve waited until he had gone, then leaned forward across the table.

"It's usually better if you don't act so surprised."

"Sorry. I've never done anything like this before."

She'd certainly never been this far away from home by herself and couldn't believe that no one was surprised to see two twelve-year-olds traveling alone. And she couldn't shake the anxiety over what exactly they were going to do if they did get caught—neither of them had any money to speak of and certainly not enough to buy two train tickets.

Steve clearly had no such worries. Instead, he shrugged off his coat, reached for his bag, and produced two large books.

"Look," he said, pushing them across the table to Belladonna, "they're books about stone circles. I thought if you looked at some of the pictures, you might see the one in your dream."

"Where did you get these?" asked Belladonna. They looked really expensive and she suddenly had an awful image of Steve stealing books from shops.

"I told you—they were my Mum's. She has loads. She was really interested in stone circles, but she left them behind when she went."

Belladonna nodded and opened the first book, trying to hide her look of surprise. His mother had been researching stone circles. Could it be a coincidence? Or was she just seeing meaning in the mundane?

She turned the pages slowly—both books had beautiful, glossy, full-page photographs of stone circles from all over Britain, from massive structures like Stonehenge and Avebury, down to the smallest ring of broken boulders, but none of them looked anything like the one in Belladonna's dreams.

"It's not like any of these," she said. "It's . . . I don't know . . . kind of new-looking, I suppose."

"Maybe you're dreaming about what one of them looked like when it was first built," suggested Steve. "Are any of the shapes similar?"

Belladonna went through the books again more slowly, but nothing seemed familiar.

"No. Sorry."

"That's okay. According to the books, only ten percent of Britain's stone circles are still standing. Your circle could be one of the ones that vanished."

"Why did they disappear?"

"Sometimes farmers moved them because they were in the way of tractors, early Christians destroyed them or used them for building materials, and some were buried."

"Buried?"

"That's what the books say."

Belladonna stared at the pictures in the books. Most of the stones in the circles were huge; she couldn't imagine trying to bury *one*, let alone the whole circle.

"Are any of them near here?"

"Just one." Steve took one of the books and flipped to a page showing a double circle of small stones overlooking the sea. "That's Sanctuary Stones. It's near Helmsea, just up the coast. According to the books, most of the earliest circles were built near the sea."

"But there weren't any in town?"

"No, but like I said, ninety percent of them have vanished, so there could have been."

Belladonna stared at the picture of the Sanctuary

Stones, perched on a moorland hill, high above the village of Helmsea. In the picture, all you could see was the top of the church steeple far below, and beyond, nothing but the gray sea and stormy clouds.

"Does anyone know what they were used for?"

"Not really. Most of the surviving ones are sort of positioned for sunrises and sunsets at midsummer and midwinter and things like that, so some people think they were built for pagan ceremonies, but the books say they probably had lots of different uses over time."

"Did you just find all this out or did your Mum tell you?" asked Belladonna, impressed by Steve's knowledge on the subject.

"I told you, I read the books last night."

"You read them? Both of them? All the way through?"

"Yeah."

"But . . . if you can read that quickly, why don't you ever do your homework?"

"It's boring." He shrugged, then leaned forward again. "There's another thing. Have you got the rhyme with you?"

"Of course." Belladonna fished her Geography exercise book out of her bag and turned to the page where she'd copied down both of the parchment's hidden clues.

Steve read it and nodded, pointing to the first line.

"Yes, I thought so. It says '*Thrice times three the cromlechs be / And thrice times three the charm.*' Well, according to the books, *cromlech* is another name for a standing stone."

"It is? Then that means . . ."

"Your dreams and the parchment are connected, like I said. There are nine stones and nine . . . whatever they turn out to be. Lancaster! Time to change."

The train eased into the station as Steve packed the books away. Belladonna followed him onto the platform where they checked for the Fenchurch train on the screen in the waiting room before making their way to platform three.

Belladonna found herself sneaking looks at Steve while they waited. For some reason it had never really occurred to her that he might actually be clever. Admittedly, he was pretty quick-witted in class whenever he was caught doing something he shouldn't, but he almost never gave in any of his homework on time and had yet to raise a hand in answer to a single question. On the other hand, it made perfect sense—a stupid Paladin probably wouldn't be much use at all, and neither would the kind of boy who always did what he was told.

"Here it is!"

The Fenchurch train clanked up to the platform. It was much smaller and quite a bit older than the first one, and even fewer passengers seemed to be climbing on board. They found another set of seats with a table near the front of the train and settled down again.

"Are you going to get the mat out?" asked Belladonna as the train pulled away.

"Errr . . . I suppose." Steve was clearly not at all keen on the idea.

"She really wanted to be here for the train ride. I

think it might be a bit much to expect her to help us if we don't let her materialize here."

"Okay," said Steve, pulling the rolled-up mat from his bag.

"I mean," continued Belladonna, "how would you feel if you hadn't been able to leave the school for nearly a hundred years?"

"Good point. But she can sit next to you."

He handed the mat across the table to Belladonna, who moved to the next seat, leaving an empty one by the window. She unrolled the rug lengthwise on the vacant seat, leaving half of it extending up the back and the rest flopping over the edge. They stared at it for a moment.

"Do we have to call her or something?" asked Belladonna.

"Oh, don't worry, she'll be here."

There were a few more moments of silence as the train clicked by wet fields full of depressed-looking sheep staring at the passing train with the resignation of commuters who have missed the 8:45 and will be late for work again.

"Oh, gosh! Corking!"

Elsie's voice rang through the carriage as clear as a bell, but she still hadn't appeared. Belladonna looked questioningly at Steve.

"Watch," he said. "It's really weird."

She turned back to the mat where, instead of suddenly appearing as she usually did, Elsie just sort of slowly materialized, starting with the parts of her that were actually in contact with the mat and ending with the tip of her nose.

"It's a bit like the Cheshire Cat, isn't it?" said Steve.

"I suppose it gets slower the further she is from the school."

"Look! Sheep! Oh, this is amazing! And fast! How fast do you think we're going? Our trains never went this fast. Is it safe, d'you think? It doesn't matter for me, of course, but I was thinking about you. Do trains crash very often? This really is fast. What a shame it isn't spring yet; it would have been nice to see some lambs."

Steve sighed heavily, but Belladonna was enjoying Elsie's excitement. It made her feel as if she were seeing everything for the first time and the fields and livestock that had seemed tedious a few moments earlier were suddenly fascinating, and it really *was* a shame that there were no lambs yet.

The train sped north through ever wilder-looking countryside, as the number of fields ploughed for crops decreased and the population of sheep grew steadily. Elsie talked almost nonstop, pausing only to gaze, awestruck, at the occasional glimpses of the sea.

"I used to love going to the seaside! Though, of course, Mother would only let me paddle. She didn't think swimming was very ladylike."

Finally, the train slowed and a sign reading ABBEY HALT eased past the window.

"This is us," said Steve. "Make yourself scarce, Elsie. I need to put the rug away."

"This is so exciting!" said Elsie, disappearing.

Belladonna rolled the rug up and handed it to Steve, then they both picked up their bags and left the train.

"She was like that *all* last night," said Steve.

"Well, she doesn't get out much, does she? And it's kind of fun to see someone who's so excited about ordinary things. How fast do you think the train *was* going?"

"Oh, don't you start."

They made their way out of the tiny station and followed the signs to the abbey a short distance up the road. The car park was empty except for two buses and two different bunches of schoolchildren who had obviously just finished their visit and were being counted onto the buses by frazzled-looking teachers. Belladonna and Steve marched past and made their way to the front door of the visitor center.

Belladonna was just about to open the door when Steve stopped her.

"Look," he said, pointing to a notice on the door, "d'you have any money?"

Belladonna looked at the sign; the admission fee was much higher than she'd expected.

"Not that much."

"Oh, rats and ferrets," he grumbled. "Well, I suppose we'll just have to walk down the road a bit and climb over the wall."

Belladonna sighed, then glanced back at the two buses. "No," she said, "I've got an idea. Come on."

She opened the door and walked in. Steve followed dubiously, but she ignored him and marched up to the ticket counter.

"Excuse me," she said.

The elderly woman behind the counter looked up from a book she was reading.

"Yes?"

"We were with the school trip, but I left my handout in the chapter house, I think. Is it all right if I go and get it?"

The woman peered at them over the top of her glasses.

"And why does that take two of you?"

Belladonna stared at her blankly.

"She's afraid of ghosts," said Steve, stepping forward quickly. "She thinks there are ghosts of monks lurking about."

"Well, that's just silly," said the woman kindly. "There's no such thing as ghosts."

Belladonna tried her best big-eyed gaze.

"Oh, alright. But be quick or you'll be left behind."

"Thank you!"

They dashed through the visitor center and out into the abbey compound, running across the wet grass, past the monks' graveyard, through the soaring nave, and into the short passage that led to the chapter house.

"Brilliant idea, that. The school trip thing," said Steve admiringly as he pulled the rolled-up mat from his bag.

Belladonna smiled, though she was a little disappointed in herself for not having the answer to the follow-up.

Steve laid the rug in the middle of the chapter house and they both stood back.

Nothing happened.

"Maybe we should—" began Steve.

"Look!"

Two faint dark shadows could be seen on the rug, slowly sharpening until Elsie's high-button boots appeared, followed by her skirt, purse belt, blouse, and curls. The last thing to appear was her awestruck face.

"This is stunning!" she said. "How old is it?"

"Um . . . 11-something," said Steve.

"1127," said Belladonna confidently.

"Look at those windows!" Elsie was slowly turning around, gazing at the dark red stone and the elaborately carved traceries. "You're so lucky. We never went on school trips."

"Right," said Belladonna, opening her exercise book. "Should we start at the beginning and work through or go for what looks like it might be an easy one first?"

"I vote for an easy one," said Elsie. "We need to find out what we're looking for."

"How about the third, then: *But twain is all the angels keep / Though none do they mistrust.*"

Steve stared at her. "That's your idea of an easy one?"

"Well, I was thinking that, as it's an abbey, there are probably some carvings of angels. You know, like those."

Steve and Elsie looked up and Belladonna couldn't help but feel a little bit pleased with herself as it slowly dawned on each of them that there were the remains of two carved angels on what had probably been supports for the roof. One angel was holding the remains of a harp and the other had a book. Both of them had been carved in the act of singing—with their mouths open.

"Brilliant!" gushed Elsie.

"And really high," observed Steve.

"Not a problem for me. Can you take the rug over to the one with the harp?"

Belladonna nodded and moved the mat over to a spot in the grass just beneath the angel. For a moment Elsie became indistinct, like a TV channel that won't quite come in, but she was soon back, as solid as ever, and staring up at the carving.

"So," she said, "do we think they might be in the mouths?"

She didn't wait for a response but began to slowly ascend, taking care to stay directly above the scrap of carpet. Once she was level with the angel, she peered into its mouth like a disapproving dentist.

"It's a bit cobwebby. I can't really see."

She blew into the hole to clear away the cobwebs and then reached inside.

"No. Nothing here. Next!"

She descended to the rug again and Steve quickly moved it to a position beneath the chorister angel.

"Aren't you worried that there might be spiders or something in there?" he asked as she rose slowly upward again.

"Nope."

Belladonna noticed Steve give an involuntary shudder as Elsie thrust her hand into the angel's mouth.

"I don't think there's anything here either," said Elsie.

Belladonna's heart sank and she began looking around the chapter house for anything else that might be described as an angel, while Elsie reached deeper into the carving.

"Oh, hang on! There is something! It's right at the back. . . . Yes, there are two! Got 'em!"

Belladonna could hardly contain her curiosity as Elsie slowly returned to the rug and opened her hand. It was empty.

"There's nothing there," said Steve, in a tone that clearly conveyed his suspicion that Elsie was playing some kind of joke.

"Yes, there is." Elsie looked from Steve to Belladonna. "You really can't see it? Hold out your hand."

Belladonna held out her right hand, and Elsie picked up the things that no one else could see and dropped them into her palm.

"Oh!"

"What is it?"

"I can feel . . . They're cold . . . they're . . . Look!"

The things in her hand slowly became visible, catching the thin winter sun and gleaming as if they were brand-new.

"They're coins!" said Steve. "But why can we see them now?"

"Maybe . . ." Belladonna turned them over in her hand. "Maybe because Elsie gave them to us. Only the dead true heart can find them, but perhaps if she gives them to you . . ."

"Then part of the gift is the ability to see them!" Elsie grinned. "It's like something out of an old fairy tale."

"My Dad says there's a kernel of truth in nearly all old stories."

"Okay, but why coins?" said Steve. "And what kind of coins are they?"

"It's a noble, I think," suggested Elsie. "Or a sovereign. Who is the king?"

Belladonna turned it over carefully. On one side was a cross with a pattern of what looked like leaves or flowers growing out of each arm, and on the other was a king in a ship. Around the edges was writing, all in capitals and crowded together.

"It's hard to read . . . um . . . Edward. But it doesn't say which one."

"It must be a noble, then. Sovereigns were created by Henry VII. And it's too big to be a florin."

"How on earth do you know that?" asked Steve.

"My father was a numismatist."

Steve and Belladonna stared at her blankly.

"He collected coins."

"Wait," said Steve. "Your Dad collected prints of anamorphic art *and* he collected coins?"

"Yes."

"I bet he collected stamps too, didn't he?"

"Well, yes, actually he —"

"Ha! Your Dad was an Edwardian geek!"

"He was not! What's a geek?"

"What else did he collect?"

"Nothing. Butterflies."

Steve opened his mouth to say something else, but Belladonna shot him a look.

"Could we concentrate?"

"Oh, right, yeah," said Steve, stifling a giggle. "Coins. We're looking for coins."

"But . . . it doesn't make any sense," said Elsie, ignoring Steve. "Why hide nine coins? How can coins help with the stones?"

"Never mind that right now," said Belladonna. "Let's find the rest quickly or we'll miss our train back."

Steve nodded as Belladonna put the coins into her pocket and consulted the rhyme again.

"Thrice the knight who failed the fight."

"I think I know this one." Steve picked up the carpet and led the way over to the alcove where Belladonna had found him talking to Edmund de Braes.

There, set into the thick walls of the chapter house, was an ancient table tomb on which lay the effigy of a knight in full armor, his hand on his sword and his shield by his side.

"Is that . . . him?" asked Belladonna.

"Yes, you can just make out the name, there: *'Hic iacet Edmund de Braes.'* "

Elsie sighed as she looked at what was left of the face. "He looks sad."

"He is," said Steve quietly. "That is, he was."

Belladonna tucked her hair behind her ears and looked at him. He and Edmund had been talking before she arrived in the chapter house, but he hadn't told her what had been said and kept changing the subject whenever she brought it up.

"But where are the coins?" she said finally. "There doesn't seem to be anywhere to hide anything."

"You really can't see them?" asked Elsie, genuinely surprised. "They're right there. Right in the open."

Steve rolled his eyes. "Of course we can't see them. They can only be seen by the Dead. That's why you're here, Miss True Heart."

Elsie pulled a face at him, then reached for the shield, which was emblazoned with a lion, rampant and roaring, above which was a bar supporting four rings. She took something from each of the two outer rings and one from inside the roaring mouth of the lion. Belladonna held out her hand and once more had the strange sensation of seeing nothing, yet feeling it land. The coins clinked in her palm and slowly appeared.

"Okay," said Steve, barely glancing at them. "Next!"

Belladonna shoved the coins into her pocket and turned to the rhyme again.

"'And thrice be mercy's balm.'"

"Ew . . . that's a bit sort of . . . vague."

They turned to look at the chapter house again. But Belladonna couldn't see anything that made her think of mercy. Well, except for the angels, but they'd already got the coins from them.

"Of course!" said Elsie suddenly. "Over there!"

"What?"

"The misericord!"

"The whosis?" asked Steve, none the wiser.

"Misericords were sort of little shelves that the monks could lean their bums on in long services," explained Belladonna. "But I thought they were only in churches. That's what Mr. Watson said, anyway."

"Well, there are some over there."

Elsie was right. Just to the left of the arched entrance

of the chapter house was a row of six carved stone seats, each with only a small shelf to rest against.

"But I don't understand—" began Steve.

"*Misericordia,*" said Elsie as if it were the most obvious thing in the world. "It's Latin for *mercy.*"

"Huh. I should've known Latin would come into it somewhere. Alright, here we go."

He scooped the rug up and marched over to the stone seats, but this time Elsie appeared a little more slowly and seemed suddenly slightly transparent.

"Are you alright?" asked Belladonna.

"I'm tired. It's harder manifesting like this . . . away from the school."

"Then let's be quick," said Steve. "Can you see anything?"

Elsie nodded, leaned forward, picked something up from three of the small shelves, and dropped them into Steve's hand. He smiled slowly as they materialized.

"That's it," said Elsie faintly. "That's all I can do. . . . I'm sorry."

She began to disappear.

"That's alright," smiled Belladonna. "We'll see you back at school."

"And well done!"

Elsie smiled weakly and was gone.

"There's a train in fifteen minutes," said Steve, who had been examining a scrap of paper with a handwritten list of times. "If we get a move on, we can make it and be back before it gets dark."

"But we've only got eight coins."

"What?"

"Two from the angel and three each from the tomb and the misericord."

She looked at the rhyme again and sighed.

"What? What is it?"

"*For the last is lost in the land of sleep / In the murksome house of dust.*'"

"The land of sleep," muttered Steve. "Great. That's the Other Side, isn't it?"

"I think so."

"*Murksome house of dust* isn't very encouraging either."

"No." Belladonna put the coins into a side pocket of her bag and hoisted it onto her shoulder. "So . . . How are we going to explain this to the visitor center lady? She'll think we missed our bus."

"We won't need to explain it," said Steve. "We'll just run."

Belladonna rolled up the mat and handed it to him, then they both walked quickly across the wet grass and into the visitor center. The lady at the counter looked concerned and was about to say something when Steve gave Belladonna a nod and they both raced out of the building, through the car park, and away up the road toward the station.

The train was already there, so they found themselves seats and settled down for the ride back.

Belladonna sighed as the train pulled out of the station. It had all been really disappointing. She had thought that once they found the nine things, everything would be clear, but it wasn't. They'd found the coins and knew they had something to do with the stones in her dream, but she had no idea what they were supposed to do with them and, anyway, they still had to get the ninth coin. She wasn't any better off than she'd been when she left the house that morning and she still had to go back to the Proctors and pretend that everything was alright.

The thought of the Proctors filled her with even more gloom, and her head had started pounding again. She reached into the side pocket of her backpack and took out the coins.

"Here," she said, holding them out, "you'd better take these."

"Why?"

"Because I don't want the Proctors to get them."

Steve nodded and took the gleaming nobles. He looked at them for a moment, shining in his hand, then placed them on the table in a ring.

"So there are nine coins. . . ."

"Nine Nomials."

"Nine Worlds."

"And nine stones."

"The coins probably have something to with the No-mials, with the Metaversal Orrery."

"I suppose they must do. It'd be too much of a coincidence otherwise. And if my Granddad was right and the orrery can give you power over the Nine Worlds . . ."

". . . and the spaces in between, then we have to go there, don't we? To the Other Side."

"Yes," said Belladonna. "Maybe someone in the Land of the Dead will know what the House of Dust is."

"It makes sense, really," said Steve, picking up the coins and putting them in his pocket. "I mean, if they're really valuable, it would've been stupid to hide them all in one place."

"I suppose."

"We'd better show up in some classes tomorrow, though, or all hell is going to break loose. And I don't think old Parker would really buy the whole mystical-doodads-Spellbinder-Paladin sketch. How about lunchtime? We could meet in the library and go down to the Sibyl. She'd let us use her lift, wouldn't she? I mean, it is to save the world . . . again."

"Good idea," said Belladonna, rubbing her left temple with a finger.

"Headache?"

"Yes. They seem to be worse the further I get from Shady Gardens. It's fine, though. I mean, it isn't, but it will be."

Steve smiled unconvincingly and turned to look out of the window as the train clacked through the countryside, retracing their steps back home. The pale February sun had broken through the gray clouds and was casting a silvery light over the fields and fells, and Belladonna settled back into her seat and watched sheep give way to crops, and drystone walls to hedgerows.

The Other Side. She could see her parents again. Perhaps they would know . . . or maybe the Conclave of Shadows could help. Her grandmother and the Eidolon Council had been sure they could help last October. And even though they had turned out to be imprisoned with the rest of the ghosts back then, perhaps this time they would be able to come up with some advice.

The Eidolon Council! Why hadn't she thought of that before? Surely the whole point of having a group of living people that could confer with the Conclave in the Land of the Dead was to deal with this sort of thing! But then . . . Edmund de Braes had told them not to tell anyone. She bit her lip and tried to convince herself that it would be alright to tell the Council, but she had to admit that she didn't know who half of them were.

No, she decided finally, they should just stick to their plan, go to the Other Side, get the final coin, and see what they could find out about the Proctors and the stones.

She tried to feel optimistic, but something told her that the last coin was not going to be easy to find and that the House of Dust, whatever it was, would not give up its secrets without a fight.

15

Crossing Over

THAT NIGHT the dreams were far worse and, for the first time, Belladonna remembered almost everything.

She remembered being woken up, but not in her bed. It was as if she had been sleeping in a large empty room. A cold room. She had never been so cold. She couldn't see who woke her; it seemed to be a person, but she couldn't quite make them out. And then there were stairs, flights and flights of stairs, all leading down into an impenetrable gloom. The dark figure led the way, but only the step immediately ahead was illuminated, so Belladonna had no sense of how long the stairs were, how far they had come, or how far they had to go. She stumbled occasionally but kept following. She wanted to stop, to turn around and run away, but it was as if she had no control, as if she were merely a passenger in the shell of her body.

After what felt like hours, they arrived at the foot of the stairs, and Belladonna found herself in a barren landscape of brush and bracken. The dark figure led her to another equally misty form. This one took her to a particular spot and placed something around her neck.

"Make them rise, Spellbinder," it said. "Make them rise."

For a moment Belladonna was confused. What was he talking about? But then she heard herself speaking.

"Sag-en-tar na szi. Sag-en-tar na szi. Sag-en-tar na szi."

She wanted to stop, but she just kept repeating the same phrase. They were Words of Power, she knew that, just as she knew that these Words were not coming to her lips in the way the others had. They had nothing to do with what *she* wanted to say or do and everything to do with what the dark figures wanted. It was as if she were a radio and someone was tuning her to a channel she had never heard before.

"Sag-en-tar na szi."

Guardians of stone, arise.

"Sag-en-tar na szi."

As she kept repeating the Words, she became aware of a low rumbling, growing louder with each repetition. At first it felt like the rumble of traffic on a distant highway, but soon it became clear that it was the earth itself shaking and tearing and eventually spewing up . . . nine standing stones.

The stones were huge, similar to some of the photographs in Steve's books, but without the erosion of age and weather. Fresh-honed by hands that understood what they were for. They formed a circle around Belladonna and the dark figures, with two stones closer together than the others, forming a sort of frame for the almost-full moon.

"Sag-en-tar na szi."

One of the figures laid a hand on her shoulder and she stopped speaking.

"Very good," it said. "Now call the Darkness."

The next morning, she could barely move. Mrs. Proctor scuttled into her room and felt her brow with just the right kind of clucking concern. If Belladonna hadn't known better, she would have thought she really cared.

"Well, you don't have a temperature," she said. "That's a mercy. You don't look at all well, though. Perhaps you'd better stay off school today."

"No!" said Belladonna, a little too quickly. "No, I'll be fine, really."

"Why don't you get dressed and come down to breakfast; then we'll see. How's that?"

Belladonna mustered a smile and nodded. Mrs. Proctor bustled out of the room and down the stairs.

Ten minutes later, Belladonna was sitting in the kitchen, trying to pretend that she felt fine and forcing herself to eat the Proctors' horrible toast. They only ate whole-meal bread and when it was made into toast, no matter what you put on it, all you could taste was the whole-wheatness of it. Belladonna couldn't understand why anyone would want that for breakfast. There was something sort of stern and puritanical about healthy food at the beginning of the day. Breakfast, to her mind, should be all about cheerful food, like Pop-Tarts or some variation on chocolate frosted sugar bomb cereal.

She finished the toast and smiled at Mrs. Proctor.

"I feel much better now."

"Alright, off you go then."

Belladonna ran into the hall, put on her coat, grabbed her bag, and was out of the house and away up Nether Street almost before the words were out of Mrs. Proctor's mouth. Her burst of energy didn't last, however, and by the time she actually got to school, she was feeling ill again and now had the worst headache she'd ever experienced. Running seemed to make it much worse, so she decided to move as slowly as she could.

She hung up her coat and dragged herself along to the classroom. Steve wasn't there, but almost everyone else was, and they all stared as she walked in and sat down. At first, Belladonna thought someone was going to say something, but the general hubbub rose again and it was only Lucy Fisher who came over and looked at her earnestly.

"Are you alright, Belladonna? You don't look very well."

"I'm fine, thanks." She smiled at Lucy and opened her bag as if she were looking for something.

Lucy seemed to want to say something else but just drifted away back to her own seat. Belladonna put her bag down. She didn't feel fine at all, but she knew that her only option was to go to the school nurse, who would probably send her home, and she didn't want to be with the Proctors any more than was absolutely necessary.

The noise in the room seemed to be pulsing at the same rate as the throbbing in her head. She reached up and rubbed her temples and became aware that she was being watched.

It was Elsie. She was standing right in front of her desk and looking very worried.

"Belladonna! What have they done to you?"

Belladonna shook her head.

"Well, they've done something. You look awful."

She was just about to pull out a notebook so she could tell Elsie to go away, when she noticed Steve standing in the doorway. If anything, he looked even more grim, and as soon as she met his gaze he nodded his head slightly toward the hall and walked away. Belladonna waited a few moments and then followed him out and down the hall. He walked quickly to the stairs and darted underneath them.

"What's happened?" he whispered, his voice anxious.

"I'm tired, that's all."

"You look more than tired," said Elsie, materializing at her elbow. "Belladonna, have you looked in a mirror?"

"Yes."

"But—" Steve's concern was starting to frighten her. Did she really look that bad?

"What was I supposed to do? Stay at home with the lovely Proctors?"

"Good point," said Elsie.

"Let's go back." She turned to go back to the classroom, but Steve held her back.

"Wait," he said, "I think we should go now. To see the Sibyl. One look at you and I'm sure she'll let us use her lift to the Land of the Dead."

"But we'll miss Math."

"I know, it's a terrible sacrifice," said Steve, managing a grin. "But, listen, you look worse every day. Those people are doing something to you, and the only clue we've got is the gold nobles. We have to do something now, today."

"Hear, hear."

Belladonna thought about it. They were right. It was obvious now that her dreams weren't dreams at all. She was really doing that stuff, standing out in the cold and calling . . . something. She shuddered. How many more nights could she do whatever it was she'd been doing without ending up in the hospital . . . or worse?

"Okay," she said finally. "But let's try Mrs. Jay first."

"Mrs. Jay?"

"Yes. I mean she knows all about the Nomials and the Land of the Dead, and she probably knows a lot more besides."

"I know." Steve hung back. "But she really gives me the creeps."

Belladonna rolled her eyes and marched off down the corridor toward Mrs. Jay's office, sure that she would know what to do. After all, she was the one who pulled them into her office last October and explained about the Nomials and why the stars went out and everything. And Mrs. Jay had known that Belladonna was the Spellbinder and Steve the Paladin (though she hadn't seemed too happy about that last part). So it only made sense that she'd know what to do about the Proctors and the Shadow People.

They had arrived at the door to Mrs. Jay's domain. Steve still hung back, but Elsie stood next to Belladonna, offering as much support as she could. Belladonna smiled slightly and rapped on the door confidently. Silence.

"Good," said Steve, "she's out. Let's go see the Sibyl."

Belladonna ignored him and knocked again. Silence.

"She's not in," said Steve again. "I don't know why you—"

"Honestly!" said Elsie, turning on him. "You've called the Hunt, fought a hell hound, and defeated Night Ravens. Why on earth are you scared of a *secretary*?"

"None of them can report me to Miss Parker or get me expelled," explained Steve.

Belladonna sighed and knocked again. Silence . . . and then the scraping of a distant chair, the click of a door, footsteps, and the office door opened.

"Yes?" said a querulous voice.

Belladonna's heart sank, and Steve grinned as though it was Christmas. It wasn't Mrs. Jay—it was the mouse-like assistant.

"Is Mrs. Jay in?" asked Belladonna, already knowing the answer.

"She's taken a few days off," murmured the assistant. "Some sort of Scandinavian holiday, I think."

"Scandinavian?" said Steve. "But she's not Scandinavian."

"No," said the assistant, who had clearly never thought of this. "Maybe it was Scottish. I can't really remember. Anyway, she's not going to be back until next week. You can see Miss Parker if you like."

"No!" said Steve, darting forward. "No, that's alright. We'll be fine."

"Okay," said the mousy woman, closing the door. "Sorry."

Belladonna stood staring at it as the sound of the footsteps padded away. Why would Mrs. Jay take a holiday now, right in the middle of term? And for a Scandinavian holiday . . .

"Right," said Steve cheerfully. "The Sibyl it is!"

They made their way to the library just as the bell sounded for the first class of the day, but to their dismay, instead of the empty room they'd come to expect, the library was full of people. Sixth formers were clustered at tables, riffling through sheets of paper. They looked up at the mere second years with disdain.

"I think you've made a wrong turn," sneered a girl with an impossibly long nose. "Finger painting is down the hall."

The others sniggered, and Belladonna and Steve backed out as quickly as possible.

"What are they doing?" whispered Steve. "No one ever goes in there!"

"Can I help you?"

They spun around. It was Mrs. Collins, the librarian.

"We were . . . that is . . . there are people in the library . . . and . . ."

"Sixth form Media Studies," said Mrs. Collins in a tone that made it clear she wasn't happy about it. "Miss Parker said they could use the library for their project meetings. Shouldn't you be somewhere?"

"Yes, sorry," said Belladonna.

She hurried away down the corridor until she was out

of sight of the library. Steve joined her, exasperation writ large on his face.

"What are we supposed to do now?"

"What about the charnel sprites?" suggested Elsie.

"I don't know . . ." Belladonna winced; the headache was making it hard to think. "No, wait—the shed!"

"The what?"

"The shed! The one by the football field. The lift from the Other Side came up there, remember?"

"But it vanished! There isn't a door, and besides, old Frank will probably be there."

"Who?" Elsie looked from one to the other. Her knowledge of the inside of the school was encyclopedic, but the outside was a mystery.

"The groundskeeper," explained Steve. "He chased us out last time after we got back. He's not likely to let us poke around looking for hidden doors."

"Well, let's at least look. If he's there, then we'll go ask the charnel sprites."

Steve thought about this for a moment.

"Okay. But keep your eyes peeled. He always seems to know when anyone's skulking about down there. It's like he's got eyes in the back of his head."

"Right," said Elsie, slowly disappearing. "It's a plan. I'll go on ahead and let your parents know you're on your way. See you in a bit!"

Belladonna smiled as Elsie vanished from view, then she and Steve set off through the school toward the door that led to the games fields, their footsteps echoing along the silent corridors. It was strange how quiet school became when classes were in session; it was as if everyone vanished for forty minutes. As if the classrooms were in some other dimension and only rejoined our own at the sound of the bell.

Steve opened the door and looked around anxiously before leading the way down the patchy grass, past the netball courts and the school vegetable garden to the lumpy green expanse of the football field.

The shed was about ten meters behind the goal and looked like it probably predated school and field by several decades. It was made of planks of wood, roughly fastened over a sturdy timber frame. A century of summers and winters had blasted the wood to a uniform gray and much of it had warped and stretched, leaving long narrow gaps between some of the planks.

Steve peeked through one of the gaps.

"Can you see anything?" whispered Belladonna.

"It's too dark."

He stood up and tried the handle. The door opened with a slight creak and they both darted inside.

"The lift was over here." Belladonna walked over to an open area between some bags of grass seed and a selection of gardening tools.

"But how do we get it to appear? Maybe you should say some Words."

Belladonna closed her eyes and concentrated. Nothing.

She opened her eyes. Steve was staring at her intently, waiting for something to happen. She closed her eyes again.

The Words still didn't come, but she heard something: a thud, followed by a rasping cough.

"Oh, no!" hissed Steve.

She opened her eyes. He was staring at something behind her.

She turned around slowly and found herself face-to-face with the tall, gaunt frame of the old groundskeeper.

Frank (no one seemed to know his last name) was an institution at Dullworth's. Belladonna had once heard Tiffany Brownlow tell someone that he'd been there back when her mother was a pupil at the school, and according to Tiffany, he'd been old even then. Of course, Tiffany had also said that her father was an MI6 agent stationed in Patagonia, when he was actually an IT specialist in Robinson's biscuit factory on the other side of town, which isn't quite the same thing.

"What's going on here?" growled the groundskeeper.

Belladonna tried a smile, but he didn't seem impressed. He just stared at her with his piercing, watery blue eyes and sucked at his teeth. The more she stared at him, the more daunting he seemed. His skin was old and sallow and seemed loose on his bones, as if he had once been a much stouter man and it just didn't fit properly anymore. His clothes hung loose as well, gray and threadbare, with a rolled-up tabloid newspaper stuffed into one pocket and the telltale greasy outline of a cigarette pack in the other.

"We were just . . ." began Steve, but his voiced trailed off in the presence of the watery blue eyes.

"It's class time, isn't it? Ain't you young hobgoblins

s'posed to be learning something somewhere? For all the good it'll do you."

"We need to get to the Land of the Dead." Belladonna could feel Steve's stunned gaze drilling into the back of her head, but she didn't take her eyes off the old man. There was something about him. Something that made her feel he knew.

"Well, I daresay you'll get there eventually. And a sight quicker if you don't get out of my shed!"

"There was a door here," persisted Belladonna. "Right here. It was a lift. It went to the Other Side and to the Sibyl."

Frank stared at her and rubbed one arthritic finger against the stubble of his gray chin.

"Who are you?"

"I'm Belladonna Johnson and I'm the Spellbinder. This is Steve Evans, the Paladin."

He looked at them both for a moment before he spoke.

"And I'm the King of Siam."

"Um . . . you don't seem surprised," said Steve. "You've heard of the Spellbinder before, haven't you?"

"I have. So if you're the Paladin, then where's this Rod of Gram I've heard so much about?"

Belladonna stared at the old man. That made *two* people at the school who seemed to know more about their new roles than they knew themselves: Mrs. Jay and now the groundskeeper. She chewed at her lip and considered that it couldn't be mere chance. Why were Mrs. Jay and Frank here? Was it to watch out for them? No, that couldn't be it. Or if it was, then they were doing a spectacularly bad job.

"It's in my pocket," said Steve, his face tense with suspicion. "But it's just an old plastic ruler. It doesn't work in this world."

"Huh. I'd always heard it works everywhere . . . if there's a supernatural creature about. Show it to me."

Steve rolled his eyes, reached into his jacket pocket, and took out the ruler. Almost immediately he found himself holding not the ruler but a large green and silver shield.

Before Belladonna even had time to register her surprise, he grabbed her and pulled her back behind him.

"What are you!?"

Frank nearly doubled over with laughter, his watery eyes streaming with tears. He shook his head helplessly as his shoulders heaved up and down, then took off his flat cap and wiped his eyes with it.

"Oh, that was good!" he gasped between guffaws. "You should've seen your face!"

Steve didn't lower the shield, but stared grimly at Frank as he laughed and laughed until the newspaper fell out of his pocket onto the ground behind him. The old man turned to pick it up and it was then that they saw it.

Or, rather, them.

Two more watery blue eyes in the back of his head.

Belladonna felt her mouth drop open as Steve lowered the shield in amazement before quickly holding it up again.

"Surprise!" yelled Frank, spinning around to face them again.

"I knew it!" said Steve. "I knew there was no way you could've seen me move the roller last term."

"I see a lot more than that," said Frank. "I see just about everything."

Belladonna was just about to ask what he meant when the old man pushed up the sleeves of his jacket and opened the front of his shirt.

She gasped and stepped back. It wasn't possible. How could they never have noticed before? Every inch of him was covered in watery blue eyes, blinking in the dim light of the shed.

"But—" Steve couldn't stop staring. "But . . . why?"

"What d'you mean 'why'?" asked Frank. "Because that's the way I am, just like you're the way you are. Though I'll never understand how you people get by with just the two. You must miss almost everything."

"How many do you have?" asked Belladonna.

" 'Bout a hundred, give or take. There's always some of 'em awake, so I generally get put to guard things."

"Like the lift."

"Like the lift. Back when I was younger, I guarded more dangerous things, but now . . . well, this suits me. I make me own hours and I get to go home and watch the telly of an evening. 'Cept this time of year, of course."

"This time of year?"

"Day of Crows. I sleep here in the shed until we're clear of the Day of Crows. Do it every year, just to be on the safe side."

"Why? What's the Day of Crows?" asked Steve.

"It's the day that's neither winter nor spring, when the

ways to Nine Worlds become little more than a veil, and as easily torn. I'm here to make sure nothing that didn't oughta tries to slide through this here door."

Belladonna glanced at Steve; she had a bad feeling about this and could see that he did too.

"And when exactly is it?"

"I told you. It's the day that's neither winter nor—"

"Yes, we got that," said Steve. "Could you be a little more specific?"

"March the second."

"That's in three days," whispered Belladonna. "That's why they're here."

"Why who are here? You'll have to speak up; my hearing's not what it was. Time was, back in the day, I could hear a satyr a mile away. And smell him too. But no more. Even the eyes aren't what they were."

"We don't know who they are," said Steve. "But we think they're using Belladonna to call pieces of the Dark. We didn't really know why, but—"

"Ah, you're thinking they'll be using the Day of Crows to slip into this world. Well, so they might. But why do you want to go to the Land of the Dead?"

"We have a . . ." began Belladonna. "That is, we think we have a charm that might stop the Dark Times. Nine coins, but the ninth is supposed to be in the land of sleep—"

"We reckoned that was the Land of the Dead."

"Yes. It's in the House of Dust, apparently. We don't know where that is, but we thought someone there would know."

"Oh, I can tell you that for nothing," sniffed Frank. "That'll be the House of Ashes, won't it?"

"Um . . . thanks," said Steve. "But that really isn't much help. House of Dust, House of Ashes—just names."

"No. The House of Ashes. *The* House of Ashes."

Belladonna and Steve stared at him, none the wiser, and Frank put his hat back on in disgust.

"What on earth do they teach you at this school? And you the Spellbinder and not knowing."

"The job didn't come with a manual, you know," said Belladonna testily.

"The House of Ashes is on an island in the middle of a lake. Grendelmere, I think it's called. It's where *she* lives."

"And she would be . . . ?" Steve was getting visibly annoyed.

"The Queen of the Abyss."

"The ruler of the Land of the Dead?"

"Yes, and more besides. But I wouldn't go there if I were you."

"Have you been?" asked Belladonna.

"Do I look dead? No, I have not."

"Well, then how do you—"

"I just know. I've heard. It's not the kind of place that anyone should go to on purpose."

Belladonna could hear the fear in his voice and for a moment she thought that perhaps they didn't have to go—perhaps there was another way. But she knew there wasn't. If the Proctors had been doing all of this in preparation for the Day of Crows, then she and Steve had to act now, and the parchment and the nobles were all they had to go on.

"We have to go," she said, stepping forward. "Please, could you call the lift?"

Frank looked from one to the other, then shook his head and sighed.

"It's your funeral." He stamped his foot once. "Going down!"

The dark marble box that was the lift immediately shot out of the ground, filling the shed with dust and grass seed. The door slid open, revealing the sumptuous interior, and Steve jumped inside. Belladonna held out a hand to Frank.

"Thank you . . . What is your real name? It isn't Frank, is it?"

"No. It's Argus, and you might want to save your thanks or otherwise until afterward," he said, shaking her hand. "If there is an afterward, that is."

"Thank you, Argus."

She joined Steve in the lift and smiled at Argus as the door slid shut.

"Ready?" said Steve, shoving the ruler back into his pocket.

"We are going to be in so much trouble," sighed Belladonna. "D'you have any idea how much school we've already missed?"

"You see," grinned Steve, leaning forward to press the button marked *U* for Underworld, "there's always a bright side."

16

Dragon Milk

"HANG ON," said Steve. "There were only three buttons before."

Belladonna glanced at the marble panel that had boasted a mere three buttons the last time they had used the lift. Now it had more than a dozen. Some were marked with letters or numbers that were familiar to her, but others were labeled with unfamiliar dots, dashes, and flourishes.

"Well," said Steve, "I suppose last time we were here, all the doors were closed."

"And now they're open," whispered Belladonna, staring at the jeweled disks. "They're all worlds. Different worlds."

"They can't *all* be worlds," said Steve. "There are only nine worlds. But I suppose the lift could stop in more than one place in some worlds. If they're . . . you know . . . busy with lots of different countries and stuff."

Belladonna looked at him and grinned. "Busy?"

"Yeah, doing stuff . . . like . . . Oh, never mind."

He scoured the panel, located the correct button, and pressed it.

For a moment after he pressed the button, it seemed as though the cold marble box wasn't going to move, but then it lurched violently to the right before springing backward, hesitating, juddering a bit, then suddenly scooping down at an alarming speed, like the first drop on a roller coaster. It then slowed, bounced a couple of times, and the doors opened. Belladonna stepped forward to leave but was hauled back violently by Steve.

"What are you —"

"Look!" he said. "I don't think we're there yet."

He was right. There was no sign of the familiar elegant entrance hall of the House of Mists, with its slowly ticking clock and glistening chandelier. In fact, they didn't seem to be indoors at all but outside, in an open expanse of steaming rocky ground surrounded by at least half a dozen volcanoes coughing smoke and flame under a dusty orange sky in which four moons of various sizes hung disconcertingly close to the horizon.

"Wow," said Steve. "D'you think this could be . . . yes! Look!"

Belladonna could do nothing but watch in open-mouthed delight as a huge, blue-scaled reptile soared across the sky, its massive wings beating slowly as it temporarily blotted out the smallest of the moons before circling lazily over one of the volcanoes.

"Dragons," she whispered, hardly daring to believe her eyes.

"Did you see the . . . the thing?" gushed Steve, tapping the center of his forehead. "It had a jewel, just like Ashe said. This must be Pyrocasta, where draconite comes from!"

Belladonna hadn't noticed the jewel; she was too entranced by the whole idea of a completely different world. A world of fire where dragons ruled the sky. Even as she was absorbing the beauty of the blue-scaled dragon, three more came into view. This time it looked like the two smaller ones were chasing the bigger one. They shot across the sky, spinning, looping, and doubling back with the ease of swallows. Finally, the large one stopped altogether, flipped itself around to face its pursuers, and let go with a stream of fire. The smaller ones tumbled through the sky, then regained their bearings and flew away.

"Did you see that?" said Steve. "It actually breathed fire. Real fire. Oh, this is amazing. We have to come back here."

Belladonna had to agree that it was a truly amazing place. Although it did occur to her that looking at it from the safety of the lift was probably the best way to go about things. She suspected that the smoking rocks and heaving volcanoes were a fairly good indication that this world was not intended for human habitation.

"Hey!"

They froze. Was that a voice? Could someone actually be walking around in this fiery world?

"Was that . . . ?" began Steve.

Belladonna strained to hear something more, but all was silence except for the steady rumbling of the volcanoes and the hiss of the hot wind.

"No," she said finally. "It must have been the wind or a—"

"Hold the doors!"

This time there was no mistaking it, and as they peered out across the rocky plain, a small figure, almost entirely swathed in what looked like a heavy black coat, emerged from behind one of the larger rocks, waving with one gauntleted hand while with the other he pushed a handcart loaded down with tall canisters.

They watched as he got closer and they began to hear the canisters clanking against one another. The man, if that was what he was, remained a mystery, however. In addition to the heavy black coat and the gauntlets, he was wearing a broad-brimmed hat and a dark scarf that was wrapped around his head and pulled up over his nose and mouth, leaving only two dark eyes sparkling beneath the hat.

"Um . . . do think this is a good idea?" asked Steve as the man hauled his cart across the last of the smoking stones toward the lift. "He could be anybody."

"I know," whispered Belladonna. "But we can't leave him here."

"Well, we *could*."

Belladonna opened her mouth to speak, then quickly changed to a smile. The man had arrived, hat, gauntlets, canisters, and all.

"Oh, bless your little cotton socks!" he gasped, heaving the cart into the lift. "I had to wait three days for the lift last time. So unreliable. I'm not convinced the button out there really works, you know."

As he spoke, he took off his gloves, unwound his scarf, and punched one of the buttons on the panel. The doors whispered shut again and the lift shot down, then sideways, before settling into a steady up-and-down motion as if it were driving across a series of small hills. Belladonna began to feel a little ill.

"I know," said the man. "Sick-making, isn't it? But it's the only way here. They're a protected species, you see."

"The dragons?" asked Steve.

"Yes, poor things. Ours died out at the beginning of the latest cold snap."

"Yours?"

"Yes. Oh, sorry! Introductions all around. Name's Burner. Well, not me real name, obviously, but that's what everyone calls me."

"Because of the dragons?" asked Belladonna.

"Yes. Not very imaginative, but there you go."

The lift lurched to a halt again and the doors opened into what appeared to be a dark room full of loud music and lights the size of cricket balls that pulsated in time with the beat and whizzed from one side to the other.

Burner looked alarmed and reached for the button to close the doors, but before they could fully close, two of the lights zoomed into the lift and hovered at head height. Burner glanced at them disapprovingly, then seemed to decide that he would pretend they weren't there and returned his attention to Belladonna and Steve.

"What about you two? Bit young to be traveling the old Transversal alone, aren't you?"

"The what?"

Burner opened his mouth to speak, but before he could say anything, one of the lights suddenly spoke up in a voice that sounded like it was being filtered through an entire hive of bees.

"The Transversal. The lift. Goes to all Nine Worlds. Don't you know anything?"

"They don't know anything," piped up the other one. "Look at them. They're small. They're probably not finished yet."

"Ignore them," said Burner. "They're just trying to wind you up."

"What are they?" asked Belladonna.

"We *are* here, you know. You needn't talk about us as if we're not."

"They're Emphots. Now, where did you say you're going?"

"Oh," said Belladonna, not really feeling any wiser. "We're going to the Land of the Dead. My name's Belladonna and this is Steve."

"Pleased to meet you," said Burner, holding out his hand. "And thanks again for holding the doors."

Belladonna shook his hand. It was hard and calloused and speckled with burn scars. He noticed her concern and grinned.

"Yes, it is a bit of a mess," he said, "but that's one of the risks of the business."

"What business?" asked Steve.

"What business? Well, what business do you think?" said Burner, patting the canisters proudly.

"I don't—"

"Dragon milk, of course!" said one of the Emphots.

"I told you they're not finished yet," buzzed the other.

"But I thought you said they were protected?" asked Belladonna, suddenly concerned about the dragons.

"I don't kill them. I just milk them. And I've got a contract, all legal and aboveboard."

"If you believe that, I've got a large bridge you might be interested in purchasing," said the first Emphot, fizzing like a dying fly.

Burner glanced at the Emphots and seemed about to say something, then took a deep breath and smiled.

"Dragon milk?" said Steve, gazing at the canisters. "What for?"

Burner shrugged. "People like it. Our world, Nidval, is going through a bit of a cold snap, like I said."

"But . . . how do you milk a dragon?"

"Very carefully, my boy, very carefully!"

Belladonna and Steve stared at him, then all three broke into broad grins.

"I love it when people ask that question!"

"You should get out more," said the second Emphot in a way that Belladonna would have described as smirking if they'd had faces.

"There's no need to be rude!"

The Emphots crackled like crinkled plastic and Burner reached out a hand and patted Belladonna's arm.

"Don't let them get to you," he muttered. "They feed off strong emotions; that's why they talk like that. Doesn't take them long to figure out which button to press."

Belladonna and Steve stared at the glittering balls of light.

"Is that true?"

"Perhaps. Tell me, half-things, do you mean to say you have never tasted dragon milk?"

"Of course not," said Steve.

"You should give them a taste."

"No."

"Go on."

"No. They could be allergic."

"Would you like a taste, half-things?"

Steve stared at the canisters. Belladonna could tell that he was really curious.

"Don't do anything stupid," she whispered.

"Are you afraid?"

"Of course it's afraid. It's not finished yet. It's just a baby."

"If you're trying to make me mad, it isn't working," said Steve in a tone that made it abundantly clear that it was.

The Emphots crackled again.

"Look," sighed Burner, "you can't let them get to you. They feed off that."

"Lots of people do," said Steve. "I'm used to it."

"No. The Emphots *really* feed off it. You'd better have a drink. It'll shut them up."

"What?" said Belladonna, alarmed. "Drink the dragon milk? How do we know it's not poisonous?"

"You see, you see!" buzzed the second orb. "Frightened."

"I'll drink some with you," said Burner. "We don't usually drink it on its own, mind. We mix it with other things, and . . . well, you never know how it's going to take people. Some people have a bit of a reaction to the neat stuff."

"A reaction?"

"Um . . . yes . . . like an allergy."

"I don't think you'd better have any," said Belladonna. "What if you're allergic?"

"What if you're allergic?" whined the first orb. "What if you're allergic?"

"I'm not allergic to anything," said Steve grimly.

Belladonna rolled her eyes. What was it with boys and always having to prove things? She wanted to say something else, something that would convince him to leave the stuff alone, but Burner had already slapped Steve on the back in approval, and she knew there was little she could say that would override a slap on the back from a real adventurer, let alone one who worked with actual honest-to-goodness dragons.

Burner smiled and opened his coat to reveal a sturdy leather belt with various tools hanging from it. He removed what looked like a small bone disk and pulled it apart so that it telescoped into a cup. Then he pried open the lid of one of the canisters, scooped out some of the contents into the cup, took a drink, and handed it to Steve. Belladonna peered over his shoulder.

"It looks sort of . . . pink," she said.

"Yup," said Burner. "That's the color it comes. Only take a sip, mind; it's powerful strong stuff."

Steve stared into the cup, then turned to look at

Belladonna. For a moment she thought he was going to back out.

"Dragon milk," he whispered. "From actual dragons."

"Go on, then," said the first Emphot. "Or are you scared now it's come to it?"

"Of course it's scared. Half-thing, half-finished."

Steve glared at the orbs, then raised the cup to his lips and gulped it all down.

"No!" Burner reached forward to stop him, but it was too late.

For a few moments, even with the undulation of the lift, it seemed as if time stood still. Burner pushed the lid back on the canister, the Emphots bobbled slightly in the air, the lights on the panel's buttons flickered by, and Belladonna stared at Steve—watching as his face went from its normal ruddy hue to white, then pink, then violently red.

"Gah!" he gasped, dropping the cup. "Hot! Hot!"

He staggered back into the rear wall of the lift, clutching at his throat. The crackling of the Emphots was almost deafening.

"Ow! What are you doing!?" Steve grasped his head and stared at the orbs as they moved toward him across the lift. "Aagh! Stop!"

Belladonna looked at Burner, her eyes wide with panic.

"What's happening?"

The dragon milker put his finger to his lips, then, just as the Emphots seemed to be close enough to Steve to touch him, he hit a button on the panel. The lift screeched to a halt with a sound like a dozen fingernails on as many blackboards. Belladonna and Steve stumbled against the back wall, but Burner stood, sure-footed, and pulled a long stick from his belt. The doors opened to reveal a vista of sun-splashed beaches and distant glistening water as he swung the stick once, then twice, hitting the orbs and sending them spinning out of the lift and across the sand. The Emphots wavered, slowed, then swung around and began flying back toward the lift, but Burner hit the button again and the doors slammed shut.

He twirled the stick happily and shoved it back into his belt.

"Nasty things. There's supposed to be a lock preventing the lift from opening on that world, but the wretched thing is always breaking."

Belladonna looked at Steve. He didn't seem to be in quite so much pain, but he was still gasping. Burner reached into a pocket and produced a large teardrop-shaped green bottle. He picked up the cup, poured some clear liquid into it, swished it around, and spilled it out onto the marble floor of the lift. Then he filled the cup to the top and held it toward Steve.

"Here," he said, "drink this. Sorry about the dragon milk, but I needed to distract them so we could get them out of here."

"Wait." Belladonna took the cup from his hands before Steve could grab it. "What's this? Is this poison too?"

"It's water," said Burner, taking it off her and handing it to Steve, who eagerly gulped it down. "And the dragon milk isn't poison, it's just very . . . spicy."

"More . . ." gasped Steve, holding out the cup.

"Drink it slowly," said Burner. "And hold it in your mouth for a bit before you swallow."

"They were from another world?" complained Belladonna. "Another one of the nine? But they were so . . ."

Burner looked at her, sniffed, and refilled the cup with water again.

"Not everything is what you expect. And there are reasons why movement between the worlds is restricted."

Steve held out the cup, and Burner filled it again. As he was gulping the third cup down, there was a melodic *ping* and the lift slowed and stopped.

"This'll be me," said Burner cheerfully, taking the cup from Steve and reattaching it to his belt.

"Will he be alright?" asked Belladonna, glancing at Steve, who still looked decidedly red in the face.

"He'll be fine! It just takes a bit of getting used to, that's all."

Steve cleared his throat and coughed. A small plume of smoke shot out of his mouth.

"Ah!" said Burner. "Umm . . . that *could* be a slight allergic reaction."

"Slight? That was smoke!"

Burner fastened his coat up tightly as the doors slid open to reveal a landscape almost as blasted as the dragon world, but this time the view was not of fire but of ice and snow. A bitter wind swept into the lift and whipped around like a mini tornado, bringing sleet and snow in its wake.

"Yes . . . smoke. So it was. Well, good luck to you both."

He heaved the cart of dragon milk out of the lift and into the blizzard.

"Wait!"

"Good-bye!" he yelled as the screaming gale almost drowned him out. "Don't take any more food from strangers!"

And with a cheerful wave he turned and began pushing the cart away across the ice.

Belladonna watched until he had vanished into the whirling snow, then turned back into the lift. She was just about to press the button to close the doors when Steve pulled her away.

"Wait!" he said, his voice sounding almost normal. "Just a sec!"

He dropped to his knees at the door and reached for the snow that was rapidly heaping in a drift against the sides of the lift. Belladonna watched as he made a quick snowball, then stood up and backed away from the doors.

"Okay. Let's go."

Steve bit into the snowball, filling his mouth with cooling ice. Belladonna hit the button to close the doors, and the lift shot down to the right, then powered away diagonally toward the Land of the Dead.

After about five minutes, Steve's face had resumed its usual color and the snowball had all but melted away.

"Belladonna?" he said.

"Yes?"

"Did you see that smoke?"

"Yes."

"Probably not a good sign . . ."

17

Coupe de Ville

"DOES THIS SEEM to be taking a lot longer to you?"

Steve was leaning against the back wall of the lift, watching the numbers or names (or whatever they were) flick by on the display above the doors, and Belladonna had to admit that it was starting to feel as if they'd been standing in the marble box for hours.

"Yes," she said. "Don't you wonder, though—"

"What it would be like to just stop it and visit one of the other worlds?"

"Yes. Not the Land of the Dead or that place with the light things, but a proper other world with people . . . or, you know, *inhabitants* who are living entire lives in another place with different countries and languages and everything."

They watched the lights flick by.

"Well," said Steve finally, "maybe after we've saved our world *again,* we'll get a chance to go and visit somewhere else instead of just being sent back to school as if nothing had happened."

"It's funny . . ." began Belladonna.

"What?"

"The name of the lake. The lake where the Queen of the Abyss lives. Frank said it's called Grendelmere."

"I know. Like the monster in *Beowulf.* D'you think there might be a monster in it?"

"Probably. It seems like almost everything I thought was imaginary is actually real."

"Yeah." Steve smiled. "It's so cool."

The words were hardly out of his mouth before the lift slowed, juddered a few times, and then came to a halt. Then . . . nothing.

"D'you think it's broken? It opened right away for Burner."

"Maybe the Land of the Dead is special," said Belladonna. "Perhaps I need to say something. You know . . . like last time."

"Okay," said Steve, taking a step back as if there was a one-in-ten chance that she might explode. "Go on."

Belladonna closed her eyes and was going to wait for the Words to come, but to her surprise she found she just remembered the Ancient Greek for "open the doors." Was that how it would be? Would she eventually just know the Words right off the top of her head without having to concentrate?

"Arate thyras!"

There was a split-second delay and then the doors snapped open with a whoosh, and Belladonna found herself staring at two familiar faces.

"Mum! Dad!" She flew out of the lift and straight into

their arms, and for the first time in what seemed like forever, she felt safe and free as her Dad hoisted her into the air and swung her around. And that wasn't all—for the first time in days, her head wasn't aching.

The familiar vast entrance hall of the House of Mists spun by in a blur as first the grandfather clock, then the massive chandelier, and finally the ornate front door sped into and out of view. It was only when her Dad finally put her down that she was really able to see that, although it was familiar, it really wasn't the same at all. The last time she and Steve had been here, the building had been little more than an empty shell, but now it was a hive of activity. Men, women, and children strode through the hall, up the stairs, and into and out of rooms, with the overly purposeful air of people who are Doing Something Important.

Somehow it wasn't quite what Belladonna had imagined when her grandmother had told her about the Conclave of Shadows all those months ago. She'd imagined elderly people in white robes, sitting in some kind of hushed chamber and being very serious, but nobody here was wearing white robes; they were all dressed in whatever had been fashionable when they died—and not a single one was old. Of course, she thought, there wasn't any reason they would be. Elsie had said that they could pick any age to be, although no older than when they had died, so why wouldn't everyone be young? The general effect of all this youth and color, of course, was that the House of Mists seemed less like a serious organ of government for the Dead and more like a rather grave costume party.

"Oh, Belladonna!" cried her mother, hugging her so tight that she could barely speak. "What have they been doing to you?"

"I'm not really sure," whispered Belladonna. "But I feel better now."

Then, as her mother let her go and looked into her face with the kind of genuine love and concern that she hadn't seen since that fatal Tuesday, she felt tears start to sting her eyes.

"Now, then," said Mrs. Johnson gently, giving her a little shake, "none of that. You've got important things to do. You can cry when it's all over."

"Why did it take so long?" asked Elsie, ignoring the family reunion.

"There were loads more buttons," said Steve. "To all the other worlds."

"Really? Did you see any of them?"

"Just two."

"Oh."

"No, but one of them was the place with the dragons! The one the amulet came from."

"Spiffing! Did you see any dragons?"

"Loads. And this man got on and he *milks* dragons! That's his job—milking dragons."

"You're joking! Like cows?"

"I suppose. We didn't actually see him do it or any-thing. But you'll never guess what I did!"

And as Steve told Elsie the story of the dragon milk, they strolled across the hall and out into the sunshine and the gardens. Belladonna blinked away her tears and took a deep breath.

"We met the last Paladin," she began. "His name is—"

"Edmund de Braes." Her father smiled in that way he had when he got the answers in television quiz shows before the contestants.

"Elsie told us all about it," explained her mother.

Belladonna nodded, relieved that she wouldn't have to go over the whole thing again.

"We have to go to the House of Ashes," she said, trying to sound like the sort of person she imagined would usually have the job of saving the Nine Worlds.

"The House of Ashes?" said Mr. Johnson. "What for? I mean . . . are you sure there isn't any other way?"

"I don't think so. Whatever the Proctors are doing, it looks like they plan on finishing it on the Day of Crows. That's the second of March—three days away. The rhyme and the nobles are all we've got to go on."

"The coins that Elsie was talking about," said Mrs. Johnson. "How are they going to help?"

"I don't know," said Belladonna, shrugging her shoulders. "But the last one is in the House of Ashes, so we're thinking that the Queen of the Abyss will know what we're supposed to do with them."

"The Queen of the Abyss!" Mrs. Johnson turned to her husband. "She can't go there!"

"Who is she?" asked Belladonna. "Elsie mentioned her last year when we were here. She said the Queen of the Abyss rules the Land of the Dead, but she didn't help much back then. Is she just a . . . you know, a figure-head?"

"No. At least I don't think so." Mr. Johnson had clearly never considered this before. "We haven't actually seen her, though. I heard she comes to the garden parties sometimes, but I think the last time was about fifty years ago. That's her in the carving outside above the front door. John Harbottle told me she rides a chariot drawn by a pterodactyl—"

"Yes, that's what Elsie said."

"But I reckon that's just a story."

"Story or not," said Mrs. Johnson, her voice tense with worry, "the woman is immortal. People like that don't look at life the same as the rest of us. We can't let Belladonna just march into her lair as if she were going to the corner shop! You have to do something! Say something!"

"I don't think I can," said Mr. Johnson sadly. "It's just . . . I'm sorry, Belladonna. I can't see any other way. I wish you didn't have to do this. But . . ."

Belladonna smiled. The idea was so tempting. The thought that she could just turn her back on the whole thing and return to the way things were, worrying about nothing more than being teased at school and keeping up with Math. She could let the Nine Worlds take care of themselves and maybe they'd find someone who was actually grown up to do all the dangerous stuff. Except she knew it couldn't happen. Something had changed in her now that she was the Spellbinder, just as something had changed in Steve—he couldn't help but protect her now, the way he had in the shed, and she couldn't help trying to prevent the Empress of the Dark Spaces from escaping. She might not have all the answers, or know why certain things were happening, but deep inside she knew that it really was all up to her.

"I know. I have to do it."

"No, you don't," said her mother, grasping at straws. "Perhaps . . . perhaps if you explained everything to the Conclave of Shadow, they'd know what to do."

"Oh, you *are* joking!" said her father disdainfully. "Don't you remember the last garden party? That lot upstairs couldn't organize a booze-up in a brewery, let alone come up with a plan to save the Nine Worlds."

A man in a toga walked by and made a sort of harrumphing noise.

"Sorry, Cicero, but really! I mean, they put alligators in the lucky dip! Just because you're dead and your hand will grow back doesn't mean you'll enjoy having it bitten off."

"That's true," said Mrs. Johnson thoughtfully. "There was an awful lot of screaming. But what about —"

"No, Mum." Belladonna took her mother's hand. "It has to be me. It's alright."

"But you're *twelve*."

"We have to hurry. There's only a few days left to stop them."

Mrs. Johnson sniffed back her tears and nodded.

"Your granddad brought his car," said her Dad, smiling. "We should get there in no time."

"If you can call it a car," said Mrs. Johnson. "When I think he could've had anything he wanted. He could've had a Rolls-Royce, for heaven's sake!"

"We'll make a day of it."

Belladonna beamed. It was just like the days out that they used to have, back when her Mum and Dad were still alive and everything was normal. She'd be sitting around doing nothing much when her Dad would bounce into the room and announce that they were going for a drive. There'd be no packing or organizing; they'd just jump into the car and take off, even if it was raining or worse. Her Dad would point the car toward the seaside and they'd park as close to the beach as they could get and eat a picnic of cold sausages, hard-boiled eggs, and fizzy drinks while the rain poured down the windshield in great rivers, and the ocean roiled beyond the sea walls, dashing itself against the stone.

"Belladonna!"

She snapped out of her reverie as Steve poked his head around the front door.

"You have *got* to see this!"

Mrs. Johnson rolled her eyes. "Typical!" she muttered.

"What?" asked Belladonna.

"Go and see," said her Dad, a twinkle in his eye.

Belladonna left them and ran outside. For a moment she blinked in the unfamiliar sunlight, but as her eyes grew used to the glare, she saw it.

The car.

Her Grandad was sitting in the front seat, but that wasn't the most remarkable thing. The most remarkable thing was the car.

"What d'you think?" gushed Steve, his eyes shining.

"What . . . is it?" asked Belladonna, trying to take the whole thing in.

It was red, for a start, but not just any red. It was the bright, wet red of a newly painted wall. It was redder than apples, redder than cherries, redder than anything she could think of.

And it was long. The longest car she'd ever seen. If it had been parked outside their house, it would've stretched from their driveway to next door's. It was wide too and seemed to hunker down close to the ground, like some kind of ravening carnivore, its front grille stretching around the sides in a grin that was more reminiscent of the dragons of Pyrocasta than a car. There were four head-lights on each side of the grille, like huge insect eyes, but that still wasn't the most remarkable thing.

The most remarkable thing was the fins.

The fins were slender and tall, and swept away off the back of the car like wings, and in the center of each were dual pointed brake lights, like torpedoes ready to launch at anyone foolish enough to get too close. And, of course, it was a convertible.

"What d'you think?" grinned her Granddad, leaning back on the white and red upholstery, his right hand ca-ressing the steering wheel.

"What . . . what is it?" she asked again, forgetting to say hello entirely.

"It's a 1959 Cadillac Coupe deVille."

"It's American," said Elsie, with the knowing air of someone who has already been told all about something.

"It's . . . huge."

"Only one thousand three hundred and twenty were ever made," said Grandpa Johnson proudly.

"Can't imagine why," sniffed Mrs. Johnson. "Come on, you lot, get in."

"Can I go in the front? Please?" begged Steve.

"Me too!" said Elsie.

"Alright. Come on, Belladonna."

Mrs. Johnson opened the passenger door, and Belladonna scrambled into the back. Even when her parents joined her on the long bench seat, there was still plenty of room. She quickly changed places with her Dad so that she was sitting between them both as Grandpa Johnson turned the ignition and the old beast sprang to life with a deep, guttural roar.

"This is probably a stupid question," said Steve as the car rolled down the long driveway away from the House of Mists, "but what does it use for petrol?"

"Nothing," said Grandpa Johnson. "This car's as dead as me."

"Well, then why is the engine running? Couldn't it just go without making any noise?"

"Of course it could. But where's the fun in that?"

Grandpa Johnson grinned as the car pulled out onto the main road.

"She's such a beauty," he whispered to no one in particular. Then he pushed hard on the accelerator and the car seemed to hesitate for a split second, then suddenly gripped the road and screamed away toward the horizon. Belladonna, Steve, and Elsie squealed with delight as hedgerows, trees, and fences melded into one long blur of speed.

"Careful!" said Mrs. Johnson. "We're not all dead you know. We've got two living children here and no seat belts."

"Sorry," said Grandpa Johnson, slowing down ever so slightly. "I got carried away."

Belladonna couldn't blame him; she felt wonderfully carried away herself, sitting in the back seat between her Mum and Dad, her hair flying in the breeze. She leaned back in the seat and looked up. The sky was blue without a cloud to be seen, and as the tops of the trees sped by overhead, she tried to imagine that she wasn't in the Land of the Dead at all but just out for the day with her Mum and Dad.

"So," said Mr. Johnson, "where are these nobles Elsie's been going on about?"

"Steve's got them," said Belladonna.

Steve reached into his pocket and handed one of the coins back to Mr. Johnson. "We've got eight, but they all look the same."

Mr. Johnson examined it admiringly. "It's gorgeous. So new-looking. And you say they've been hidden for how long?"

"Since the time of the last Paladin," said Belladonna. "Around six hundred years or so."

"Amazing."

"Yes, but we don't know what they're for," said Steve. "We're just hoping that the Queen of the Abyss can tell us."

Mr. Johnson glanced at his worried-looking wife, then leaned forward to hand the coin back. "Well, if anyone knows, I imagine she does."

"Hang on." Belladonna reached for the coin. She'd seen something, or thought she had. Something glimmering in the sunlight.

She took the noble and turned it over, examining the edge.

"There's something written here."

"What, like on a pound coin?"

"Yes . . . but it's just one word. It looks like . . . *Gwerfyl.*"

"Gwerfyl?" said Steve. "What is that?"

"It sounds Welsh." Mrs. Johnson was suddenly interested. "Is the same thing written on the others?"

Steve reached into his pocket and handed three more to Belladonna, then rummaged around in another pocket for the other four.

"No, they're different," said Belladonna, turning each of the coins over and examining them. "This one says *Paderau.* Then *Morwenna* and *Rhianwen.*"

"This one says *Lowri,*" said Steve.

Elsie took one of the coins from his hand. "*Briallen.*"

"*Aerona* and *Caniad.*"

"I think they're names," said Mrs. Johnson. "At least, I know *Rhianwen* is a name."

"Are they all Welsh names?" asked Elsie.

"I think so. They sound Welsh anyway."

"Why would English coins have Welsh names written on them?" asked Steve.

"I don't know. . . ."

"Perhaps because they're not coins," said Belladonna.

"They look like coins to me," said her Dad.

"I know, they are. But . . . maybe they're not. Maybe

they're something else. Something that's been made to *look* like coins."

"So they'd be ordinary," said Steve, suddenly understanding what she was getting at.

"What?" Mrs. Johnson looked from one to the other.

Steve hung over the front seat and explained, "Well, they seem special now, but six hundred years ago when they were made, they would have just been coins."

"I get it," said Mr. Johnson. "So if anyone found them, they'd just think they'd found money."

Belladonna nodded, then sighed and handed the glittering nobles back to Steve.

"But we still don't know what to do with them."

"Yes, but it's something, isn't it?" said Steve. "Maybe they're the names of gods or famous warriors or something and you're going to have to call them to fight the Proctors."

"Nine gods to fight one couple seems a bit like overkill," said Grandpa Johnson.

"Well, maybe it's not to fight the Proctors," suggested Elsie. "Maybe it's to fight the Empress. Perhaps these are the gods or the warriors who defeated her the first time around."

"Maybe." Belladonna wasn't convinced. "But why would the names be hidden? I mean, if it was a great battle, wouldn't everyone have known their names? Why hide them?"

"I don't know," said Elsie, slightly crestfallen.

"I think the Ninth Noble will tell us," said Steve confidently. "There has to be a reason that one wasn't hidden with the others."

He put the coins back in his pockets and turned back to enjoy the ride. Grandpa Johnson smiled and started pointing out items of interest along the way, but eventually silence settled over the car, as it usually does on long trips.

Belladonna was still thinking about the coins and the names. She felt that she ought to know, it ought to be one of those things that would just come to her, like the Words. But she couldn't think how coins could stop the Proctors or the Empress and she seriously doubted that the ninth coin would make everything suddenly clear.

"Don't worry," whispered her Dad. "It'll be alright."

Belladonna smiled, though she wasn't convinced.

"Have a sleep. You need one. Everything always looks brighter when you've had a rest."

Her Mum and Dad put their arms around her, and Belladonna hunkered down and let herself enjoy the feeling. She didn't ask how far the House of Ashes was. She didn't want to know. She closed her eyes and started to drift off, listening to the purr of the engine, the whistle of the wind, and Steve and Elsie eagerly questioning Grandpa Johnson about the car.

It felt like only moments had passed when her Dad gently nudged her awake, but it must have been ages because the whole landscape had changed. Where before there had been gently rolling hills and hedgerows, there were now towering knife-edged sand dunes as far as the eye could see.

"Look, Belladonna," said her Dad. "Isn't it beautiful?"

"Yes," she muttered, still dopey with sleep. "Is this a desert?"

"No, it's a jungle," grinned Steve.

"Look over there," whispered her mother.

Belladonna sat up, turned, and peered out across the undulating sands. Something sparkled. She glanced at her mother before turning back, a smile blossoming on her face. It was so beautiful, and so unlikely: a cluster of trees, deep green grass, and the unmistakable glimmer of water, all shimmering in the desert sun.

"It's an oasis," said Elsie authoritatively. "I've read about them. Sometimes when people have been stranded in the desert and they're dying of thirst, they start imagining they see them, but when they get there, there's nothing but sand."

"I take it this wasn't a natural history book," said Grandpa Johnson.

"No, it was a ripping yarn, though," gushed Elsie, ignoring his ironic tone. "It was about this chap who left England after the love of his life married someone else. Only it turned out she wasn't the love of his life, because later in Algiers . . . But that happened later. First he joined the—"

"—French Foreign Legion?"

"Yes!" said Elsie, turning and looking at Mr. Johnson with newfound respect. "And it wasn't what he expected at all and he had to escape, but he ended up going back and it was just in time because the fort was being attacked and he saved nearly everyone, but then they had to make their way through the desert and the nearest fort was miles and miles away. The men were dropping like flies and then some of them started seeing water and oases and wanting to lead everyone off into the heart of the desert and certain death, and the hero had to stop them at gunpoint and keep them going on until they reached the other fort!"

Mr. Johnson rolled his eyes, and his wife gave him a sharp dig in the ribs.

"That sounds brilliant!" said Steve.

"I know! It was absolutely ripping. And that all happens in just the first half of the book."

"What was it called?"

"Oh. Um . . . I don't remember."

Mr. Johnson leaned down and whispered in Belladonna's ear, "Is she always like this?"

Belladonna smiled and nodded.

"Fantastic!" said her father, clearly impressed.

As they drove, the knife-sharp dunes slowly gave way to rough scrubland, which in turn became first thick brush and then a dense, verdant forest. The day had all but turned to night, and the starless sky was almost obscured by the canopy of trees. Steve was asleep in the front seat, and Belladonna let her head fall against her father's shoulder as it became more and more difficult to keep her eyes open. But just as she was about to slip away, her mother leaned down and whispered in her ear.

"We're here."

18

The House of Ashes

BELLADONNA SAT UP. They had left the forest and were now coasting down a dirt track toward the edge of a vast dark lake ringed by jagged mountains that seemed torn and wounded as they strained toward the ink-black sky. In the center of the lake was a small island almost entirely occupied by a rambling fortress that spread across the rocky outcrop like a fungus.

Belladonna's stomach flip-flopped as she tried to remain outwardly calm. She peered at the back of Steve's head, wondering if he was awake.

He was. He turned and glanced back at her, smiling thinly.

"It looks just like school."

Belladonna smiled back. The shore of the lake was visible now, the water lapping gently over a pebbled beach and a small boat bobbing at a decrepit dock.

The closer they got, the more dilapidated the dock appeared. It had clearly been a fairly robust structure in its day. But its day had long since passed and now the boards and piers were black and rotted. With each movement of the tiny waves, small bits of wood could be seen breaking off and dropping into the water. The boat wasn't much better — Belladonna had seen more impressive craft on the lake in the park at home. The fact that this one didn't have a pedal paddle wheel was just about the only factor in its favor, so far as she could make out.

They had almost reached the dock before they saw the boatman. He was swathed in a black coat that was tied around his waist with a piece of rope, and an old blue muffler was wrapped around his throat. He sat on the edge of the dock, eating sunflower seeds and watching their approach.

Grandpa Johnson brought the car to a halt and they all got out. Was it Belladonna's imagination or were they all moving more slowly, as if they could delay the inevitable end of the journey? They walked down the last ragged bit of track toward the boatman.

"Hi," he said when they were close enough that he didn't have to raise his voice.

"Hello," said Mr. Johnson, smiling.

"What can I do for ya?"

"We need to get to the island," said Belladonna nervously.

"Do you, now? And why would that be?"

"We have to see the Queen of the Abyss."

"Really? Old family friends, are ya?"

"Well, no . . ."

"Because otherwise you'd have to be totally loony tunes to deliberately put yourselves in the way of that one."

He hoisted himself to his feet and stomped down the dock toward them. Belladonna winced at each footfall, expecting the whole structure to give way completely and dump him into the drink. As he came closer, she was able to make out his face. It was friendlier than she'd imagined, wide-browed and open, though he had a fairly impressive scar that ran down one cheek and right across his chin. His hair was thin on top and grizzled gray. The overall effect was of a professional wrestler who had fallen on hard times.

"We still need to go," she said.

"Yes, well, there's a price."

"No, there isn't," said Grandpa Johnson. "And you can drop the act. You're not Charon and this isn't the Styx. You're Hank Miller from Philadelphia; you used to drive a bus, and this is Grendelmere."

"What if I am?" grunted the boatman defensively. "And what if I did drive a bus? Everyone paid for a ticket back then, and half the time the buses weren't even clean. Why should the trip to the House of Ashes be any different? It's a lot harder, I can tell you that. There's no engine, for a start. I have to row and this water's like molasses."

"Did you do something wrong?" asked Steve.

"Wrong? What makes you think I did something wrong?"

"Well, most of the Land of the Dead seems to be really nice and . . ."

"Nice?" barked the boatman. "*Nice?* It's all sunny and full of happy people and animals and . . . things. I mean, look at that car you pitched up in!"

"What's wrong with it?" demanded Grandpa Johnson a little defensively.

"Fins!" sneered the boatman. "That's all I gotta say. Fins!"

"You don't like the sunshine, then?" asked Elsie.

"The sunshine's fine. The sun shines here, as matter of fact . . . occasionally. No, it's the people. I drove a bus. I seen enough people. I like it here. I sit by the water. I row people over when they want. Not that anybody much wants. And I fish. It's pretty good."

"You fish?" said Mrs. Johnson, looking at the gray-green water. "What kind of fish do you catch?"

"Kind of weird ones, to tell the truth. Big eyes. Lots of teeth. They don't taste great."

"I wouldn't think so."

"But it's not about the fish. It's about *fishing*."

"I can understand that," said Grandpa Johnson. "Used to like a bit of sitting on a riverbank myself."

"Okay," said the boatman, somewhat mollified. "Enough talking. I'll take the kids over. It's not like I'm doing anything else."

"The kids?" Belladonna turned and looked at her parents.

"We can't come," said her mother, smiling softly. "The Dead aren't permitted to cross the waters of Grendelmere."

"But . . . I thought she was the ruler of the Dead," said Steve. "You said she was immortal."

"She *is* old," explained Grandpa Johnson. "Older than anyone who has ever lived. Older than any*thing* that has ever lived. She has been here, in that house on this lake, since the dawn of time itself."

"But she doesn't rule?"

"Not really. She has seen more, felt more, done more than anyone else. They say that nothing happens that hasn't happened before, so she always knows what to do."

"But you can't speak to her?" said Steve skeptically.

"No. But sometimes she comes to us."

"Well, that's just stupid. I mean, it's like that staff room rule."

"Staff room rule?"

"Yeah. We can go to the staff room, but we're not allowed to knock on the door. We're supposed to wait until a teacher comes out or goes in and then we can say who we want to see. You could end up standing there all through lunch; it's the most stupid rule ever."

"I'm guessing you don't just stand there?" said Mr. Johnson, who was really starting to like Steve.

"No, I don't. I knock on the door. They're just teachers."

"Look," said the boatman, "are you going to the House of Ashes or not?"

"Yes, we are," said Belladonna.

"Right. Follow me."

He stomped off to the boat and jumped in. Belladonna was sure he'd go right through the bottom of it, but it just bobbed about a little more.

"Come on!" he yelled. "Move it along! It's safe!"

Belladonna turned to her parents and her grandfather and hugged each in turn.

"I wish you were coming," she whispered.

"You'll be fine," said her Dad.

"But what if—"

"Don't worry," said her mother. "We'll be waiting for you."

Belladonna smiled and turned to Elsie, who held out a hand and shook Belladonna's and then Steve's firmly.

"Good luck," she said. "I wish I could go too. It looks really scary. Should be topping fun!"

They turned and made their way along the rotting dock to the small boat.

"Okay," said Hank, "ladies first."

He held out a massive hand and helped Belladonna into the boat. To her surprise, it felt perfectly sturdy once she was in it. She glanced around to see if anything had changed, but it looked just as rickety. Steve clambered in and sat next to her while Hank did some stretches with his arms and shoulders as if he were about to compete in some sort of athletic event.

"Ready?"

Belladonna nodded, and Hank set the oars into the rowlocks and pushed away. The boat bobbed against the piers for a moment before he heaved it to port and hauled the oars back. The small vessel lurched forward with surprising force, leaving a bubbling wake.

Belladonna waved to Elsie and her family and watched the shore until she could no longer make them out.

"You know what I'm going to do?" said Steve matter-of-factly.

"What?"

"When I see this Queen of the Abyss character, I'm going to ask her where she was last October. I mean if she's so old and powerful and clever, how could Ashe have practically destroyed everything?"

"That's a good point, kid," said Hank. "You might want to phrase it a bit more polite, though. She sprinkles kids like you on her cereal for breakfast."

"What?"

"Just so y'know."

Hank winked at Belladonna, who grinned and turned away from the receding shore to look forward over the prow of the boat toward the looming black silhouette of the citadel on the island's shore. It looked like there was quite a bit of open ground between the shore and the great wall around the palace, but from that point the fortress thrust skyward, with palisade upon palisade punctuated by towers, spires, and flying buttresses. It was impossible to make out any detail, however. The House of Ashes seemed to absorb what little light there was and stand stark on the skyline like a shadow.

"Here's the thing," said Hank suddenly.

"What?"

"You need to know this. There are seven gates between here and the Queen of the Abyss. Each one has a guardian. You gotta give each of them a gift."

"A gift?" said Steve. "*Seven* gifts?"

"Well, offerings, really. You'll get them all back. And they don't have to be anything big. Not wrapped or anything. Pencils are fine. Well, so I've been told. I've never actually been in there myself, you understand."

The boat was halfway to the island now and Bella-donna was starting to feel a little apprehensive. Gifts. The guardians would want gifts. She started to mentally list all the things she had in her backpack. Were there seven? Why hadn't he mentioned this before they left her Mum and Dad? They could've brought more stuff with them.

She heard Steve coughing at the back of the boat and saw a faint wisp of smoke curl away.

"Are you alright?" asked Hank.

"Fine. A bit of a sore throat. I might be getting a cold."

Yes, thought Belladonna, *or you might be allergic to dragon milk.*

The more she thought about it, the more she was convinced that drinking the dragon milk had been a really bad idea. And it wasn't just that Steve had drunk it, it was that she hadn't tried hard enough to stop him. And after all that stuff with the Night Ravens!

"Hank . . ."

"That's my name."

"What do you know about the Empress of the Dark Spaces?"

"Not much. Before my time."

"Yes," said Belladonna, "but empresses are more important than queens, aren't they? Did the Empress once rule over the Land of the Dead? Or did she rule over some of the other worlds?"

"She did not."

"But—"

"Look, alls I know is that she was nobody. Nothing.

At least to start with. Professor Gadge up at the Panoptic Library says she was an aberration. I don't know much about that, or where she came from, but the prof said she didn't give herself the title until she heard where she was going to be exiled. Nice guy, the prof. Got me this gig. . . . Empress! As if!"

"Well, then why is everyone so scared of her?" asked Steve.

"You don't need some old-fashioned title to be scary. Plenty of people all through time have been plenty scary without so much as a 'sir' or 'duchess' between 'em."

"Yes, but—"

"Right," said Hank cheerfully, as the boat knocked gently against the dock on the island, "stay where you are."

He jumped out of the boat and tied it to the dock before reaching a hand down to Belladonna and helping her out. Steve scrambled out behind her and for a moment they all stood awkwardly.

"Thank you," said Belladonna.

"Yeah, well, you guys be careful. You wouldn't believe the stories I've heard about this place."

"You've brought other people over before, though, haven't you?"

"Yeah. A few, like I said."

"How many . . ." Steve hesitated, then continued: "How many have you taken on the return journey? Back to the shore?"

"Not a single one," said Hank, smiling. And with that he stepped back into the boat, untied it, and pushed away with one of the oars. "So long!"

They watched him as the ramshackle boat eased through the black sludgy waters of Grendelmere and back to the far shore.

"I wonder what happens if you fall in?" mused Steve.

"Nothing good," said Belladonna as a bubble appeared on the surface, expanded slowly, and then burst with a thick *pop*. "Come on."

They turned and walked across the open ground toward the House of Ashes. The walls were dark gray and massive, streaked with the accumulated dirt of centuries and punctuated every hundred meters or so by sturdy, crenellated towers. At first it looked as if there was no way in, but then Belladonna realized that what she had first thought was a shadow cast by one of the towers was actually an open gateway.

"It's that way, I think," she said, nodding toward the gap.

"Great," said Steve grimly. "It looks like a missing tooth."

Belladonna smiled—it really did.

"How old d'you think she'll look?" mused Steve as they strode across the rock-strewn ground toward the gate.

"I've no idea," said Belladonna. "Maybe she'll be like the Sibyl—so old that there's nothing left but her voice."

"Huh. I reckon if you're going to give yourself a title like Queen of the Abyss, you're going to have to look properly scary."

This was almost certainly true, thought Belladonna. The kings and queens they'd read about in History at school had all been real sticklers for the right combination of respect and awe from their subjects. Particularly Elizabeth I. Maybe the Queen of the Abyss would be like her. Belladonna admired Elizabeth I, but she had a feeling that she was almost certainly "properly scary" in real life.

"Who dares approach the realm of the Lady of Death?" boomed a voice just ahead of them.

There was no obvious speaker, so Belladonna and Steve walked on a bit further and saw that there was a fire burning in a great bronze brazier just to the side of the gate. Next to the fire was a small temple constructed not of marble but of some sort of black stone. Belladonna could just make out a white-robed figure inside.

"We need to see the Queen of the Abyss," said Belladonna, peering into the darkness of the interior.

She was about to step inside, when there was a yelp.

"No! Stay where you are!" said the voice. "I'll come out."

There was a pause and a rustle of frantic activity inside the temple.

"That voice sounds familiar," whispered Steve.

The guardian of the first gate emerged, irritated and pressing a mask onto her face.

"What's the rush?" she said in a deep, feminine, and very familiar voice.

Belladonna stared, openmouthed. The guardian was tall, very tall, and wore a long robe of white that flowed with every movement, but it wasn't her voice or stature that was striking. It was the snakes.

They writhed around her head, knotting and re-knotting, slithering over her shoulders, tongues flicking in exploration and mouths occasionally gaping to show deadly venom-dripping fangs. On her face was a blank mask of white, with simple holes for eyes and mouth.

"Well?"

"We're . . . that is . . . are you the gorgon?"

"*A* gorgon," she corrected. "A. One of, well, not many, but a few. Well, three actually. I'm Euryale."

Belladonna had the feeling that behind the mask was a face she knew, but she couldn't quite place the voice no matter how hard she tried.

"Hello," she said, "I'm Belladonna. This is Steve."

"And you want to see the Queen of the Abyss."

"Yes."

"Why?"

"Because we need to find the Ninth Noble."

"The noble?" said Euryale with a start that seriously alarmed the snakes, which went into a tongue-flicking frenzy.

"To stop the—"

"The Empress, I know. Has she found the Circle?"

"The what?"

"The stones, the standing stones? Has she found them?"

"I don't . . . maybe . . ." stammered Belladonna, remembering her dream.

"Typical," muttered Euryale, wringing her hands and glancing up at the walls of the citadel. "I told her not to choose someone so young, but did she listen to me? Noooo. And now look where we are."

"Where?" asked Belladonna, suddenly hoping that perhaps they'd found someone who could actually tell them what was going on.

"What?"

"Where are we? And who did she choose? Me? Are you talking about me?"

Euryale looked at her like someone who didn't realize she'd been speaking aloud. She shook her head sharply, making the snakes writhe and hiss in discomfort.

"Yes. No . . . It's not for me to say."

"Um . . . are we going to have to go through this with all seven guardians?" asked Steve, rolling his eyes. "Because if we are, then it's going to take a really long time to save the Nine Worlds . . . *again.*"

Euryale spun around and glared at him. "You are a very annoying boy," she hissed.

"I know," said Steve, smiling. "Everyone says so."

The gorgon continued staring at him, and Belladonna began to get the uneasy feeling that she was considering removing her mask, but she turned to Belladonna instead.

"Do you have a gift?"

"Yes," said Steve, reaching into his bag and producing half a pencil and a ballpoint pen. "Here."

Euryale's mask was stark and plain, but her stunned contempt for the proffered gift came through loud and clear.

"What," she said slowly, "is that?"

"It's a gift. Hank said that—"

"Hank is an idiot. The gift does not need to *have* value, but it must be *of* value to one of you, at least."

"Sorry?"

"Pencils and pens would not fall into either category."

"What if it was a really nice pen, like one of those fountain pens they sell in the posh stationery shop in town?"

"Do you have such a pen?"

"No. But if I did, then it would *have* value, wouldn't it? So when you say that pencils and pens don't have any value, that's not strictly true."

The gorgon just stared at him.

"I'm really tempted to just take off my mask and turn you to stone."

"Don't do that!" said Belladonna quickly. She rummaged through her bag and produced the Wild Hunt's horn. "How about this?"

"What is it?"

"It's a horn. It calls the Wild Hunt."

"Don't give her that!" said Steve. "We might need it."

"It has to be of value. Here. Take it."

"Fine," said Euryale, snatching it off her without even looking. "Off you go, then."

"Great!" said Belladonna in an artificially cheerful way that she knew would fool no one. "Thanks very much!"

Steve looked like he was about to say something else, so she gave him a shove toward the opening in the wall. The important thing now was to find the final coin. They'd just have to manage it without the help of the Hunt.

The gorgon watched them for a few moments, then made a disapproving smacking sound with her teeth and disappeared inside her temple.

"Hey!" said Steve, turning around. "Did you hear that? I've heard that before. . . ."

"Oh, come on," said Belladonna.

They clambered over the last few rocks to the gap in the wall, which turned out not to be a gap at all but two dark pewter-colored metal gates that rose, smooth and unmarked, to the full height of the walls.

"How are we supposed to—" began Steve, but before he could finish, one of the great gates ground slowly open, just enough to let them pass.

"Yowza," he whispered.

"Yes," said Belladonna, "yowza."

They looked at each other, took a deep breath, and walked into the House of Ashes.

The Guardians of the Gates

EVEN AS BELLADONNA and Steve passed under the massive lintel at the entrance of the House of Ashes, the door began to swing shut, and as it crashed into place, Belladonna couldn't help feeling that there was a finality to the reverberating sound, a sense that from here there could be no going back.

She hesitated for a moment and stared at the gray metal of the door with its eight massive iron hinges and six rusty bolts.

"This is weird. I thought there'd be a courtyard."

"What?" She turned around, but Steve wasn't really speaking to her.

He was right, though. She had assumed there'd be a courtyard too. In almost every castle she'd ever visited, either with her parents or on school trips, once you passed through the main gate, you were either in a central courtyard or in a passageway leading to a central courtyard. But the gates of the House of Ashes opened onto a street.

Not like a street at home, of course. This one was

more like the pictures she'd seen of medieval towns, with buildings huddled close together and upper stories hanging so far out that they seemed about to tumble down from their own weight. At ground level were shops that opened directly onto the roughly cobbled street, where the worn tracks of millennia of cartwheels could be seen on either side of a wide stone gutter. Every detail was clear and it took a few moments for Belladonna to realize that it shouldn't be like that. It was night. Or it had been night outside the walls. Inside, it was something else altogether. It was as if the citadel were stuck in a perpetual dusk, like a rainy afternoon on a winter day, but without any actual rain.

"Come on," she said, trying to sound grim and confident, "let's go."

Steve nodded and they both took a deep breath and started to walk down the street. Their feet echoed in the stillness that lay over the place, and Belladonna imagined that this was what it must have been like for the first people who discovered Pompeii. The silence enveloped them as they passed by bakers, butchers, grocers, and garages. Nothing moved within the looming houses and shops, no breeze caught the awnings, and no birds or animals foraged or sang.

But Belladonna knew she and Steve weren't alone.

She knew that eyes were watching their every move, watching them glance into the shops and peer down the narrow passageways. They were watching from doorways and windows and craning to see them from the upper stories.

"Do you feel like someone's watching us?" whispered Steve, glancing left and right and trying to walk as quietly as possible.

Belladonna nodded. Once, she slowed down, convinced that someone was about to come out, but no one did. She imagined that this was what life was like for people who couldn't see ghosts: feeling the prickle on the back of the neck, the slight movement out of the corner of an eye, but never seeing a single spirit. For Belladonna, however, it was a totally new experience. It was as if these eyes and their owners were another class of ghost altogether, ones who hovered not between this world and her own but between this world and somewhere else entirely.

She decided to pick up the pace—there was no point in dwelling on who (or what) was watching them. They just needed to get to the Queen of the Abyss as fast as possible.

"Wait!" hissed Steve, raising a hand to hold her back. "There's someone there."

"No, I think it's just our—"

"Who seeks to enter?" boomed a hollow, sickly voice.

Belladonna froze and looked at Steve, who was staring intently ahead. She followed his gaze and realized that what she had thought was just another shop door was actually a narrow iron gate that extended upward until it became lost in the general gloom. She looked around for the source of the voice and was finally able to make out a shadowy figure standing to the left of the gate, so completely swathed in black that he almost seemed to become one with it.

"Who seeks," he repeated sternly, "to enter the home of She Who Watches?"

"Um . . . Belladonna Johnson," said Belladonna.

"And Steve Evans."

Belladonna flinched as their voices echoed up and down the street. The black-clad figure stepped forward, but she still couldn't make out any details of his face or figure.

"Are you living children?" he asked.

"Yes," whispered Belladonna.

"Why would living children wish to enter the domain of the Mistress of Death?"

"We've come to ask for the Ninth Noble."

"The what?"

"The Ninth Noble," said Steve. "It's a coin."

The black-clad creature stared at them. At least, Belladonna assumed he was staring. It really wasn't possible to tell *what* he was doing.

"Do you think," he hissed finally, "that this is some sort of shop?"

"Well, obviously it's not really a coin," said Steve testily. "It just looks like one."

The black figure stared again, then turned and walked back to his post next to the gate.

"You must leave something with me," he said.

"I know . . . um . . ." stammered Belladonna.

She swung her backpack to the ground and pulled out Dr. Ashe's bell.

"Will this do?"

The creature leaned forward, then seemed to nod.

"It is adequate. Place it on the ground before me."

"But—" began Steve.

"It calls the Dead," whispered Belladonna. "I really don't think we're going to need it here."

"Oh. Right. Good point."

"Place it on the ground!"

Belladonna did as she was told, and the guardian reached down and picked it up.

And then he was gone. He seemed to have melted completely into the shadows.

"Whoa," whispered Steve. "These people are creepy."

The tall iron gate slowly creaked open. Steve pulled it wide and they stepped through.

The street was gone. Now they were on a dirt road bounded by high stone walls. The path curved up toward the towers of the citadel like a massive spiral stair, and every hundred feet or so, torches burned in braziers set into the rock.

"I don't like this," said Steve. "It's a bit too much like that thornbush thing of Dr. Ashe's."

"Maybe we should find another way."

Steve nodded and they turned back, but the iron gate had gone. In its place was just another piece of gray wall. It was as if the gate had never existed.

"Great."

He glared at the wall as though he could make the gate reappear by sheer force of will.

"Come on," sighed Belladonna. "This is going to take forever if we keep stopping."

Steve reluctantly joined her and they began walking along the path.

"Have you got enough in there for all seven guardians?" he asked, nodding toward her backpack.

"I think so," she said. "I've got a roll of Parma Violets, um . . . some ginger snaps, a photo of my Mum and Dad . . ."

"I've got my Geography homework, my thermos . . . the ruler."

"You can't give the ruler away," said Belladonna. "We might need it."

"I know, but—"

Belladonna was destined never to know what he was going to say because at that moment, something else spoke. Something with a sibilant voice. Something that clearly thought it was whispering.

"These ones are alive!"

"No, they're not!"

"Yes, they are! Look, that one's tired. The climb is making it pant a little. Only the live ones do that."

Belladonna and Steve stopped and stared at each other.

"Uh-oh," said Steve.

Belladonna put her finger to her lips to stop him talking and strained to look ahead. There was nothing there, just more wall, but the voices had been real, and she could hear something else as well.

"Can you hear that?" she whispered.

Steve nodded slowly. The sound was like sliding or

rumbling. They looked up. Above their heads the walls were topped with crumbling battlements, just like the ones Belladonna remembered from old films on television or the tops of castles on family holidays to Wales. But there was nothing there that could have spoken.

"Did you see that?" whispered Steve urgently. "There! Look!"

Belladonna looked up at the top of the wall where there was a larger break in the ramparts and she saw it. The shimmer of green scales and the flash of three-lidded eyes.

"What should we do?" whispered Steve.

"Walk."

He nodded and they marched forward, straining to hear whatever was behind the wall.

Finally, after what felt like hours of hard slog up the steep pathway, they rounded a corner and found themselves facing another door. This one was set into the stone wall and its surface was smooth and gray. But there was no sign of a guardian. Belladonna glanced around, confused.

"Hello?" called Steve hopefully.

"Just a minute!" came the reply. "We'll be right there!"

"No, we won't," muttered another voice. "And if you think I'm slithering over that wall, you are sadly mistaken!"

This time Belladonna knew where the voice was coming from—it was directly overhead.

They tilted their heads up to the top of the wall and saw three reptilian faces staring back. Belladonna smiled hopefully. The creatures looked very big, but not unfriendly, with their iridescent green scales and pointed faces. Their eyes were dark yellow flecked with black, and each had a narrow red stripe that ran over the top of its head across its nose and down to its mouth where a needle-like purple tongue continually tested the air.

"Hello," said Steve again. "Are you the guardians of the gate?"

The creatures glanced at each other, then vanished from view, but Belladonna could hear them arguing in hushed, angry tones as they moved along the inside of the wall toward the door.

This was followed by silence, some scrabbling, the grind of shooting bolts, and a scraping sound as the door slid slowly open. But instead of finding themselves facing three reptilian creatures, Belladonna and Steve were face-to-face with one reptile and three heads.

The creature tumbled out of the door in a cascade of coils the size of tree trunks and came to a halt about two meters in front of them. The heads eyed their backpacks expectantly before turning their attention to Belladonna and Steve themselves.

"Did you bring a present?" said the middle head.

The other two heads looked irritated and swung themselves around in such a fashion that they managed to push the offending head into the background.

"Sorry about that," said the left-hand head. "Rude."

"Are you alive?" asked the right-hand head.

"Yes," said Steve. "We're alive."

The reptile heads looked impressed, and the left-hand one adopted an I-told-you-so expression.

"I knew you were," he said. "I told them so, but they wouldn't believe me."

"Only because live people would have to be madder than leverets on a hot day to come anywhere near the House of Ashes," said the right-hand head.

"No offense," he added.

"None taken," said Belladonna, trying to remain serious as Steve did his best to stifle a giggle.

"What is your gift?" asked the left-hand head.

"Present! Present! Present!" enthused the middle head, bursting between the other two and eyeing the backpacks.

"Something edible would be nice," said the right-hand head quietly.

Belladonna nodded, rummaged through her pockets, and emerged with the Parma Violets.

"What is that?" asked the middle head suspiciously.

"Sweets," said Belladonna. "They're violet flavored. There are twelve in a pack, so you get four each."

The heads looked at each other, then nodded.

"Alright," said the left-hand head, "you may pass."

"Thank you," said Belladonna, picking up her backpack and beginning to move toward the door.

"Just a moment," said the middle head. "Could you unwrap them, please? We don't have any fingers."

Steve smiled and picked up the packet. He opened it carefully and set the sweets out in three piles of four each. The reptile looked pleased, so far as reptiles can, and began to sniff the sweets expectantly.

Belladonna and Steve walked quickly to the door and

through the opening, past coil after coil of the reptile's body. The only sound from the creature now was the crunch of Parma Violets and the occasional wet click of a happily flicking tongue. The coils curled around the doorjamb almost at right angles and down a passageway that ran parallel with the outer walls. A perfect lair for a snake, thought Belladonna.

"Which way?" she said, looking down the passages on either side.

"Neither," said Steve. "I think it's this way."

He stepped forward and lifted the latch on a small wooden door directly in front of them. Belladonna couldn't understand why she hadn't noticed it right away, but she was prepared to believe that he was right and followed close behind as he cautiously pushed on the roughly hewn timber. The door swung inward to reveal almost complete darkness—they could just make out the first three steps of a steep staircase leading upward.

"Oh, great," said Steve. "More stairs."

"At least they're going in the right direction," said Belladonna. "Up is definitely the way we need to go, after all."

Steve sighed.

"Three down," he muttered, "and four to go."

Belladonna peered up the stairs. It looked dark. And steep.

"Oh, well," she sighed, "if we don't start, we'll never get there."

She began to climb with Steve slogging along close behind her.

The stairs were bounded on each side by stone walls, roughly hewn from granite. Belladonna felt that they were inside the island rather than in a building on top of it. She reached a hand out to feel the wall—it was dry and cold, with the sort of deep chill that struck right to the bone. She shoved her hand into her pocket to try to get it warm again and noticed something else: She always seemed to be able to see three steps ahead.

"Are you using your flashlight?"

"What?" said Steve.

"Your flashlight. On the key chain. To light the way."

"No. It's not dark. I can see where we're going."

"I know. Weird, isn't it? It ought to be dark."

There was light, but from where?

They kept climbing and after a few moments Belladonna heard a dull groan from behind. She stopped and turned around.

"Don't stop!" Steve pushed her forward, his voice tense. "Keep moving!"

"What? What is it?"

"Look up."

She looked up and at first saw nothing. Then a movement. And another one. Something was up there.

It was an insect. No, insects. There were lots of them. She strained to see and was gradually able to make them out. There was a small ledge above their heads and there were white insects, like crickets or grasshoppers but with extremely long legs and no eyes at all. As they passed, the insects scuttled to the edge of the ledges and crevices where they lived and lit up, casting a sickly yellow light down into the stone corridor.

"Amazing."

"You *would* say that," said Steve, shuddering. "Have you seen how long their legs are?"

"They're only insects," said Belladonna, loving the idea that Steve was more scared of them than she was. "What do you think makes them glow? Maybe it's our breath."

"This is me not caring," he grumbled. "Would you get a move on?"

After about half an hour of slogging up the stairs, they came to a large wrought-iron gate with rusty hinges and a broken lock. Was this one of the gates? She looked around for any sign of a guardian, but no one spoke or barred their way, so she reached forward and pushed at the gate. It creaked loudly and swung inward.

"At last!" said Steve.

They stepped inside. Above their heads was a domed iron grille that was open to the sky, casting weird checker-board shadows over roughly constructed stone terraces. On closer inspection, she realized that the terraces had actually been thrown together from odd bits of poorly painted concrete stacked into imitation rocky outcrop-pings.

"What is this?" she whispered.

"It's like an enclosure in a zoo," said Steve.

He was right, but if it was a zoo, it was a rather run-down one. The replica rocky outcroppings were gray and striped from years of rain, and the dirt floor was littered with large bones that Belladonna really hoped weren't human.

She took one glance around and knew that this wasn't the sort of place where you should linger if you had any common sense at all.

"Let's get out of here," she whispered, and led the way toward a dark opening in the far wall.

"Not so fast!" said a cracked, high-pitched voice.

Belladonna and Steve stopped and peered around for the source of the voice, but all they could see was dark concrete and the barred roof. Steve took an exploratory step forward, keeping his eyes on the gray terraces.

"Stop!" said the voice.

This time Belladonna knew exactly where it was coming from: There was some sort of cave halfway up the wall. She didn't say anything but pointed out the spot to Steve. They both shaded their eyes and peered into the space, but all they could see was the faint sparkle of eyes.

"Oh," said the voice, "so you want to see me, is that it? You want to *stare*."

"No," said Belladonna quickly. "That is . . ."

"Well, have a good look, then! You've paid your admission. It's your right, I suppose!"

Belladonna was about to protest that they had no desire to stare and that they hadn't paid any admission for anything, but the words died on her tongue as the creature stepped out of the shadows.

"Oh, wow," muttered Steve, his eyes like saucers.

The first thing Belladonna noticed was the feet. They were the talons of a bird of prey but easily a hundred times larger than any hawk or eagle she'd ever heard of. The ribbed toes and curling claws were designed to cling to branches and to grab and rip flesh. Belladonna shuddered.

"Yes, horrible, aren't they?" said the creature.

"No . . . I mean . . ." Belladonna looked up as she spoke and found herself face-to-face with a creature she couldn't even begin to identify. She glanced at Steve, hoping for assistance, but he was just staring, his mouth slightly open.

Which was quite an understated response when you considered what they were both looking at.

The feet and body were those of a bird of prey, that was certain, but the head was human. An old lady, in fact. All yellowing skin and cascading wrinkles. She looked fed up and angry at the world and, given her situation, Belladonna couldn't blame her one bit.

"Hello," she said, hoping that she could start again.

The creature looked at them, cocked her head sideways, and fluttered down.

"We brought a gift."

The bird-woman turned around. She was half in shadow now and Belladonna was able to see that the bird part of her really was spectacularly beautiful. The feathers were golden brown and tan and shone in the moonlight like satin.

"What are you thinking?" snapped the woman.

"That your feathers are really beautiful," answered Belladonna truthfully.

The creature paused for a moment, then preened a wayward feather before returning to Belladonna.

"My name is Aello," she said, ignoring Steve entirely. "Have you heard of me?"

Belladonna shook her head.

"No," said Aello sadly. "All is forgotten. There were three of us. Sisters, you know. I'm all that's left. I don't know what's happened to the others. That's families for you."

"I'm sure if they knew—"

"They'd laugh. That's what they'd do if they knew. Laugh. Pathetic, isn't it? People used to live in fear of our approach, quake at the sound of our wings, and now look at me—a glorified porter!"

The bird-woman looked at her feet sadly and scratched small circles in the sand with a claw.

"Why were they scared of you?" asked Steve.

"You're joking, right?"

"Well, I can see that you don't look . . . that the way you . . . but that's just a first impression, and—"

"We're *harpies*," said Aello irritably. "We stole their food, ripped the unsuspecting from their beds, and dragged them here to the Land of the Dead. There were no *first impressions*, only final ones."

Steve stepped backward in surprise at the venom in her voice, and Belladonna began to realize that she'd probably made a mistake in trying to chat with Aello and that perhaps the time was right to ease the conversation back to the gift.

"I was wondering—" she began, but the harpy had already fixed her with a hungry, gimlet eye.

"You understand that I'm going to have to eat you

both," she said in a resigned tone of voice that implied a sort of bored regret. "No offense."

"We'd prefer that you didn't," said Belladonna, backing slowly away.

The harpy sighed, walked slowly toward her, and examined her closely.

"I'll tell you what," she said finally. "If the present is good, if it's something pretty, maybe I'll let you go."

Belladonna's heart sank. She didn't have anything even remotely pretty.

The harpy looked at her expectantly and cocked her head on one side again. Belladonna swung her backpack onto the ground and unzipped it. She stared into it, as if something might just materialize through sheer strength of will, then reached in and took out half a packet of ginger snaps.

"What's that?" snapped Aello.

"Ginger snaps," said Belladonna, who was sort of hoping that the orange packaging might qualify as "pretty" in the Land of the Dead.

It didn't. Aello shook her head and peered over the bag.

"What else?" she asked, turning to Steve.

Steve opened his backpack and showed the harpy the contents. She glanced in without much interest and was about to turn her attention back to Belladonna when something caught her eye.

"What's that? There's something shiny."

"Um . . ." Steve reached into the bag. "House keys."

"Show me."

He removed his massive key ring, loaded down with the keys to his house, the shop, his Dad's storage unit, and the tiny pen light.

"Oh!" gushed the harpy. "Lovely! Put it around my neck!"

Steve looked at the keys and then Belladonna, who nodded eagerly.

Steve reached into a pocket and extracted a small bundle of string from the collection of random objects that he'd shoved into his pocket over the previous week. He untangled it and looped the keys onto it. Aello grinned with delight as he tied the keys around her feathered throat, revealing a mouth that had barely half its full complement of teeth. Then she scurried away to gaze at the effect in a small puddle near the middle of the enclosure. Belladonna watched as she preened, smiling and muttering to herself.

"Can we go?" she asked finally.

"What?" Aello looked up, surprised to see that they were still there. "Yes! Yes! Go."

They didn't need telling twice. They both scooped up their backpacks and ran for the dark opening beneath the concrete outcroppings. This led into a dank tunnel, which quickly revealed a narrow hallway that, in turn, opened into a large room with windows that looked across Grendelmere.

Belladonna realized that they must finally be in the actual House of Ashes. Steve ran to one of the windows and looked outside.

"What can you see?"

"Nothing. The lake, the trees. Walls."

She joined him by the window and for a moment they stood, gazing over the labyrinthine streets far below and reveling in the feeling of the soft night breeze against their faces.

"What is today?" asked Steve.

"I don't know. Friday by now, I should think."

"No, the date. What's the date?"

"The twenty-eighth of February."

"Huh."

"What?"

"It's my birthday."

"Really?" Belladonna was surprised—not that he had a birthday, of course; obviously, he had to have one of those—but that he told her about it. For some reason, he was never particularly forthcoming about the non-Paladin side of his life. She knew about the shop and she knew that his mother had disappeared, but other than that, she didn't know very much. She'd always just assumed that he saved his real conversations for his football-chess-club-tormenting friends.

"It's not really on the twenty-eighth," he said, "it's on the twenty-ninth."

"You were born in a leap year?"

"Yes." He turned to her and grinned. "I'm really only three."

Belladonna laughed, "Happy birthday."

"Thanks."

The clouds parted and the bright blue moon of the Land of the Dead shone down on the glistening lake and the dark fortress.

"It feels so far away," said Belladonna.

"I know. Like the Proctors and the Empress and the school don't exist at all."

"What if we can't figure it out? If we don't know what to do to stop them . . . and her?"

Steve turned away from the window and looked at her.

"We can't think about that now. If you start thinking about all the things that could go wrong, you can't do anything. You just have to pretend that everything's okay and then just deal with things when they come up."

"Oh, I see," said Belladonna, smiling. "That's how you manage at school, isn't it? You just don't think about how late your French homework is or how you're going to explain when Mr. Fredericks and Miss Venable actually compare notes."

"Yes, I suppose it is. It's just *school,* you know. They're only teachers. It isn't the end of the world."

Belladonna glanced at him sharply.

"Okay, yes, *this* could be the end of the world. But we can't worry about things we have no way of knowing. Right now we just have to concentrate on getting to the Queen of the Abyss. We'll figure everything else out later."

Belladonna nodded. She felt envious of Steve's ability to set things aside and just tackle the problem at hand. It might not serve him well in the long run, but she'd give anything, right now, this minute, to be able to stop worrying—about the Empress, the Proctors, the names on the coins, and whether the Queen of the Abyss would be good or bad. She leaned further out of the window, examining the walls, the lake, anything to try to take her mind off it all.

"Um . . . having said that. There is one other thing," said Steve.

"Yes," said Belladonna, closing her eyes and letting the soft breeze riffle through her hair. "The day after to-morrow is the Day of Crows."

She opened her eyes, turned away from the window, and smiled at Steve.

"Onward and downward?"

"Yes."

They left the window and walked toward an open door on the far side of the room.

"Maybe the Queen of the Abyss will have a birthday cake for you," said Belladonna.

"Oh, I'm sure she will. And balloons."

They continued on their way, passing from one vast empty room to another. There was no furniture anywhere, no decoration on the walls, and barely any light, but they kept marching on through the great fortress toward the Queen of the Dead.

Hours seemed to pass, but just as Belladonna was be-ginning to think she might need a rest, she saw something up ahead. Something shiny, something that glistened in the moonlight. And it seemed to be swaying slightly, like fabric.

"Look! What's that?"

As they got closer, she could see that it was a curtain set into a carved stone archway. A slight breeze wafted in from a narrow window high on the wall and gently fluttered the material. Belladonna reached forward to push it aside.

"Ow!"

She snatched her hand back.

"What is it?"

"Something bit me!"

Steve peered at the curtain, then suddenly jumped backward.

"Oh, yagh!"

Belladonna rolled her eyes and leaned forward, then it was her turn to start in surprise—the curtain wasn't fabric at all, but a rippling sheet of spiders. Thousands of tiny black spiders.

The small creatures were linked together by their legs and small pieces of web, each grasping the next. Separately, they were nothing more than rather unimpressive spiders no more than half an inch across, but together they made an impressive symbiotic life-form. (Belladonna remembered symbiosis from Miss Kumar's Biology class, though she did wonder why she remembered it now when she couldn't recall it for the life of her during the test last month.)

She considered the problem, then slowly moved her hand toward it again. This time she noticed how the spiders moved toward the point where her hand would reach the curtain.

"Hello?" she said tentatively.

The spiders were just spiders, however, and declined to respond.

"You're talking to spiders," said Steve drily.

"I think they're guardians."

She considered the problem for a moment, then swung her backpack onto the stone floor and began rummaging through it. She pulled out the half-empty packet of ginger snaps again, then hesitated. It was the last food they had (other than whatever was in Steve's thermos), and if it took too long to complete the journey, there was a possibility that they might be forced to eat the food of the Dead. Or starve. But the results would probably be the same. On the other hand, if they didn't leave a gift for the spiders, they'd be stuck on this staircase until the crack of doom.

She put the cookies on the floor and pushed them toward the spiders with her toe. At first, nothing happened; the packet just lay there, rocking back and forth slightly. Then, with a movement so fast that Belladonna wasn't even sure she saw it, the curtain was gone and the spiders were on the cookies, a single pulsating mass of shining black.

Steve shuddered and Belladonna had to agree that the heap of spiders was definitely much worse than a gently wafting sheet of them. She gave them as wide a berth as she possibly could and walked through the archway.

"Come on!" she urged, as Steve hung back, staring at the spiders.

"I'm coming," he said, rather unconvincingly. But he closed his eyes, got as close to the wall as he could, and inched through the arch.

"I'll bet Edmund de Braes wasn't afraid of a few spiders," said Belladonna.

Steve ignored her and moved further into the new room and away from the spider arch.

"We're outside!"

He was right. A cold breeze whipped around their faces and there was suddenly light and air. It was still dark, of course, but at least now they were outside with the blue moon shining above and dusky clouds trailing across the sky.

Belladonna breathed deeply, feeling as though she had been trapped in a dismal cellar for weeks. And now they were in a garden.

Sort of. Or maybe it was a patio. It was obviously in the middle of the palace and was the size of a small lawn. Just about the size of the back garden at home, actually. Only here, instead of a border of skinny rhododendrons, the whole garden was bounded by a covered marble walkway, its coffered roof held aloft by elegant columns. In the center was a narrow path, bisected by a small reflecting pool. On either side of that, clusters of herbs released their heavy fragrances into the night. Without realizing what she was doing, Belladonna moved into the garden, reaching for the plants. She brushed their leaves gently and drank in their aroma.

She had never been a particularly garden-y person. Weeding and planting and water features held no charms for her. But ever since last October, when she'd seen what a truly dead world could be like, she'd had a new appreciation for everything green.

"Belladonna . . ." Steve was whispering and his voice sounded strange.

Then she sensed it.

They were being watched.

The Manticore

ßELLADONNA SPUN AROUND—there was nothing there, but Steve moved in close behind her.

"We need to move," he whispered.

She noticed that he had the plastic ruler in his hand and wondered how he knew. How did he know that now was the time for the Rod of Gram? He hadn't taken it out when the harpy had threatened them, or when Euryale had first appeared, with her mask and head of venomous snakes.

"There's a door. Over there. Let's go."

Belladonna nodded. They started to move slowly across the garden toward the door.

This time she really thought she saw something. A movement, just to her left, but too far back to be sure. They stopped and waited. Nothing.

But it was still there.

They took a few more steps. This time there was no question. She saw a tail—a long, muscular tail—vanish behind one of the columns.

"Was that a cat?" whispered Steve. "It sort of moved like a cat."

"A really big cat," said Belladonna warily.

They stood still and listened . . . and watched. Nothing.

"Okay," said Steve finally, "this is stupid. We'll just go to the door, leave something for whatever it turns out to be, and carry on."

Belladonna nodded and they both marched forward with what she hoped were looks of steely determination, but before they reached the end of the short garden, there was the crisp clicking sound of claws on stone, and the creature that had been stalking them leapt in front of the door.

Belladonna gasped and stumbled back, almost falling into the reflecting pool. Steve backed up slowly, standing between her and the creature while she scrambled to her feet. She was really impressed with his unruffled reaction because this was a creature like no other she'd ever seen.

Its body was that of a lion, but bigger than she remembered from trips to the zoo, and its fur was a weird sort of red color that darkened almost to burgundy on the legs and tail. The claws were dark and metallic, and clearly didn't retract, scraping the stonework and leaving white marks wherever the creature went. But it wasn't the body or the claws that were most striking about this guardian. It was the head and tail.

At first glance the tail seemed to be just the tail of a lion, thick, powerful, and twitching irritably. But as it moved, Belladonna became aware of something else, something at the end, where there should have been a small brush of fur.

It was only as the creature took another step forward into the moonlight that they could see what it was — spines. An egg-shaped cluster of spines, each about four inches long, that generated a high-pitched whistle as the tail whipped through the air.

And then there was the head.

It was the head of a man, his bald pate glistening in the pale moonlight, eyes black and shining with the kind of bloodthirsty anticipation she'd seen on hyenas in nature documentaries, right before they ripped some unsuspecting antelope to shreds. He had a beard, short and ragged and the same shade of red as the body. But it was the teeth that really got her attention.

She didn't see them at first. The mouth was closed as he paced back and forth in front of the door, his tail whistling through the night air. Then he stopped and smiled, but this was no ordinary smile. The mouth was far wider than a human mouth could ever be, and the teeth that the smile exposed were narrow and sharp, more like needles than teeth, and like the claws, they appeared to be metallic. All of which was bad enough, of course, but then he opened his mouth as if tasting them on the air, and revealed three rows of the murderous daggers, each row tipping slightly backward to make absolutely certain that any prey, once caught, would never escape.

Belladonna thought of the Venus flytrap that she used to have on the windowsill in her room and was suddenly filled with sympathy for the flies. She glanced back at the archway with the spider curtain, every instinct telling her to run. Steve shook his head.

"He'd get us long before we reached the spiders," he whispered, then turned to the creature. "Are you . . . the guardian of this door?"

The tail whipped back and forth as the creature stared at them. It occurred to Belladonna that it might not be able to talk, human head or not.

"Because—"

"I am," it said suddenly, as if the act of speaking was an annoying postponement of the eating portion of the evening, "I am the *only* guardian."

Belladonna had to agree with him there. So far the guardians they'd encountered had been little more than glorified ticket takers.

"We're trying to reach the Queen of the Abyss," she said, feeling more confident now that he had spoken.

"No," he spat. "You both die here."

He stepped forward. Belladonna and Steve stepped back.

"What . . . are you?" asked Steve.

"I am a manticore," he said. "My name is of no concern to you. Stand still. You'll only make it worse by running."

Belladonna thought that was very unlikely. She took another step back and her foot went straight into the reflecting pool. She ignored the feeling of the cold water seeping into her shoe and up her sock, and slowly removed her backpack.

"We were told that if we left a gift with each of the guardians, we would be allowed to pass."

"You were told wrong," said the manticore.

Belladonna glanced at Steve, but the ruler was still just a ruler. She reached a hand into her bag and removed Dr. Ashe's book.

"What is that?" demanded the creature.

"It's a book."

"I can see that. How can a book help you now?"

"It's a book of magic," said Belladonna, opening it slowly.

"Is it, now?" said the creature, scornfully.

It drew back its tail as Belladonna turned the first page, then suddenly flicked it in her direction.

"No!"

Steve leapt in front of her and raised his hand. The ruler immediately turned into a heavy leather shield just as the manticore's dart found its target and embedded itself deep into the circular, worked surface.

He lowered the shield slowly and looked at the dart. A small trickle of dark goo was leaving a pale track down the leather.

"Surprise!" said the creature, smiling. "And they're poisonous too."

Steve grabbed the spike and started trying to work it out of the shield. The manticore watched, pacing, as he struggled. It was in no hurry. It knew that these small creatures were no match for the might of an animal older than time.

Eventually, Steve worked the dart loose, but just as he got it out, Belladonna saw the tail pull back for another strike. There was no time to think: She kicked her backpack at the creature and she and Steve ran for the shelter of the pillars on the opposite side of the garden.

They dodged behind the nearest one just as the manticore released the spike, which screamed through the air, hitting the pillar and dropping to the ground.

Steve reached forward and picked it up.

"You needn't bother collecting them," said the manticore confidently. "I'm not susceptible to my own poison."

"Keep him talking!" whispered Belladonna as she leaned against the pillar and opened the book.

"Didn't think you were," said Steve, as she desperately turned the pages.

"Then what are you doing?" asked the manticore.

Belladonna heard the telltale rustle of leaves and stalks and knew he was crossing the herb garden. Steve nodded his head and they ran two pillars to the left as quietly as they could. She opened the book again and tried to find a clue.

The untidy pages were scrawled with notes in English, Latin, and Greek as well as snippets of several languages she didn't recognize. Sketches, drawings, and diagrams further cluttered the pages, and copious notes in the margin made it almost certain that no one but the creator of the book would ever be able to glean anything useful from it.

It had been the last of Dr. Ashe's notebooks, a handwritten record of all his attempts at magic and of the secrets he had discovered. Belladonna had found it in a hidden cupboard at the back of the launderette that had once been his apothecary shop, but her first experience with using it and attempting to call up the Dead had made her cautious of trusting anything that Ashe had written. Still, it might offer their best chance of getting past the manticore.

"You know," said the manticore wheedlingly, "it is entirely possible I might let you go."

She looked up; the creature was in the walkway, zebra-striped by the shadows of the pillars. It hunkered close to the ground and was moving imperceptibly, with just the up-and-down slices of its shoulder blades revealing any forward motion at all. Belladonna wasn't fooled — she'd seen cats moving just like that when they were stalking birds in the garden, and it never ended well for the bird.

Steve had crept around the far side of the pillar, so she leaned back, pretending she hadn't noticed it, then slowly rolled around out of its line of sight. They both backed slowly toward the spider curtain while she still struggled to find something, anything, in the book.

She stood in the shadows near the curtain and froze.

"There *is* something!"

"There is?" Steve didn't dare take his eyes off the manticore.

"It's a drawing. It looks like the dart."

She was trying to read the text next to it and keep an eye on the creature's current location at the same time, when she suddenly became aware of something on Steve's shoulder. Something that was sort of crawling.

Steve obviously felt it and reached up to brush it off.

Only the tiny spider gave more resistance than he expected, and when it hit the floor, there was a definite *thunk*.

He spun around. The spider was huge. Bigger than anything Belladonna had ever seen on television documentaries, and across its abdomen were black and yellow stripes like a wasp. Steve looked pale and he was staring at the curtain. She followed his gaze and shuddered: What had been an airy net of tiny black arachnids was now a heavy brocade of interlocking tarantula-sized spiders. He backed away, stumbled over the one that he'd knocked off his shoulder, and fell to the ground. The shield flew out of his hand and landed a few feet away. Belladonna glanced quickly at the manticore, but it was just watching. A long black tongue lolled out of its mouth and licked the shining metal teeth.

"Have you met my friends?"

"They were . . . they were tiny," gasped Belladonna.

"That was the lining," said the manticore. "All well-made curtains have linings, you know."

Steve pushed himself backward with his feet, shuffling toward the protection of a pillar while feeling for the shield. He grabbed it and picked it up as Belladonna helped him to his feet, then they both ducked behind the temporary safety of the marble column The manticore seemed amused. It extended a paw, hooked a spider on its claws, and conveyed the unlucky creature to its mouth. Belladonna winced as the jaws closed on the struggling spider until all that was left was a uselessly twitching leg dangling from the manticore's greasy beard.

She began leafing through the book again, searching

for the drawing of the dart. But it was useless; her hands were shaking so much she could barely read a word. She dropped the book onto the floor and leaned her head against the cold stone of the pillar.

"It's not going to end like this," muttered Steve. "You stay here; I'm going to try to get behind him."

"To do *what*?"

"I don't know," he said. "*Something*. We're not going to end up like that spider."

Belladonna watched as he crept away down the colonnade. Was this how it was going to end? She closed her eyes and thought back to the Chemistry class where she'd first got to know Steve. She still couldn't believe that Mr. Morris hadn't noticed that he was mucking about, and she had to admit that making his shoes emit little explosions with every step was definitely a cut above the practical jokes that most of her classmates came up with. Still, she thought, her mind rambling in the face of almost certain death, there wasn't really any reason Mr. Morris would notice. Steve's concoction had only added one more ingredient to Mr. Morris's experiment, so it probably all looked quite normal to him. Plus he had those really thick glasses, so . . .

"That was the appetizer," whispered the manticore, its breath hot on her ear.

Belladonna opened her eyes. The creature was right next to her! She could smell its fetid breath and all but count its rows of teeth.

She leapt away and ran. The manticore laughed, and stalked slowly in pursuit. Belladonna made it to the far end, to the door that would take them closer to the Queen of the Abyss. She grabbed the great bronze handle and pulled desperately.

It didn't open. She glanced back to see where the manticore was now, and then it hit her: Steve's solution had only had one different ingredient.

Where was he? She scanned the garden and saw him behind a pillar at the far end.

The manticore was immune to its own poison, but what if they added something to it? She looked at the small herb garden. Perhaps something from there.

"Steve!" she shouted. This was no time for whispering; the manticore was coming in for the kill. "Remember last year? In Chemistry?"

"What?"

"Do you remember!?"

"Yes, but —"

"How Mr. Morris's experiment got all messed up when you added just one extra ingredient?"

"What does . . ."

And then the penny dropped. Steve peeked out at her from behind the pillar and she nodded her head toward the herb garden.

"Please let this work," she whispered, as Steve hunkered down and began to creep across the open space toward the herbs.

"You're talking to yourself," said the manticore from the shadows. "That's never a good sign."

She took a deep breath and ignored the creature. She knew what it was doing. She'd once seen the Williams's cat playing with a mouse it had caught. The sport for the cat was clearly in the game, not the kill. She tried to resist the temptation to look at Steve. It would be better if the manticore just focused on her.

She could see him, though, out of the corner of her eye. He was in the herb garden and examining each of the plants. Why was he doing that? None of them looked like anything from the herb gardens at home, with their neat rows of basil and oregano. Most of these plants were dark and slightly bluish, with feathery leaves or foliage like tiles. Some had small fruit dangling beneath their stems, while others spat forth spores and pods as you brushed against them. What was he doing? Why didn't he just pick one?

The manticore padded out of the shadows and stopped in front of the gate.

"It's time," it said.

Belladonna tried to look calm, but inside her head she was screaming at Steve: *Pick one! Pick one!*

He did it. He reached down and grabbed a handful of something, shoved it into his mouth, and chewed on it.

Belladonna backed away from the manticore, splashed across the reflecting pool and darted behind a pillar again. Steve joined her, spat the green goo into one hand and carefully rolled the darts in it.

"It might not work," he whispered, "but at least we'll go down fighting. See if you can get it to come out into the open."

"What??"

"I've only got two of his darts," explained Steve. "I need a clear shot."

"With what?"

"With this."

Belladonna hadn't noticed that the shield had gone, but it had, and in its place Steve was brandishing a long narrow tube.

"Promise you'll hit it?"

"I promise."

She smiled briefly, then stepped out into the moonlit garden again and stared at the manticore.

"Dinnertime," it simpered.

The creature leapt forward, pushing off the ground with its powerful haunches, its front claws stretched toward its prey, the mouth gaped wide, and anticipatory drool dripping from the rows of glistening teeth.

Steve crouched and slid one of the darts into the end of the tube.

Belladonna held her breath. Every instinct told her to close her eyes, but she kept them open, watching as the creature flew toward her.

Closer.

And closer.

At the last possible moment, Steve stepped out from behind the pillar, put the tube to his mouth, and blew.

The manticore flinched in pain and dropped to the ground. Belladonna leapt up and ran toward the spider curtain and behind the nearest pillar before daring to look.

The manticore sat in the garden and removed the spike, laughing softly.

"Didn't you hear me?" it said. "I'm immune to my own poison. Stupid boy!"

It threw the spike aside and prowled toward him, its tail twitching dangerously. Steve slowly exhaled and carefully put the second dart into the blowgun.

He started to raise it to his lips, but the manticore was already upon him, its claws clacking on the stone walkway and its teeth shimmering in the half-light. This time there was nowhere to go. This time the creature had won.

Belladonna closed her eyes.

Nothing happened.

She opened them slowly and saw the manticore clawing at its own stomach, a look of surprise on its face.

"What have you done?" it hissed.

Then it stumbled, the front paws buckling under the back ones. Belladonna watched, horrified, as its eyes rolled upward and the massive creature crashed to the cold stone floor in front of Steve.

"I killed it!" he whispered, looking from the manticore to Belladonna.

Belladonna started to cross the garden.

"Wait!" He held up a hand. "It's still breathing!"

They both froze, staring at it, as deep, long breaths echoed through the colonnades.

"It's asleep!" said Belladonna.

"Let's go," said Steve, his voice tense.

"What's the matter?"

"It's asleep. We don't know how long it'll last."

"Right," said Belladonna. "Good point."

They both ran for the door and seized the handle, but it still wouldn't open. Belladonna pulled on the handle, twisted and yanked at it, but the door might as well have been part of the wall. They looked back at the manticore. It was snoring softly. Steve examined the door, felt around its edges for a hidden switch, like the one in the school library, but there was nothing.

The manticore rolled over on one side and sniffled for a moment before settling into a deep sleep again.

Then Belladonna knew—there still had to be a gift. The gift wasn't for the guardians at all—it was for her, for the Queen of the Abyss. Belladonna ran back to the manticore and retrieved Ashe's book from the walkway where she'd dropped it. She took it to the door and put it on the stone floor.

There was a soft click as the latch released and the massive bronze doors swung slowly open.

They stepped forward, triumphant in the knowledge that there was only one more gate to pass and that maybe (just maybe) they would get the Ninth Noble after all.

The Queen of the Abyss

BELLADONNA AND STEVE paused in the doorway while their eyes adjusted to the darkness of the room. Behind them, the doors closed softly, gently nudging them inside.

"Heads up, girls," whispered a throaty female voice. "Someone's made it past Louis."

They peered into the darkness, trying to locate the owner of the voice, but couldn't see anything—which was strange because the room wasn't very big at all. It was about the size of the classrooms at school, though it was difficult to be sure, as the corners all disappeared into shadow. The walls were covered in a dusty red flocked wallpaper that left Belladonna with the impression of being inside an old jewelry box and, unlike the other rooms she'd seen in the House of Ashes, there was some furniture. A tall black grandfather clock stood against the wall to their right, though it didn't appear to be going, and a large red velvet sofa crouched in the center.

But there were no people. Or creatures.

On the far side, she could see an elaborately carved mahogany door covered with endless knots of sculpted wood. Two carved women stood sentinel on either side of the door, tall and straight with enormous feathered wings, one wing at rest behind the back and the other extended up over the doorway where they crossed at the top, forming a pediment.

"You know what they look like?" whispered Steve.

"Yes."

They took a few steps into the room, then stopped and listened. Silence.

"Hello?" said Belladonna finally.

"They speak." The voice was female, velvety and languid.

Belladonna and Steve spun around. The voice was definitely behind them.

"And they're alive," said a second voice.

Belladonna's fear was quickly replaced by irritation, and then anger.

"Look," she said, "we don't have time for any more stupid games! Show yourselves and let's get this over with!"

There was silence for a moment, and then she heard soft laughing from the far side of the room. They spun around again, just in time to see that the carvings of the winged women weren't carvings at all. The left-hand figure had folded her wings elegantly behind her back and stepped down from her station at the side of the door. She was soon joined by her opposite number, and then by two more from either side of the entry door.

They were unmistakable, with their long bloodred hair, their sleek black dresses that pooled on the floor like oil, and their wings. Above all, the wings. Massive and black, shining blue like the wings of crows and draping behind them like half-discarded cloaks.

"Keres," muttered Steve.

"Clever boy," cooed one of the Keres. "Have you seen our kind before?"

Steve nodded.

"We need to see the Queen of the Abyss," said Belladonna, eager to get the encounter over and done with. "We have to leave a gift."

"You are in a great hurry," said the Kere who was lingering behind them.

"Yes, well, it's just that—"

"Life is short," said another. "Often shorter than you think. It's a mistake to hurry things."

"Why don't you both sit down?" asked a third, gesturing toward the red sofa.

"N-No," stammered Belladonna, "we're . . . We really can't wait."

The fourth woman stepped closer to them. She seemed slightly taller than the rest and leaned forward, staring at Belladonna with eyes that were completely black—there was no white in them at all.

"Now," she said gently, her red lips revealing perfectly white teeth, "if you've come this far and managed to get past our little pet next door, you must be at least a bit tired."

Belladonna shook her head and started to speak, but

as she did so, one of the great black wings swept up and out over her head, making a small warm breeze, and she realized that she was quite tired after all.

"Do sit down," said the tallest woman.

Belladonna glanced at Steve, but he seemed tired too and gratefully took the hand of one of the Keres when it was offered. This seemed wrong, somehow, but her mind was eager for sleep and she couldn't think why.

"Come," said the tall Kere softly, holding out a long pale hand, the wrists of which were wreathed with ebony bracelets that rattled gently as she moved, like wind chimes on a summer day.

Belladonna smiled, took the hand of the woman, and allowed herself to be led to the sofa.

It had looked uncomfortable before, but as she sat on it, she realized that it was softer than anything she'd ever known. She sank into the downy cushions next to Steve and, although she tried to sit up straight, she kept finding herself slipping backward into the burgundy depths.

"So . . . you know who we are," said the tallest one, sitting next to her on the couch.

"Do you know what we do?" said one of the others as they swept across the room, surrounding the couch and hemming Belladonna and Steve in with their wings.

"No," said Steve.

"Why don't you take that off?" said another, moving behind the couch and gently removing Belladonna's back-pack. "It can't be comfortable and it must be heavy."

"It was, but it's alright now," said Belladonna, retrieving the backpack and placing it carefully on the floor at her feet. "It's nearly empty."

"I see," said the tallest one, smiling. "You left everything as gifts."

"Yes."

"Did you save anything for us?" asked another.

"I think so . . ." began Belladonna.

"I'm sure you have," said the tallest one quickly, "but there's no rush. Would you like some sandwiches? You must be starving."

She waved a long-fingered hand to the left and Belladonna saw a tea table, laden with food.

"No . . . thank you," she said.

"Of course not," said the one behind her. "What child wants sandwiches when she can have cakes?"

Belladonna blinked as the table was suddenly covered in cakes, plates and plates of them. Her mouth watered at the sight of all the pastry, cream, and tiered dishes of multicolored iced macaroons.

"No," said Steve, as if speaking was an incredible effort. "No. We can't eat the food here."

The tallest woman seemed momentarily taken aback, but quickly regained her composure and her friendly smile.

"Good boy," she said. "Very wise."

Belladonna was beginning to feel better and thought they really needed to get off the couch and go through the last door.

"I think we'd better go," she said.

She was about to jump off the sofa when one of the women readjusted her wings, brushing one of them against her cheek. The feathers felt like satin, and Belladonna suddenly felt slightly breathless. She gulped for air and fell back into the cushions again.

"I think she sat up too suddenly," said one of the women.

"Yes," said the tallest one, stroking Belladonna's forehead with an icy hand, "you should be careful of that. Just sit for a moment. I'm sure your friend could do with the rest . . . in his condition."

"My condition?" whispered Steve.

"Well, your arm," said the tall one, as if it was the most obvious thing in the world. "The manticore. It must hurt quite a bit."

Steve was clearly about to tell her that there was nothing wrong with his arm, when he suddenly seemed to realize that it did hurt. It was his right arm. Belladonna looked at it and saw that one of the tallest woman's wings was covering it. Steve tried to move it away and winced in pain; it looked heavy and almost useless, as if he'd broken it.

"Ow," he said, drawing it into his chest with his good arm. "I don't remember the manticore doing that."

"That's often the case in battles," said one of the other women. "It just becomes a blur."

"No," he said, "I think I remember everything. I have a very good memory."

"Of course you do," whispered the tallest one. "You're just tired."

"Why do you keep telling us that we're tired?" said Belladonna, but the words were hardly out of her mouth before the wings rose again and stirred the air.

This time she felt more than tired—she felt as if she were falling into a pit. A deep, red, soft pit. She looked up, but the women and the room seemed to be far above, like something at the top of a well. She could see them looking at each other and smiling.

"What are Keres?" she thought.

"She still speaks," said one of the women far above.

The tallest one smiled slightly and Belladonna realized that she hadn't just thought it. She had spoken.

"What did she say?" said another of the women.

"What . . ." Belladonna marshalled all her strength, but her lips were dry and the effort of speaking seemed almost too much. "What are Keres?"

Had she managed to say it? She wasn't sure. But she knew it was important.

The tallest one leaned down and suddenly she too was in the pit, her lips against Belladonna's ear.

"We are the takers of souls, of course," she whispered. "We come where people die in violence. In battles we are there, at accidents, at the scenes of murders. At the last we are always there to rip the souls from their bodies and take them to the Dark Spaces. Our mistress needs minions—dead but not dead, bereft of breath and yearning to return."

Belladonna turned her head and stared at the beautiful face with the glistening black eyes, and realized that the breath was foul and the white teeth a little too pointed.

"But sometimes," continued the tall woman, her voice purring, "sometimes, we don't like to wait."

The black wings closed above Belladonna and Steve,

forming a feathered dome at the top of the red pit. Belladonna gazed helplessly up at the pallid faces as she felt her heart beat more and more slowly, until she wasn't sure it was beating at all. She could see Steve at her side, his eyelids fluttering as he slipped into oblivion. Belladonna wanted to close her eyes too, to sleep, to let everything go. Her lids felt so heavy, and it was only with a superhuman effort that she kept them open.

"She's a fighter," the voice drifted down to her, though she had no idea who spoke.

"They're the only ones worth having."

She breathed in slowly, but the air seemed thin. It didn't fill her lungs with life but with the chill of death. She was so tired and the red pit was so soft.

"She's going," said another voice.

Belladonna looked up and, with an effort, made her eyes focus on the faces above. They were no longer beautiful, but old and gaunt. Their red lips were thin and cracked, and as they drew them back, Belladonna could see that the teeth that had seemed a little too pointed a few moments before were now gaping maws of rotting fangs.

She wanted to do something, but her mind seemed incapable of concentrating on anything. She kept imagining she was back at home with the aroma of dinner drifting into the sitting room as she watched television with her father; or up in the attic at school sorting through the trunk of papers with Steve and Elsie; or finding Ashe's book in the wall of the launderette; or touching the handle of the scenery door that had led them to the Other Side; or sitting on the train to the abbey, listening to Elsie; or laughing in the old Cadillac, the wind rushing through her hair; or . . .

The door. There was something about that. She opened her eyes again and looked at the faces of the Keres.

"The door," she whispered.

"What did she say?"

"I couldn't hear."

"Why won't they die?"

She remembered the door. She reached for the handle.

"What's she doing?"

"Nothing. Reaching for her mother, I suppose. Lots of them do that."

She could see it shining just in front of her, the brass handle of the fake door. She touched it and gasped. Air rushed into her lungs. Good air, not the Kere's breath of death. She sat up and pushed the women back as the Words poured from her mouth.

It was the same ancient language she always spoke, but this time, more than any other, she understood exactly what she was saying. She knew she was sending them back to the black place where they waited and forbidding them to set forth from that place unless they were called.

The women screamed and reached for her with their long thin hands, but Belladonna had strength now and she backed away and repeated her command.

"This is not the end!" spat the tallest woman. "The walls between the worlds are coming down! And then will come a day when such mewling words from the mouth of a child will have no power! None!"

And then there was silence. The women were once

more nothing but carved wood on the doors, and Bella-donna was alone in the dark.

"What happened?"

She turned around. Steve was sitting on the couch, rubbing his eyes and looking as if he'd just woken from a long sleep and had no idea where he was.

"Keres," said Belladonna grimly, hoping she'd never see them again, but suspecting that she would.

She went back to the couch, helped Steve to his feet, and picked up her backpack. She opened it and peered inside.

"It's okay," said Steve. "I'll do this one."

He pulled out his thermos, marched to the door, and placed the thermos carefully in front of it. It swung open and they both ran through, eager to leave the sickly pres-ence of the Keres far behind.

This time they emerged into a narrow passage with flowery green wallpaper and tall wainscoting. There were lights here, flickering gas lights behind amber globes high on the walls. They stopped running and looked ahead. There was one more door.

It was simple and poorly made, with a wrought-iron handle. Belladonna reached for the handle and turned, but it was locked.

"That's not right," said Steve. "Seven guardians. There were supposed to be seven. We've passed them all. This door should open."

"I know. See if you can find a key or something."

Steve ran his hands over the surface of the door as Belladonna felt in the corners for hidden keys.

"Wait," said Steve. "There's a button."

Belladonna looked up—he was right; there was a small button to one side of the door. A doorbell?

Steve pushed the cobwebs away.

"Ready?"

"Yes," she said firmly. "Ready."

Steve pressed the button. There was a pause, then the sound of a distant buzz followed by silence. He looked at Belladonna.

"Try it again."

He nodded and was about to press it again when something inside the door clicked softly.

Belladonna reached out and turned the handle once more and this time the latch gave way and the door swung slowly inward. It was heavier than she had expected, and she had to lean hard to get it to open wide enough for her to get through, but she could already see that this room was light. Bright, even. And there was carpet.

She stepped into the room and blinked at the sunlight streaming in from the two windows on either side of her. There was a large desk and a Picasso print. A woman was sitting at the desk and staring at her.

As her eyes grew accustomed to the light, Belladonna froze, her mouth hanging open in astonishment.

"Miss Parker!"

22

The Chariot

MISS PARKER DIDN'T seem stunned at all, beyond an expression that seemed to indicate mild surprise that Belladonna hadn't knocked first.

They stared at each other for a full minute, Miss Parker not moving from her desk and Belladonna frozen in the doorway that she now realized was behind the tall narrow bookcase that she'd examined so closely while trying to decide what to say when she and Steve had been sent there after Chemistry last October.

Then it occurred to her—that wasn't possible. The bookcase was between two windows, and Miss Parker's office was on the second floor.

She spun around. There were the windows alright, with their not very impressive view of the street outside and the run-down buildings opposite. And there was the bookcase and the door. There should be nothing but a long drop, but Belladonna could still see the narrow corridor with the green wallpaper stretching into shadow.

"Hey, let me in!"

Steve gave her a sharp shove and half stepped, half tripped into the room.

"Whoa!" he blurted. "You have got to be kidding me!"

"My feelings exactly," sighed Miss Parker, standing up. "I'd been rather hoping that Mrs. Jay was wrong."

She walked around the desk and took the old lacrosse stick down from its display case, then turned and looked at them both critically.

"You look a mess," she said. "I don't suppose it occurred to either of you to pack a comb in those backpacks of yours?"

Belladonna and Steve shook their heads. Miss Parker opened a drawer in the desk and handed a comb to Belladonna.

"There's no excuse for slovenliness," she said as she pushed the bookcase back against the wall. "Particularly when you are in school uniform."

"Are you the . . ." began Steve, ignoring the whole comb thing, but his voice trailed off before he actually asked the question.

"Thank you," said Belladonna, running the comb through her hair and handing it back. "We got the nobles . . . and there was a rhyme . . . so are . . ."

But her voice trailed off as well. For some reason the question seemed so ridiculous, looking at Miss Parker, with her sensible shoes, her ill-fitting navy blue suit, and her helmet of dark hair trimmed so precisely just at her jawline.

"Oh, for heaven's sake," said Miss Parker impatiently. "Yes, I am Ereshkigal, the Queen of the Abyss. There. Now you know."

Belladonna tried to absorb the information.

"But . . . you're Miss Parker. The head of our school."

"How terribly observant of you, Miss Johnson," said Miss Parker drily. "Were either of you intending telling me something useful, or did you think you'd just stand there with your mouths hanging open?"

"The guardians —" said Steve suddenly. "We were nearly killed! Twice!"

Miss Parker looked at him as if she were going to impose detention or issue one of those letters to parents that fill all schoolchildren with unnameable dread. But she stopped.

"Of course!" she said, her eyes opening wide and displaying a rather unsettling amount of white around her green pupils. "You got past my manticore —"

"And the Keres!" interrupted Steve. "Who nearly killed us, in case you're interested!"

Miss Parker's eyes narrowed, as if she were seeing them both for the first time.

"How did you do it?" she asked.

"Well," said Steve, "with the manticore I just added something to the poison on his darts and it became poisonous to him."

"From the herb garden?"

Steve nodded.

"Wolfsbane? Helibore?"

"Dunno," said Steve. "I thought I'd killed him, but I think he's just asleep, so . . ."

"You don't know?" said Miss Parker in a voice that was a little too loud.

She glanced at the door, then strode over to Steve and lowered her voice.

"You defeated him with a herb? Whatever gave you that idea?"

"I . . . that is, we thought that adding something to the poison might change it, that's all."

Miss Parker looked at him and sighed. "So it was luck."

Steve nodded.

"And the Keres?"

"Their wings . . . they—" began Belladonna.

"I know about their wings," snapped Miss Parker.

"I thought we were going to die, then I thought of the door. The first door, the one in the theatre. I reached for its handle and I said the Words."

"What words?" Miss Parker's eyes bored into Belladonna.

"The . . . my grandmother says they're . . . um . . ."

"You said Words of Power," said Miss Parker.

"Yes."

Miss Parker looked at her sharply, then strode to the office door and locked it. Belladonna watched her quick movements and impatient glances and realized that they were taking a chance on Miss Parker being a force for good.

"Has anyone ever made it before?" Belladonna asked, trying not to sound nervous.

"No," said Miss Parker in a matter-of-fact manner, "except for Old Ones, of course. But no living people."

"But why do you . . . Are they your friends?" Steve

was clearly still suspicious and Belladonna could see him fingering the plastic ruler, just in case.

"Who?"

"The Keres . . . the manticore."

"No," said Miss Parker. "No, they are not. And you can put that ruler away right now."

Steve reluctantly slid it back into his pocket, but he was far from convinced, and Miss Parker seemed to realize that she was going to have to provide a bit more detail if these particular students were ever going to trust her again.

"There was a Chinese thinker," she said. "He wrote a rather tedious and obvious treatise on war. Well, I thought it was obvious, but then I've been around since the Beginning. Anyway, he said, 'Keep your friends close and your enemies closer.'"

"So the Keres are your enemies?"

"Their loyalty does not lie with me," she said, as if that was sufficient explanation. "Now, what brought you here?"

"You don't know?"

"Would I have asked if I did?"

"But why not?" asked Steve. "If you're such a big deal, why don't you know what's going on?"

"Do you have any idea how big the Land of the Dead actually is?" she asked, in that way that teachers have of making you think that maybe they already told you this and now there was going to be a test. "Everything that ever lived and died? Can you even begin to comprehend?"

"Well, I . . ."

"And there's this school, which seemed like a good idea at the time but I have to tell you is more trouble every day, what with government requirements and inspections, parents constantly wanting meetings about their dull children, who they are inexplicably convinced are 'gifted,' and pupils who seem utterly incapable of just sitting still and learning things."

Her gimlet eye settled on Steve as a prime example of just that kind of recalcitrant pupil and he squirmed uneasily.

"I got taken into care," said Belladonna.

"I know. I'm really sorry about that, Belladonna, but Mrs. Warren has always poked her nose where it really doesn't belong. She was like that as a child and hasn't changed a bit."

"You knew her when—"

"She went to school here."

"Well, maybe you don't know her as well as you think. I got put with these foster parents and they seemed really nice at first, but it turns out they might not be human."

"What makes you think that?"

"They're living in a building that doesn't exist and using Belladonna to bring pieces of the Dark Spaces into this world, apparently," said Steve.

Miss Parker looked at him for a moment, her face calm but her eyes slightly narrowed.

"Say that again."

"I was having really strange dreams," said Belladonna. "Only it turned out they weren't dreams; the Proctors were drugging me and then taking me out during the night to . . . I don't know . . . make the bits of Darkness come. And now they're everywhere, all over Shady Gardens, standing in sort of groups and waiting."

"Shady Gardens?" said Miss Parker quietly. "That's where you're living?"

"Yes, but Steve has video of—"

"So they've found the Circle," muttered Miss Parker.

"Belladonna's been getting really sick, with headaches and things and the Wild Hunt said—"

"You called the Hunt?"

"Yes."

"Do you have any idea how dangerous they are?"

"Well, yes, but Belladonna needed to get away from the Proctors and we thought they might know where her Aunt Deirdre had gone."

"And did they?"

"No." Belladonna picked up where Steve left off: "But they said that it was probably me, that I was the one making the stones come and . . . well, all the things in my dreams. But they're not dreams, so we thought the best thing would probably be to look for the nine thingies that the parchment talked about."

"The parchment?"

"Edmund de Braes gave it to us. They turned out to be coins, nobles—"

"But they can only be seen by—"

"We know," said Steve. "We took Elsie with us."

"Elsie? But she can only haunt the school."

"We took a bit of the school along too," said Belladonna proudly. "It was Steve's idea. We took that little rug from the front door."

"Anyway," continued Steve, "we found the nobles, but there were only eight and the rhyme said that the other one was in the House of Ashes, so we went to the Land of the Dead to find it. Which is a bit annoying, really, because we could've just come upstairs instead of wandering all over creation and nearly getting killed."

Miss Parker looked at them both for a moment, then strode over to her desk and pressed a button.

"Hold my calls, Jane," she said. "Something's come up. I'll be out the rest of the day. See if Watson will cover sixth form Latin for me."

"Yes, Miss Parker," said the distant voice of Mrs. Jay's mousy assistant. "Is there anything I can —"

"No. Thank you."

They watched as Miss Parker clicked off the button and walked back to the bookcase. She was still carrying the lacrosse stick, and nothing could have looked more unlikely. Miss Parker may once have been the sporty type, but now it was hard to imagine any situation in which she would run. *I mean*, thought Belladonna, *she keeps her glasses on a little chain around her neck!*

"Stand back," said Miss Parker.

Belladonna and Steve backed away toward one of the windows.

"Oh, and close the blinds. We don't want anyone seeing this."

They obediently shut the window blinds. Miss Parker nodded, then held the lacrosse stick in front of her.

"*Aturrha-hadar,*" she intoned.

Belladonna jumped at the guttural sound. It was like the Words she spoke, and she knew what it meant.

"Darkness," she whispered.

"Very good," said Miss Parker. "Your Ancient Sumerian is coming along well."

Only she wasn't Miss Parker anymore. The lacrosse stick had collapsed in and telescoped up, until it was little more than the length of Steve's ruler, and her pointy bobbed hair seemed to shiver to its roots before running down her neck, over her shoulders, and nearly to the floor in two fat black braids, while the frumpy blue suit stretched and moved across her body like liquid until it re-formed again as dark blue robes clinging to Miss Parker's thin frame and dusting the floor. The sleeves trickled down her arms and draped themselves over her long white hands and her face assumed the pallor of death. Once the metamorphosis of her appearance was complete, the remains of the lacrosse stick retracted into her hand for a moment before emerging again and expanding into a huge silver-capped ebony staff inlaid with gleaming ivory and festooned with shreds of mourning veils.

Miss Parker stretched her arms and sighed happily.

"Oh, that feels good!" she said.

Belladonna and Steve just stared. Any relief they'd felt at Miss Parker's assurance that the Keres were her enemies vanished at the transformation—because now she looked like one of them.

"You're a Kere!" whispered Belladonna.

"What? Oh, don't be ridiculous, child. Open the door, Evans."

Steve did as he was told and heaved the bookcase open again. Miss Parker marched through, followed by Steve, but Belladonna hung back.

"You've done well," said Miss Parker, glancing back. "Now come with me."

Belladonna glanced back at the office door. She didn't want to follow Miss Parker down the green corridor that led to the Keres, but she took a deep breath, turned her back on the office, and walked back into the House of Ashes, pulling the door closed behind her. It was only after it clicked shut that she realized they weren't in the green corridor at all but in a vast obsidian hall bounded on each side by a forest of pillars six or seven deep. The ceiling was so high that it was lost in shadow, although she could see something moving up there, making slow languorous circles in the night air. The hall itself appeared to be empty, though Belladonna was aware of dozens of eyes watching in awe as the Queen of the Abyss strode through.

She ran to catch up with Miss Parker, who suddenly stopped and peered into the shadowy pillars on her right. Belladonna followed her gaze but could see nothing. Miss Parker waved a hand and the shadows crept away as if they were living things, revealing a man clad all in black, sharpening a large scythe.

"Hello, Edward," said Miss Parker.

The man in black bowed his head and continued working on his scythe.

"Busy day?"

"Not too bad."

Miss Parker smiled briefly and walked on to the center of the room, where she was suddenly surrounded by several small, hunched creatures that seemed more like rounded piles of old clothes and trash bags than anything else. She spoke quietly with them for a few moments, after which two scuttled off in different directions. She turned around, obviously expecting Belladonna to be right behind her.

"Come over here!" she said. "This is no time to be dawdling. Tell me about your foster parents."

Belladonna told her about Mr. and Mrs. Proctor and about Grandma Johnson trapped in a nonexistent room in the nonexistent building.

As she spoke, the two small creatures returned, each carrying a tray covered with a black cloth.

"How interesting," said Miss Parker, in a tone that suggested it wasn't interesting at all. "These are your things; take them."

She pulled the cloth from the trays and revealed the gifts that Belladonna and Steve had left for the guardians. They eagerly put everything back into their bags and raced to catch up with Miss Parker as she strode across the cavernous hall.

"Hurry," she said, without looking back. "We have to go."

They passed out of the hall and through a succession of dismal rooms.

"And these bad dreams . . . describe them to me."

"They lead me outside and Mr. Proctor puts something around my neck. Then . . . I say some Words, but it doesn't feel like it's me. It's as if I'm watching from a corner inside my head."

"Hm. Clever," muttered Miss Parker as they reached the foot of a spiral staircase. "Carry on."

"And then these stones appear. A stone circle. But it's not like any of the ones in Steve's mum's books. It looks new. And I keep saying Words and the Shadow People come."

They climbed the staircase in silence and Belladonna found herself staring at another of the spider curtains. She glanced back at Steve, who was on the stair behind her, and saw him shudder at the sight of the entwined arachnids.

"Bartamakh," muttered the Queen of the Abyss.

The spiders immediately sprang to life, crawling over one another away from the right-hand doorjamb. The effect was like a curtain drawing itself, and as soon as the opening was wide enough, Miss Parker marched through.

Belladonna felt the cold sting of night air on her cheek as she followed, stepping out onto the roof of one of the soaring towers of the House of Ashes.

"We must go to Mynydd Anhrefn," said Miss Parker calmly.

"Where?" said Steve.

"It's a mountain. Hop in."

Just as Belladonna was wondering what, exactly, they were supposed to hop into, the clouds parted and the bright moonlight illuminated the top of the tower.

Steve's mouth dropped open, and Belladonna felt for a moment as though her heart had stopped. She'd never seen anything like it. There, on the roof, a mere two meters away, was a large black chariot inlaid with gold and dripping with mourning crepe and the braided loops and tassels of funeral passementerie. It had two huge black wheels, the outer spokes of which were studded with deadly curved blades that glistened in the moonlight.

"Get a move on," said Miss Parker, in a tone most people use when they're urging the reluctant family dog to jump into the back seat.

Belladonna and Steve stepped into the chariot and looked around. There was no seat, just a narrow bar across the top, over which a set of black reins had been loosely draped. Belladonna peered into the darkness in an effort to make out what would be pulling the chariot, but all she could see was something large and dark shifting about in the shadows.

Miss Parker jumped in beside them, picked up the reins, and gave them a sharp tug.

"Come on, Odysseus!" she snapped. "Wake up!"

A growl issued from the shadows. The sort of growl that Belladonna had once heard from the lions at the zoo right before they had been fed. It was deep in the throat and so low it was felt more than it was heard.

The creature in the shadows slowly uncoiled itself and shuffled into the light, stretching its great leathery wings and tasting the air through its open beak.

Steve gasped and stepped back from the front of the chariot.

"That's a pterodactyl!" he whispered.

"Yes," said Miss Parker. "He's rather magnificent but terribly bad tempered."

She snapped the reins again and the pterodactyl hissed

at her, his deadly white teeth catching the moonlight and sending a shiver down Belladonna's spine, but he obediently took his place at the front of the chariot.

Belladonna shifted uneasily; she couldn't see how the whole heavy equipage was ever going to get airborne, but before she had time to really think about it, Miss Parker struck the chariot sharply with her staff.

"Aðhu-bakha!" she commanded.

The chariot slowly rose up and hovered about three feet above the top of the tower. Miss Parker snapped the reins again and the pterodactyl spread its huge wings and launched itself off the battlements, dragging the chariot behind as it plummeted toward the ground. Belladonna held her breath as the crenellated walls beneath rushed up to meet them. But just as she'd decided that there was no way they'd ever be able to pull out of their dive, the dinosaur caught an updraft and soared up and away, his wings beating lazily in the darkness.

The chariot shuddered as he hauled it upward, gaining altitude with each strike of his wings.

"He does this on purpose," said Miss Parker. "Always so dramatic."

The mourning cloth and passementerie snapped and fluttered in the wind as the chariot circled the House of Ashes twice, while clouds of bats poured from the tops of the towers and formed a throbbing escort.

Belladonna looked down as they sped over the lake, the inky waters shimmering in the moonlight. Ahead were the forests that bounded the lake and the sweeping expanse of desert with its huge, knife-edged dunes.

The journey to the lake seemed so long ago and she wondered what Elsie and her parents were doing now. Had they stayed at the lake, waiting for their return? Or had they driven back to the spectral version of the town? She glanced up at Miss Parker, the Queen of the Abyss, as she stood tall and regal, her hair and robes barely moving in the icy wind, the black reins wound around her long white fingers, and for the first time she thought that everything really might work out alright. After all, the Proctors were nothing, less than nothing when compared to this woman who had seen the worlds born and would probably see them die. How could they even think that whatever they had planned could possibly work?

"Miss Parker?" she yelled, straining to be heard above the clash and clatter of the wind and the chariot.

"Yes?"

"What did the Keres mean when they said the walls between the worlds were coming down?"

Miss Parker turned her head slowly and looked at Belladonna.

"What?" she said.

And in that moment, that split second, Belladonna noticed something in the eyes of the Queen of the Abyss. Something that didn't belong, something that she immediately knew the ruler of the Land of the Dead had never experienced before, and something that shattered her new optimism.

She saw fear.

23

The Ninth Noble

THE CHARIOT RATTLED and hissed as it flew through the night sky. Belladonna stared into the darkness, afraid of what she had seen in Miss Parker's eyes and unwilling to make things worse by asking any more questions.

Steve seemed not to have noticed. He was gripping the bar at the front of the chariot as though he were on the best fairground ride ever, his eyes shining as he watched the powerful beating of the pterodactyl's wings. He noticed Belladonna watching him.

"This is superb!" he yelled, straining to be heard above the howling wind.

Belladonna smiled. She had to admit, all things considered, that it actually was pretty superb. *I mean,* she thought, *that's an actual dinosaur!* And they were flying. Really flying.

She looked up at the starless sky of the Land of the Dead and at its shining blue moon, half hidden behind burgundy clouds. All was quiet except for the wind, the steady thump-thump of Odysseus' wings, and the occasional high-pitched chirp from the bats that crowded on either side of the chariot. It was all so beautiful. She held on to the crossbar, closed her eyes, and leaned back, drinking in the wind and the freedom of the flight. Tomorrow she would have to face the Proctors, but tonight she was flying with the Queen of the Abyss and she decided that she really needed to take a page out of Steve's book and just enjoy the moments that were fun without thinking too much about a future over which she really had no control.

"We're here," said Miss Parker eventually, her voice cutting through the sound of the chariot and the roaring wind with no more effort than if she were back in her office.

The pterodactyl wheeled to the left and shot toward the jagged peak of a huge black mountain. It circled the summit twice, then plunged toward the ground with a sick-making lurch. As far as Belladonna could make out, there was nowhere to land on the massy crag, but the great beast knew otherwise and brought the chariot in to a surprisingly gentle landing on one of the few areas that was reasonably flat.

Once they were on the ground, the bats flew off to roost in the caves and canyons of the mountain while Odysseus wrapped his wings around his muscular body, hissed once at his mistress, and curled up under an overhanging boulder.

"We'll have to climb the rest of the way," said Miss Parker, stepping down lightly. "Follow me."

She marched off, leaving Belladonna and Steve running to catch up. The ground was littered with rocks and boulders of various sizes, but the Queen of the Abyss seemed oblivious. She strode through the wasteland as if it were nothing more than a park on a summer's day, and even when she started to climb, it seemed to take no effort at all, while Belladonna and Steve lagged behind, struggling to find hand- and footholds in the crumbling black rock.

Belladonna strained to see the summit. It had seemed clear when the chariot had circled it, but now it was shrouded in dense black clouds that roiled around the serrated pinnacle, and the closer they got, the darker it became. Soon rain began to fall, then sleet bit into their faces and fingers, but still the Queen of the Abyss climbed on as lightning flashed among the clouds, and the thunder rumbled around their ears.

Belladonna had to admit that the mountain was certainly a great hiding place—no one would come here unless they absolutely had to. But the sheer effort involved made her wonder all the more about the coins. English coins with Welsh names. Why were they so important? When was *someone* going to let them in on the secret?

She was wet and freezing and the more she thought about the coins and the cryptic "explanations" they got from everybody they spoke to, the more irritated she became. She glanced over at Steve. His teeth were clenched in an effort to stop them chattering and he seemed to be trying to concentrate on the next handhold rather than looking ahead into the storm. This seemed like a good idea, so she made an effort to drive all speculation about the coins from her mind, put her head down, and just get on with it.

She was still trying to think only about the next step when the howling of the wind and the rumble and crash of the lightning were shattered by laughter. She looked up. Miss Parker was standing above them, completely dry and composed.

"Get a move on," she said. "I've got a parent/teacher meeting at four."

"We're going as fast as we can!" yelled Steve. "It's freezing up here and I think the storm is getting worse!"

"Oh, it is," said Miss Parker. "I designed it that way."

She smiled briefly, then turned toward the storm and raised her staff.

"Megar!"

It was like turning off a switch. No sooner was the word out of her mouth than the rain, thunder, and lightning stopped and the clouds dispersed through the sky like ink in water.

Belladonna didn't know what she expected to see, but it certainly wasn't what she was looking at: a small rocky waste without even a cairn to mark it as the summit.

"There's nothing here," she said, trying to keep the disappointment out of her voice.

"That's the idea."

Miss Parker held her staff out and pointed it at the ground in the center of the mountaintop.

"Erpaд!"

At first nothing happened and Belladonna wondered

if it was going to work. She knew that the word meant "reveal," but the barren ground seemed to be unwilling to show whatever it was Miss Parker wanted to see.

Crack!

The noise was loud, like the snapping of a heavy branch, and Belladonna watched as the ground in front of them seemed to split. At first the opening was slight, nothing more than a thin strip, but soon there was a second crack and a third and a fourth and before long, there was a gaping wound in the plateau, a chasm into the mountain's heart.

The Queen of the Abyss stamped the earth twice with her staff, and the earth began to shake beneath their feet. Belladonna and Steve almost lost their balance, but Miss Parker never had so much as a single hair out of place as slowly, painfully, something began to rise out of the hole. It was a rock, a black boulder, eroded into an almost perfect sphere but in every other way no different from any of the other rocks on the mountain.

Belladonna watched as it rolled slowly across the ground to the feet of Miss Parker, who just stared at it.

"I had thought," she said, "when I concealed this here, that there would never be a need for it to be seen again."

She sighed and stared at it for a few moments. Moments stretched to minutes, and Belladonna and Steve glanced at each other. Why didn't she just get on with it?

Apparently the same thought had been going through Miss Parker's head, because she turned and looked at Belladonna.

"Well, go on. What are you waiting for?"

"What?"

"I concealed it, but it can only be opened by a Spell-binder. It was agreed . . . we agreed that it should be so."

"Why?" said Steve.

"It was thought best that no one should be able to re-trieve all the nobles, and without all, they are useless. It was decided that only a Spellbinder should be able to do so and then only to prevent a return of the Dark Times. Open the rock, Belladonna."

"Hang on." Steve stepped in front of Belladonna. "I've seen this sort of thing in films. How do we know you're not just going to take it and kill us? Or leave us here, which would probably be the same thing."

"Are you questioning me?" Miss Parker looked as though she could barely grasp the idea that someone might be so foolish.

"No, he's not! It's fine!" said Belladonna, trying to get around Steve to the rock.

He was having none of it, however, and demonstrated some of the guarding skills he'd picked up in football—no matter which way she tried to move, he was always in her way.

"Steve!" she hissed. "Stop it!"

"So what do they do? The coins. We found the names on them. Welsh names."

"Amazing," said Miss Parker. "Really amazing."

"What?"

"You, Mr. Evans. After untold millennia in all of the Nine Worlds, I finally find myself genuinely surprised."

"Why?"

"Because a few months ago I doubt whether you had ever noticed Belladonna Johnson, and yet here you are, a true Paladin, putting yourself between her and me when you have to know that I could destroy you utterly with the merest movement of my little finger."

"Isn't that my job?"

"So it is. However, questioning me is not. No Paladin has ever dared to question the Queen of the Abyss."

"Well, maybe he should have," said Steve. "It seems like you made a right mess of things last time. Maybe if Edmund de Braes or the last Spellbinder, whatsername . . . Margaret something . . . anyway, if they had asked what the heck you thought you were doing, maybe we wouldn't have to be here now."

"He has a point," said Belladonna. "If this is all really so important, why doesn't anyone tell us what's going on? Why do we have to keep figuring out these stupid rhymes?"

"Everything is there for a reason, Spellbinder, even the rhymes. The journey is as important as the destination—"

"Look!" said Steve. "See? There you go again! What on earth is that supposed to mean?"

"It means," said Miss Parker, her teeth gritted in an attempt to stay calm, "that when the time comes for you to take on the Empress, you must be prepared and we must be sure that you are the right ones for the job."

"Wait . . ." Belladonna glanced sharply at the Queen of the Abyss. "The rhymes are part of the test?"

"Of course. As I said, all Spellbinders must be tested.

We must know that they and their Paladins have the mettle for the challenges that lie ahead. Too much is at stake to merely hope for the best."

"But what do you mean, the 'right ones'?" asked Steve. "Are there other Spellbinders? Other Paladins?"

"Not at the moment. There can be only one at a time. One girl is chosen as needed."

"By who?"

"Decisions that affect all Nine Worlds are made by the Old Ones, and whenever the fabric that holds the worlds together is threatened, we designate a Spellbinder from among the Chime Children."

"The Chime Children?"

"Children born in the chime hours, or more correctly on the striking of the chimes."

"No," said Steve. "That wasn't really an explanation. You can't explain a word with the same word. That's not how it works."

"The chime hours, Mr. Evans, are midnight and three o'clock in the morning."

"Wait, you mean all children born at that hour are Chime Children? There must be an awful lot of them."

"There are. Why do you think I run a school?"

Belladonna had to admit that it seemed rather an odd hobby for the Queen of the Dead.

"Are we all Chime Children, then?" she asked. "Everyone at Dullworth's, I mean."

"No, but there are more than the average number."

"And what does it mean? What makes Chime Children special?" asked Steve.

"They can see ghosts," said Miss Parker matter-of-factly. "That is, they have the *ability* to see ghosts. Most go through life without seeing a single one, of course. You, for one, Mr. Evans, I rather imagine would never have seen a single spirit if it hadn't been for Belladonna here. Didn't you ever wonder why, once you saw one, you could suddenly see them all?"

"Umm . . . Not really."

"It's still difficult to believe that you, of all people, are the Paladin," sighed Miss Parker.

"Didn't you choose me too?"

"No, we did not," she said, as if the very idea were ludicrous. "We can only choose the Spellbinder; the Paladin chooses himself."

"But I didn't," protested Steve, as if he'd been accused of breaking something.

"Not consciously, of course," snapped Miss Parker.

"Well, what does seeing ghosts have to do with saving the Nine Worlds from the return of the Dark Times?"

"The Spellbinder and Paladin must be able to move between the worlds. The ability to see the Dead is merely the outward indication of that ability."

"Hang on," said Steve. "If loads of people have the ability to see ghosts, like you said, then why don't they? Why isn't everyone just having nice afternoon chats with all their dead relatives and inviting them over for Sunday dinner?"

"You really are obtuse sometimes, Evans," sighed Miss Parker. "A person may have an innate ability to play the piano or the violin, but they'll never know it unless they get the opportunity to play, and even then, it will take plenty of practice before they realize their true potential."

"But I could already see ghosts," said Belladonna. "I didn't just start when this started."

"I know. We couldn't believe our luck."

"Your luck?"

"Someone who can already see ghosts as easily as you has the potential to be the greatest Spellbinder of them all, and we knew that to defeat the Empress of the Dark Spaces, we would need a most extraordinary girl. That was why we took the risk on one so young."

"Because you thought there would be time."

"And now there is none, so I strongly suggest you open the rock."

"So what you're saying, really," began Steve, "is that if something happens to Belladonna or me, you'll just pick somebody else?"

Miss Parker sighed again and rolled her eyes. "Yes."

"Okay. So you don't really have our best interests at heart, then, do you? I mean, if you're just thinking, 'Oh, I broke this one, let's go and get another,' then how are we supposed to believe that the things you tell us to do are really the best way of going about things?"

"That's true," said Belladonna, suddenly regarding the Queen of the Abyss in a whole new light. "I mean, we've only been doing this since October and now you're going to send us off to tackle the Empress head-on. If she can only come through on the Day of Crows, and can only do *that* if I'm there saying the Words, then why don't Steve and I just hide out for a day until it's over?"

Miss Parker looked from one to the other. "Alright. Alright. I'll think about it. But could you *please* open the rock now so that you are armed just in case. And I am not deliberately trying to get you killed, Mr. Evans, nor am I going to leave you on top of this mountain, tempting though the idea may be."

Belladonna glanced at Steve, who nodded and stepped aside. She stood in front of the round stone and stared at it.

"What am I supposed to do?"

"Oh, in the name of all that's holy! I don't know! I told you—the rock can be opened only by the Spellbinder. If I knew how to open it, I would have done it already!"

Belladonna bit her lip and turned her attention back to the rock. She closed her eyes and tried to concentrate, waiting for the Words. Then she knew. She kneeled down, placed a finger on the stone, and whispered the Words. They were in the ancient tongue, but she knew their meaning: *Give to me what is mine!*

For a moment it seemed as if nothing would happen, but then the boulder suddenly swelled, like a cake in the oven, and just as suddenly collapsed in on itself, leaving only a pile of black dust. Belladonna waved her hand slightly and a breeze surged across the plateau, blowing the dust away and leaving a gold coin, the Ninth Noble, gleaming on the ground.

"That is just so cool," said Steve in a tone of awestruck wonder.

Belladonna picked up the coin and turned it over in her hand.

"What name is on this one?"

"Skatha."

Belladonna stood up and put the coin in her pocket. The Queen of the Abyss muttered something about pulling teeth and strode to the edge of the plateau.

"Odysseus! *Аðhu-bakha!*"

There was a distant hiss, then the sound of claws on rock, then a grinding noise and the thumping of massive wings as the pterodactyl took to the air. Belladonna watched as the chariot made a slow circle through the sky in front of them, then came in and stopped, hovering a foot above the summit.

"Climb in," said Miss Parker. "There's no time to waste."

They scrambled into the waiting chariot beside her and took a firm hold of the crossbar. The Queen of the Abyss picked up the reins and gave them a sharp snap.

"Home!"

Odysseus hissed once, then pulled the chariot around, circled the mountain once more, and headed out into the night sky as the clouds of bats emerged from their caves and crags and escorted their queen back across her domain to the House of Ashes.

24

The Last Spellbinder

THE RETURN JOURNEY seemed much shorter, as return journeys usually do, and it wasn't long before they were crossing the great hall of the House of Ashes once more.

The man in black who had been sharpening his scythe had gone and Belladonna couldn't suppress a shudder. He had seemed so ordinary when he had spoken to Miss Parker before, but she knew he was what most people dreaded.

Miss Parker must have seen the expression on her face because she put one long, elegant white hand on Belladonna's shoulder and patted it gently.

"It isn't always dreadful," she said. "For some it is a longed-for release and for others just the final curtain on a well-lived life."

"But not for everyone," said Belladonna.

"No, not for everyone. There will always be those whose deaths are untimely, but there you go. Such is life, as the French say."

She smiled cheerfully, but Belladonna felt far from comforted. It reminded her too much of the car crash that killed her parents.

She turned away. She needed to think about something else.

"Miss Parker?"

"Yes?"

"What do the names mean?"

"They are the names of the stones," said Miss Parker, the sharp click of her footsteps echoing through the hall.

"The ones in the circle in my dream?"

"I think you will find that you were not dreaming."

"Wait." Steve stopped walking. "So there really is a stone circle in Shady Gardens?"

The Queen of the Abyss stopped striding through her palace and turned around.

"Indeed."

"The Wild Hunt said the stones were important to her. To the Empress."

"The Hunt is dangerous and not to be trusted."

"But are they right?" asked Steve. "Is this circle special in some way?"

"They are all special. Or they were, but together they were too powerful. That is why we got rid of most of them. She was searching for the Fortress of the Sisters, you see."

"The what?"

"She didn't find it. But she did find out about the stones. She realized that some were more powerful than others, those at the junctions."

"Hang on," said Steve. "Are you talking about ley lines?"

"What are ley lines?" asked Belladonna.

"Some people think that there are sort of invisible lines joining all the stone circles and megaliths and that the lines themselves have some kind of power. Of course, most people think those people are nutjobs. But they're not, are they?"

"Not entirely," said Miss Parker. "The lines do connect the circles, but for the most part their effect is negligible. However, some circles are intersected by many lines."

"Like circuits?"

"Yes. She discovered that these had more power than she had ever imagined. We had, of course, taken the precaution of destroying many of them, but as her power increased, she discovered that she could call them back. As the circles were restored, so was the power of the few great circles at the junction of the lines. No matter where she was, there was always a stone circle nearby. She became quite adept at harnessing their power to her will. Impressive, really, if it weren't so disastrous."

She sighed, then drew herself up and continued striding through the great obsidian hall. Belladonna and Steve ran to catch up.

"Wait!" Belladonna caught at the shreds of mourning veils that trailed behind her. "Wait!"

Miss Parker spun around. "What!? Time is of the essence."

"She called the stones. You said she called the stones."

"Yes."

"Well, how did she know . . . How could she . . . Was she a Spellbinder?" Belladonna hardly dared ask the question, though deep inside she already knew the answer.

Miss Parker hesitated, then nodded. "Yes, she was. She was the last Spellbinder. Margaret de Morville."

"You're joking!" Steve's eyes were wide.

"No. It was a misjudgment on my part. A disaster. It won't be allowed to happen again."

She marched off once more, to the far end of the hall, through the hidden door and into her office. Belladonna and Steve followed, their minds racing.

"The Empress of the Dark Spaces was originally just human? Like me and Belladonna?"

"Well, not really like you, Evans. But yes. Her character, however, was not all that we had hoped."

"No duh!"

"But how can we . . ." began Belladonna.

"Yes, how can we defeat her when she's a Spellbinder as well?" said Steve. "And shouldn't you have picked someone older?"

"Of course. But I was sure the Empress was safe for a few more years, a decade at least, and that would have given us time, you see. But that wretched necromancer ruined everything."

"Doctor Ashe?"

"Yes."

"But we stopped him," said Belladonna. "And the Hunt carried him off."

"Yes, well done, by the way. But the thing is, he weakened the boundary between the worlds and the Dark Spaces and created a hole. A small hole, no more than a pinprick, but that is all it takes, isn't it? One area of weakness. We had known it was coming; that's why we decided to select a new Spellbinder, but we didn't know about Ashe. His plan to bring the Empress back may have failed, but he succeeded in accelerating events and making the Empress's escape all but inevitable."

"But why does she want to return?"

"It doesn't matter. We will defeat her again. In any case, to do what she wants, she would need to find all nine Nomials. You have already found two of them, and without those she cannot succeed. All we need to do now is prevent her from wreaking any more havoc in your world and ensure that she is never again able to even contemplate escaping from the Dark Spaces."

She tapped her staff lightly on the ground and the Queen of the Abyss fell away from her like dust, leaving the familiar figure of Miss Parker in her ill-fitting navy blue suit. She returned the lacrosse stick to its frame and sat down at her desk.

"But that's just stupid!" said Steve.

Miss Parker turned around. "I beg your pardon? Are you suggesting that you, a mere human child, have more insight on this matter than I, the Queen of the Abyss, who has lived since time began?"

"Um . . . well, yes, actually."

Miss Parker looked him up and down, then turned back to her desk and removed some paper from a drawer.

"The thing is," said Steve, "the Nomials are just in Mrs. Jay's desk drawer. Anyone could get them. I mean, I could probably do it and I'm no master thief or anything. And, honestly, in films whenever there's a secret place that can't be found and the world would be destroyed if it *was* found, the bad guys *always* find it."

"This is real life, Mr. Evans. Real life is not like films."

"Actually, it kind of is," said Steve. "Well, so far, anyway."

"I think he's right," said Belladonna.

"No, he is not," said Miss Parker. She looked from one to the other, then seemed to relent. "You are right about tonight, though. There are dark times ahead and it would be foolish to risk the Spellbinder at such an early stage. Without you they cannot open a portal."

"Tonight? But the Day of Crows is tomorrow!"

"It is the eve that is important. And tomorrow begins at midnight. Here are notes excusing you from classes for the rest of the day. Mr. Evans, I suggest you take Miss Johnson to your home and stay there until tomorrow. At three o'clock tomorrow morning, the veil between the Worlds will be little more than smoke. That is when she will try to ride the Darkness in. If you are not there, Miss Johnson, they will have to wait. I'll send someone else to deal with the Proctors. By tomorrow morning, Shady Gardens will have vanished once more and we will have bought one more year in which to prepare you both."

Belladonna took her note. Steve reached for his, but as he did so, he started to cough again and this time, in addition to the wisp of smoke, a few sparks flew from his mouth and ignited the note.

"What on earth . . . !?" Miss Parker blew the flames out. "Have you been drinking dragon milk?"

"Um . . . Just a bit. A taste."

"Have you no sense at all? I despair, I really do. To think the fate of the Nine Worlds depends on you two! Go. Now. Get out of my sight."

"Why can't *you* do it?" asked Steve, not moving. "I mean, you're the ruler of the Land of the Dead. Why can't you just go out there and stop them?"

"I cannot leave my domain."

"But you can be here in school and this isn't the Land of the Dead."

"And what makes you think that?"

"Well . . . because . . . it isn't . . . is it?"

"It is both of the Living and of the Dead. We created it for a purpose, but I cannot go beyond its doors."

She pulled a stack of exercise books toward her, opened the first, and began marking. Belladonna and Steve glanced at each other, then walked to the door.

"Miss Parker?" said Belladonna, turning back.

"Yes?"

"Would you have let the manticore or the Keres actually kill us?"

"Of course. There's no point in tests if you don't adhere to the results, is there? I had to know whether you were worthy. Now get off with you; I have work to do."

Steve stepped out onto the science lab landing at school, but as Belladonna followed, she suddenly felt a searing pain in her left temple. It was more than a headache, greater than anything she had ever felt. She raised a hand to her head, but even as she did so, she felt herself stumble. Steve looked back, then leapt forward to catch her just before she hit the ground.

"Belladonna!"

"Owww." Belladonna slowly opened her eyes. The pain wasn't as intense, but it was still more than anything she'd ever felt.

"Are you alright?" said Elsie, suddenly manifesting behind Steve's shoulder and peering into Belladonna's face. "You look awfully pale."

"And that's really something, coming from a ghost," grinned Steve, clearly relieved.

Belladonna smiled weakly and scrambled to her feet.

"I'm fine."

"You really don't look fine," said Steve.

"Don't make a fuss," said Belladonna, tucking her hair behind her ears. "Let's go."

They started downstairs and Elsie disappeared, only to reappear at the bottom.

"Let's go? Let's go where? What's happening? What was the House of Ashes like? Come on, I'm falling behind! Did you find the Queen of the Abyss? What did she say about the coins? And how did you end up back here?"

"Well, there were —" began Belladonna.

"Wait," said Steve, his eyes narrowing with suspicion as he looked at Elsie. "Did you know about Miss Parker?"

"Know what about Miss Parker?" asked Elsie, all wide-eyed Edwardian innocence.

"That she was the Queen of the Abyss."

"You're joking! Miss Parker? The one with the dreadful suits and the positively criminal haircut?"

"Yes."

"She was here all the time?"

"Yup."

"Then why did you have to go through all that palaver with the lift and the drive and the House of Ashes and . . ."

". . . and guardians. There were seven guardians in the House of Ashes and at least three of them tried to kill us. And all the time, we could've just gone upstairs and pressed the buzzer."

"She said it was a test," said Belladonna. "She had to know if we were 'worthy.'"

"Could you have died?" asked Elsie.

Steve nodded. Elsie thought about this for a moment and then smiled, her eyes sparkling.

"That is absolutely topping!" she gushed. "It's like something out of an adventure story. Did you have to use the plastic ruler thing? I wish I'd been there!"

Steve rolled his eyes, then suddenly coughed again. More smoke and a few more sparks.

"Crikey!" said Elsie. "Is that from dragon milk?"

Steve nodded. "Yes. My throat's really raspy." He noticed Belladonna's expression and shrugged. "I know, I know . . . it's my own fault. But, you know, if you don't try new things, you'll never learn anything."

"There's a bit of a difference between trying a vindaloo or duck-web soup and slurping down dragon milk," pointed out Belladonna.

"But not much. Duck-web soup? What on earth is that?"

"Never mind. Come on, let's get out of here."

"Where?" said Elsie. "What's happening? You still haven't told me what's going on."

"Miss Parker . . . the Queen of the Abyss . . . she told us to just hide out until after the Day of Crows. She said they can't bring the Empress through without me there to say the Words."

"But . . . what about the Proctors? They're still your foster parents."

"She said she'd send someone else to deal with them," explained Steve.

Elsie looked from one to the other. "Did she tell you what to do with the coins if it doesn't work?"

"No."

"Well, that doesn't sound right." For once Elsie seemed genuinely worried. "There should always be a plan B. Look . . . why don't you take the rug. Please."

"But . . ."

"I'll see what I can find out . . . just in case. I mean, I'm sure it'll be alright. But I'll see what I can find out. So take the rug, in case I need to find you."

"Okay, but . . ."

"No. Promise me."

"We promise," said Belladonna.

Elsie nodded and watched as Steve got the old piece of carpet from its tray inside the front door and rolled it up.

"Good luck," she said and vanished.

"Right," said Steve. "I think we should go the back

way through the park and stay off the streets as much as possible."

Belladonna nodded and followed him through the school, out the back door, and down to the park gate.

"Belladonna?" he said, pushing the gate open.

"Yes?"

"You won't tell anybody about this, will you?"

"About what?"

"About staying at mine."

"Oh, criminy. Right, like I'm going to go back to school and brag about staying at your house. I don't think."

Steve grinned, clearly relieved, and they made their way across the small park, striding through the wet grass and pausing only once—to watch the ducks in the lake.

Belladonna breathed in the wintry air. It was still overcast and cold but seemed positively springlike in comparison to the gloom of the House of Ashes.

"I'm thinking about trying out for the under-15s," said Steve.

"Football?"

"No, tiddlywinks. Of course football! D'you think it'll be okay?"

"Why wouldn't it be?"

"Well, with practices and everything. D'you think I'll be able to do that and . . . you know, save the world from time to time?"

Belladonna grinned. "Maybe you'll need a special permission note from the Queen of the Dead."

Steve laughed as they left the park and started walking up Spicer Street.

"You live here?" asked Belladonna. "I always thought you lived above the shop."

"Eugh. That would be depressing. Though my Dad spends so much time there, he might as well. No, we live up at the top here. It's a bit of a walk, I'm afraid. I don't usually go this way. It's faster to go by town."

"That's okay."

Belladonna gazed up at the mottled gray sky and considered the events of the past few days. It had been a surprise discovering that Miss Parker was actually the Queen of the Abyss, but it made her feel safer. Just knowing that she was at the school, right there where they could speak to her whenever they wanted, seemed to make everything a bit more manageable. She felt less alone, less stranded with a role she didn't truly understand and a responsibility she was only beginning to appreciate. But now Miss Parker was going to fix everything, and once the Day of Crows had passed, she felt confident that her grandmother would return and she'd be able to go back to living at home with her parents. She smiled to herself and tucked her hair behind her ears. There were the first glimmerings of green on the branches of the trees along the road, and in the afternoon quiet she could hear birds singing and courting as they sensed spring in the air.

She didn't hear the car at all.

It was just suddenly there, screeching to a halt in front of them.

"Belladonna! Run!" Steve dropped his bag and reached for the ruler, but before he could get his hand on it, Mr. Proctor was out of the car and hit him hard across the face.

Steve staggered backward and stumbled, dazed, to the pavement.

Belladonna tried to run, but it was no good. Mr. Proctor grabbed her and threw her into the back of the car, jumping in after her and slamming the door as Mrs. Proctor turned the wheel and sped away.

"Stupid girl," spat Mr. Proctor, grabbing her backpack and throwing it out of the window.

Mrs. Proctor reached back.

"Give me her hand!"

Belladonna struggled as Mr. Proctor tried to force her arm toward his wife's hand.

"No! Leave me alone!"

He slapped her hard once and thrust her wrist into Mrs. Proctor's grasp.

Belladonna gasped, suddenly breathless as the cold grip sapped her strength. She twisted and strained to see out of the back window. She could just make out Steve in the distance, scrambling to his feet, the sword in his hand. Then she began to feel the darkness enveloping her, and felt herself slipping away.

She knew that he would go back. That he would get Elsie and that they would try their best. But there was nothing they could do. Only the Nine Nobles could stop the stones, stop the Shadow People, and stop the Empress. And Steve only had eight.

The ninth, Skatha, was in her pocket.

25

The Day of Crows

BELLADONNA WOKE UP slowly. She was back in her room in Shady Gardens, lying on the bed, her head pounding. She got up and tried the door, which was locked, of course. She went back to the bed and sat listening as the clock on a nearby church struck every hour and every quarter hour. It was half past two. Only half an hour to go.

She took the Ninth Noble out of her pocket. She had to hide it. She couldn't believe they hadn't found it already, although there wasn't much she or they could do with just one. Still . . . she took off her shoe, dropped the coin into it, and put it back on again, then she went to the window and looked down. Mr. Proctor was in the center of Shady Gardens, setting up a little table. It was very dark.

She sat back on the bed and tried to think positively. Miss Parker had said that she would send someone. It would be alright. The someone would arrive and defeat the Proctors and then she would go home.

She was still trying to convince herself when there

was a loud noise outside and a sudden flash. She ran to the window again, but there was nothing to see—just Mr. Proctor and his folding table and a faint smell of fireworks.

She went back to the bed and racked her brains. Fireworks. There hadn't been any fireworks in her dream. . . .

At two forty-five she heard the lock on the bedroom door click and Mrs. Proctor stepped inside.

"It's time," she said. "Come on."

Belladonna got up and followed her down the stairs.

"Are you a Kere?" she asked.

"Yes."

"So that's how you can make people think they remember things? Like Mrs. Lazenby and the policemen?"

"Humans are laughably weak," said Mrs. Proctor.

"You're going to call the Empress."

"No, you are."

"And then . . . can I go?" She had a feeling her cause was lost, but a flicker of hope remained.

"No, my dear," laughed Mrs. Proctor. "The Dark Spaces cannot give up one of its own. There must be balance. A life for a life. It will give us the Empress but will take another in return. I doubt you'll last long; the legends say it is a hard place."

Belladonna stared at her. This couldn't be happening. There had to be something she could do. She was the Spellbinder. It was supposed to mean something. She was supposed to be special. But there was nothing. No Words came, just desolation and the faintest of hopes that Mrs. Parker's "someone" would arrive in time.

Mrs. Proctor held the front door open and followed Belladonna down the concrete steps to the central garden.

"Ready?"

Mr. Proctor nodded. Mrs. Proctor turned to Belladonna.

"Raise your hands."

Belladonna looked around, searching the shadows for any sign that someone was waiting for their chance to strike and save her. Mr. Proctor grinned.

"Expecting help?"

Belladonna looked at him sharply. He stepped aside and revealed a pile of mangled black feathers.

"It'll take more than a few Night Ravens to stop us," he cackled. "The centuries have dulled the skills of the Queen of the Dead, but we have been waiting and honing ours. We are sharp as damascene swords and this time the Empress will rise. When the—"

"That's enough," snapped Mrs. Proctor. "Raise your hands, Spellbinder."

Belladonna did as she was told. All hope was gone. There was nothing she could do.

Mrs. Proctor leaned over her and went through her pockets. She smirked at the packets of Parma Violets and put them on the table. Mr. Proctor led Belladonna to a spot near the center of the gardens and turned her until she was facing the moon. She looked up; it wasn't as bright as the blue moon in the Land of the Dead, but it was full and shining, though partially obscured by clouds.

"Wait!"

Mrs. Proctor scuttled over to them.

"Shoes."

Belladonna's heart sank. Mrs. Proctor took her right shoe, shook it, and put it back. Then she took the left shoe and smiled at the rattle. She tipped it up and the coin dropped into her hand.

"Well, well," said Mr. Proctor. "I always wondered what those things looked like."

Belladonna's mind was racing. She knew she couldn't save the world, that these were almost certainly her last moments, but she wasn't going to let them have that coin. That, at least, she could do.

She spun around as they were admiring the noble and struck it from Mrs. Proctor's hand. Mr. Proctor grunted and hit her hard. She fell to the ground, gasping, but it was too late—the glittering coin twirled above their heads, fell to the ground, and was gone.

"Where is it?" screamed Mrs. Proctor.

"There! It landed right there!"

"I can't see it!"

They turned on Belladonna.

"What have you done? Where is it?"

"You can't have it," muttered Belladonna.

"What?" Mr. Proctor grabbed her and hoisted her off the ground. "What have you done to it? Bring it back!"

"I can't," said Belladonna, smiling. "It can only be seen by the Dead. The Living can only see them when they touch our skin."

"Only be seen by the Dead?"

"By someone with a true heart. I'll bet you don't know a single person like that."

Mr. Proctor dropped her to the ground in disgust, stalked back to the table, and picked something up. Belladonna slipped her shoes back on and stood up as he returned and placed it around her neck.

It was an amulet. A triangular amulet with a dark stone at its center.

"It's a Nomial!" whispered Belladonna.

"Shut up," said Mr. Proctor.

She reached up and touched it, but Mr. Proctor slapped her hand away.

"Begin!" intoned Mrs. Proctor, her human disguise falling away like oil until she stood in her true form: a sleek, black-eyed, ebony-winged Kere.

"Begin!" said Mr. Proctor, as his form too fell away, revealing what at first seemed to be another man, but as he turned toward the center of the circle, Belladonna could see that he was yet another creature from mankind's collective nightmares.

He was tall and thin, thin enough for his bones to be seen stretching against their dark red envelope. His legs were mere spikes that dug into the ground like spear points, and his hands were bony claws. But it was his face that struck terror into her heart.

He didn't have one.

It was just an oval, with no features whatsoever, dark red and smooth, and framed by greasy locks of long brown hair.

"What . . . what are you?" was all she managed to say.

"I am an Allu," he said, though Belladonna had no idea how he was able to speak. "Like the Kere, we wait for death. We have waited since the sons of Marduk ruled the Mesopotamian plains. Waited for the Darkness to take its rightful dominion. Waited for this night."

As he spoke, Belladonna became aware of the Shadow People. They were moving closer and were much more solid than they had ever been before. She could see them clearly as they crossed the open space of the gardens and formed a huge circle around Belladonna and the demon creatures.

The Kere and the Allu raised their hands, as if in supplication, and the Shadow People began to move. Around and around, always at the same speed and without a sound.

At first, Belladonna just watched, fascinated, but slowly she became aware of a low rumbling, as if a heavy truck were driving by. She looked at the Shadow People. Were they causing it? They never changed their pace, never wavered, just walked around and around.

Gradually, almost imperceptibly, the rumbling became louder, and soon Belladonna could see the dirt at her feet dancing with the vibration. And still the Shadow People walked.

"Make them rise, Spellbinder! Make them rise!"

Belladonna was about to refuse when the central stone in the Nomial around her neck began to glow. It was becoming hot too; she could feel it through her clothes. But it wasn't the comforting warmth of a winter fire or the life-giving heat of the sun—it was the stifling heat of fever, like a disease coursing through her veins. She tried to ignore it, to concentrate on what was happening, but she felt sick. Hot and sick. Her ears were ringing and she began to shiver. And then, suddenly, she had the sensation of something crawling on her skin. No, not on her. *In her.* There was someone inside her head, shoving her aside, and she no longer had the strength to resist.

Then the Words came. The Words from her dream.

"Sag-en-tar na szi."

Guardians of stone, arise.

"Sag-en-tar na szi."

She kept repeating them, over and over, until their meaning seemed gone and the syllables were just sounds rolling around the circle, joining with the steps of the Shadow People and disappearing into the dark. Then, suddenly, directly opposite where she was standing, two stones suddenly broke through the earth and shot up, framing the moon between them. They were each about eight feet high and roughly carved.

Belladonna gasped and stepped backward, but the Allu moved her back into position facing the two stones. As he did so, other stones broke the surface until she was standing in a circle of nine mighty megaliths.

And still the Shadow People walked. Then, slowly, some of their number separated themselves from the ring and stood on either side of the two central stones.

Belladonna knew this was the end. She wanted to turn and run, but the someone else inside her mind was speaking different Words now. She could hear herself speaking them unhesitatingly in a voice that was not quite her own.

It was only with a supreme effort that she was able to focus, to gather enough energy to look out through her own eyes and see what was happening.

The clouds had cleared from the sky, and the moon seemed to sit on top of the two largest megaliths, closing the space between them. She could see the swing set through the gap, and then she couldn't. There was just blackness.

And there was something else. Something between the steadily moving Shadow People and the mighty stone circle. A small figure with dishwater blond hair, running from stone to stone.

The creature within her hadn't noticed, though. It just kept talking, kept saying the Words, and slowly, as she watched, the two lines of Shadow People on either side of the megaliths came together. They seemed to melt, like chocolate on a sunny day, into one formless mass. But the mass was gaining a shape and Belladonna knew what it was.

It was Margaret de Morville, the last Spellbinder and Empress of the Dark Spaces.

"Belladonna!"

The voice whispering into her ear was familiar.

"Belladonna! Can you hear me? It's Steve! Where's the Ninth Noble?"

Belladonna's heart leapt; she forced herself forward, pushing the other thing aside.

"Over there . . ." Her voice sounded husky, as if she hadn't spoken for weeks. "I threw it . . . I can't see . . . They can't see it either . . . Elsie . . ."

She glanced across the circle, but the Kere and the Allu were lost in adulation of their returning Empress.

"It's alright. She's here. Belladonna, you have to say

the names. The names of the stones. When I tell you. Do you understand?"

"Yes . . ." And then the fever rose again and the thing inside her head shoved her aside. Her head spun as the unfamiliar Words echoed across the ancient circle once more.

She watched as Steve crept over to the place where the coin had fallen and spread the scrap of carpet from the school. Everything seemed slow, as if she were watching a film that was running at the wrong speed. Elsie materialized on the carpet and quickly found the coin, picked it up, and handed it to Steve, who ran to the last stone and placed it on a carved ledge.

"Now!"

The thing inside her heard the voice but didn't recognize it. But it was afraid.

It was afraid.

Belladonna felt its fear and in that moment knew that it could be defeated. She called on every ounce of strength she had ever had: the strength that had seen her through the worst times in her life; the strength she had needed when her parents had left her alone forever; the strength she had called upon to fight Dr. Ashe; and the strength she had used every day at school when she had been taunted and teased just because she was different.

The names of the stones, she thought, *I must say them!*

The thing in her head seemed surprised, but Belladonna had no time to think about it. She had to speak.

"Aerona!" she blurted.

The thing fought back. Belladonna fell to her knees.

"Aerona!" she yelled, and no sooner was the name out of her mouth than one of the stones shot back into the earth, leaving a small gold coin spinning in the air where it had been.

"Morwenna! Gwerfyl!"

Two more stones vanished from the circle and two more coins spun, sparkling in the night.

"No!" screamed the Kere, running toward Belladonna with her bloodred hair flying and her teeth bared.

Belladonna looked up, unable to move away, waiting for the impact.

"Oh, no, you don't!"

Steve jumped in front of Belladonna, a gleaming sword in his hand. The Kere laughed derisively, then leapt back in surprise as Steve wielded the mighty weapon as if he'd been training for this moment all his life.

"P-Paderau!" yelled Belladonna, scrambling to her feet. "Caniad!"

"Get back, little girl," hissed the Allu, "and let my mistress in!"

He drew back his hand and hit her across the face again. Belladonna fell to the ground, stunned, and in a moment the thing was back and she could hear herself saying the Words once more.

And once more the ground rumbled and two of the stones rejoined their sisters.

"Belladonna!" yelled Steve. "Don't give up!"

She struggled to regain control of her own mind, and

as she did so, she saw the Allu creeping up behind Steve.

"Watch out!"

Steve glanced back, then deftly rolled away, springing to his feet and tossing the sword from hand to hand as he looked at the two creatures.

"Morwenna! Paderau!" yelled Belladonna. "Briallen!"

Only three stones remained and she could feel the thing in her head getting weaker, but the melting form on the other side of the circle was becoming more defined. She reached up and pulled the burning Nomial from around her neck. The thing inside her head vanished and she could think again.

"Steve! I think you have to break the circle! The Shadow People!"

Steve looked from the Kere and the Allu out to where the Shadow People continued their relentless circuits of the stone circle. He hesitated for a second and then the sword was gone and in its place he held what appeared to be a long pole that seemed far too unwieldy for him to handle easily, but once more he brandished it as if he had been born to it. He held it in the middle, like a tightrope walker, then spun around and swung it through the ring of Shadow People, scattering them to right and left like mown grass.

"Lowri!" yelled Belladonna. "Rhianwen!"

Another two stones disappeared and she became aware of something else. As the stones returned to the earth, Shady Gardens was vanishing too. She could see right through it, right to the church in the distance. The clock was striking—it was three o'clock.

"Belladonna!" Elsie was kneeling on her piece of carpet, desperate to help. "Look out!"

But the Kere had already grabbed her and thrown her to the ground, and Belladonna felt the weight of the goddess pinning her down.

"You will not defeat us a second time, Spellbinder!"

She looked into the pale face and the black eyes and for a second, for just a split second, it was gone. Like a television changing channels and then immediately changing back. One second it was the Kere holding her down in the dirt of Shady Gardens and the next second it was . . . Mrs. Evans. Steve's mother! Belladonna gasped, but as soon as she'd seen it, it was gone and the Kere was back.

"Let's see how well you resist with a little less blood in your veins!"

The Kere held up her index finger and ran it across Belladonna's wrist. The long black nail was so sharp that at first she thought nothing had happened, then she saw the blood—her blood—running out and into the dirt.

"How are you feeling now?" sneered the Kere.

"I'm feeling fine, no thanks to you!" said a familiar voice.

Thwack!

The Kere slumped to the ground, and Belladonna found herself looking at the one person she had been longing to see.

"Gran!"

"The very one," grinned Grandma Johnson. "Good job I always carry a spare crystal ball."

She pulled her scarf from her neck and tied it tightly around Belladonna's wrist.

"But how did you—?"

"The building is going. It's nothing but mist. Now get up—you have something to finish, I think."

Belladonna scrambled to her feet. On her right she could see Steve still scattering the Shadow People. The Allu was stalking across the circle toward him.

"Never you mind that, Belladonna, he can manage."

Belladonna looked at her grandmother. She felt woozy from the loss of blood and was still shivering from the fever that the Nomial had induced, but she knew her Gran was right—the main thing was to get rid of the stones.

"Where was I up to?" she asked.

"The last one was Rhianwen, I think."

Belladonna nodded and closed her eyes for a moment, letting the Words come. Then she opened them and stepped forward, but before she could speak, another voice cracked through the air.

"Spellbinder!"

It was the faceless Allu. One claw was around Steve's neck and had hoisted him into the air. The quarterstaff lay at his feet and as Belladonna watched, the weapon shrank back to an ordinary plastic six-inch ruler. He was defense-less.

"Restore the stones or your Paladin dies!"

She hesitated and looked back to Grandma Johnson

and then to Elsie, but both just stared in horror at the scene before them.

"Say the last name, Belladonna, say it!" gasped Steve.

Belladonna bit her lip, then turned back to the melting mass and the final stone.

"Skatha!"

The stone vanished and the last anchor for the opening to the Dark Spaces was gone. The opaque blackness that remained in the space between where the tallest stones had been began to swirl and writhe, like a whirlpool, and slowly the Shadow People, the pieces of the Dark Spaces, began to be pulled back into its vortex.

"Idiots!" screamed the Allu. "What have you done? You will pay with your lives. Starting with you, you sorry excuse for a Paladin."

"I'm not done yet," whispered Steve.

"You have dropped the Rod of Gram. Everyone knows that is the Paladin's strength. That is the way they have all died in the end."

"I'm not like everyone else," said Steve, coughing slightly.

Belladonna stepped closer, holding her breath. She glanced at Elsie, who had her hands clasped in front of her, willing him to win.

"Stay back, Spellbinder!" commanded the Allu.

Steve coughed again. He looked over at Belladonna and Elsie and grinned.

"Watch this."

He took a deep breath, opened his mouth, and let go with a withering blast of white-hot fire. The Allu screamed, dropped Steve, and clawed at its faceless head, staggering around the circle until it came too close to the vortex and was grabbed by the Dark Spaces.

"Nooooo!" it howled.

But it was too late; the Allu was gone.

Belladonna smiled as Steve retrieved the ruler, but as she turned to speak to her grandmother she found herself face-to-face with the last of the Shadow People. For a moment they just stared at each other, then it grabbed her by her wounded wrist and started to drag her toward the vortex. She felt she should have been able to break its grip, but it was like a vice and was dragging her toward an eternity of nothing.

Whap! Crack!

The quarterstaff hit it squarely on what would have been its chin. It staggered back, letting go of Belladonna's wrist. Steve hit it again, and this time it reeled back toward what little remained of the vortex, which grabbed the last of the Shadow People before dribbling away, like water down a drain, leaving only a fenced-in demolition site and a billboard promising "new luxury residential units soon."

"Thanks."

"Belladonna," whispered Steve, helping her to her feet. "Don't tell anyone it touched you."

"What?"

He led her over to Elsie. "Tell her."

"They said . . . the Conclave said that it was really bad. The Shadow People *are* the Dark. You can't let them touch you."

"But it's alright, see?" Belladonna showed them her wrist. "It grabbed the scarf; it didn't touch me."

"That looks like an awful lot of blood, Belladonna," said Steve.

She looked at the scarf. He was right.

Her grandmother put her arms around her. "Don't worry. You'll be fine."

Then everything went black.

26

Secrets

*S*HE WOKE UP in her own bed at home, with her grandmother by her side and her parents hovering anxiously near the foot of the bed. She looked at her wrist, which had been expertly bandaged.

"I did that," said Grandma Johnson proudly. "I was in the St. John's Ambulance Brigade once. Great way to get into football games for free."

Belladonna smiled, then remembered Mrs. Lazenby. She looked at her grandmother, suddenly anxious.

"Don't worry," she said. "They have no record of you or the Proctors. Miss Parker may not be able to leave the school, but her reach is still very long."

"How do you feel?" asked her mother.

"I feel . . . actually, I feel fine," said Belladonna, surprised. "This hurts a bit."

"You're staying off school this week," continued Mrs. Johnson. "I just can't believe these people. Putting children in the way of danger like that! They should be arrested! I'm going to make the dinner."

And with that, she disappeared, followed within moments by the sounds of rattling pans and silverware in the kitchen.

"You did very well," said her Dad. "And that young lad. Very good."

Belladonna smiled and closed her eyes. She was home.

"Mr. Evans."

No answer.

"Mr. Evans!"

Steve was staring out of the window at the trees and the clouds, the end of a pencil in his mouth and absolutely nothing on his mind.

Madame Huggins strode up to his desk and rapped on it loudly.

"This is a classroom, Mr. Evans! It is for learning."

Steve's eyes came into focus and he shrugged.

"Sorry."

"Right. Now I asked if you could conjugate—"

Steve was never to find out what he was going to have to conjugate because at that moment the classroom door opened and Mrs. Jay stepped inside. Twenty-five pairs of eyes shifted their attention from Steve's inevitable dressing-down and detention to the bulldog face of the school secretary.

"Sorry to interrupt," she said, not looking sorry at all, "but Miss Parker would like to see Belladonna Johnson and Steve Evans in her office."

"What, now?" asked Madame Huggins.

"Yes. Now."

Belladonna and Steve got up and followed Mrs. Jay out of the classroom, through the school and up the stairs to Miss Parker's office. As they reached the landing, there was a loud bang as the office door slammed shut and Sophie Warren, her face like thunder, pushed past them on her way down the stairs.

"Score," whispered Steve, grinning at Belladonna.

Mrs. Jay pretended she hadn't heard, opened the office door, and leaned in.

"Johnson and Evans."

They stepped inside and Mrs. Jay closed the door quietly behind them, returning to whatever it was she usually did.

"Sit down," said Miss Parker.

Two chairs had been placed in front of the huge desk. Belladonna sat in one and Steve perched nervously on the other.

"You have done very well. Much better than I had expected. I was quite sure we'd be looking for a new Spellbinder by now."

She smiled somewhat disconcertingly. Belladonna wasn't sure she liked being thought of as disposable.

"There are a couple of things, though. . . . Um . . . Mr. Evans, I am told that you breathed fire. Is that correct?"

"Yes," said Steve, unable to suppress a grin.

"I despair, I really do," sighed Miss Parker. "Do you still have this ability?"

"No, it went away," said Steve ruefully. "It was totally cool, though! You should have seen that faceless thingy! Aaaargggh!!!"

He grabbed his face and did a passable impression of the injured Allu. Miss Parker rolled her eyes, and Belladonna tried to suppress a giggle.

"And you used a quarterstaff?"

"Yes," said Steve, grinning. "Actually it was a buck-and-a-quarter staff, but don't tell anyone."

Belladonna giggled. "I am him for whom thou theeketht!" she lisped in her best Daffy Duck voice.

"What about the nobles?" asked Miss Parker, ignoring them.

Belladonna reached into her pocket and handed them over.

"Good."

Miss Parker placed them on the desk in front of her and pushed them into the shape of a circle, then she waved her finger over them and sat back as the coins slowly rose above the desk and began to spin slowly around. Belladonna and Steve watched, mesmerized, as the coins spun faster and faster.

Miss Parker whispered a Word, then clapped her hands together sharply. The coins immediately shot in toward one another. There was a brief flash and something heavy fell to the desk.

"It's a Nomial!" said Belladonna.

"Yes," said Miss Parker, picking it up. "It's a toad-stone. Now we have three."

"Four," said Belladonna.

"Four?"

She reached into her pocket and removed the amulet that Mr. Proctor had placed around her neck.

"Ah," cooed Miss Parker, "the Cornerinal. The blood-stone. Some call it the fever stone. A rather nasty thing. Excellent. Good. Now."

Silence. She looked from one to the other, and Belladonna could see Steve bracing himself for the worst.

"I have arranged for some extra classes."

"What!?" blurted Steve, horrified.

"Ancient languages, mythologies, self-defense, that sort of thing. It really was irresponsible of us to select a Spellbinder so young, and you have both proven that you have a great deal of natural talent. It just needs honing."

"But . . . didn't we win?" asked Steve.

"Yes, you did."

"Well . . . then, isn't it over?"

"No. She got through," said Belladonna quietly, realizing the truth. "Mrs. Proctor . . . the Kere . . . she said that the Empress could only escape if the Dark Spaces took another body. She said there had to be balance. But the Allu . . . the Dark Spaces took the Allu. It got its body and she's . . . the Empress is still here."

"Yes. Yes, that would seem to be the situation. She's got a lot to learn, though. Your world has changed a great deal since she was last here, and she wasn't able to bring any of her minions from the Dark Spaces with her, so there should be plenty of time. Classes start next Monday. That is all. You may go."

They drifted out of the office and stood on the landing, staring at the floor.

"We failed," said Steve finally. "After all that, we failed."

Belladonna thought about it for a moment. "No. We stopped her doing what she wanted. Now she's just stranded here, isn't she?"

"She's very powerful, though."

"Yes."

"We should probably take the classes."

"Yes."

They smiled and started to walk down the stairs, then Steve turned back to look at Belladonna.

"How is your wrist?"

Belladonna instinctively grasped at it. "It's fine."

"Really?"

"Yes, it's fine."

"Okay." He turned and continued down the stairs just as the bell sounded for lunch. "Yes! We missed the rest of Latin. See you!"

Belladonna smiled as he raced outside. The corridors were suddenly full of children as everyone dashed outside or in to lunch or loitered near the radiators. She made her way to the library, where it was quiet and she was sure she could be alone. She needed to think.

The Empress was here, and that was really, really bad. But she had started out as just another girl, plain Margaret Morville. A girl in a priory. She was probably supposed to become a nun. Then she had been chosen to be the Spellbinder. But what had happened to make her turn against everyone, even the Queen of the Abyss? Had just being the Spellbinder changed her so much?

Belladonna chewed on her lower lip and let her hair fall in front of her face. Outside she could see Steve playing football with his friends, jackets off in the near-freezing temperatures and oblivious to everything except that game and that moment.

She wished she could feel that way, but she never had. Steve was the sort of person who could set things aside to worry about later or not at all, but now that she knew the Kere had not only disguised herself as Mrs. Proctor but had also lived for years as Steve's mother, it changed everything.

What did that make Steve? Looking at him running across the field, she couldn't imagine that he was anything more or less than human. So why had the Kere posed as his mother?

She knew she ought to tell Miss Parker. Now that the Empress was here, even ordinary secrets could be dangerous, and this one was far from ordinary.

But she had a secret of her own.

She pulled back the sleeve of her cardigan and looked at her left wrist where the creature had grabbed her. There, beneath the skin, there was a shadow, like a wisp of smoke.

And it was moving, wreathing around her wrist like a slender bracelet.

A piece of the Dark Spaces.